Rising Tiger

RISING TIGER

A THRILLER

Brad Thor

EMILY BESTLER BOOKS

ATRIA

New York   London   Toronto   Sydney   New Delhi

EMILY
BESTLER
BOOKS

ATRIA

An Imprint of Simon & Schuster, Inc.
1230 Avenue of the Americas
New York, NY 10020

First Emily Bestler Books/Atria Books hardcover edition July 2022

EMILY BESTLER BOOKS / ATRIA BOOKS and colophon are trademarks of Simon & Schuster, Inc.

For information about special discounts for bulk purchases, please contact Simon & Schuster Special Sales at 1-866-506-1949 or business@simonandschuster.com.

The Simon & Schuster Speakers Bureau can bring authors to your live event. For more information, or to book an event, contact the Simon & Schuster Speakers Bureau at 1-866-248-3049 or visit our website at www.simonspeakers.com.

Manufactured in the United States of America

1 3 5 7 9 10 8 6 4 2

Library of Congress Cataloging-in-Publication Data has been applied for.

ISBN 978-1-9821-8215-1
ISBN 978-1-9821-8218-2 (ebook)

For Jill Thevenin—
Who lovingly gave me a room in her Paris flat
so that I might try my hand at writing.
I will be forever grateful.

Every neighboring state is an enemy
and the enemy's enemy is a friend.

—KAUTILYA, *THE ARTHASHASTRA*

CHAPTER 1

GALWAN VALLEY, WESTERN HIMALAYAS

The battle had been barbaric. Forbidden from using firearms in the disputed border region, the Chinese soldiers had crept across the "Line of Actual Control" in the middle of the night armed with spike-studded bats and iron rods wrapped with concertina wire. The brutal, medieval-style hand-to-hand combat had lasted more than six hours.

In the early light of dawn, a bitterly cold wind—like the breath of death itself—blew down the steep valley from the glaciers above. Bodies lay everywhere. The jagged stones along the banks of the chalky blue Galwan River were covered in blood.

Despite China's gruesome surprise attack, the Ladakh Scouts had courageously charged into the fight. Known as the "Snow Warriors," they were one of the Indian Army's toughest, most fearsome, and most decorated regiments. They had only one primary objective—to guard against the Chinese invading India via this section of the Himalayas.

The Snow Warriors had succeeded in their mission, but their success had come at a devastating cost. Twenty Indian soldiers had been killed and almost twice as many Chinese. Amid escalating tension between the two nations, it had been one of their deadliest altercations yet. And once more, China had been the aggressor. The reason for the aggression, at least to those paying attention, was obvious.

Dramatically unpopular among its people and facing a myriad of social and economic problems, the Chinese Communist Party was weaker than it had ever been.

The CCP's grip on power was increasingly tenuous. The panic of its members was palpable. Many in the party believed they were only one Tiananmen Square away from full-blown revolution. It was why they had crushed the prodemocracy movement in Hong Kong and why they continued to flex their military muscle over Taiwan. One more crack in their hull, one more leak in their sagging, waterlogged boat, and the CCP would slip beneath the surface of the waves and be dragged violently down to its death.

To prop up the party and prevent such a demise, Beijing needed to fog the minds of its people—to convince them that they were locked in an existential struggle, that the world was out to destroy China.

The course of action they decided to adopt was a form of virulent nationalism—the likes of which hadn't been seen since the Italian Fascism and German National Socialism of the 1930s.

For their plan to take root and grow, Beijing needed bogeymen—both big and small, near and far. The United States and its Western allies were a natural fit. Another exceptional contender, however, lay right at China's doorstep. *India.*

As the world's largest democracy, not only were India's ideas a threat, but so too were its growing economy, increasing military, and deepening ties with the United States. The CCP feared India's burgeoning power and was willing to do whatever necessary to diminish it.

Coercive statecraft to drive wedges between India and its neighbors, bloody cross-border raids to capture and hold disputed territory—China was feeling weak, and that weakness made them dangerous. Anything and everything was on the table—including the most contemptible and horrific acts of aggression.

The Snow Warriors' commander, Major Shaukat Banu, was a tall, sinewy man with a thick mustache. As he surveyed the carnage, his skin was still inflamed and sensitive to the touch. The weapon the Chinese had unleashed was unlike anything he had ever experienced.

At the end of the battle, when it had become obvious that they were going to lose, the Chinese had called their soldiers into retreat, and had activated some sort of directed-energy device.

The weapon had heated up the water molecules beneath the Indian soldiers' skin, causing them to vomit and experience excruciating pain. The Ladakh Scouts had been left with no choice but to abandon any pursuit of the Chinese and to pull back out of the range of the weapon.

With their retreat secure, the Chinese had fled, leaving their comrades to the mercy of the Indian Army. Banu directed two of his medical officers to attend to any of the enemy in need of care. Despite the brutality shown by the Chinese, it was the honorable thing to do and, at his core, Major Shaukat Banu was first and foremost an honorable man.

Both in his training from the Indian Army and as a guest of the United States military, he had been schooled in battlefield tactics and ethics.

The Snow Warriors had cross-trained with some of the United States' best high-altitude, cold-weather experts, including the U.S. Army's Tenth Mountain Division, the Marine Corps Mountain Warfare Training Center, and the Naval Special Warfare Cold Weather Detachment.

Those men, like Banu, who had proven themselves exceptionally distinguished had been invited to further participate in special hand-to-hand training normally available only to America's most elite operators. The major credited the edged-weapons portion of the program not only for the reason he was still standing, but also for why he had been able to slay so many Chinese.

On the left side of the belt encircling his bloodstained uniform hung an American-made tomahawk popular with the U.S. Navy SEALs. On the right hung a custom, hand-forged knife carried by many of America's Delta Force operatives. Banu had been taught how to wield both, simultaneously—how to cut, and thrust, and strike his way through the enemy, which was exactly what he had done.

Eleven of the Chinese casualties had been at his hands. But as proficient as his skills had proven to be, they hadn't been enough to prevent the slaughter and injury of so many of his own men. Never had he so heavily felt the burden of command.

But beneath his sense of loss lay something else—a deep sense of foreboding. China had raised the stakes dramatically. It was probing; testing what worked and just how much India would absorb. Once the Chinese had their answer, they would strike again.

And like the cold wind that blew through the valley, the next attack would be more chilling, more deadly, than anything that had come before.

Major Shaukat Banu's only question was whether India would be able to stop it.

CHAPTER 2

A pistol, much less one with a suppressor, was not a common sight on the streets of Jaipur—especially not during Diwali, the Hindu festival of light.

As the largest celebration in India, Diwali represented the triumph of good over evil, knowledge over ignorance, and hope over despair. Tonight, however, victory was about to be handed to evil, ignorance, and despair all wrapped up in one.

American Eli Ritter had been encouraged to accept a security detail. Nothing too obvious, just something light, a buffer in case anything bad happened. He had declined.

Understanding his reluctance, the president's national security advisor had suggested pairing him with an Athena Team operative from the U.S. Army's all-female Delta Force unit. Once again, Ritter had declined. And with good reason.

Per his orders, he was supposed to be operating not just "under" the radar, but altogether off of it. No one was to have any idea what he was up to. That was why he was in Jaipur and not in New Delhi, and why he had been in Adelaide and Osaka rather than Canberra and Tokyo. Popping up in the capitals of India, Australia, and Japan—drawing attention to himself with bodyguards—could have jeopardized everything.

The president and his team, however, didn't like their shadow diplomat operating without protection. Reluctantly, after much debate, they had acquiesced. Ritter, after all, was a man who knew how to handle himself.

After leaving the United States Marine Corps, he had gotten a master's degree in economics and had joined the State Department. Over the years, he had been posted at various diplomatic missions around the world as an "economic development officer."

Officially, his job had been to help hammer out trade agreements and secure favorable environments for American corporations looking to operate abroad.

Unofficially, he had functioned as a highly regarded intelligence officer, skilled at recruiting foreign spies and building outstanding human networks.

Ritter had been so successful that his identity had been kept secret from all but a very select few in the U.S. government. Even after he had retired and moved into the private sector as an international business consultant, his identity had been protected.

While no one in the diplomatic arena was ever completely beyond suspicion of espionage, Ritter had come pretty damn close. None of his assets had ever been compromised and none of his colleagues had ever screwed up and revealed his true occupation. By all appearances, he had led a rather unremarkable career at the State Department, which was fine by him—just the way a true and professional spy would have wanted himself to be seen.

After opening his consulting business, Ritter had kept his nose clean. Any time someone from his past had come around with an intelligence contract, he had politely refused. The espionage chapter of his life was closed. Or so he had thought.

Everything had changed when he showed up for a "new client" meeting and had found himself face-to-face with the president of the United States.

When the president explained the nature of the mission and what hung in the balance, Ritter had agreed to come out of retirement.

Other than his Marine Corps commitment to a lifetime of fitness, there was nothing about Ritter that said "military." He was in his early sixties and stood about six foot two. With medium-length gray hair swept behind his ears, trademark stubble on his face, casual yet well-tailored designer clothes, a TUDOR Black Bay Chrono, and a pair of Ray-Ban

Aviators, he had looked like any other well-heeled tourist or stylish entrepreneur exploring India's tenth-largest metropolis.

In an effort to cement his relaxed-visitor image, as well as to pick up any potential surveillance, he had spent two days "sightseeing" and purchasing small gifts for his family back home.

The exquisite Pink City—so named for the pink blush of so many of its buildings—had much to offer.

He took in the big sights, like the stunning City Palace, the Jal Mahal, and the Hawa Mahal, as well as the impressive Amber Fort, the Nahargarh Fort, and the Galta Ji. At random, he wove in and out of countless lush gardens, in addition to bustling, colorful marketplaces selling everything from spices, textiles, and shoes to perfume, jewelry, and crafts.

He used taxis, buses, and the colorful, open-air autorickshaws to get around. The air was scented with incense mixed with the winds that blew from the Thar Desert. He drank chai from sidewalk tea shops and ate food from street vendors—always keeping his eyes and ears open. Never once did he notice, or sense, anyone following him. When it came time for his meeting, he felt confident that he was in the clear.

Even so, he continued to maintain his situational awareness. Leaving his hotel, he ran a series of surveillance detection routes through Jaipur's affluent Vaishali Nagar neighborhood.

The Diwali festival was in full swing and even more spectacular at night. From courtyards and rooftops, fireworks were being launched high into the night sky. Beautifully decorated homes were framed by the illumination from tiny, flickering clay oil lamps called *diyas*.

People walked down the street waving sparklers, dressed in their most elegant clothing. Bursts of firecrackers could be heard coming from all directions. There were musicians on every corner. The traffic was thick and noisy. Everything in Jaipur was electric . . . thrumming . . . alive.

Ritter was meeting his contact in a part of Vaishali Nagar popular for its food scene. The Tansukh fine dining restaurant, with its gleaming white floors and polished wooden ceilings, specialized in authentic Rajasthani cuisine. It was one of his contact's favorites. Though they had serious business to discuss, the man had assured him that he was in for a meal he would never forget.

His contact had been right. From the Mohan Maas—meat stuffed with dried fruit and cooked slowly in milk, cardamom, and cinnamon— to the Bajra Roti flatbread, a never-ending parade of chutneys, and ice-cold bottles of Kingfisher beer from Bangalore, it had been an outstanding dinner.

Even better than the food was his counterpart's agreement on almost everything he had come to discuss.

It wasn't a total fait accompli, however. Ritter would have to convince the man's boss. And it would not be easy.

What's more, setting up the meeting was going to be extremely difficult and would require an unparalleled level of secrecy. India was on edge.

China had become much more belligerent. Pakistan, despite its massive internal problems, was also stirring up trouble. And the Kashmir region, after an unusually protracted calm, was beginning to overheat.

Those elements alone had the makings of a perfect storm. Throw in an upcoming election, and the danger level only skyrocketed. Politicians seldom liked taking risks. They liked risk-taking even less when their political careers were sure to hang in the balance.

Complicating matters even further was the fact that India's democracy was backsliding. Illiberal forces were amassing power at an alarming rate. The incumbent party was doing all it could to hang on to office. There were fears that a state of emergency might be declared, the constitution suspended, and all elections postponed.

It was against this difficult backdrop that Eli Ritter had been sent to work his quiet magic. And based on the success of his dinner, he appeared—so far—to be off to a solid start.

So that they would not be seen leaving together, his contact stayed behind and ordered a digestif.

Stepping outside, Ritter smiled. Jaipur's citizens were still out in force celebrating. He also felt like doing a little celebrating.

Removing one of the Cohibas he had purchased earlier in the day, he snipped the end and fired it up.

The communists may have fucked up everything else in Cuba, he mused, *but they've been wise enough to keep their hands off Cuba's exceptional cigar industry.*

Filling his mouth with a heady draw of peppery smoke, he struck off toward his hotel.

Two blocks later, a string of firecrackers exploded close by, taking him by surprise.

Out of instinct, he turned toward the noise. That was when the assassin stepped up from the opposite direction, placed the suppressed pistol behind Ritter's left ear, and pressed the trigger.

CHAPTER 3

Ducking back behind cover, Scot Harvath slammed a fresh magazine into his weapon. Out on the street, Taliban gunmen—about twelve in total and most of them armed with American M4s—continued to fire on his position.

The amount of U.S. military equipment that had been abandoned to the bad guys after Afghanistan's collapse made him sick to his stomach. The fact that it was now being used against his team made it even worse. Two of his people were already dead.

They lay in pools of their own blood no more than twenty feet away. There had been nothing he could do for them. Things had escalated that quickly.

The pair had been fierce, anti-Taliban resistance fighters, recruited specifically for this operation. Dressed in plain clothes and supplied with envelopes full of cash, their job had been to negotiate roadblocks and to smuggle their American colleagues into the city.

While the key phase of the mission took place, they were to stand guard. Then, once the objective was complete, they were to smuggle everyone back out again. Ideally, no one would ever know the team had been there. But when a roving Taliban security patrol had passed through, everything had gone south.

What had started as a shakedown, with the Taliban angling for bribes, had rapidly turned into a bloodbath.

The men were initially accused of being out too late. Next, questions were raised about their vehicle, then their driving permits and other documents.

It didn't matter that everything was in full compliance. That wasn't how things worked in a failed state. The law didn't matter. The rights of the individual didn't matter. The only things that mattered were brute force and one group's ability to successfully impose its will upon the rest of a society.

It was the antithesis of everything the United States had hoped to help the Afghans achieve. Sadly, and at tremendous cost, America had learned the painful lesson that democracy couldn't simply be handed to a people on a silver platter. The people themselves had to want it so badly that they would do anything for it. They had to be willing to fight and die. And not just some of them. *All* of them. Anything less than a complete commitment to their own freedom was a recipe for defeat and subjugation.

That only added to the sickness Harvath felt. He knew and had worked with courageous Afghans. Men and women willing to go the distance and do whatever needed to be done. Unfortunately, the nation's tribalism and rampant corruption had doomed even the most noble of freedom fighters to a near-impossible battle against the Taliban and other terrorist organizations that had taken root once again like weeds throughout the country.

It wasn't his problem, however. Especially not now. He and his team had been sent on a specific mission—the extraction of a high-value Afghan intelligence asset.

Unlike many Afghans who had dragged their feet and had postponed getting out, this Afghan, code-named "Topaz," had selected to stay behind.

At great personal risk to himself and his family, he had continued to willingly serve as a well-placed, loyal set of eyes and ears for the American government. The man had gone above and beyond what anyone could have asked of him. Now, with murder, rape, starvation, and so many other evils falling like a poisoned, unstoppable deluge, all he wanted was out.

While the United States was sorry to have to pull him, the man had more than earned it. And so, Harvath was called in.

The former SEAL Team Six member turned covert intelligence operative was no stranger to extracting individuals from hostile, war-torn places, including Afghanistan. If there was one thing he had learned, it was that if something could go wrong, it would. That fact had just gruesomely played out right before his eyes.

In an effort to deescalate the situation with the Taliban, one of the resistance fighters had pulled out an envelope filled with currency and had offered a contribution to the cause. Normally, after a little haggling, such an overture—referred to as *baksheesh*, a Persian word for bribe—would be enough to settle everything and see the thugs move on in search of their next victim. This time, unfortunately, things had taken a deadly turn.

The security patrol's commander was seasoned and possessed of above-average intelligence. *Where there was one envelope of cash,* he had reasoned, *there were likely more*. He initiated a search of the men and their vehicles.

Not only did the Taliban uncover the rest of the money, but they also found weapons and equipment hidden in the resistance fighters' truck that clearly suggested they were up to something. Discovering what that something was had been the patrol commander's next goal.

He gave the first fighter an opportunity to explain. When the man didn't answer to his satisfaction, the commander removed his pistol and shot him point-blank in the head.

Harvath's sniper, Jack Gage, had been poised on a rooftop halfway down the block. Gage had been ready to let loose, but Harvath had held him back, wanting to give the resistance fighters a chance to do what they had been hired to do—smooth things over and convince the Taliban to move on. As it turned out, Harvath had held out hope a fraction of a moment too long.

The moment the commander fired, Harvath cleared Gage to shoot and joined the fight himself. It was too little, too late.

Gage managed to drop the commander with a head shot of his own, as well as another Taliban standing nearby.

Harvath laid down cover fire, but before the remaining resistance fighter could get to safety, another gunman from the security patrol had popped up and shot him dead.

The fight was on and it was vicious. Whatever concerns the Taliban might have had, running out of ammo wasn't one of them. The onslaught was intense.

It was only a matter of time before more Taliban showed up and pinned them down. It wouldn't have shocked Harvath if more men were already headed in their direction.

Three hours on the ground, *tops,* was all that they had budgeted for the operation. If the extraction took any longer, they would miss their window and would have to move to Plan B.

Nobody—not a single member of the team—wanted to activate Plan B. Fighting their way north, in hopes of escaping through high mountain passes on horses and donkeys, via dangerous opium routes, with smugglers as their guides, limited supplies, and no backup, would be like poking death in the eye with a sharp stick. It was not how Harvath wanted this to end.

He needed Plan A to work. But for that to happen now, he was going to have to take an even greater risk. The team had to move—get off the X, as it was known in their business—because even more troubling than the potential of reinforcements arriving was the fact that the Taliban were big fans of rocket-propelled grenades.

He had no idea if the men out on the street had any RPGs, but if they did, it would take only one, fired directly into the small house, for it to be game over.

As delegation was one of the most important components of leadership, he'd made that Gage's problem. From his vantage point, with the powerful optics on his rifle, he had the best odds of not only seeing someone with an RPG, but of taking the person out before he could mount and launch the weapon.

That said, the clock was running for Gage as well. He wasn't safe on that rooftop. The security patrol would have called in the presence of a sniper and would have given his approximate location. Harvath needed to evacuate his whole team, along with Topaz and his family, and get them all to the extraction point. To do that, he was going to have to offer himself up as bait.

Radioing his plan to his team, he leaned back out from behind cover and let loose with another volley of shots. He drilled two Taliban, who dropped like sacks of wet cement. Whether they were dead made no difference. They weren't moving, which meant they were out of the fight.

When he retreated back to cover, his teammate Mike Haney shouted from his position, "Nobody else wants to say it, but your new plan *sucks*."

"It's a good thing nobody else gets a vote," Harvath replied. "Make sure the family's ready. I want everyone prepared to exit in sixty seconds."

CHAPTER 4

Everything now was about speed, surprise, and overwhelming violence of action. Slinging his suppressed, short-barreled Heckler & Koch 416 A5, Harvath grabbed two fragmentation grenades from his chest rig. The moment the team signaled that they were ready to go, he pulled the pins and threw the devices into the street, yelling, "Frag out!"

They exploded with a deafening roar, showering the Taliban with red-hot shrapnel.

From his rooftop perch, Gage recommenced firing, and Harvath rushed forward, finding concealment behind a parked car. Removing a pair of smoke grenades, he yanked their pins, rolled them across the road, and transitioned back to his rifle.

As soon as the visibility was sufficiently impaired, he gave the order for his team to move out.

He used the engine block of the car he was hiding behind for partial cover and, popping over the hood, began firing on the Taliban position.

Two of their vehicles had been badly damaged. They were both on fire and from what he could tell, were definitely out of commission. That was the good news.

The bad news was that only a couple of blocks away, headlights could be seen racing in their direction. Reinforcements were arriving. He wouldn't be able to hold all of them off. In fact, it would be a miracle if he could hold off the gunmen he was already engaged with.

Over his earpiece, he heard teammate Tyler Staelin radio that they had successfully made it to the truck. That was Gage's cue to get off the roof and get down to the street up ahead so he could be picked up.

As the truck fired up and peeled out, Harvath—per his own orders—was left alone.

What he hadn't told Haney was that he didn't much like this plan, either. It was suicide. It was also the only way.

He needed to keep the Taliban at bay long enough for Topaz, his family, and the rest of the team to escape. It was the only thing that mattered. Ducking back behind the car, he prepared himself.

Once he was ready, he grabbed his next-to-last frag, pulled the pin, and sent it hurtling through the air toward his attackers. The moment it detonated, Harvath charged.

He used the smoke, as well as the shock of getting fragged again, to his advantage, allowing them to veil his movements.

Sprinting to the other side of the street, he slid soundlessly along the parked cars until he reached his objective. It was a flanking position from which he was going to launch his final attack, but the Taliban had a surprise waiting for him.

A skinny, sickly-looking kid, no more than sixteen, had been positioned between the last two parked cars to protect their left flank. He had his weapon ready, and the moment Harvath came into view, he pressed the trigger. There was just one problem. The teen hadn't properly seated a round in the chamber.

The sound of the rifle's metallic *click* caused a wave of panic to crash over his features. Before the boy could cry out to his comrades, Harvath butt-stroked him with his weapon, knocking him out cold.

He took no joy in doing it, but it beat the alternative. The kid was a combatant. He could have shot him. That, however, wasn't something he wanted on his conscience.

Dragging the teen behind one of the parked cars, Harvath laid him down, disabled his weapon, and helped himself to the young Taliban's spare magazines.

With his impromptu resupply complete and the approaching reinforcements only seconds away, he then made ready for his final push.

Ripping the pin from his last fragmentation grenade, he tossed it through the air, dropping it right at the feet of the remaining members of the security patrol. As soon as it detonated, he sprung.

Harvath moved quickly through the smoke, double-tapping each of the Taliban gunmen. It didn't matter whether they were moving. It was the only way to be absolutely certain that they were dead.

Once he was done, he changed magazines and ran toward the only thing with four wheels that wasn't on fire.

The beat-up, former Afghan National Police pickup had massive steel bumpers, an M60 machine gun mounted to a roll bar behind the cab, and keys that one of the Taliban had left in the ignition. With a phalanx of likely enemy vehicles barreling down on him, Harvath wasted no time. Placing his suppressed rifle on the seat next to him, he took off as fast as he could.

At the end of the block, he jerked the wheel hard to the left and headed north. He had no idea where he was going; he just knew that he had to get out of the area as quickly as possible.

"Moonracer. This is Norseman. Do you copy?" he said over his radio as he sped through the dusty streets of Kabul.

"Roger that, Norseman. Lima Charlie," a voice replied from an operations center thousands of miles away in Northern Virginia.

It was military slang for *loud and clear*. And while the little man, known only as "Nicholas" to his friends, had never served, he had made it his goal to be proficient in the language his colleagues spoke—especially when they were engaged in life-or-death tactical operations.

"What's the status on Beach Ball?" Harvath asked, wanting an update on his team as they made their way toward Kabul International Airport.

"En route. Seven klicks out. Zero contact," Nicholas replied.

So far, so good, Harvath thought to himself. Now all he had to do was get himself to the airport. Glancing at his watch, he felt pretty good about his chances.

Good, that was, until he flicked his gaze up to his rearview mirror and noticed several sets of headlights closing in on him from behind. His only chance was to move fast enough that he could outrun them.

Approaching the next intersection, he gripped the wheel with both hands and turned to the right with such force that the pickup rose up onto two wheels. He almost thought that he had gone too far, that he was going to flip it over, when he adjusted and gravity helped bring the way-ward tires crashing back down onto the road. The moment they did, he pressed down on the gas even harder.

Storefronts whipped past, their façades forever altered in the post-Kabul-collapse era. Beauty salons had painted over pictures of women wearing makeup and sporting the latest hairstyles. The same thing had happened at boutiques for women's clothing; images of fashionable models erased out of fear of incurring the wrath of the Taliban.

It wasn't just a "step" backward. It was as if the entire culture had been loaded into a catapult and launched decades into the past. The Taliban were like a cancer, destroying everything they touched. And for what? All of it simply in service to their abhorrent, radical religious beliefs.

In Harvath's experience, the Afghans were good people. His heart ached for them. Not only for what they were suffering, but also because they had lacked the collective will to stave off and ultimately fight back against the monstrous regime that now ruled over them. They could have had a different future. They *should* have had a different future. It had been within their grasp.

He wasn't very optimistic about their future. If there was one thing he knew, it was that once freedom had been lost, it was almost impossible to get back. That was one of the biggest reasons he had chosen the career that he had. As a previous U.S. president had stated, "Freedom is never more than one generation away from extinction. We don't pass it on to our children in the bloodstream. It must be fought for, protected, and handed on for them to do the same. And if we don't do this, we will spend our sunset years telling our children, and our children's children, what it once was like in America to be free."

That responsibility, Harvath had learned, required vigilance at home and abroad. There was no American Dream without those willing to protect it. Every citizen had a role to play. It required commitment, truth-telling, and a belief not only in what America was, but what it *could* be—a belief that its best days were always in front of it.

It also involved danger. For as long as America stood apart as a beacon of liberty, a place where the dignity and rights of the individual were prized above all else, it would attract the scorn and enmity of tyrannical governments and malevolent actors the world over.

To combat those threats, the United States needed citizens like Harvath, men and women willing to take on additional risk; who would put their lives on the line and fight America's enemies, no matter where that fight might take them.

It was what had brought him to Kabul. He wasn't thrilled to be back, but he had a job to do, a mission to complete, and he was going to do it. Failure wasn't an option.

It wasn't enough for his team to escape with Topaz and the man's family. Harvath had to get out of the country as well.

If he couldn't get out, he would die trying. He wouldn't allow any lives to be risked coming back for him. He understood what he had signed up for, and he was going to see this mission through to its very end—one way or the other.

His focus now was on losing the vehicles on his tail. Once that was done, he could plot a new course and bolt for the airport. Whether he'd be able to get in the gate, much less whether the plane would even still be there, was anybody's guess. He'd have to jump off that bridge when he came to it.

Up ahead, he could see a traffic circle. The roundabouts in the city were famous for congestion. But due to the late hour, there was only a smattering of cars. Nevertheless, it was going to be his best, and possibly only, option for ditching his pursuers. They were closing the gap and almost on top of him.

He hit the traffic circle hard, easing up on the gas only enough so that he didn't roll the pickup. As he disengaged the clutch and then put it right back into action, his rear tires smoked as he oversteered and drifted the truck through the turn.

It was a difficult maneuver, especially with such a high center of gravity, but he had nailed it.

The only thing that would have made it better was if he had noticed the SUV flying down the next feeder road into the roundabout.

But by the time he saw it, it was too late.

CHAPTER 5

The vehicle hit the side of Harvath's truck with such force that it felt like he had driven over an IED. The windows exploded in a hail of glass and his helmet struck one of the pillars so hard, it caused him to see stars.

The SUV pushed his pickup all the way across the road, slamming it into a concrete barrier and pinning it in place.

Harvath scrambled for his rifle, but he couldn't find it. It had been ejected at some point in the crash. Reaching for his belt, he drew his SIG Sauer pistol and pointed it at the bearded occupants of the SUV. All were wearing black Taliban turbans. As soon as he saw one of them raise a weapon, he pressed his trigger.

He fired in controlled pairs, again and again, not stopping until all four men were dead.

Unfortunately, there wasn't any time for a breather. The vehicles that had been chasing him had just entered the traffic circle.

Quickly sliding out of the cab, he holstered his pistol and leapt up into the bed of the pickup.

The machine gun mounted on top of the truck's roll bar was an old M60. It was all scratched up and looked totally beat to shit, but that was par for the course in a country where everything aged rapidly and locals still cleaned their AK-47s by running knotted shoelaces through their barrels.

There was no telling how many ammo cans had originally been in the bed of the pickup. Right now there was only one, which, mercifully, had been strapped down.

Opening it up, he snatched the two-hundred-round belt of 7.62 ammunition, loaded the weapon, and made ready.

"Moonracer, this is Norseman," Harvath said over the radio. "My vehicle has been disabled. I'm at a roundabout approximately three klicks north of the initial objective. Multiple hostiles inbound. I'm going to need some help getting out of here."

"Roger that," said Nicholas, who had been monitoring the team's GPS trackers via a National Security Agency satellite overhead. "Can you activate your IR beacon so I can get a positive ID on your position?"

Prior to the Taliban "inheriting" shipping containers full of American night-vision goggles from the Afghan Army, Harvath would have had no problem activating the infrared strobe attached to the back of his helmet. Now, however, it could end up being the equivalent of bathing in gasoline and lighting himself on fire.

Once he turned on the beacon, if any of his pursuers were using the goggles, he'd be as eye-catching as a disco ball hanging over the altar at a midnight mass. But as he needed Nicholas to find him a way out of there, he didn't have a choice.

What's more, the belt of ammunition was studded with tracers. Every fifth round included a pyrotechnic that caused the round to glow. From the shooter's perspective, it allowed a visual means to trace the flight path of the rounds as they streaked through the sky in order to see where they were landing.

From the enemy's perspective, it allowed them to see, rather precisely, where their attacker was shooting from.

In other words, it wasn't going to matter if the Taliban were wearing night-vision goggles. The moment he started firing, they'd be able to zero right in on him.

He had agreed to bring a beacon only in case of emergency, and if this didn't qualify as an emergency, he'd be hard-pressed to know what did. Reaching atop his head, he turned it on.

He was just about to instruct Nicholas to start looking for it, when he heard Haney's voice over his earpiece. "We're almost at the extraction point, Norseman. Once we hand off our package, we're coming back for you."

"Negative," Harvath ordered. "None of you are coming back for me."

"We exfil together," said Staelin, adding his voice to the proposed change of plans, "or we don't exfil."

"I appreciate the sentiment but stop screwing around. You have your orders. Now clear the net."

As Haney and Staelin obeyed and fell silent, Nicholas said, "I've got a visual on you. Nice and bright."

Leaning his shoulder into the M60, he took aim at the approaching Taliban vehicles and began applying pressure to the trigger. "It's about to get much brighter. If you have any rabbits in your hat, now's the time to start pulling them out."

"Roger that," Nicholas replied. "On it."

The little man suffered from primordial dwarfism and stood just under three feet tall. What he lacked in physical prowess, however, he more than made up for in mental capacity. He was, quite simply, one of the most brilliant people Harvath had ever met. If anyone could find him a way out of this, it was Nicholas.

But regardless of how smart and how talented the man was, none of it would make a difference if Harvath didn't neutralize the threat that was heading straight toward him. It was time for business.

Reaching up to his helmet, he turned off the beacon. There was no sense in giving the bad guys any more of an advantage than they already had.

The most important thing now was his timing. The attack had to be perfectly launched. The words of William Prescott, cautioning his soldiers at the Battle of Bunker Hill not to fire until they saw the whites of the British soldiers' eyes, played in Harvath's mind.

As the first vehicle entered the roundabout, he could feel his pulse quickening. Every fiber of his body tightened. It took everything he had not to put a single extra ounce of pressure on the trigger.

Instead, he took a deep breath and then slowly let it out of his lungs.

When the second of the two vehicles came into range, he was officially in "whites of their eyes" territory. Unleashing the M60, he rained hell down on them.

Swinging the machine gun back and forth on its mount, he lit up the night, shattering their windows and windscreens, sending rounds ripping through their doors, and sawing the Taliban trucks—as well as everybody inside—to pieces.

It was a frightening display of firepower, made even more so by the use of the tracer rounds.

One of the vehicles was on fire, and the other was smoking so heavily that it looked like it was actively trying to combust.

The bed of his pickup was filled with hot shell casings and the spent links that had held the ammo together.

His work was done. It was time to get moving. Hopping down from the truck, he took a moment to make sure no more vehicles were immediately inbound and hailed Nicholas. "Talk to me, Moonracer. What are we doing?"

"You picked the right neighborhood," the little man replied. "Head north and take the road that branches off at two o'clock."

"What am I looking for?"

"Three blocks down, there'll be a side street. I'll call it out to you when you get there."

"And then?" Harvath asked.

"There's an old CIA safe house. The Agency mothballed it on its way out of Kabul."

"Do we know what's inside it?"

"Negative," Nicholas responded. "It might be a dry hole, but it'll get you out of sight until we can figure out our next move."

Harvath didn't like the idea of rushing toward a building he knew next to nothing about, but the sooner he was off the street the better. His gunfight, along with the burning vehicles, was going to act like a brand-new bug light and draw even more Taliban into the neighborhood.

He just hoped the safe house wasn't a mistake, that it hadn't been taken over by a group of armed squatters or wasn't across the street from some militant recruiting station.

Someone up above seemed to be listening, because no sooner had he started heading in that direction than he was given what appeared to be a very positive sign.

Fifteen yards from his truck, he looked down and saw his rifle. Picking it up, he gave it a quick once-over. It was dirty, but that was all. Nothing was bent. Nothing was broken. The optic was working and still appeared to be zeroed.

After making sure the magazine was firmly seated and a round was chambered, he picked up his pace. He knew better than to be lulled into thinking that one piece of good luck meant that more were on the way. That wasn't the way things worked.

In fact, it was usually quite the opposite. The more difficult and dangerous the mission, the more likely Murphy's Law would come into play. He had seen it too many times to count. He had also learned from it.

The trick was not letting Murphy capture the momentum. No matter what happened, you had to keep pushing. You had to keep fighting. "If you fall," as his mentor used to say, paraphrasing Wild Bill Donovan, founder of the CIA's precursor, the OSS, "fall forward in service of the mission."

It was good advice, even noble, but Harvath preferred *not* falling. That was why he had worked so hard to develop a very deep set of skills. It was why he trained like hell and wasn't above taking performance-enhancing substances. Considering the operations he was called on to carry out and the kinds of people he had to go up against, he needed every advantage he could lay his hands on. He wasn't expected to fight fair. He was *expected* to win. And getting Topaz and his family out wouldn't be seen as a bona fide "win" if he ended up getting his ticket punched on some darkened side street in Kabul.

He had been in worse scenarios before and had always found a way out. There was no reason to expect this time would be any different.

But as Nicholas directed him to make a left at the next corner, a bad feeling began to build in the pit of his stomach.

As he drew even with the former CIA safe house, he took everything in, and what he saw caused him to stop dead in his tracks.

CHAPTER 6

The building looked like a bomb had been dropped on it. Part of the façade of the second story had been completely shorn away. The ground-floor doors and windows, from what he could see through the gate, were covered with metal security shutters, all of which had been scorched by fire. The walls of the compound were pockmarked from bullets. This not-so-OK-Corral had seen *much* better days.

Unfortunately, it was "any port in a storm" time, which meant beggars couldn't be choosers. Having tried the gate and having found it locked, he raised Nicholas over the radio. "Any chance the Agency left a hide-a-key?"

"In the wall, immediately to the right of the gate," the little man replied, reading from a file he had accessed, "there should be a green tile with a white teardrop in the center."

Harvath searched until he found it. "Got it."

"Behind it there's a keypad."

He pushed on the tile, releasing a lock and allowing it to swing open on an internal hinge. Nicholas read the combination to him.

Harvath punched in the numbers, but nothing happened. In the distance, he could hear the sound of more trucks. They were headed his way. He tried the combination again. *Nothing.*

"It's not working," he said. "Are you sure we've got the right combo?"

Nicholas repeated the digits and then added, "Does the pad have power? The keys will be backlit. They should glow when you touch them."

"Negative," Harvath responded. "They're definitely not lighting up."

"You're going to have to open it up."

Harvath glanced in the direction the vehicles were coming from. "I don't have a lot of time here. Likely hostiles inbound."

"I can see them on my screen," Nicholas stated. "It looks like an SUV and two pickups. Don't worry. Just focus on the keypad."

That was easy for him to say. "What am I supposed to be doing?"

"There are four screws on the faceplate. Take them out and then you can pop it off."

Harvath slid a Leatherman multitool from its sheath, found the Phillips head bit, and began to remove the screws.

He was on the last one when its head stripped. "Damn it," he cursed under his breath.

Switching to the multitool's blade, he tried to pry the steel faceplate the rest of the way off, but could get it to move only so much.

He tried not to think about the approaching vehicles. They sounded like they were almost on top of him.

Flipping open the needlenose pliers, he grabbed the corner of the plate and began wrenching it away from its base. Finally, he heard a snap, the faceplate came free, and he could see inside the unit.

"Faceplate's off," he said over the radio.

"Based on the spec sheet," offered Nicholas, "that lock runs on four double-A batteries. The first thing you should do is power-cycle the lock and—"

Harvath had already tuned him out. Reaching in, he stripped all four batteries and tossed them aside.

Everything from his night vision to his optics ran on double-As, and he always carried spares. Pulling four of them out of a waterproof holder, he slid them into the unit and tried the combination again. *Bingo*.

Closing the tile that hid the keypad, he pushed his way through the gate and entered the rubble-strewn courtyard. "I'm in," he said.

"Good copy," Nicholas replied. "Stay dark. Those vehicles are almost to you."

"Roger that," said Harvath. Flipping his night-vision goggles down, he headed for the door of the main structure.

The keypad was easy to find and, unlike the one at the gate, had power. As soon as he entered the combination, the lock released; he swung back the thick metal door and slipped inside.

His first priority was to clear the structure and make sure it was secure. As he moved from room to room, his weapon up and at the ready, he could see that the CIA guys had left in a hurry. Some clothing still hung in the closets, there were toothbrushes in the bathroom, and a stack of dishes sat in the kitchen sink.

The stench wafting from the garbage can was like something out of a crime scene. There could have been a million dollars hiding in there and Harvath wouldn't have dared lift the lid—not without some level 4 hot-zone respirator on.

While it would have been the perfect place to hide something valuable, nothing inside the safe house suggested anyone was doing that kind of thinking. Up on the roof, two charred-out burn barrels and a pair of empty jerry cans served only to put an exclamation point on how fast the previous occupants had bugged out.

Risking a glance over the parapet, he looked down onto the street. Several buildings over, he could see the SUV, as well as the two pickups, both of which appeared to be mounted with a .50-caliber machine gun.

And as if that wasn't bad enough, the vehicles' heavily armed occupants had dismounted and were going house to house. He doubted they were door-knocking to register voters for the next Taliban election. They were looking for someone, and that someone was *him*. He was sure of it.

Having a fortified position and holding the high ground were two items very much in his favor. The walls of the compound were high enough that he wasn't worried about them being scaled—not without a ladder or getting one of the vehicles close enough that his opponents could scramble up and over. The weak point of his position, however, was the gate.

If they had chains and could get a man close enough to attach them, they could tear it out. Or they could simply use the truck-mounted .50-cals as can openers and hammer the gate until it dropped.

This was starting to look a little like the Alamo. With his limited ammo, he was going to be able to keep them at bay only so long. He needed to come up with a plan. *Quickly*.

Retreating inside the building, he returned to the first floor and started tearing through everything.

While the Agency team had left a lot of personal items behind, the one thing they hadn't left was anything *professional*—specifically weapons. He would have given a year's salary at this moment for a single RPG, or some more frag grenades.

Near the front door, he noticed something that had briefly caught his eye on the way in. It had looked like a small fuse box of some sort, but seeing it again, he realized that it was actually a key box.

Opening it up, he saw there were six pegs. Two had keys. One of them had a handwritten label hanging from a piece of wire that read "shed." The other key had a black plastic head and was instantly recognizable. He grabbed them both and headed outside.

The shed was a small, concrete utility building on the other side of the courtyard. Keeping one eye on the gate, he unlocked the padlock on the shed door and opened it up.

It was filled with junk—buckets, hoses, mops, brooms—nothing useful. Except, over in the corner, something had been hidden under a plastic tarp. He moved to it and pulled it back. Underneath was a dirt bike— a red-and-white Honda XR.

He checked the wheels, the tires, and then the chassis—all of which seemed to be in decent shape.

There was no fuel gauge, so, straddling the motorcycle, he rocked it from side to side and listened. It didn't sound good.

Opening the gas cap, he turned his flashlight on low and peered inside. The tank wasn't very large to begin with, probably less than three gallons, but even half a tank of fuel would have made him feel better. By the looks of it, there was less than a quarter.

Placing the cap back on, he did a quick scan around the shed for any extra gas. He didn't find any and guessed that whatever reserve stock they'd had had been used for the burn barrels and destroying sensitive documents up on the roof.

He hailed Nicholas as he wheeled the bike out of the shed. They had an insider at one of the entrances to Kabul Airport—a man who helped facilitate the ingress and egress of aid organizations.

Crippled by a shortage of food, fuel, and medical supplies, Afghanistan was staying alive only thanks to international assistance. As the SEALs had used aid flights as a ruse in the past, it had been Harvath's idea to employ the same tactic for this operation.

They based out of Tajikistan and chartered an old Antonov An-26 from Tajik Air. The flight crew were highly experienced and had run multiple operations into Afghanistan for the CIA.

Because of instability under the Taliban, it wasn't unusual for aid organizations to have to stage outside the country and bring in supplies via smaller, regional aircraft.

For their part, the Afghan government didn't care where the flights were coming from as long as the critical aid kept flowing.

The facilitator at the airport was named Hamza. He had quite the side hustle going. While aid organizations enjoyed a special, somewhat "protected" status, the treatment aid workers saw could be dialed up or dialed down. This was still Afghanistan, it was still corrupt, and baksheesh still ruled the day. Hamza had been prepaid a healthy amount of it.

He was responsible for getting the rest of Harvath's team into the airport and out to their plane unmolested. At that point, he would receive an additional envelope filled with cash.

Hamza, however, wouldn't be at the airport all night. When his shift ended, he would be gone. What's more, the Tajik flight crew had already filed a flight plan and were expected to return home. That's why a hard time frame had been placed on the mission.

The dreaded Plan B of having to make it all the way up north, linking up with the smugglers, and traveling through the dangerous mountain passes into Tajikistan was beyond unappealing. Harvath was praying he could catch the plane.

Nicholas wasn't so sure. "Dalton," as Hamza had been code-named—after the bouncer in the movie *Road House*—"has already delivered the team. I don't know how much longer he'll be on-site."

Before Harvath could reply, Haney's voice came over the radio. "Just get here," he said. "We'll take care of everything else."

"Not if it means jeopardizing the exfil," Harvath replied.

"You're breaking up, Norseman," the man responded. "Say again."

Harvath didn't believe for a second that Haney was having issues with his radio. "You have your orders," he said to the man. "Follow them."

"Roger that," Haney replied, before handing communications back to Nicholas.

Out of time, Harvath explained what he was about to do and what he needed from Nicholas.

When the little man confirmed, Harvath prepped the bike, propped open the front gate, and counted down.

Three. Two. One.

CHAPTER 7

There had been nothing in the main house, or in the shed, that Harvath could have used to cobble together some sort of a distraction device. He had only one thing going for him, and that was the element of surprise.

The moment he fired up the dirt bike, however, his element of surprise would be gone. At that point, his only chance for escape would be to outrun his pursuers. It was a serious gamble considering how low on fuel he was. Nevertheless, it was a gamble he was going to have to take.

With the gate propped open, he was about to start the motorcycle when he heard voices approaching and, simultaneously, Nicholas radioed him a warning.

"Two tangos, just south of your location, fifteen yards and closing," the little man said.

There was no time to close the gate. There was no time to hide the bike. The only thing he could do was to hide himself.

Flipping down the kickstand, he got off the bike. He moved as quietly as he could to the shed, crouched down, and readied his rifle.

It wasn't optimal. Unlike in the movies, suppressed weapons weren't totally silent. They still emitted a *crack* when a round was fired; it was just at a partially reduced decibel level.

But maybe the courtyard's high walls would help dampen the sound. Maybe the rest of the Taliban down the street wouldn't hear anything.

With the gate wide open, however, it wasn't a wager Harvath would have been willing to put a lot of money on.

He would have much preferred using his knife. Cutting throats was a lot quieter. The only problem was that it wasn't scalable. You couldn't slice two throats at once. That meant he was going to have to use his rifle.

Thankfully, the EOTech holographic sight mounted atop it was compatible with his night-vision goggles. That would allow him the advantage of hanging back in the darkness and attacking from there. It took only moments for the men to arrive.

He watched as the pair entered the courtyard and did a terrible job of "slicing the pie." They seemed more interested in the abandoned motorcycle than clearing all the angles a threat might be coming from.

Applying pressure to his trigger, he fired at both Taliban in rapid succession. One shot apiece, each in the face.

The first man received his round right between the eyes and it tumbled out the back of his skull. The second took his just underneath the nose and it exited out the top of his head.

A spray of red mist hung in the air as their lifeless bodies collapsed to the ground with bits of bone and bloody brain tissue splattered across the wall behind them.

Slinging his weapon, Harvath radioed Nicholas as he sprung out of hiding and raced for the bike. "Tangos down."

"Whatever you did, you just stirred the hornet's nest," the little man replied. "There are multiple tangos inbound to your location."

"How many?"

"*All* of them. Get out of there. *Fast*."

Harvath didn't need any additional encouragement. Leaping onto the motorcycle, he began the very specific process of starting a cold Honda XR.

Turning on both the fuel switch and the ignition, he adjusted the choke all the way forward, pulled in the decompression lever located above the clutch, and rapidly pumped the kick-starter.

He raced through several more steps until he was ready to go.

Finally, he stood up on the kick-starter, pushed straight down, and the bike came roaring to life.

No matter how fast the Taliban were coming at him, hearing the motorcycle firing up would only cause them to double their pace. Opening up the throttle, he popped the clutch and shot straight through the courtyard gate.

As soon as he hit the street, the shooting started. He got as low as he could over the bike and gave it as much gas as possible.

The red-and-white Honda was fast, capable of reaching speeds of over 110 miles per hour. Bullets, however, could reach speeds of thousands of feet per second. He needed to put as much distance between himself and his opponents as quickly as possible.

"I'm going to need a route to the airport," he said over his radio. "Preferably one with no checkpoints."

"Can do. The problem is going to be getting you on the other side of the fence once you arrive. Dalton has already left for the night."

"Tell him to come back."

"We have. He's holding just off the property, not far from the main terminal. But we've got another problem."

"Naturally," said Harvath as he swerved around a pile of garbage someone was burning in the street. "What's the rest of the good news?"

"The team tried to push back the departure to buy you extra time. They were denied. As the last flight out, they're either wheels up as scheduled, or they'll be forced to deplane, remain overnight, and depart in the morning."

That was definitely *not* good news. In fact, it was absolutely untenable. If Topaz and his family were discovered trying to escape, they, along with Harvath's entire team, would be shot well before morning. That plane had to take off. On time. Tonight.

"Wheels up as planned," Harvath ordered, swerving the motorcycle again for another obstacle. "With or without me. Is that clear?"

"Good copy," Nicholas responded.

Another barrage of bullets ripped through the air overhead and chewed up the road around him. The sound from the heavy .50-caliber machine guns was so loud that even at this distance, it was earsplitting.

Any moment, one of the Taliban gunners was going to make the right adjustment and drive one of those massive rounds through either him or the bike. Either would end up being game over for him. He needed to leave these guys behind once and for all—and he needed to do it before he ran out of gas.

At the next intersection, he leaned away from the bike and skidded into the hardest left turn he had ever made.

For a moment, it felt like the motorcycle was going to be ripped right out from underneath him. Then he felt the tires bite into the dirt and, almost as if by magic, the bike defied gravity and began to right itself.

He flew down the road, weaving from side to side, making himself as difficult a target as possible.

At the next intersection, he made an impossibly hard right, his knee grazing the road. It should have hurt like hell, but he was too amped up to notice.

When the next intersection appeared, he pulled another dangerous, hard left turn and opened up the throttle as far as it would go.

He barely registered the houses and storefronts as they whipped by on either side of the street.

He blew through the next intersection without slowing down and then another. It was only after he passed the third that he eased off the throttle.

It had been a few minutes since he had heard gunfire. Risking a look back, he glanced over his shoulder. No one was in sight. He had lost them.

Nevertheless, he was still in hostile territory, behind enemy lines. If he didn't make it to the airport in time to evac with the rest of the team, he was in for a lot more trouble.

CHAPTER 8

P ulling another right turn, Harvath instructed Nicholas to plot him a route. His destination, however, had changed. He wasn't going to the airport, at least not directly.

Instead, he wanted Dalton to meet him at an infamous gas station nearby.

Known by the codename "Oxygen," it had been a rally point manned by Afghanistan's elite "02" paramilitary unit in the final days of the U.S. occupation.

It sat on a quiet piece of road, on the north side of Kabul International, not far from where the Central Intelligence Agency had opened a secret passage through the barrier fencing called "Glory Gate."

While the Taliban controlled the main commercial entrance to the airport, Glory Gate was how the CIA had evacuated high-value intelligence assets and embassy personnel. The gas station was where everyone had been processed and gathered up. Its existence had remained a secret all along. The Taliban never had a clue.

If Harvath could make it there, he might have a chance of making it the rest of the way onto the airfield. There was just one thing he needed from Dalton—*two* if you also included fuel.

Nicholas had routed him via back roads, helping avoid any checkpoints. When he arrived at Oxygen, he coasted in on fumes.

The gas station looked like it had been abandoned for years. In exchange for allowing them to use it, the owner had convinced the CIA to take him with them when they left.

Almost anywhere else, someone would have tried to step in and restart the business. Not here. What little fuel that did make it into the country was quickly commandeered by the Taliban. No matter how great the demand, without a somewhat predictable supply of product, running any business was next to impossible.

The place looked well picked over. Harvath doubted there was a single can of gas just lying around. What's more, he didn't have a moment to spare to search for it.

Leaning against a brown Toyota sedan, waiting for him, was Dalton. He had a thick, gray beard, gnarled hands, and a weather-beaten face.

According to his file, he was forty-seven years old. He looked seventy. Yet another example of how everything aged rapidly in Afghanistan.

Pulling up next to him, Harvath placed his right hand over his heart in a sign of respect and quickly greeted him with the Arabic phrase common in most Islamic countries, "Salam alaikum."

Dalton returned the gesture and replied, "Wa'alaikum salam."

Normally, some back-and-forth pleasantries took place before getting down to business, but in this case there wasn't any time. His plane was minutes away from taking off.

"What have you got for me?" he asked.

Dalton beckoned him to come look inside his trunk.

Putting down the kickstand, he turned off the ignition, climbed off the bike, and walked over to the rear of the car to peer inside.

The Afghan fixer had a little bit of everything. Pulling back a ratty blue towel, he showed off three frag grenades and a roll of duct tape.

"Good?" he asked.

For opening up a solid steel gate that had been welded shut as the last CIA personnel left the country? It was hard to say. Maybe. But maybe not. This wasn't a situation in which you wanted to underdo anything. He was going to get only one crack at it.

Seeing the tip of something he recognized peeking out from under a blanket, Harvath pointed at it.

Dalton held up his hand, shook his head, and stated, "No, no, no."

"Yes, yes, yes," Harvath replied, reaching in and pulling the blanket back. Underneath was an older but hopefully still-functional RPG with an armor-penetrating HEAT warhead.

"Very expensive," Dalton insisted. Covering it up, he picked up the towel with the grenades and encouraged Harvath to take them. "Good. Good."

Whether this guy liked it or not, Harvath was leaving with that RPG in the next sixty seconds, if not sooner.

Withdrawing his own envelope of cash—meant to see him through Plan B if necessary—he held it out and offered it to Dalton. The man's eyes widened, both at the sight of the stack of American currency and the watch strapped to Harvath's wrist. He indicated that he wanted the time-piece as well.

Harvath wasn't in any position to haggle. Unbuckling his Seaholm Offshore Dive Watch, he handed it, along with the cash, to Dalton. The Afghan then gestured for Harvath to help himself to the RPG.

The weapon had a frayed sling and only the one grenade. If it didn't work, he was screwed.

Strapping it to his back, he thanked the man, hopped back on the bike, and tried to start it. Nothing happened. There wasn't enough fuel.

Harvath hurriedly rocked it from side to side. He could faintly hear some gas sloshing in the tank. Once more he attempted to start the machine and once more, he failed.

Dalton seemed to understand the problem. Signaling for Harvath to get off, he grabbed the bike by the handlebars and laid it on its left side. It took Harvath only a fraction of a second to figure out why.

The gas tank was built over the frame like a set of saddlebags. The fuel, however, entered the carburetor via the left side. Without tipping the bike all the way over, a small remnant of gas would slosh at the bottom of the right side and never be used.

Raising the motorcycle back upright, Dalton indicated that Harvath should try again.

Harvath got back on the bike and it fired up on the first try. Thanking the Afghan one last time, he took off toward the Glory Gate.

Halfway there, he could hear Haney's voice over his earpiece. The pilots were done with their preflight check and about to fire up the engines. "What's your status?" his teammate asked.

"I'm still three klicks out," Harvath replied. "Minimum."

"The pilots are going to request permission to warm the engines—do a little back-and-forth on the tarmac before takeoff. It may buy us a couple of minutes."

"Good copy. Just remember—with or without me—you go wheels up."

"Roger that," Haney replied. "I saved you a seat in first class, so make sure you get here on time."

The Soviet-era aircraft was anything but first class. It was amazing to him that not only had it gotten off the ground, but that it had cleared all of the mountains between the Tajik capital of Dushanbe and Kabul. Fingers crossed it would do the same on the return trip.

Watching from the tactical operations center back in Northern Virginia, Nicholas kept Harvath up to speed on everything he could see via satellite.

Eventually, after stories appeared in the American press, the Taliban had learned about the covert entrance the CIA had created on the backside of the airport. But, because Glory Gate didn't serve any purpose for them, they had left it sealed and unguarded. The Taliban had neither the imagination nor the manpower to treat it as a potential weak point, which was exactly what Harvath was banking on.

Nicholas guided him to a spot halfway between the main road and the secret gate. There, Harvath turned off the bike's ignition and laid it on its left side just in case there was even a single drop of fuel that could still be reclaimed.

He then quickly field-stripped the RPG and examined its components, before reassembling it and getting himself into a safe firing position.

The most important consideration was not to be right on top of the target. The warhead needed five meters of travel in which to become armed.

After about ten meters, the rocket's internal motor ignites, its stabilizer fins pop out, and the round is pushed to full velocity, reaching a blistering speed of approximately three football fields a second.

At its top speed, the warhead was capable of penetrating eleven inches of solid steel. The RPG's reputation as one of the deadliest and easiest-to-use weapons on the battlefield was well deserved. This one was going to go through the Glory Gate like a red-hot screwdriver through a butterfly's wing.

Confirming that the back-blast area behind him was clear, Harvath sighted in his target, pressed the trigger, and sent the deadly projectile screaming toward the gate.

Less than two seconds later, it hit *hard* and detonated in a brilliant explosion. Harvath didn't wait to assess the damage. Lifting the bike, he fired it up and drove straight for it.

The nearer he got, the better he could see how well the RPG had done its job. The warhead had blown half of the massive steel gate clean off its hinges. He couldn't have hoped for a more perfect opening. Gunning the throttle, he drove right through it.

"I'm inside the wire, but black on fuel," he radioed, letting his team know that he was almost out of gas. "What's your location?"

"We're on the runway, ready to take off," said Haney. "East end."

"*East* end?"

"They changed the takeoff direction. There's a headwind."

Harvath wasn't a pilot, but he had flown in enough aircraft to know that taking off into a headwind created more lift, allowing the plane to get off the ground at a lower speed and in less time.

His problem, however, was that the east end of the runway was on the other side of the airport, over three and a half klicks away.

"That's too far," he said, the bike already beginning to sputter. "I'm not going to make it."

"You may not have a choice," Haney replied. "It looks like using the world's biggest door knocker on that gate has drawn you some unwelcome attention. I'm counting six heavily armed security vehicles, all with lights and sirens, rolling in your direction."

Sitting near the pilots, Tyler Staelin chimed in with more bad news. "The tower has just ordered a full ground stop. The entire airport is shut down. We've been told to taxi off the runway and immediately return to our parking apron."

"That's not happening," Harvath stated. "Tell the pilots to ignore the tower."

"You want us to take off?"

"Affirmative."

"What about you? We're not leaving you here."

"No, you're not," he responded. "We're going to compromise and you're going to meet me in the middle."

•   •   •

Harvath didn't have time to do the math. He had kicked the hornet's nest and had a phalanx of vehicles headed toward him. Increasing his speed, he risked burning through what little gas he had left in the tank.

This was an absolute, last-ditch effort and there was zero room for error. If he was off by even a hair, there was no contingency plan.

Over the radio, Nicholas called out distances. "Five hundred meters. Four hundred meters. Three hundred meters." Then finally he said, "One hundred fifty meters. *Brake now*."

Harvath braked and leaned the bike into a hard right turn. A massive plume of dust was thrown into the air. He couldn't wait for visibility to improve. The props of the Antonov An-26's engines could be heard as the aircraft came screaming up the runway toward him.

Hitting the throttle, he sped down the taxiway and onto the main runway. The plane was behind him and they were both headed in the same direction. Once again, Nicholas began calling out distances. In his peripheral vision, Harvath could see the column of security vehicles closing in.

When the little man called out, "Seventy-five meters," Harvath steered the bike as close to the edge of the fifty-meter-wide runway as he dared.

As soon as the plane zoomed past, he could see Haney and Gage, harnessed up, on opposite sides of its lowered tail ramp.

Haney directed Harvath in, while Gage had his rifle at the ready, manning overwatch.

Harvath leaned into the center of the runway and lined up with the Antonov's ramp. The security vehicles behind him were so close, he could hear the blaring of their Klaxons over the roaring of the plane. Their strobes pulsed the aircraft in bursts of hot light.

When Haney announced, "Now!" over the radio, Harvath opened the throttle the rest of the way as Gage began firing toward the security vehicles, sending them scattering off the runway.

The plane then slowed, just enough, and Harvath raced up the ramp. As soon as he was inside, Haney radioed, "Got him! Go for wheels up!"

"Roger that," Staelin responded, relaying the command into the cockpit. "Going for wheels up."

The pilots revved the plane's enormous engines as Haney closed the tail ramp and Gage secured his weapon.

Before Harvath could turn off the motorcycle, it sputtered one last time and died, totally out of fuel.

Haney grinned. "I told you your plan sucked."

Harvath grinned back as he hurriedly climbed off the bike. "A bad plan executed with balls always beats a good plan that's gone to shit."

"Classy. Clausewitz?"

"Bismarck," interjected Gage, as he joined the pair and helped quickly strap down the motorcycle.

As the plane lifted off, the men grabbed the closest seats they could find. Most of his teammates eventually closed their eyes and tried to get some sleep. It had been a long, hard night.

Harvath, however, found it difficult to drift off. Even the deep, meditative-like state he often dipped into before missions was proving elusive.

He was still wound pretty tight from the operation. That was to be expected. Nevertheless, he had always been capable of shutting off that part of his brain and powering down.

Was he concerned about the plane making it back to Tajikistan? He had flown on much worse aircraft and statistically, the odds were in their favor. What's more, the Taliban had very few functioning aircraft, and even fewer pilots, that they could call on to give chase. And even if they did, Afghanistan's radar monitoring system was all but defunct.

As an added layer of protection, the Antonov's pilots had filed a phony flight plan, taking them east into Pakistan, rather than north to Tajikistan.

Minutes after takeoff, they shut down their transponder and changed course.

The Taliban wouldn't have just been looking for a needle, they would have been searching for the actual haystack—and they would have had to do it blindfolded.

So, what was it then? What was eating away at the back of his mind? Harvath couldn't put his finger on it. All he knew was that something was coming.

Something very bad.

CHAPTER 9

Military intelligence for the People's Liberation Army was handled by the Joint Staff Department of the Central Military Commission Intelligence Bureau. It was quite a mouthful.

Only six years into the name change and Colonel Yang Xin still hated it. He much preferred when the organization was known as the Intelligence Bureau of the General Staff, or more simply, the Second Bureau.

Even the acronym, JSDCMCIB, was a tongue-twister. China, like so many of the Western nations it despised, was being choked to death by bureaucracy. When your "rebrand" ended up lengthening your name, rather than shortening it, Yang figured things probably weren't headed in a positive direction.

China, via its horribly conceived one-child policy, was heading straight for a demographic tsunami. Though the program had been jettisoned right around the time his organization got its name change, the damage had already been done.

The buckets of water next to birthing beds, ready to drown female babies, had not only been immoral, but had also been a form of slow-motion suicide for the nation.

Every single day, somewhere in China, there was civil unrest—often in multiple places. Now, with hundreds of millions of men coming of age, unable to find wives and girlfriends, things were only going to get worse.

With Russian men dropping like flies from drug and alcohol addiction, a professor from the Chinese Academy of Social Sciences had put forth the idea that China and Russia each had fifty percent of a puzzle that needed fixing.

While the men of China quite liked the idea of blond-haired, blue-eyed brides, the feeling was unrequited. In a poll of Russian women, they said they'd rather Moscow enact polygamy than they marry Chinese men.

It was a simple-minded suggestion for a complicated problem for which Beijing had only itself to blame.

Yang, for all intents and purposes, was secure, but only as long as the Communist Party and the country were secure. He was married and had two children—a boy and a girl—permission for which had come as a perk of his position. His car, the apartment block he lived in, the excellent schools his privileged children attended, all of it was made possible by the state. Its survival was his survival and so, despite disagreements on some governmental policies, he was nevertheless a fierce defender of his motherland.

The Intelligence Bureau was highly compartmentalized and, because of the nature of its operations, extremely secretive. Yang's division was one of the IB's most covert and most protected. Its codename was *Yaomo*—Chinese for "demon."

Yaomo's job was to terrorize China's enemies—to be the stuff of bloodcurdling nightmares.

A slight, sickly-looking man with thinning hair and dark circles under his eyes, Yang wasn't exactly what came to mind when one thought of an architect of human horrors. But it wasn't his appearance that he had been selected for. In fact, being unremarkable, even forgettable, was actually a plus in the espionage business.

No, Yang had reached his position via his ability to conceive of spectacular operations and to see them carried out to completion.

The attack on Indian troops in the Galwan Valley had been one such operation. And in typical Yang fashion, there had been an added element of surprise.

The Science and Technology Commission had been working on a suite of directed-energy weapons and had wanted to test their latest under actual battlefield conditions. Yang had been all too happy to provide the opportunity.

The weapon had exceeded expectations, repelling all of the enemy combatants while providing exceptional cover for the Chinese soldiers to escape. Today they were going to employ two different weapons, six and a half hours apart, on two different sides of the world. One in the United States and another, once again, in India.

It was why he had come into the office so early. He had been given an enormous task and was spinning a significant number of plates.

Coordinating the assassination of the American in Jaipur had been difficult, but not impossible. The heightened tensions between China and India had drawn added attention to all of its diplomatic personnel, especially its intelligence officers.

Whether you worked at the Chinese Embassy in New Delhi, or one of the consulates in Kolkata or Mumbai, you couldn't move without being smothered by a blanket of surveillance.

Even using NOCs—intelligence operatives without official ties to Beijing—you could not employ anyone even remotely Chinese. "Chindians"—persons of mixed Chinese and Indian lineage—existed in India, as did some expatriate Chinese, but their numbers were so low compared to the overall population that they always drew attention and, after what had happened in the Galwan Valley, were the objects of suspicion and sometimes downright hostility.

Indians were a stubborn, patriotic people. Their dislike and distrust of all things Chinese were only growing. So, Yang had been forced to adapt—but adaptation was one of his strong suits.

While he could use Chinese operatives in the United States, pretty much at will, he had recruited an exceptional, non-Chinese operative to coordinate things on the ground in India.

The excellence of his operatives was imperative, because the next steps in his plan were more complicated and required even more caution. There could be no loose ends; nothing that might trace back to Beijing.

If anything went wrong, he wouldn't have to worry about the Americans or the Indians coming after him. His own government would put a bullet in the back of his head and send the bill to his family.

He couldn't let that happen. Yang needed to obsess over every detail. He needed to be sure that every person he put into the field was at the top of their game, the absolute best.

And once he had done all that, he needed to pray that none of his adversaries fielded anyone better.

Because if they did, all bets would be off. He would bring every deadly tool at his disposal to bear. And he would do it without giving a second thought to the cost. Nothing was going to stop him from accomplishing his task.

CHAPTER 10

The Indian Air Force helicopter had taken off from Sulur Air Base en route to the town of Wellington, in India's southern state of Tamil Nadu. There were a total of fourteen people aboard, including the chief of Defense Staff of the Indian Armed Forces. Twenty minutes into the twenty-seven-minute flight, all communications were lost.

Air traffic control had tried desperately to reestablish contact with the Soviet-designed Mi-17V-5 aircraft but had been unsuccessful and had feared the worst.

When calls started coming in about a fire, not far from Wellington, in the hilly, forested township of Coonoor, their anxiety mounted.

It took a local rescue crew half an hour to mobilize and cut their way through the trees and thick underbrush to get to the site. Once they did, they found the wreckage of the helicopter still engulfed in flames. There was only one survivor—a group captain of the Indian Air Force named Khattar. He was conscious, but horribly burned.

They worked quickly and carefully to remove him. Carrying him to a road at the edge of the forest, they loaded him into a waiting ambulance.

As the ambulance raced toward the military hospital in Wellington, state police officers established a cordon and waited for crash scene investigators to arrive.

Fifteen hundred miles north, in New Delhi, Asha Patel was about to leave for lunch, when the phone on her desk rang.

"The secretary's conference room," a curt voice on the other end of the line said. "Now."

The Research and Analysis Wing, also known as RAW, was India's foreign intelligence service. Established in 1968, it was structured similarly to the American CIA and had been entrusted with a very broad mandate.

At its core, RAW was responsible for gathering foreign intelligence and advancing India's strategic interests abroad. Among its additional responsibilities, it handled counterterrorism operations, psychological warfare, and direct-action assignments such as assassinations and assisted in safeguarding India's nuclear program.

Its premier department was also its most clandestine. The Special Operations Division, or simply "The Division" as it was referred to by insiders, handled RAW's most dangerous and most sensitive assignments. Asha Patel was one of the Division's top operatives.

The youngest of six children, she had been raised in a solidly middle-class family in Mumbai. Both of her parents had been college professors— her father at the Indian Institute of Technology and her mother at the Institute of Chemical Technology. None of the Patels were lacking in brainpower. In fact, her brothers and sisters had all gone into either accounting or the tech sector. Asha, however, answered a different calling.

Despite having an uncle in the film industry who was convinced that he could make her a star, with her long legs and striking good looks, she chose to pursue a career of public service.

She believed in the promise of India. And while that promise was not perfect, she believed in both its power and its potential.

She had seen, firsthand, what education and hard work had done for her family. She wanted all families in India, regardless of their religion or caste, to have access to the same opportunities.

What they did with those opportunities was up to them. No nation-state or political philosophy could guarantee an equality of outcomes. People were simply far too different. Some were born with minds for mathematics and science, others for literature and the arts. Some were predisposed to alcoholism and addiction, while others were blessed with a capacity for entrepreneurship. The greatest thing India could do for its people was to keep the playing field as level as possible and work tirelessly to see to it that everyone was following the rules. After that, it was up to the individual to succeed based on their talent and hard work.

Of course, there would always be those who, because of infirmity or just bad luck, would require more help. The family who loses their house in a flood. The child born with debilitating mental or physical liabilities. The mother or father who is earnest and struggling to find work.

Asha had watched in awe growing up as families and communities had rallied around such people in need. She understood, however, that sometimes the need was greater than what one's extended family or community could provide. She believed that the state had a role to fill in these rare instances.

Her father had called her his "little idealist." Her mother had called her a "brave and powerful realist." Both parents had believed she was destined to do good and noble things for the people of India. Neither would have ever expected it would be in the realm of espionage.

In fact, had you put the possibility to her as she had begun her studies at the Lal Bahadur Shastri National Academy of Administration—India's preeminent institute for civil service training—she would have squinted at you with her dusty brown eyes, her mouth would have turned up into a radiant smile, and she would have laughed out loud at the ridiculousness of it all.

But that, of course, was if you had asked her at the beginning. By the time Asha was ready to graduate, she had developed a much more nuanced view of India, its promise, and what was necessary to preserve it.

Lal Bahadur Shastri was a prime recruiting ground for RAW. It not only had agents posing as students; it also had multiple professors and teaching assistants who functioned as talent scouts, seeking out the best and brightest potential candidates.

Through their embedded proxies, RAW also ran a subtle, ongoing information campaign.

It was important that tomorrow's civil servants understood their responsibilities not only to the governmental organizations they would be serving, but also to India and its citizens. They needed to understand the threats the country faced and the importance of combatting malign foreign influence.

Having secured its independence from the British in 1947, when it was separated into two dominions—Hindu-majority India and Muslim-majority Pakistan—India was less than one hundred years old. In that period, however, it had gone to war five times—once with its neighbor China and four times with its other significant neighbor, Pakistan.

Similar in many ways to Israel, India lived under a constant state of threat, both from outside its borders, as well as from a wide range of terrorist organizations operating within.

During her studies at Lal Bahadur Shastri, Asha's eyes had been opened and her priorities more keenly focused. She realized that if India itself was not zealously protected, its promise would cease to exist—*for everyone*. The opportunities for education, prosperity, and advancement that her family had enjoyed depended upon India remaining strong and free. In the aftermath of the three days of terror attacks across Mumbai that had killed 171 people, she had known what she needed to do.

Upon her graduation, RAW had given her one day to celebrate with her family. After that, it was time to get to work. The *real* work.

Her parents and siblings had thought she was undergoing training and would ultimately be placed in the Indian Administrative Service, focusing on governmental policy. She had not been allowed to inform them that she was employed by RAW or to discuss any of the operations she would ever be involved in. As far as her family was concerned, she was a busy civil servant up north in New Delhi.

Her training was brutal—both physically and psychologically. She had been told how tough it was and had done her best to get herself into peak condition, but nothing could have prepared her for what she experienced—especially when it came to her instructors.

Ironically, the female instructors turned out to be much tougher on her than the men, and she learned on day one that "sisterhood" wasn't something that existed in RAW training.

The lead drill instructor—an unattractive woman, who reeked of body odor—seemed to have it out for her and rode her day and night.

That was fine by Asha. She hadn't signed up to make friends. She had signed up to defend India.

With four older brothers and a somewhat vindictive older sister, she was no stranger to being picked on. Instructors being "tough" wasn't something she objected to. What she couldn't abide was unnecessary cruelty.

The woman undercounted Asha's pull-ups and push-ups, lied about her obstacle course performance, and falsified her run times. It was as if the instructor was trying to get her to drop out. That, however, wasn't going to happen. Asha simply bit her tongue and redoubled her efforts.

When they got to the hand-to-hand portion of the training, however, things got considerably rougher. The instructor appeared to take a perverse pleasure in making an example of Asha, embarrassing her and causing her pain.

Asha had wanted to strike back, to really kick the woman's ass, but she had pushed her anger down and had summoned every ounce of patience she could muster. But then her patience ran out.

It was an oppressive, exceptionally humid afternoon. Everyone was dripping with sweat. They had been given very little sleep for the past several nights. The food had been terrible, the coffee and tea little more than brown water. Not that any of that justified what she did. She should have better controlled her emotions.

They were working on how to take a weapon away from an opponent. As always, the instructor called Asha forward to help demonstrate the process.

The instructor walked the group through it slowly a couple of times, then racked the pistol's slide. Looking at Asha, she told her that they'd now be doing it for real.

Asha's eyes widened. Doing it for real? *Right here? With a loaded weapon?* The instructor had to be insane.

Drying her palms on her BDU pants, Asha made ready. When the instructor moved in and presented the pistol, Asha went through the steps, just as she had been taught. That was when everything had gone wrong.

The instructor changed up her approach. Instead of allowing Asha to step off the line of attack and get out of the way of the muzzle, she had shifted her weight and had driven right at her, taking Asha totally by surprise.

Asha went for the gun, but her hands were still slick with perspiration and they slipped while trying to take control of the weapon. It was at that moment that the instructor fired.

The crack of the round was so loud that it felt like someone had hammered spikes into each of her ears. But that wasn't the worst of it. As the weapon attempted to cycle, the web of her left hand, between her thumb and forefinger, was bitten into as the slide came racing forward. The white-hot pain was excruciating.

Instead of trying to help extricate her student, the instructor fought to maintain control of the pistol. That was the point at which Asha absolutely lost it.

Bringing her free hand up, she used it to twist the weapon and create a massive amount of torque and subsequent pain in her instructor's wrist.

She then pulled down, causing her instructor to stumble forward. That was when she let go of the weapon and punched the woman in the jaw, following it up with an elbow to her nose.

Bone and cartilage cracked. Blood sprayed. A fellow student rushed over to help Asha apply enough pressure to retract the slide and reclaim her hand. Another grabbed a towel to help stanch the bleeding. No one moved to assist the instructor, who had fallen, unconscious, onto the ground.

They ran lots and lots of laps after that and conducted lots and lots of forced marches with backpacks loaded down with BFR (big fucking rocks), but no one complained to Asha about it. She had become a rock star to her fellow cadets.

More important, she never had a problem with her drill instructor— or any instructor, for that matter—again. In fact, she graduated at the top of her class.

The reputation she had developed in training as a smart operative able to take care of herself was what had made her so attractive to the Division. Their agents were expected to perform with little to no support in a constantly changing battlespace. They needed to function as their own cavalry and rapidly adapt as circumstances dictated. They were the best that India put into the field.

Hanging up the phone, Asha sent a quick text to the friends she was supposed to have met for lunch, picked up the leather-bound notepad her parents had given her as a graduation gift, and headed toward the secretary's conference room.

Unlike other agents in the Special Operations Division, she had never let her boss's brusque style get to her. Onkar Raj—an average-looking man in his late fifties with thinning hair, a pencil-thin mustache, and boxy eyeglasses—was short with people because he needed to be. India had countless knives to its throat and more popping up daily, if not hourly. It was Raj who was responsible for handling the most serious among them. The stress of his job was said to be akin to juggling bottles covered in razor blades. Asha wouldn't have traded places with him for all the money in the world.

While many saw him as a colossal prick, he was *their* prick and she appreciated that he got things done. No matter what his people needed, they always received it.

Even more important, he stood behind them one hundred percent and would go toe-to-toe with the prime minister himself if ever need be. Raj was a good man and India's foreign intelligence service was lucky to have him.

"Close the door," he said as she entered the conference room.

Asha did a quick scan as she obeyed his command. No one else was present. It was just the two of them. "Are we waiting for anyone else?"

"No," the man replied, gesturing for her to sit. "It's just you and me."

"Then why didn't we meet in my office or at least in—"

He held up his hand and cut her off. "Because our offices are no longer safe. In fact, this is the last meeting you and I are going to have in this building."

"What are you talking about?"

Removing a piece of paper from the folder in front of him, he slid it across the table to her.

She looked at it in disbelief.

"Asha Raveena Patel," he stated, "you are hereby terminated. Effectively immediately."

"But this is a letter of resignation."

"I know what it is," he replied, dyspeptic as ever. "Sign it."

"I don't understand. I haven't done anything wrong. Is this some kind of a joke?"

"It is not," he responded, removing his pen and pushing it toward her. "You have been given a direct order. Quit asking questions. Sign the document."

Several moments passed. Then, slowly, she picked up the pen and scratched out her signature.

Securing the cap, she passed the pen back to him, along with the piece of paper ending her career.

Raj took out his phone and showed her a photograph. "Do you recognize this location?"

Dumbfounded and trying to process what was going on, Asha nodded.

"I want you to clean out your office. There's already a security team waiting to accompany you. Only take what you can carry. Drop everything back at your apartment and then meet me in an hour. Do you understand?"

How could she? Against her will, she had just been forced to resign. None of this made any sense. What the hell was going on?

"I'll explain everything in an hour," her boss continued. "In the meantime, I want you to be very careful. Don't talk to anyone. And even more important, don't trust anyone."

Asha nodded once more. It was the only response she could manage.

"Good," Raj replied. Standing up, he put his hand on her shoulder. "Keep eyes in the back of your head. Do not, under any circumstances, let your guard down."

With that final warning, he left the conference room.

CHAPTER 11

The photo on Raj's phone was of a multistory concrete office building approximately fifteen minutes' walk from RAW headquarters. It was part of a complex of buildings that sat, surrounded by trees, at the southwest corner of the Delhi Golf Club. Next door, a mere one hundred meters through the woods, stood the stunning Oberoi—one of the finest and most luxurious hotels in the city.

By contrast, the Blind Relief Association of Delhi was quite plain. Most people passed without even noticing it.

Its buildings were nothing special. Neither were its grounds. The true beauty was to be found inside.

With more than eight million visually impaired people, India was home to a quarter of the world's blind population. The Blind Relief Association of Delhi existed to help them "develop their latent talents and realize their fullest potential."

It was begun in the 1940s by a local couple who wanted to do more than create a charity. They wanted to give India's visually impaired purpose, self-confidence, and fulfillment. The facility provided vocational training for a wide swath of industries—from textile manufacturing and massage therapy, to furniture-making and call center staffing.

In addition to job placement and ongoing support, the organization offered medical care, secondary school education, and tireless, around-the-clock advocacy. There was no more noble, nor greater, friend to India's visually impaired.

But as wonderful as the organization was, Asha had no idea why Raj had requested that she meet him there. It was a highly unusual location.

Even so, she had done as her boss had requested. She cleaned out her desk, endured the humiliating escort out of the building, and took the cardboard box filled with her belongings back to her apartment.

As instructed, she spoke with no one. She kept her head on a swivel and was careful as hell. Whatever was going on, it had to be massive. There was no other way to explain all of the subterfuge.

After changing into street clothes, she lifted up her shirt and placed a Glock 19, with an inside-the-waistband holster and a spare magazine holder, into her jeans. If things were bad enough that she wasn't supposed to trust anyone, she definitely wasn't going anywhere unarmed.

She grabbed a nondescript backpack and threw in a few appearance-altering items like a hat, sunglasses, and a jacket. Slinging the bag over her shoulder, she left the apartment.

Delhi was different in so many ways from Mumbai, where she had grown up. It was the capital of India and the center of politics and culture. With more than eighteen thousand parks, there were green spaces—and birds—everywhere. At the same time, the air pollution was some of the worst in the world and crime was so bad, many people would go out only at night if they were in a group. It was also very, very crowded.

Even in the middle of the day, the streets and sidewalks of Delhi were packed. It made it almost impossible to tell if you were being followed. Asha, however, had been trained by the best and knew what to do.

She threaded her way through multiple bustling neighborhoods. Cars honked and motorbikes buzzed past. With it being Diwali, the air was filled with the delicious aroma of feasts being prepared.

Intricate works of art made with brilliantly colored powder and fine sand, known as *rangolis,* could be seen everywhere.

In houses and businesses, offerings were being made to Lakshmi, the goddess of prosperity and wealth.

All of these sights, sounds, and smells were enough to overwhelm a person's senses. Nevertheless, Asha maintained her focus and used all of her tricks to flush out anyone who might have been following her. She didn't see anything that gave her pause.

The only thing that caught her attention was a television, inside a shop, that was broadcasting reports of a helicopter that had gone down in the southern Indian state of Tamil Nadu.

Arriving at the Blind Relief Association with a few minutes to spare, she found Raj already waiting for her near the front desk.

He didn't smile. He didn't greet her. He merely tilted his head toward a hallway and began walking. Asha followed.

The walls were lined with photographs of famous celebrities, sports figures, and politicians who had visited over the years. All of them showed the visitors meaningfully engaged with the students or staff. There were no autographed vanity headshots provided after the fact by a press or media relations person.

In one photo was a Bollywood actress whom many of Asha's friends thought she resembled, Chitrangada Singh. In it, the actress could be seen helping students make candles by pouring wax into small clay molds. In another photo, the wife of Japan's foreign minister had paused to admire the school's foundation stone, which had been laid by Helen Keller.

There was a shot of a famous cricketer who had been blindfolded and was being taught how to navigate using a support cane. A well-known industrialist could be seen trying his hand at one of the machines in the sewing school, while all three mayors of Delhi—North, South, and East—were shown, together, preparing and serving food in the association's kitchen. Asha took it all in as they walked.

At the end of the hall was a locked metal door. Raj removed a set of keys from his pocket and opened it. Three flights of stairs led down to the basement level and another corridor. This one was different from the one above.

There was no ornamentation. The lights were simple and much dimmer. Everything was gray—the walls, the floor, even the ceiling. The doors were metal, like the one at the top of the stairs, and also gray. A letter and a number had been painted in white upon each one.

When they arrived at D7, Raj reached back into his pocket for his keys. As he did, Asha detected the faint scent of some sort of smoke coming from the other side. Opening the door, Raj stood back and allowed her to step inside.

It was a long, low-ceilinged storage room that had been turned into some sort of makeshift operations center—and it appeared to have been done on a very low budget.

There were plenty of desks and desk chairs—none of which matched. Dented, and in some cases rusted, steel bakery shelves had been used to mount aging flat-panel monitors around the space. The workstations, printers, and telephones also appeared to be at least ten years out of date.

At one of the desks, under a lamp that looked like it had come from a charity shop, was the source of the smoke. Asha recognized the man immediately.

Gopal Gupta was a legend. In his day, long before he had retired, he had been considered one of RAW's most brilliant thinkers. His understanding of India and its enemies was said to have been unrivaled. He had served for decades, and rarely did a general or a prime minister make a major move without consulting him for his analysis.

There were two additional things he was also known for. The first was for his pipe smoking. Long after government workplaces had gone smoke-free, he was the only person who had continued as if the rule had never been enacted. So valuable was he that RAW created a special exemption for him. He was the only government employee in the whole of India to be allowed to smoke in any government building.

The other remarkable item about Gopal Gupta was his appearance. The joke had been that his thirst for knowledge was equaled only by his hunger for food. He possessed a quite robust double chin. He also had an unusually long and pointed nose. This combination of features, coupled with jealousy over his special position in the Indian intelligence community, had earned him a rather unkind nickname. Behind his back, he was referred to as the "Pelican."

Asha had never met him. As she was working her way up the ranks at RAW, Gupta was preparing for his retirement. By the time she came into her own, he had already left. Even though he had been out of the game for several years, it was incredible to see him sitting there, poring over maps of some sort, puffing away on his pipe.

"Senior Field Officer Asha Patel," Raj began. "I'd like to introduce you to—"

"Special Secretary Gopal Gupta," she stated, finishing his sentence for him. "I am honored to meet you, sir. I've heard a lot about you."

"Which, depending on what you've heard," Gupta said, smiling as he stood and walked over to shake her hand, "is probably true."

Despite his girth, and his age, there was a power in how he moved. His hand was large, but as it enveloped hers, he applied just the right amount of firmness.

He was measured and confident. His eyes were bright, and in them she could see a bit of the Machiavellian gleam that had allegedly made him so good at his job.

"I have heard a lot about you, too," he said, releasing her hand. "We're lucky to have you here."

Her eyes shifted from Gupta to Raj. "Now that I'm *here,* what is all of this? What's going on?"

"Let's sit," Raj replied, pointing at a ramshackle wooden table. "And I'll fill you in. As promised. On everything."

CHAPTER 12

Gupta poured tea as Raj started his PowerPoint briefing via the large flat-panel monitor hanging from a set of shelves at the head of the table.

"Because of repeated Chinese provocations along the Line of Actual Control, we worked with the Army to make sure that drone operators were embedded with all units of the Ladakh Scouts. The footage I am about to show you comes from an attack at the river in the Galwan Valley. Even recorded in night vision, it is extremely difficult to watch."

Asha nodded and Raj pushed PLAY.

She had heard about the horrible, barbaric attack in the Himalayas. Everyone in India had. But right now, seeing it play out on-screen, she was at an utter loss for words. The brutality of it all was beyond description.

The footage had been edited down, but it was apparent that the vicious, hand-to-hand combat had raged for hours. She had never seen anything like it. The Snow Warriors had fought with exceptional valor and, in her estimation, were all deserving of medals.

"Wait," she said as the footage fuzzed out and went to black. "What happened there?"

"We believe the Chinese engaged some sort of microwave weapon to cover their retreat."

"Why do you think that?"

"The Ladakh Scouts," Raj answered, "complained of vomiting and being boiled alive from the inside out."

"Which, if it was microwave energy, probably would have also knocked out the drone."

"Precisely."

"Is there any other footage?" Asha asked.

"Only of the aftermath," Raj answered, advancing to the next slide and playing a new video.

This footage had been captured by a video camera or a cell phone camera. It was daylight, and the full, horrific toll of the battle could be seen. The rocky, bloodstained ground. The dead bodies. The terribly injured. All of it.

"So what does this have to do with why I'm here?"

Raj gestured for her to be patient and advanced to his next slide. "This is American diplomat Eli Ritter."

Asha studied the photograph on the screen. "He doesn't look like any diplomat I've ever seen."

"That's because he's not like any diplomat you've ever seen," Gupta explained.

"I don't understand. What kind is he?"

"He was involved in a form of shadow diplomacy, similar to intelligence operatives doing business without official cover."

"What happened to him?"

"This," said Raj, clicking to his next set of slides. "These are from last night in Jaipur."

Asha stared at each of the crime scene and autopsy photos as they slowly scrolled by.

"It was a .22 round," Raj continued. "We believe subsonic. No one heard or saw anything. The weapon was probably suppressed and, based on the evidence, was pressed right up behind his ear when it was fired."

"A suppressed .22?" she said. "Right behind the ear? That's a mafia-style killing."

"Agreed," Gupta responded.

"What was this American shadow diplomat doing in Jaipur, and what does it have to do with the Chinese attacking our troops at the Galwan River?"

"In answer to the first part of your question, Ritter was here pursuing a military alignment," said Raj.

"What kind of military alignment?"

"Before I go any further, I want to remind you that despite the severance document you signed just over an hour ago, you still remain bound by all of your previous national security nondisclosure agreements."

"So stipulated," Asha stated.

"To counter China, the Americans are working to create an Asian version of NATO," explained Gupta. "The founding nations would include the United States, Japan, Australia, and India."

She couldn't believe her ears. "The Chinese would go ballistic over something like that—maybe even *literally*."

"Which is exactly why all of the diplomacy was being handled in the shadows."

Suddenly all of the pieces in her brain tumbled into place. "You think the Chinese killed Ritter."

"We do," said Gupta. "We just can't prove it yet."

"What happens when you can?"

"That's a decision that gets made at desks much bigger than ours."

"There's also another, very serious development that has taken place," interjected Raj, bringing the focus back to his PowerPoint. He advanced to the next slide. "Two hours ago, a military transport helicopter crashed in Coonoor."

Asha held members of the Indian Armed Forces in very high esteem. She knew the critical role they played in the country's survival. Any loss of personnel, for any reason, was tragic. "That's terrible. I saw something about it on my way here. But the reports didn't identify the aircraft as military."

"Because the press doesn't know—at least not yet. For the time being, all of the details, including the manifest, are being withheld."

"*Including the manifest?* Who was on board?"

"General Mehra," said Raj, breaking the news.

"The chief of Defense Staff?" Asha asked. "*That* General Mehra?"

Both men nodded.

"Do we have any reason to believe the crash was deliberate?"

"We do," Gupta replied. "General Mehra, who is close to the prime minister, was very much in favor of the U.S. proposal. He and several members of the senior staff were en route to the Defense Services Staff College, where they were going to be discussing it with colleagues, when the helicopter went down."

"Do you have any direct proof of sabotage?"

"Not at this moment," Raj responded. "That's why I'm sending you to investigate."

"Me? In what capacity? I don't work for RAW anymore."

"You still work for RAW. You just no longer work *at* RAW."

Asha had no idea what he was talking about. "Meaning?"

"Because RAW is a 'wing' of the cabinet secretariat and not an 'agency,' it enjoys a certain unorthodox legal status."

"*Meaning?*" she pressed.

"Meaning," Gupta clarified, "that RAW is not answerable to Parliament and can, within reason, carry out black operations at will."

"Is that what this is?" she asked, sweeping her hand in front of her as she took in the room again.

"Yes," said Raj.

"And its objective is?"

"Stopping the Chinese," Gupta stated. "No matter who in the Indian government we have to burn down to do it."

"Whoa. Wait a minute," Asha balked. "What are you talking about?"

Raj gestured for his colleague to pause and took over the conversation. "We believe that the Chinese not only know about the proposal, but are actively working from inside our own government to kill it."

"As well as anyone associated with it," she said, chilled by the thought.

"It's very much looking that way. Which is why we needed to set up things here. It's of the utmost importance that we remain unseen by both the Chinese and any elements within the Indian government that have been co-opted."

"In this place," offered Gupta, "no one sees us."

Asha wondered if he was referring to being in such an obscure, non-governmental location, or that this was literally a facility for the blind. Either way, the foundation was a curious choice.

Looking at Raj, she asked, "How was this site selected?"

"I have a prior relationship with the organization."

"What kind of—"

"My son was a student here," he said, cutting her off.

"I didn't know that."

"No one at RAW does. And I expect it to be kept that way."

"Of course," she replied.

She was about to launch into a new line of questions, when Gupta's phone chimed. Removing it from his jacket pocket, he read the message and announced, "The plane has arrived."

"What plane?"

"Your plane," Raj stated. "The one taking you to Sulur Air Base. That's where General Mehra took off from. You'll begin your investigation there. Gupta will continue your briefing on the flight down."

Asha held up her hand. "I'm just going to land at an Indian Air Force base and start asking questions? Under what authority? Even if I was still 'officially' with RAW," she said, making air quotes, "this wouldn't fall under our jurisdiction."

Raj picked up a light brown envelope with a string-tied closure and handed it to her. "Open it."

She did. Inside was a cell phone, cash, and two credit cards. There was also a new set of credentials, with her service photo, identifying her as a senior investigator in the Defense Security Corps. The DSC was responsible for securing India's military installations against sabotage. Coupled with the credentials was an official set of orders empowering her investigation. Raj had seen to almost everything.

But before she could raise her next point—that she was hardly dressed to pose as a uniformed DSC operative—Gupta said, "There's a change of clothes waiting for you on the plane."

She should have known better than to underestimate two of India's most accomplished spymasters. Apparently they *had* thought of everything.

"The same rules still apply," Raj reminded her. "Watch your back and don't trust anyone. If this was intentional, they're going to be keeping a close eye on anyone who comes to investigate. Don't linger. Get in, get what you need, and get out as quickly as you can."

"Understood," she replied, gathering up her things as Gupta picked up his briefcase and they prepared to depart. "Anything else?"

"If you cock this up, if you get caught—there won't be anything we can do to help you. RAW will disavow any knowledge of your operation. You will be completely on your own."

"Then you, and India, have nothing to worry about," said Asha as she opened the door. "Because that's when I do some of my best work."

CHAPTER 13

When the Antonov An-26 touched down at Ayni Air Force Base, ten kilometers west of the capital, Harvath could feel the weight being lifted from his shoulders. He had been wound so tight that he hadn't slept a wink, not even after they had safely entered Tajik airspace and were largely in the clear. He was exhausted.

They taxied for several minutes until they arrived at a large hangar occupied by a sleek, Gulfstream G700 private jet and pulled inside.

Once the large hangar door had been closed, Haney dropped the Antonov's ramp, while Gage and the other team members prepared to transfer their gear.

Despite having pulled out of Afghanistan, the United States government still pursued close, albeit very quiet, ties with Tajikistan. The government in Dushanbe didn't want any trouble with the Russians or the Taliban. The more covert the relationship, the better. That suited Harvath's needs just fine.

It allowed the private intelligence agency he worked for to land its jet at Ayni, park inside the hangar, and conduct the transfer of the passengers and equipment from the Antonov out of the sight of any prying eyes. There was no passport control or customs checks. In short, what happened in the hangar, stayed in the hangar.

This was the Carlton Group's preferred method of doing business. Harvath's tactics in Kabul notwithstanding, his agency was paid to remain in the shadows, unseen and unheard, as much as operationally possible.

He was looking forward to climbing aboard the Gulfstream, pulling off his boots, and finally getting some shut-eye as the plane made its way back to the United States.

As Harvath bent down to grab one of the equipment cases, Staelin picked up the other end. "How's everything feeling?" he asked. "Head? Neck? Back?"

A former Green Beret in the Fifth Special Forces group, Staelin had been a medical sergeant known as an 18D before moving on to Delta Force and ending up at the Carlton Group. As such, he was immediately voted in as the team's medical officer.

"No change. All good," Harvath replied. Staelin had checked him over shortly after they had lifted off from Kabul. He had been concerned about the force of impact Harvath had experienced at the roundabout.

"Sure," said Haney as he and another operative named Preisler passed, carrying an even larger case. "'All good' until the incontinence and erectile dysfunction set in."

"Yeah," Preisler stated. "That much trauma, mixed with that much adrenaline, can be downright debilitating for a man your age."

Harvath used his free hand to give them both the finger.

"At least we know what to get him for his wedding gift," added yet another operative named Johnson. "Adult diapers and a case of Viagra."

Harvath kept his middle finger up and kept giving it to everyone as they laughed good-naturedly at the joke.

The only time the team stopped busting each other's chops was when they were in the thick of an operation, and sometimes not even then.

Harvath took it all in stride. They could make fun of him all they wanted. The fact that he was engaged to a younger, extremely intelligent, and very attractive woman gave him the last laugh. His teammates not only envied him, they also thought she was fantastic.

As an original member of Norway's first all-female special forces team and now a deputy director at its premier intelligence agency, Sølvi Kolstad could go toe-to-toe with any of them. She also had a fabulously dark sense of humor, which only endeared her to them more. Harvath had definitely won the lottery with her.

He and Sølvi were planning to get married in a couple of months—

between Christmas and New Year's, when things would hopefully be slow and no one would have to take any extra time off.

The plan was to throw two parties—one for friends and family in the United States and one for friends and family in Norway. After that, Scot and Sølvi would take a short honeymoon.

With neither quitting their job anytime soon, that meant they would still be bouncing back and forth between the two countries.

Harvath, however, was working on a plan to establish a quick reaction force in Europe.

Because the Carlton Group was a private organization, it would continue to allow the White House plausible deniability, while providing a highly skilled, forward-deployed team that could carry out assignments, from reconnaissance and surveillance all the way to direct action.

The plan was still in its infancy, and there were a lot of kinks to be ironed out, but he was making headway.

After loading their gear aboard the G700, Harvath made sure Topaz and his family were comfortable and then headed straight for the bar. A friend in Kentucky had helped him source one of the best bourbons he had ever tasted.

The fifteen-year-old Pappy Van Winkle was expensive, but it was worth every penny, especially as Harvath had found a way to dip into the team fund and essentially let the office pay for it.

The "bribe box" was a locked footlocker in the forward closet that contained everything from cigars, cash, and sports watches to cigarettes, gold coins, and cognacs. Whether it was an overzealous customs official or a greedy warlord, the Carlton Group prided itself on being prepared to deal with any situation. Baksheesh, after all, made the world go round.

A little creative accounting opened up the money for more high-end liquor, and the friend from Kentucky was even kind enough to provide a receipt.

It was, admittedly, several orders of magnitude above pilfering office supplies. But it wasn't like Harvath was sneaking a Cadillac out of the factory one day at a time, one part at a time, in his lunchbox. They had been sent into Afghanistan—one of the worst and most dangerous places he could imagine them having to go—and they had successfully achieved their mission. His team deserved a little Pappy Van Winkle, and then some. It was time to celebrate.

Lining up glasses for everyone, he uncorked the bottle and carefully poured. Spilling even a single drop would have been an unforgivable sin. Then, calling his teammates to the bar, he handed one to each of them.

Fans of the Viking toast, they raised their glasses in unison and proclaimed, "Till Valhalla," before savoring the rich, brown liquid.

"The first person who asks for a Coke to mix with this gets a bullet in the mouth," declared another operator on the team, ex-SEAL Tim Barton.

Matt Morrison, a former Force Reconnaissance Marine like Haney, said, "There's one problem with bourbon: you can never drink down. Thanks a lot, Harvath. When we get back, I guess I'm going to have to start robbing banks."

"Or you could stop dating strippers," said Johnson.

"Or," offered Preisler, "maybe glue a bunch of razors to an ice scraper instead of paying the salon for all those back waxes?"

This time, it was Morrison's turn to give everyone the finger.

Harvath smiled. They were the best team he had ever worked with. He couldn't think of anyone else he would want in a battle.

Once the pilots had completed their preflight, the hangar doors were opened and a tug pushed the aircraft out onto the tarmac.

The men found seats and settled down, sipping their bourbon as they got ready for takeoff.

As the plane's engines powered up and the tug detached, the Gulfstream headed toward the runway. Then suddenly it came to a stop.

Everyone leaned into their windows, trying to figure out what was happening.

"This probably isn't good," said Staelin.

The captain came over the PA system and told Harvath there was a call for him on the encrypted satellite phone.

Harvath picked up the nearest handset. It was Nicholas. "You need to deplane."

"All of us?"

"No," said the little man. "Just you. Step out clean. Leave your phone, passport, and anything else that can identify you. Don't bring any weapons."

"Why? What's going on?"

"On your port side, you should be able to see a vehicle approaching. The man inside is named Leahy. He'll explain."

CHAPTER 14

The United States Embassy to Tajikistan was north of the Ayni Air Base and just west of central Dushanbe. It was a sleek, newer facility that reminded Harvath a lot of the U.S. Embassy to Norway.

America took great pride in being one of the first countries in the world to have recognized Tajikistan's independence after it split from the Soviet Union in the early 1990s. In the three decades since, the United States had invested more than two billion dollars in the Central Asian nation and had established strong security cooperation. They were an important partner in the region and Washington remained keen to enhance the relationship in whatever manner it could.

Leahy, the twentysomething CIA operative who had picked Harvath up, had been in-country for less than a year.

"What's it been like?" Harvath had asked, making small talk as they left the airport and headed toward the embassy.

"Dushanbe? A bit like Mos Eisley."

Harvath grinned at the *Star Wars* reference to the spaceport on Tatooine. "You will never find a more wretched hive of scum and villainy," he said in his best Obi-Wan Kenobi voice.

Leahy nodded. "There's a bit of everything going on here and everyone is on the make—jockeying for position—especially the Russians and the Chinese. The older Tajiks, unfortunately, still have a somewhat limiting Soviet-style mind-set. The younger generation, born after independence, are much more optimistic and open to entrepreneurship. The best people to deal with here, however, are the Indians.

"They're smart, clear-eyed, and understand how their interests are aligned with the Tajiks', especially when it comes to Chinese expansionism. India even set up its first-ever overseas base at Farkhor."

"For its air force, right?"

"Correct," said the young CIA operative. "Around 1996, India's Research and Analysis Wing negotiated rights to use it in order to support the Afghan Northern Alliance against the Taliban. The Indian Air Force has been here ever since."

"Which puts them in close striking distance of the Pakistani-administered portion of Kashmir, as well as the Pakistani city of Peshawar."

"Like I said," Leahy replied with a smile, "they're both clear-eyed and smart."

Harvath didn't disagree. "How's the food?"

"If you're in the capital, not bad. Chinese, Mexican, Italian, there's a little bit of everything—even burgers. But as soon as you leave Dushanbe, the quality and selection drops off a cliff."

"Par for the course in the 'Stans.' A post like this builds character. What do you do for fun?"

"I like to fish," said Leahy.

"Is the fishing any good in Tajikistan?"

"You'd be surprised. Even though it's the smallest of the Central Asian nations, it's covered with rivers and lakes—more than a thousand of them. And thanks to all the breeding and stocking they're doing, the fishing is excellent."

You learned something new every day. Fishing wasn't exactly the first thing Harvath normally thought about when he thought about Tajikistan. Not even top ten. But it would be now.

When they arrived at the embassy, Leahy badged Harvath in and took him to their SCIF. A table with food, coffee, and waters had been set up outside.

"You've got about thirty minutes before your videoconference," the young man said. "There's a bathroom, with a shower, down the hall to your left. My desk is the one with the Chicago Bears flag. If you need anything and I'm not here, pick up my phone and have the embassy operator track me down."

Harvath thanked him, grabbed a mug of coffee, and wheeled his bag toward the bathroom in pursuit of a nice, hot shower. It wouldn't make up for his lack of sleep, but it would be the next-best thing.

He then returned to the sensitive compartmented information facility showered, shaved, and in a fresh set of clothes. He poured more coffee and assembled a small breakfast of yogurt, hard-boiled eggs, and fresh fruit, which he carried into the SCIF.

Via the sat phone aboard the Carlton Group jet, Nicholas had said that Leahy would explain why Harvath was staying behind while everyone else was taking off and headed back to D.C. All the young CIA operative had told him was that Harvath was needed for a secure videoconference, after which Leahy would be transporting him from the embassy to Dushanbe International. It wasn't much of an explanation of anything.

A few minutes before the appointed time, Leahy entered the SCIF and fired up the encrypted videoconferencing system. Harvath had assumed he'd be interacting with his office, but when he saw a screen saver on the other side indicating that the call was going to be with the White House, he quickly retrieved a travel blazer from his bag and put it on. Whatever this was about, it was happening at the very top.

He took a couple of bites of food, chugged some water, and, grabbing a pad and pen, made sure he was one hundred percent ready for the meeting. When the clock hit the top of the hour, the video went live.

Harvath instantly recognized the interior of the White House Situation Room. It was a ten-hour time difference between Dushanbe and D.C. He guessed most of the people gathered around the long, polished table had probably already called home to let their families know that they were going to be missing dinner. And judging by who was assembled, he knew that whatever they wanted to talk about was extremely serious.

President Paul Porter, a Montana native who resembled a modernized version of the Marlboro Man, got straight to business. "You did a hell of a job in Kabul. Well done."

"Thank you, sir," Harvath replied.

"I have a packed schedule tonight, so I'm going to make my part of this short. First, I want to extend my condolences. I know you had occasionally worked with a State Department employee named Eli Ritter and that the two of you were friends. His death comes as a shock to us all and we are sorry for your loss."

Harvath was stunned. He and Ritter had indeed worked a handful of assignments together and had developed a friendship. But Ritter had gone into the private sector. Why was he on the president's radar? "What happened?"

"He was murdered. Yesterday, in Jaipur."

"Do we know who killed him?"

"Not yet. The Indian Police are leaning toward it being a robbery gone bad. We're not so sure. So, that's what we want you to find out," said Porter. "The team here will fill you in. I just want to express how serious Mr. Ritter's work was *and* how important it is that you get to the bottom of what happened."

"I understand, Mr. President," Harvath replied, even though he had very little to go on. "You can count on me."

"Good. I believe you already know our new chairman of the Joint Chiefs."

"I do, sir. The admiral and I go back many years."

"Then I'll leave you to it."

The other participants stood as the president left the room. Once they were settled back in their seats, Admiral David Proctor took over the meeting.

The man had worn many hats in his long and storied career. Until his most recent promotion, he had been NATO's SACEUR, or Supreme Allied Commander Europe. Harvath had worked with him both in his NATO capacity as well as back when he headed up the United States Special Operations Command.

But most important was when Harvath had been taken prisoner in Russia. It was Proctor who had sent in the planes that had saved his life and had gotten his whole team out. He would be forever in his debt.

As this was an official meeting and there were multiple other people in the room, they kept their interaction professional.

Proctor began by echoing what the president had said about Ritter.

When he segued into his briefing and saw Harvath pick up his pen, he stated, "No notes. Nothing on your end can be written down."

Harvath set down the pen and leaned forward, all ears.

The admiral began with an ominous question. "What do you know about the Chinese military strategy referred to as the String of Pearls?"

CHAPTER 15

Harvath was familiar with the String of Pearls strategy. It was the maritime extension of Beijing's Belt and Road Initiative, but much more dangerous.

With the Belt and Road Initiative, China was investing in infrastructure projects from East Asia to Europe—ports, roads, bridges, highway, and rail networks—in order to purchase influence and create dependence across sixty countries. It was in the process of spending north of twenty trillion dollars and would end up reaching nearly sixty percent of the world's population.

Once a country took China's money, it was like being on the hook to a particularly nasty loan shark. At that point, Beijing had its nose inside your tent and could begin to push for what it wanted to have happen in your country's affairs—both domestic and international.

In addition, Beijing was always on the hunt for territorial toeholds. That was what made the String of Pearls so unsettling.

The "string" was a route that wound from mainland China, through the Indian Ocean, around the Horn of Africa. The "pearls" were stops along the way where the Chinese had invested heavily in "port projects" and, in return, had been granted docking and staging rights.

Under the guise of commercial shipping, China had been building up these ports so that they could accommodate Chinese warships. And as China had just leapt ahead of America in the size of its navy, anything that helped the Chinese repair, refuel, or resupply its battle force vessels was of added strategic concern to the United States.

In short, as the Belt and Road Initiative had taken off, so had China's navy—both through modernization and the construction of new ships. Among all their other global superpower ambitions, they were hell-bent on maritime domination. The United States was right to be concerned.

Harvath shared with Proctor what he knew.

"We're not the only ones worried about the String of Pearls," the admiral replied. "New Delhi is, too. The Indian Ocean has always been within their sphere of influence. The Chinese, however, have muscled in and are boxing them out of relationships with regional partners. But that's not the worst of it.

"We also have reports that China has been angling to base combat task force units at each of the pearls, as well as to construct high-end surveillance outposts. Essentially, they are working with amazing speed to solidify control of the Indian Ocean and upend the balance of power. China's goal is quite clear—to encircle India in order to choke it off."

Proctor put up a map of the region and highlighted each area as he continued speaking: "India shares a massive border to its north with China, which is rife with territorial disputes and increasing Chinese hostilities.

"The String of Pearls, as we've discussed, surrounds India to the south. To the west is India's long-standing enemy, Pakistan. Here, China has cemented a strategic alliance by investing over sixty-two billion dollars in projects referred to as the China-Pakistan Economic Corridor.

"Finally, there is Bhutan to the east, where China has been slicing off land from a strategic plateau where India, China, and Bhutan meet. It overlooks a thin strip of Indian territory known as the 'Chicken's Neck,' which functions as a corridor connecting India to states in its northeast.

"Even though the terrain is extremely rugged and virtually inhospitable, China has been constructing buildings there, ostensibly to house military units that will be able to cut off access to this vital Indian corridor. Once that's done, the noose will be complete and China can choke India to death. All it has to do is squeeze."

"And, as India is a nuclear power with more than a million troops,"

Harvath stated, "that's not going to end well. But what does this have to do with the United States and what Ritter was doing in Jaipur?"

"He has been covertly negotiating an Asian version of NATO. The plan is to bring the United States, Japan, Australia, and India together to counter the growing threat from China."

It was an ambitious plan and made sense on multiple levels. Harvath could understand why it was being discussed.

He could also understand why the Chinese would hate it and want to put a stop to it at all costs.

"So, my job is to figure out what happened to Ritter. And then what?"

Admiral Proctor looked at the other people around the table and then back at Harvath. "Your official tasking will come from your organization. My job was solely to present the briefing."

"Understood. Is there anything else I need to know?"

"You've tangled with the Chinese more than once," said the chairman of the Joint Chiefs. "You know how dangerous they are. And while I shouldn't have to warn you, I'm going to say it anyway—watch your back. I'm serious."

"I know you are. And I will. Thank you."

The men said their good-byes, the feed went dark, and a moment later there was a knock at the door of the SCIF.

Sticking his head in, Leahy said, "Everything go okay?"

"I thought the ads along the bottom encouraging me to sign up for premium encrypted video via White House TV+ were a bit much," replied Harvath, "but other than that, it was fine."

The young CIA operative smiled. "Your office is up next. They asked to be notified once the call was complete. If you want to stretch your legs or grab another coffee, I can put them off for a few minutes."

Harvath had almost a full mug. Holding it up, he thanked Leahy and said, "I'm good. Let's go ahead and put them through."

"Roger that," Leahy responded, closing the SCIF door.

It took less than a minute for the screen to come alive again. This time he could see the faces of Nicholas and his "boss," Gary Lawlor.

He used the term *boss* lightly when it came to Gary. Before his death, Reed Carlton had made it clear that he wanted Harvath running the organization, but Harvath hadn't been interested. He had no intention of giving up fieldwork. As such, someone needed to run day-to-day operations and Lawlor had been offered, and had accepted, the position.

He was ex-FBI and had helmed the first completely black program Harvath had worked in after leaving his stint as a Secret Service agent at the White House. But they had known each other much longer than that. Though in a different branch of service, Lawlor had saved Harvath's father in Vietnam. The men had remained friends and Gary had become like a second father to Scot.

He had also been one hell of a covert operative with Army Intelligence during the Cold War. The joke around the Carlton Group was that Lawlor was the only person with hands calloused enough to handle someone as "rough" as Harvath.

"U.S. Embassy Tajikistan," the older man said with a smirk when the video feed went live. "I hope we'll be able to pry you away."

"If you can't immediately arrange for transportation, I'll be fine. I have it on good authority that the fishing here is exceptional."

"That person probably also wants to sell you a bridge and some ocean-front property."

"I don't know," Harvath replied. "He seems okay to me."

"Well, tell him to mail the proposal to your *Gettysburg* address. It's time to move."

"Where to?"

"Jaipur," said Lawlor.

"I figured as much. What's my assignment?"

"To find out who killed Ritter."

"And then?"

"The powers-that-be want a Rembrandt."

Harvath was familiar with the term. It meant a very public, very eye-catching execution.

"But," Lawlor added, "your brushes don't touch the paint until you've figured out who sent the killer."

"So, we're going to work our way up the ladder?"

"All the way to the top. This is priority one. You get whatever you need. And you do whatever needs to be done. Are we clear?"

"Crystal," said Harvath.

It was now Nicholas's turn to speak. "As Dushanbe to Jaipur is a bit too far to travel via motorbike, even with a full tank of gas, I've found you a flight."

Harvath smiled.

"That said," Nicholas continued, "I have good news and I have bad news. Which do you want first?"

He hated any question that started this way. "Give me the bad news."

"The only commercial flight available takes fourteen hours, it has only one seat left—in economy class, and you have to change planes in Delhi."

"What's the good news?"

"The Indian Air Force is moving a transport plane this morning from Farkhor Air Base to Jaipur. It'll save you several hours."

"Great. What about getting to Farkhor? It's about one hundred and thirty klicks from here."

"In that respect, you're in luck. When Afghanistan fell, half of its helicopter pilots fled to Tajikistan and brought their aircraft with them. The U.S. has been paying to keep their skills sharp. You get to choose your means of transit to Farkhor. Either a Russian Mi-25 or a UH-60 Black Hawk."

"No contest," Harvath said with a laugh. "The last Russian helicopter I flew in turned into a submarine. It's going to be made in the U.S.A. for me. I opt for the Black Hawk."

"Good choice," Lawlor replied, taking back control of the conversation. "Leahy is going to provide you with a new phone, diplomatic passport, ID, and some walking-around money. As far as the government of India is concerned, you're a State Department specialist sent to look into what happened, and to arrange repatriation of Ritter's body."

"Where am I staying?"

"Jaipur is booked solid for Diwali, but we managed to get you into the Fairmont. That's where Ritter had been."

"Any support on the ground?"

"In a normal situation," said Lawlor, "the CIA station in Delhi would be reaching out to their contacts in the Indian Intelligence Bureau, trying to back-channel whatever information they could get. You'd also have the FBI legal attaché in Delhi involved, as well as the regional security officer from DSS. Basically, all the heavy hitters at the embassy."

"But this isn't a 'normal' situation."

"No, it's not. The White House wants this kept as quiet as possible. They're willing, however, to get the FSN/I involved."

FSN/I was U.S. government–speak for Foreign Service National (FSN) Investigator. At most embassies, it was a retired, local law enforcement officer who had held a senior rank, had good connections, and was able to navigate the old-boy network.

In the case of the U.S. Embassy in New Delhi, the position would likely be occupied by a former member of the Indian Police Service—and he, or she, would have been thoroughly vetted by the CIA to make sure everything was aboveboard and that they weren't compromised by a hostile foreign government such as the Russians or the Chinese.

Their job was to help untangle or navigate in-country law enforcement issues where American citizens or American interests were at stake. This could be done by the FSN/I traveling to a location in person, making calls from the embassy, or linking up American personnel in that jurisdiction, such as consular staff, with a trusted local source.

But when the case in question involved a dead American citizen, everyone at the embassy would expect the FSN/I to be on-site and to personally oversee every facet of the investigation. And it wasn't just the powers-that-be at the embassy who would expect it; so would the entirety of the Jaipur police force. Appointing anyone else in the FSN/I's stead would have been highly suspicious. What's more, as far as Harvath was concerned, it also could have been dangerous.

No matter how trusted the FSN/I was, the minute he handed the case off to a colleague in Jaipur, Harvath would be dealing with an unknown entity. It didn't matter if it was the FSN/I's uncle, cousin, brother, sister, son, or daughter; that person was someone who had not been fully vetted by the CIA. Add in the high levels of police corruption in India, and the risks only grew.

In a perfect world, Harvath would have had his own trusted source in Jaipur—someone he knew, who was well connected and plugged into everything.

But this wasn't a perfect world. Jaipur was completely uncharted territory for him and was going to be extremely difficult to navigate. Anything that might give him the edge was worth grabbing ahold of.

"I'll take the FSN/I," he said.

"Roger that," Lawlor replied. "I'll contact the embassy in Delhi and get everything in motion. By the time the helo arrives to take you to Farkhor, you'll have, at the very least, a bio and a photo. In the meantime, based on the information we have, Nicholas is going to brief you on Ritter's movements in Jaipur."

• • •

As always, Lawlor was a man of his word. Ten minutes before the Black Hawk touched down on the embassy's soccer field, Harvath not only had his new cell phone, passport, documents, and cash from Leahy, but he also had a full dossier on the FSN/I who would be picking him up in Jaipur. And from the looks of it, Vijay Chabra was exactly the person Harvath needed.

CHAPTER 16

Nicholas had pulled an all-nighter getting ready for the Kabul op. When it was over and Harvath had been briefed on his next mission, he collected his gear, gave his two enormous, white Caucasian Ovcharkas the command to walk with him, and headed for the Carlton Group's private elevator that delivered him to the underground parking level.

Similar to a Tesla, his highly customized black Mercedes Sprinter van was covered with sensors and tiny cameras. If anyone had come near it, that person would have been recorded and an alert would have been sent to his phone.

Even though he hadn't received such an alert, he still gave Argos the command to sniff the van for explosives. One could never be too careful. Nicholas had made a lot of enemies over his lifetime.

When the dog was done, he rejoined his master, as well as Draco, who had never left the little man's side.

Climbing into the van together, Nicholas slid into the driver's seat and drove out of the garage. The ride home, without traffic, was only twenty minutes.

In his previous life, before going legitimate, he had amassed a staggering amount of money. When it came time to purchase a house in the United States, price wasn't a problem. The challenge was in finding the perfect property.

Nicholas had very specific tastes. He wanted something that reminded him of Europe. Something solid. Something that felt like it had been around forever, but had all the modern conveniences. Most important of all, it had to be safe.

On forty extremely private, wooded acres he found the perfect place. It had been built just a decade earlier by a furniture magnate. The thirteenth-century, Scottish-inspired fortress was constructed from more than four thousand tons of local, hand-hewn stone. It boasted five bedrooms, a chapel, a pool, a walled garden, an elevator, and a fourth-floor observation deck with an outdoor fireplace and one of the most stunning views he had ever seen.

The entire property was like something out of a fairy tale. And after the hardships he had endured, Nicholas deserved a happy ending.

More important, he wanted to give Nina the fairy tale. All of it. She had made him so incredibly happy. And soon she was going to give birth to their baby.

At first, he had been beside himself with worry, concerned that the child might suffer from his rare genetic disorder of primordial dwarfism. Testing, however, had put his mind at ease. Everything was on track for them to have a beautiful, healthy baby.

Nicholas looked forward to filling the house with love, warmth, and the sound of laughter.

Having been abandoned as a child in Soviet Georgia and raised in a brothel near the Black Sea, he had always longed for a real family of his own. Now that it was coming true, he often felt like he was living in a dream. In fact, that was what he had named his home—Castle Mechta, from the Russian word for "dream."

Parking in his large, impeccably clean garage, he waited for the overhead door to close before climbing out of the van with the dogs.

Inside the house, he turned off the rest of the alarms and headed for the kitchen. He loved to cook and tonight he was making a very special meal.

Nina, unfortunately, was terribly allergic to shellfish. But because he loved her so madly, he had sworn it off as well. No easy task for a gourmand who had eaten himself into a food coma on countless occasions via towers of crab, shrimp, and oysters that were taller than he was.

Tonight, however, Nina wasn't home. She had gone away for a few days to see friends—one of her last trips before the baby was due.

Nicholas had the entire house to himself and was going to prepare Lobster Thermidor with pommes soufflé on the side and a 2002 bottle of Dom Pérignon.

After getting out one of his Riedel Dom Pérignon glasses, he retrieved the champagne and gently uncorked it. The sound, he had been taught, should never be louder than a lover's sigh. He thought people who popped their corks or sabered the tops off of their bottles were savages.

Pouring a glass, he opened the music app on his tablet and scrolled through his many playlists. The only thing more diverse than his taste in food was his taste in music. He and Harvath had bonded over their shared love of funk—and that was what they often listened to when he came over. That, or classic rock. Tonight, however, he was in the mood for something different.

His finger hovered for a moment over the list titled "Great American Songbook." But the likes of Nat King Cole and Dinah Washington wasn't exactly what he was in the mood for at the moment. He wanted something with more passion, more power. *Opera* was what he wanted. And not just *any* opera.

He tapped the playlist of his favorite arias and turned the volume way up. Soon the overhead speakers began to rumble as "Ebben? Ne andrò lontana" from Alfredo Catalani's *La Wally* tumbled lusciously from them.

Taking a sip of champagne, the little man drew a custom stepladder up to the island and got down to the business of preparing his meal.

• • •

Two hours later, after he had eaten and had let the dogs out, he stood at his liquor cabinet, trying to decide what he would have for an after-dinner drink. He was reminded of the line by Samuel Johnson, "Claret is the liquor for boys; port for men; but he who aspires to be a hero must drink brandy," and selected his rare bottle of Louis XIII Black Pearl.

The cognac came from a single cask of the Hériard Dubreuil family's private cellar. Only 775 bottles, made out of Baccarat crystal, were ever released worldwide.

He poured a measure of the amber liquid into a Lalique cognac glass and, dogs in tow, headed to his elevator.

The previous owners had spared no expense. The home was filled with beautiful hardwoods—maple, cherry, walnut, and oak. From the hand-carved millwork to the paneling in the elevator carriage, it was first-class.

He and the dogs rode up to the fourth floor of the tower and exited out a set of French doors to the observation deck. From here, he could see for miles.

It had been a warm, Indian summer. But as autumn crept ever closer to winter, the evenings were beginning to bite. He decided to light a fire.

Cooler nights were actually something they had been looking forward to. At the end of the day, before dinner, he and Nina had a ritual. They would meet on the roof to unwind, reconnect, and enjoy a cocktail to-gether. A fire only made it more romantic.

Setting his glass down, he selected a couple of logs for the fire, turned on the starter, and lit a match.

A bright flame leapt up as the gas ignited and, slowly, the logs began to crackle. As the dogs lay down near the fireplace, Nicholas went to pick up his cognac.

But as soon as he reached for it, he began to feel sick. A piercing sensa-tion was radiating through the left side of his head—something he could both hear and feel. The pain in his ear was off the charts. Soon everything started spinning.

He tried to make it to the French doors, but lost his balance, crashing onto the slate pavers, his glass of cognac shattering in his hand.

He attempted to call out to Argos and Draco, to get them to drag him inside to safety, but they were experiencing it as well.

The last thing he took in before everything went black was the dogs writhing and howling in pain.

CHAPTER 17

The flight from New Delhi to Sulur Air Base took just under three hours—more than enough time for Gupta to complete Asha's briefing and answer plenty of her questions. She wasn't, however, crazy about all the answers.

Their operation, despite all of the mismatched desks and out-of-date computers at the Blind Relief Association of Delhi, consisted only of the three of them. Raj had no intention of bringing anyone else on board.

The reason he had made her sign a resignation letter and clean out her desk was so that in case she was caught, RAW could disavow any connection to her, as well as any knowledge of what she was working on. It was, essentially, their get-out-of-jail-free card.

It didn't come as a shock. Being expendable—within reason—was part of the job description. What had surprised her was how much Raj was gambling on her. Of all the agents he could have chosen, she was *the* one.

Gupta had told her she should be proud, which she was. He had then reinforced the importance of her assignment by quoting from a popular movie, based on real events, that had fictionalized RAW: "India is not just a country. It is an ideology. And the enemy wants to use every method to defeat this ideology."

The "enemy" referred to in the quote was Pakistan, but it could have been any of India's enemies—especially China. The example set by India's Western-facing democracy was as dangerous to Beijing as Ukraine's Western-facing democracy was to Moscow. Totalitarians couldn't abide freedom blossoming on their doorstep. It was an ever-present reminder to their citizens of what they were being denied. As such, it was a contagious, corrosive, existential threat that needed to be extinguished at all costs.

Asha understood what was at stake. The fact that Gupta had been drawn out of retirement to work on this assignment only served to hammer the point home. That and the additional fact that their operation had been limited to only three people.

If they were successful, the benefit to India would be incalculable. Perhaps a movie would be made about them. Knowing her siblings' love of cinema, that would probably impress them even more than a medal presented to her in secret.

Not that any of that made any difference. That wasn't why she had signed up with RAW.

Before landing, she pinned up her hair, changed into the Defense Security Corps uniform that had been hung on the back of the lavatory door, and checked the name tape on her uniform to make sure it matched her ID, which of course it did.

She secured her Glock inside the waistband of her fatigues, hiding it under her "jacket," as the camouflage uniform shirt was called, and re-joined Gupta in the cabin. There was one last question she wanted to pose.

"Tell me about Raj's son," she said.

The older man shrugged as he packed his pipe with tobacco. "There's not much to tell."

"Until today, I had believed he and his wife were childless."

"Which is exactly what they wanted people to believe. Even if they'd had ten children, no one would have known. Our attachments—the people and things we care about—are what make us vulnerable in this line of work."

"What was the cause of the boy's blindness?"

"I don't know," said Gupta. "He doesn't talk about it."

"Where is his son now?"

"He has a job, in a small workshop in Ghaziabad. It's an easy drive from New Delhi, so they're both able to visit him on a regular basis."

"How old is the boy?"

"The boy is now a man. Twenty-five. He has a fiancée. She's nineteen and works in the same shop weaving chair caning. They'll be getting married in the spring. They want to have children."

"Raj and his wife must be very happy," said Asha.

"For the first time in a long time, it would appear," he replied. Then, fastening his seat belt, he gestured for her to do the same.

Minutes later, they touched down at Sulur, India's second-largest air base, responsible for protecting all of the country's ocean territory. It could handle both fighters and transport aircraft—the only air force station in India capable of doing so.

The weather was overcast. A thin fog lingered over the airfield.

"Ready to go?" Gupta asked as he accompanied Asha to the forward door and a crew member lowered the airstairs.

She nodded.

"You've got this," he told her. "And we've got you."

"All *two* of you."

Gupta held out his hands. "If you think you can pick two better, you know how to reach us."

Asha pulled the cell phone she'd been given from her pocket and shook it. "You're both on my speed dial. In fact, you're the only ones on my speed dial."

"Relax. You're going to do a good job. Raj has faith in you."

"Just Raj?"

The older man smiled. "Faith involves trust. Trust is based on experience. And experience is arrived at over time. I look forward to developing faith in you," he said, lighting his pipe and stepping back so she could descend the stairs. "The clock starts now."

Asha smiled back and shook her head. It was an odd pep talk. She didn't have any time, however, to dwell on it. Waiting at the bottom of the stairs for her was a green Maruti Gypsy—a jeep-like vehicle popular with the Indian military. Standing next to it was a young Defense Security Corps soldier.

After saluting her, he raised his voice so he could be heard and introduced himself as Lance Naik Kamal Khan. *Lance Naik* was the Indian Army's equivalent to a lance corporal.

Asha returned his salute and handed him her backpack, which he placed behind the Maruti's passenger seat.

The air was thick with humidity and the scent of jet fuel. Around them the base roared with activity. Planes taxied, took off, and landed. A trio of helicopters thundered overhead in formation. A fleet of Boeing P-8s, the elite long-range maritime reconnaissance and antisubmarine warfare aircraft, sat nearby—the first ever to be sold by the Americans to an international partner. India had the fourth-largest air force in the world, and it always filled her with pride to see it at work.

"We have an office prepared for you," said Lance Naik Khan, holding the door open for her. "Major Badal is back at the crash site, but has instructed that you receive full cooperation. Where would you like to begin?"

Asha consulted her watch. "I'd like to start with the chief flight mechanic."

"Sergeant Siddiqui. Yes, ma'am. Let me radio the base repair depot."

Lance Naik Khan then closed Asha's door, walked around the rear of the vehicle, and hopped in behind the wheel. Firing up the Maruti, he put it in gear and headed for the BRD as he attempted to raise them on the radio.

It took a moment before they reached someone who could answer their question. The news that they delivered wasn't good.

As the person who had signed off on the flight-worthiness of General Mehra's helicopter, Siddiqui had been subjected to questions and interviews all day. The command staff had wanted to talk with him. His boss, and his boss's boss, had then spent hours with him, going through every detail over and over again. After that, crash scene investigators had arrived and the process started all over.

Through it all, he had been calm, professional, and thorough. That had changed, however, when a call came in for him.

The person over the radio said he didn't know who he had been speaking with, but that Siddiqui had become agitated and had rushed out of the depot. The chief flight mechanic had last been seen getting into his personal vehicle, a late-model, white Tata Tigor, and speeding off toward the main gate.

"How long ago?" the lance naik asked.

"Three minutes tops," the voice replied.

"Get me to that gate," Asha ordered the young DSC soldier.

She had no idea who had called Siddiqui, nor what had been said, but the fact that it had shaken him so thoroughly that he had taken off—before the end of his shift—disturbed her. It was critical that she get to him before he did something stupid, or disappeared altogether.

Lance Naik Khan deftly navigated the airfield and got them to the main gate just in time to see a white Tata Tigor exiting the base and accelerating as it turned right onto the main road.

There was a backup of cars ahead of them. Asha told Khan to go around them. When Base Security tried to wave them down and halt their vehicle, she had the lance naik give a quick hit of the strobes and bark the Klaxon. They weren't stopping for anything. She wasn't going to risk losing sight of Siddiqui.

Wherever the man was headed, he was hell-bent on getting there as fast as possible. Traffic was light, but as they got closer to the main part of town, it began to pick up.

Siddiqui started weaving in and out. It was not only making it difficult to follow him, but it was also incredibly dangerous. He was going to get somebody killed.

When the flight mechanic blew through a red light, Khan was forced to follow and missed being in a collision by mere inches.

Asha had had enough. She instructed the lance naik to reengage the strobes and Klaxon. Technically, any authority the DSC had ended at the exit of the base. At this point, however, all she wanted to do was get him to pull over and stop.

Siddiqui wasn't interested. In fact, he sped up and began executing even more aggressive maneuvers. *What the hell is wrong with this guy?* Asha ordered Khan to stay with him.

In a narrow street in the Ganapathy neighborhood, the chase ended—at least the vehicle portion.

A delivery truck was stopped and there was no getting around it. There was no backing up, either. Siddiqui was boxed in and decided to abandon his car.

Pulling out her cell phone, Asha activated the voice memo feature and had the lance naik quickly rattle off his number. Then she exited the vehicle and headed after Siddiqui on foot.

He was significantly older than her and nowhere close to her level of physical fitness, yet he was as quick as lightning and moved like a man possessed. A car crash, she was realizing, was going to turn out to have been the least of her worries. This guy was going to drop dead any moment from a heart attack or a stroke.

Like Mumbai, the streets were packed with people coming and going, getting ready for another evening of Diwali. It made it difficult for Siddiqui to navigate. Asha was closing in on him.

They ran past a small hardware store and a popular party-themed chain called the Cake Point.

Near a shop that sold refurbished car and motorcycle tires, she was close enough for him to hear her. Yelling out his name, she ordered him to stop. He glanced briefly over his shoulder, but kept going. That was the last straw.

Kicking it into high gear, she ran as fast as she could—a full-out sprint. She didn't slow down until she was close enough to reach out and grab the back of his collar. But that wasn't what she did.

Instead, on a piece of rough, uneven pavement, she thrust both arms out and gave him a massive shove.

Siddiqui hit the ground so hard, he bounced.

Before he could get to his feet, Asha had her boot on the back of his neck and her gun drawn.

"Sergeant Siddiqui," she said. "What you do in the next several moments will impact the rest of your life. I urge you to choose very carefully. Why are you running?"

On the ground next to him was his phone. He began to move his fingers toward it. Asha applied pressure to his neck, sending a bolt of pain through his body.

"Please," he begged. "Help me."

She eased off, but only by a hair. He picked up the phone and offered it to her. On its cracked screen, a video was being livestreamed. The comments were abominable.

Taking her boot off his neck, she helped the flight mechanic to his feet. "How far?" she asked him.

"Three more blocks."

"Run!"

CHAPTER 18

Securing her weapon, she took off along with Siddiqui. Arriving at a scene like the one playing out on the livestream, with a gun in your hand, was a very dangerous idea. If she did have to pull her Glock, it was going to be because all other possibilities were exhausted.

They covered the three blocks quickly, slowing down only when they began to see the crowds. This is where Asha was forced to take over.

Removing her cell phone, she pulled up the voice memo from Khan, punched in his number, and told him where they were and what the situation was.

Then she turned to the flight mechanic and told him the words she knew he wouldn't want to hear. "Sergeant Siddiqui, you must remain here."

"But my family—" he began.

Asha held up her hand. "If this mob sees you, they will tear you apart. You are no good to your family dead. I will get to them and I will protect them. I promise you. Wait here for my colleague. He will see to your safety."

Siddiqui knew she was right, but being this close to his family and not doing anything felt incredibly wrong. It was his job to protect them, not hers. They were under attack and there was nothing he could do. It made him feel ashamed.

"What is your wife's name?" she asked.

"Ismat."

"Call her. Tell her help is coming. Remind her to stay inside the house, stay away from the doors and windows, and to remain calm. Everything is going to be okay."

The flight mechanic nodded and Asha headed toward the inflamed mob. She hated the internet for this very reason. *Everyone* in India had a cell phone. The rapidity with which rumors could be started and her fellow citizens could be whipped into a frenzy was disgusting.

Very few people ever stopped to ask, "Is this story true? Is it propaganda? Am I being manipulated to serve someone else's agenda?"

Rumors that exploited ethnic and religious hatreds seemed to animate mobs the fastest. It was a cultural weakness in India, especially in its body politic—and one that cynical Indian politicians did more to encourage than to discourage and dismantle. The easiest road to electoral power was also its most corrosive. More energized blocs could be built by telling voters what was wrong with their lives rather than what was right.

Instead of seeing each other as fellow countrymen and women, India's citizens were walling themselves off, sorting themselves into silos based on party affiliation. They were banishing friends, neighbors, coworkers—even family members—from their lives, anyone who didn't support the same political "team" that they did. Asha hated to see it.

Democracy wasn't about how you were *different,* it was about how you were the *same.* It was about the rights and freedoms everyone enjoyed, and how everyone protected them.

Democracy was also about your responsibilities, your duties, as a citizen. When people began to see themselves as members of a subset first, it was a flashing red light—a warning that a nation's democracy was in peril. Factionalism was the opposite of patriotism.

Asha had no idea who had started the rumor that sent the mob to Sergeant Siddiqui's home, but it was someone with two key pieces of information.

One—that Siddiqui had been the flight mechanic who had signed off on the flight-worthiness of General Mehra's helicopter. Two—that Sergeant Siddiqui was a Muslim.

In Hindu-majority India, it didn't take much to spark religious violence. The same could be said for Muslim-majority Bangladesh next door. Oftentimes violence against the Muslim minority in India sparked violence against the Hindu minority in Bangladesh. It was a vicious cycle.

The mere suggestion that Sergeant Siddiqui, a Muslim, might have sabotaged a helicopter carrying General Mehra, a Hindu, was all it took to light the fuse. Arriving on the scene, Asha could see plenty of potential "accelerant."

The crowd was made up of about seventy-five angry people and was growing. Police had arrived but were hanging back. It was reprehensible.

Identifying the commander, a fat and obviously lazy cop, leaning against his patrol vehicle with a baton under his arm and a lit cigarette in his mouth, she approached him and said, "Do something."

"Excuse me, ma'am?" the officer said, taken aback.

"You heard me. *Do something*."

"Ma'am, the Rapid Reaction Force has been alerted. We are not equipped to deal with mob actions."

Asha glanced at the front seat of his cruiser, where an array of crowd control devices had been stacked. "What's all of that, then?"

"That's for our protection. If the need arises."

"*Your* protection?" she shot back. "What about protection of the Siddiqui family and their home?"

"Ma'am, you are interfering with my ability to do my job. Please step back."

"As far as I can see, you're not doing anything."

"We are monitoring the situation, ma'am," the officer replied.

"That's not good enough," said Asha. "Sergeant Siddiqui is a member of India's armed forces."

One of the other cops standing nearby said derisively in Hindi, "He's also a Muslim."

It was an unprofessional slur and should have immediately been rebuked by the commander, and the offending officer reprimanded. Instead, the lead officer continued to lean on his cruiser, smoking.

"Our troops work around the clock to keep you and your families safe, *regardless* of religion. You owe them the same respect and obligation in return," she stated.

The commander looked at her, took a deep drag from his cigarette, and held it for a moment before exhaling. Dropping the butt to the ground, he crushed it out with his boot and then motioned for his men to follow him.

Asha watched, expecting them to start breaking things up and pushing people back, away from the Siddiquis' home. That wasn't what happened.

The cops walked over to another cruiser, where the fat commander struck the same, lazy pose and lit another cigarette. The message being sent to the crowd was obvious—*we're not here to do anything*.

Asha had only a handful of options—none of them good. She had promised the flight mechanic that she would protect his family. Right now, however, she couldn't even make it to the front door.

Complicating matters was the lack of action by the police. The mob would only grow angrier and more emboldened. Some in the crowd were already throwing rocks at the house, which caused Asha even more concern.

The most common trigger, worldwide, that tripped an angry mob into violence was the sound of breaking glass. It was like a starting gun that opened a destructive and potentially deadly set of floodgates.

When one of the rock throwers in the street succeeded in shattering an upstairs window, Asha knew she had run out of time. She had to act.

Opening the passenger-side door of the cruiser, she grabbed a 40mm launcher, slung a bandolier studded with less-lethal munitions, and headed toward the crowd.

Before the cops even realized what was going on, she had loaded the four-shot launcher and had taken aim at the mob.

The first device she fired was a warning munition. Holding the launcher at an angle, she pressed the trigger and sent the projectile high into the air. It detonated twenty feet above the crowd with an earsplitting, 170-decibel explosion and a blinding, five-million-candela flash.

A collective panic spread through the mob. People started screaming and running away.

There was a handful of about fifteen who had decided to charge the house and were trying to kick in the door. Asha advanced and turned her attention on them next.

The next three shots to erupt from the launcher were called WASPs.

Each munition contained fourteen rubberized projectiles accurate to fifty feet with an eight-foot spread. In other words, none of the rioters were spared. Each was struck multiple times and each strike caused excruciating pain.

By the time any of the mob realized where the shots had come from, Asha had already reloaded and was firing at them again as she closed the rest of the distance.

Those who could, ran. Those who couldn't, limped. The rest had to be helped away by their comrades.

In the end, Asha had succeeded in her objective. She had cleared a path to the house and had made it to the front entrance.

Banging on the door, she called out to Mrs. Siddiqui, using her first name and telling her it was safe to let her in. A moment later, Ismat did just that.

After reloading her launcher, Asha turned and fired an aerial-burst pepper spray grenade that detonated overhead of where the mob had reassembled, halfway down this street.

It wouldn't keep them away forever, but it would have to do for now. Scanning the street before retreating inside the house, she caught the astonished gaze of the overweight police commander. He stood there with his mouth agape, the lit cigarette barely hanging on to his lower lip.

"The Indian Armed Forces thanks you for your assistance," she shouted, maintaining her professionalism, while fighting the urge to give him the finger.

She then went inside to join Mrs. Siddiqui, closing and locking the door behind her.

CHAPTER 19

"Everything is okay. You're all safe. Nothing is going to happen to you," Asha said, trying to calm Mrs. Siddiqui and her young children down. "Is anyone injured?"

They all shook their heads.

"Good," Asha replied. "I need everyone to pack an overnight bag. No suitcases. Something small that you can easily carry. Okay?"

The family nodded and Asha set them on their task as she searched the rest of the house, making sure it was secure.

Once her job was complete, she took out her phone and called the lance naik.

"Do you have Sergeant Siddiqui?" she asked.

"Yes, ma'am. He's right here."

"Tell him his wife and family are safe, but he must remain with you. It's still not safe for him down here."

"Yes, ma'am," Khan replied and then relayed the information to the flight mechanic.

"What's your position?" she asked.

"We're a block down the street in the opposite direction of the crowd."

"How many cops do you see?"

"At present, I count ten, but there could be more."

"Be very careful. I don't trust them."

"Yes, ma'am," said the lance naik. "I understand."

"What is the crowd doing? Is it dispersing?"

"They scattered after you fired that last round, but they appear to be regrouping."

Damn it, she thought. *How the hell am I going to get all of them out of here safely?* And then it came to her.

"What kind of air assets does Sulur have on standby, crewed and ready to go right now?" she asked.

"Fixed wing, ma'am? Or rotary?"

"Rotary."

"Surely, ma'am, you're not thinking of trying to land a helicopter on the street outside. It is much too dangerous. With the proximity of the buildings, not to mention the power lines—"

Asha cut him off and explained precisely what she wanted him to arrange. Once Khan assured her that he understood what it was she wanted, she disconnected the call and went to check on the progress Mrs. Siddiqui and the children were making.

As she did, she offered up a silent prayer that her plan would work. If it didn't, with a less-than-compliant police force, she had no idea how she was going to pull this off.

• • •

When Khan called back, she could already hear the sound of the inbound chopper. It was a sleek, new HAL Dhruv, manufactured by Hindustan Aeronautics Limited and operated by the Indian Air Force.

The Dhruv took its name from the Sanskrit word for "unshakeable," but today it was going to do some of the most serious shaking of its career.

Asha had rejiggered her launcher with a different set of munitions. Checking them one last time, she told the lance naik that she was good to go.

"As soon as you give the signal, then," Khan replied.

Lining up the family, she gave them one final set of instructions, literal marching orders, and then unlocked the front door.

Even though she couldn't see the helo, she knew where it was. Once the crew received her signal, it would move in.

Out on the street, the mob had not only regrouped: they were moving forward, back toward the house. Many had tied pieces of cloth around their faces in anticipation of another salvo of pepper spray.

Asha raised the launcher and fired one of the flash-bang-style warning rounds. It exploded over the heads of the crowd with another thunderous bang and a searing flash of light. A handful of shocked rioters skittered away, but after a chorus of surprised screams, the mob pressed ahead. That was when she loosed another aerial burst of pepper spray.

Those who thought cloth masks were going to protect them from the chemical irritant were sorely mistaken. Wave after wave of coughing and choking could be heard coming from the mob, which had appeared to have gained considerably in size. It was time to launch her third round—a smoke grenade.

Gathering up the family behind her, she counted to three, pressed her trigger, and began her evacuation of the Siddiquis.

Out on the street, they broke left, led by Ismat, while Asha covered them from the rear.

Upon seeing the cloud of blue smoke, the Indian Air Force pilots swooped in and provided what the local police wouldn't—riot control.

In a maneuver known as a "hot wash," the Dhruv came in low, less than fifty feet above the mob. Using the storm-strength downwash of its rotors, it created a hurricane of pain by whipping up dirt, sand, and debris, sending it everywhere.

The rioters tripped over and knocked each other down as they scrambled to get away.

Asha, Ismat, and the children were almost to Khan's vehicle, when the police commander caught sight of Asha and shouted for her to stop.

When she refused and kept on running—urging the Siddiquis forward—the officer ordered his men to move in.

Asha had one more round in her launcher and she let the commander and his men have it.

Just as she had done earlier in holding back from flipping him the finger, she maintained her professionalism. She didn't use a WASP munition or one packed with pepper spray. Rather, she used another blue smoke grenade.

Whether the commander and his men chose to stand there as the helo barreled down on them to deliver another hot wash was their problem.

By the time the helicopter had arrived overhead, Asha had reunited Sergeant Siddiqui with his family, they had all wedged into Khan's Maruti Gypsy, and they were on their way back to Sulur Air Base.

CHAPTER 20

Asha was well aware that Siddiqui was upset and wanted to console his family, which made this the right time to question him. He owed her and she was ready to collect.

The fact that the rumor had spread so quickly and had sparked such a horrible reaction bothered her. But not as much as the fact that someone with inside information, someone connected to the air base, had leaked it.

When she asked the flight mechanic who he thought it might be, he didn't have a clue. In fact, he hadn't even known who was going to be on the helicopter, only that it was some sort of VIP group. He had assumed that meant politicians or military personnel.

According to Siddiqui, he and his team were always meticulous, regardless of who was flying. Every life was precious and it was his duty to see to their safety.

However, because of the VIP designation, they had not only done their standard, focused tip-to-tail preflight examination of the helo; they had also done a much more intensive inspection, sampling fuel and hydraulic fluid, swapping out certain electronic elements in advance of their expiration, and undertaking a host of other abundance-of-caution items. In short, the helicopter was in above-tip-top condition.

When Asha then asked Siddiqui what he thought had happened, he hung his head. "I knew the pilots. I respected them. They were my colleagues. I do not wish to disparage them now that they have died."

"But it is critical that we figure out *how* they died," she replied, trying to coax him. "If nothing else, to prevent something similar from happening in the future."

The flight mechanic exhaled a long breath through his nostrils and then said, "CFIT."

Asha was unfamiliar with the term. "*CFIT?*"

"Controlled flight into terrain."

"You're saying you believe it was pilot error?"

He nodded. "Maybe different evidence will be found at the crash site, but from my perspective, there is nothing to suggest a technical issue. Nor sabotage."

"Why would you think sabotage might be a possibility?"

"You're DSC," the flight mechanic stated, pointing at her uniform. "That's the kind of thing you handle, isn't it?"

Asha nodded. "Yes."

"I think your investigation is going to be short-lived."

"Why is that?"

"Because I was with that helicopter the entire time. I never took my eyes off of it until General Mehra boarded and he and his party took off. Not even the invisible man could have made it past me."

"You would have been able to see the invisible man?" she asked.

"No," Siddiqui replied, "but I would have seen the fog swirl as he tried to access the aircraft. And that's why I believe the cause of the crash was"—he began to say CFIT again, but stopped himself midsentence and said—"pilot error. Because of the terrain and the way in which the weather changes here, visibility likely worsened as they traveled closer to Wellington."

It was possible, Asha reasoned. It was probably even the most likely explanation. But it didn't explain Siddiqui being publicly identified as the chief flight mechanic, along with his religion. That part felt too coordinated, too prepared in advance.

She put the question to him again, told him to take his time, but the man remained unable to come up with any names of anyone who might have exposed him.

Asha believed him—both in that the helicopter hadn't been sabotaged and that he had no clue who had outed him.

She debated whether it was worth her time to visit the crash site. That type of investigation was largely outside her realm of expertise.

There were trained investigators on scene who, ostensibly, would be able to spot any indication that a bomb or a missile of some sort had brought down the helo.

But barring that sort of evidence, she was leaning heavily toward Sergeant Siddiqui's assessment—pilot error coupled with poor visibility.

She was about to release Siddiqui so that he could take his family over to the temporary base housing that had been arranged for them, when Khan knocked and stuck his head into the office.

"Phone call, ma'am. Line two. Major Badal."

She picked it up. "Yes, Major?"

"I need you to come to Coonoor."

"To the crash site?"

"No," Badal responded, "to the police station. There's something you need to see."

• • •

She was flown up on the same HAL Dhruv, with the same Indian Air Force crew, that had hot-washed the rioters and the Coimbatore police.

At her request, the pilots flew the same route as General Mehra's helicopter and then circled the crash site for several minutes so that she could take it all in.

There were few words she could have chosen to describe it. Wreckage was scattered everywhere. Trees had been snapped like toothpicks. The surrounding forest had been charred black.

On a large patch of grass near the town of Coonoor police station, the Dhruv touched down and disgorged its sole passenger. Major Badal was waiting for her.

She saluted the superior officer and followed him inside. Like every other police station she had ever set foot inside, it smelled like stale chai mixed with cigarettes that had been not-so-covertly smoked in the station restroom. There was a ton of activity going on, no doubt in response to the crash.

Badal led her to a small, empty conference room that had been set up as a war room and closed the door behind them. On the desk was a laptop computer with two attachments—a projector and what appeared to be some sort of SD card reader.

"Next to the head constable, who processed this evidence when it arrived, and the inspector in charge of this station, no one else has seen what I am about to show you," said Badal.

Asha nodded and, after turning out the lights, Badal pushed a button on the computer, which projected a video on the whiteboard at the front of the room. "We believe this footage is the last sighting of General Mehra's helicopter before it went down."

The video appeared to have been taken from a rooftop, in a crowded neighborhood, somewhere on the outskirts of town. She could see a mix of commercial and residential buildings. There were laundry lines, old satellite dishes, and a smattering of billboards. There was also fog, but not as thick as she had expected.

Badal narrated: "The footage was captured by a young man who thought it might be cool for his social media accounts. In a moment, you'll see the helicopter enter screen left."

As was true in most cases, you could hear it before you saw it. When the helicopter finally materialized, everything appeared normal. But after a few seconds, it began to dramatically lose altitude. It also began swinging violently from side to side.

She could only imagine how terrifying it must have been for everyone on board, especially the pilots as they fought to bring it under control.

The video stayed with the aircraft until it disappeared from view. Shortly thereafter, an explosion could be heard and a plume of black smoke could be seen on the horizon.

"Wait a second," said Asha, walking over to the whiteboard. "Rewind it, please."

Badal did as she asked.

"Right there. Stop." Pointing at one of the rooftops, she then asked, "Can you tighten in on this?"

The major was impressed. He had watched the video several times, but hadn't noticed what she had. He'd been focused on the helicopter and what he was certain was a mechanical failure of some sort. "What is that? A sniper?"

"Not in the traditional sense."

"Meaning?"

Asha used her finger to outline the backpack the figure was wearing, the odd features of his rifle, and what appeared to be some sort of a hose tying it all together.

The tighter Badal zoomed in, the fuzzier and more difficult the image was to view.

"I don't understand," he said, zooming out. "What are we looking at?"

"The cause of our crash," she replied. "And quite possibly an act of war."

CHAPTER 21

Yang Xin was exhausted. It had been a long, hard day with a lot on the line. His jaw ached from being clenched and his stomach hadn't been right since before even stepping into the office. The stress of the job was getting to him. By all accounts, however, today's operations had been a total success.

The helicopter carrying the head of India's armed forces had gone down in a fiery crash and the Yaomo operative in the United States charged with raining down "Havana Syndrome," as the Americans had come to call it, on the first member of the Carlton Group had been wildly successful.

The Science and Technology Commission had no research from which to gauge how severely the weapon would impact the little bastard known as the Troll. They had advised against going too strong with the initial attack. Yang, however, had instructed his operative to go with a full dose. He wanted the attack to be extremely painful and for it to leave a deep psychological scar. He wanted the little man to live in fear of it happening again. Which it most definitely would.

Yang had a plan for all of the members of the Carlton Group, but he had a very special plan reserved for one employee in particular—Scot Harvath.

Harvath had not only single-handedly disrupted several of China's most important, highly sensitive strategic missions, but he was also suspected of recently assassinating a ranking member of China's Ministry of

State Security and one of its top operatives, who had been a former military colleague of Yang's.

There would be quite the reward and untold accolades for whoever managed to capture or kill Harvath.

Yang's hope was that in staging attacks on members of the Carlton Group, he could weaken the organization and flush Harvath out into the open. The man had been impossible to find.

But as much as Beijing considered Harvath a special target, the priority right now was to put a stop to any potential Asian version of NATO. Yang was free to go after Harvath on the side, but not at the expense of his primary mission. Beijing would absolutely not stand for a military alliance in their backyard anchored by the United States and India. It was a nonstarter—one they would risk anything to stop, even going to war.

That meant that the next operation was critically important. And even though he knew his man in Mumbai knew that, he wanted to drive the point home once more. He didn't want any mistakes. *Zero*.

Looking at his watch, he computed the time difference. They were coming up on another communications window.

Opening his encrypted laptop, he activated the app that would encode his communications and send a signal to his contact that he was online. Minutes later, Basheer Durrani entered the chat.

He was a deep-cover operative from the Pakistani Inter-Services Intelligence agency, or ISI for short. Pakistan had been one of the first nations to recognize and formally establish diplomatic ties with the People's Republic of China. It had also played a pivotal role in making Richard Nixon's historic state visit to China possible.

China was Pakistan's largest trading partner and lavished the country with massive investments, including the over $62 million worth of upgrades to Pakistan's infrastructure, economy, transportation networks, and energy sector, via a program known as the China-Pakistan Economic Corridor—Beijing's biggest overseas investment, which fell under its global Belt and Road Initiative.

Islamabad loved the money and expertise that the Chinese provided. They also loved that China hated India as much as Pakistan hated India. It was a match made in heaven. In exchange for Beijing's largesse, Pakistan not only looked the other way when it came to the ethnic genocide of Uyghur Muslims, but actively spied on them in the northern regions of Pakistan and fed the intelligence to the Chinese.

It wasn't lost on Beijing that the China-Pakistan Economic Corridor was viewed by Islamabad as Pakistan's economic lifeline—and so China did what they did in every nation where they had gotten an investment foothold: they pushed for everything they could get in return. This went double for help in undermining and weakening India.

Beijing referred to the arrangement as a strategic intelligence partnership—a relatively benign-sounding title. What it was, in fact, was China being granted access to, and the ability to task, Pakistani intelligence operatives inside India.

In any other scenario, this would have been untenable—the geopolitical equivalent of bobbing for hand grenades. Pakistan was running Chinese operations against India. Whatever went wrong would not only blow back on China, but on Pakistan as well. Islamabad didn't have a choice. Pakistan was simply too desperate for Beijing's cash to say no.

It was via this "relationship" that Yang had been made aware of Durrani. The more he had dug into the ISI operative, the more he knew he wanted to recruit him. He was not only extremely talented, he also had some very dark, very compromising things in his past that would make him easier to control.

Yang wanted a full debrief on the downing of the helicopter, but then he wanted to get down to more important business—how the next attack would unfold.

For that, he had something very special in mind.

CHAPTER 22

When Harvath stepped off the aircraft, Vijay Chabra—ex–Indian Police Service officer and current U.S. Embassy Foreign Service National/Investigator—was on the tarmac waiting for him. Harvath liked him the minute he laid eyes on him.

The man had swagger. He looked like he had been frozen in the middle of a stylish, 1980s Bollywood action movie and brought back to life.

He was fit for his age, which Harvath pegged to be somewhere in his mid-sixties. He was tall, with his hair parted on the left side, and he had a thick, almost porn-star-style mustache that must have been dyed, as it was such a dark shade of black.

He wore khaki trousers and a linen safari jacket, belted at the waist. His leather shoes were highly polished and he wore a gold signet ring on the pinky finger of his left hand. Capping it all off, he wore a gold watch, and a fashionable pair of dark, gold-rimmed sunglasses hung from his shirt at the neck.

From top to bottom, the confident Vijay Chabra radiated a powerful "Fuck you" vibe. This was a man who got things done.

"Welcome to India," he said as the two met at the bottom of the airstairs and shook hands.

"I wish it was under better circumstances," said Harvath. "I appreciate you coming to meet me, Mr. Chabra."

"Only my mother-in-law calls me *Mr. Chabra*," he said with a grin. "Please call me Vijay."

Harvath laughed at that one. "And you can call me Joe," he offered. The name in the passport that had been created for him was Joseph John Sampson.

When Harvath took an alias, he liked to base it upon the name of someone from the OSS. "Jumping Joe" Savoldi, codename "Sampson," was one such man.

Famed for his language and hand-to-hand combat skills, he had been a highly lethal and highly successful covert operative during World War II.

"You don't look like an investigator," said Vijay. "You look more military to me. Maybe I should call you GI Joe."

"You can call me anything you like," Harvath replied with another smile. "But as someone who spent a little time in the Navy, maybe you can come up with something better than *GI* Joe."

"I knew it," the man replied. "I am *always* right about these things. What's your middle name?"

"John."

"Then I'll call you JJ. It's perfect. Vijay and JJ. There, it's settled. End of that piece of business. Now, the next item for discussion. You just got off a very long flight. Have you eaten?"

"No," Harvath answered. "I have not."

"Do you mind a working dinner?"

"No, I don't mind. What are you thinking?"

"You and I are at the same hotel," Vijay said. "You can check in, get cleaned up, and then we'll retrace Mr. Ritter's last steps. And if you don't find it too off-putting, we could even eat in the same restaurant."

"That sounds like a plan."

They left the airport via the cargo terminal, where, via his diplomatic passport, Harvath was sped through customs and immigration.

Parked outside was Vijay's 1990s-era Jaguar XJS convertible in British racing green. It was so clean that even under the lights of the parking lot, it shone like a mirror. It was obvious that he took very good care of it.

"Nice car," said Harvath. "How was the drive from New Delhi?"

"Not bad. It's only three and a half hours. I have a cousin in Behror, which is about halfway. We had a cup of tea together."

Popping the trunk, he stood aside so that Harvath could place his bag inside and then closed the lid and asked, "Top up or down?"

It was a beautiful, warm evening. "Top down," Harvath replied.

"Excellent choice. Because of Diwali, you will see lots of fireworks."

· · ·

The man hadn't been kidding. There had been tons of them. It was the ultimate way to be introduced to a city.

They made small talk along the way, with Vijay acting the proud tour guide, pointing out places of interest and providing a brief history of Jaipur. It was the first planned city in India, but it was the story behind its becoming the "Pink City" that was so fascinating. In 1876, the Prince of Wales and Queen Victoria were coming for a state visit. The maharaja who ruled Jaipur decreed that all of its buildings should be painted pink—the color believed to represent hospitality and vibrancy—and that same tradition was still being followed nearly a century and a half later. Indians were a proud people, Vijay explained, and tradition was very important to them.

Harvath good-naturedly asked if that commitment to tradition also applied to car stereos. "I can't remember the last time I saw a CD player in the wild," he joked.

Reaching behind his seat, Vijay pulled out a black nylon CD wallet and handed it to him. "You are my guest, so I will let you choose the music."

Harvath was a bit uncomfortable, yet oddly interested to see what CDs the ex-cop had inside. Taking the plunge, he opened it up and began flipping through the translucent sleeves. He was shocked to find one he had owned himself.

"Earth, Wind and Fire?" he queried, pulling it out.

"You're familiar with them?" Vijay asked.

Harvath laughed. "After George Clinton and Parliament, one of the best funk bands ever."

The ex-cop clucked and shook his head. "Most definitely not. They are an R-and-B band. Everyone knows this."

"Everyone?"

"Yes, and this is the problem with you funk people. You want to plant your flag everywhere. I am here to tell you that the R-and-B world will hear nothing of it."

This guy was a legit piece of work. "Okay," Harvath replied. "Out of respect, as your guest, I'm not going to have this fight with you."

"Because you know I'm right."

Harvath laughed again and removed the CD from the sleeve. Inserting it into the CD player, he pushed PLAY and settled back.

As the iconic vocoder opening of "Let's Groove" slid out of the Jaguar's speakers, Harvath realized he had been wrong. Fireworks *and* Earth, Wind & Fire was the ultimate way to be introduced to a city.

Harvath played DJ the rest of the way to the Fairmont, selecting as much funk music as he could find in Vijay's CD wallet. And to be fair, he had to hand it to the man, there was a good amount of it—the S.O.S. Band, Kool & the Gang, and even the Bar-Kays—all of whom Vijay argued were R&B and most definitely not funk.

When they arrived at the perimeter of the hotel, they were greeted by a security checkpoint. Two guards in berets checked the vehicle, including using a mirror to inspect the undercarriage. Satisfied that neither the Jaguar nor its occupants posed any threat, one of the guards removed the metal bollard just ahead of them and waved them in.

Harvath had stayed at a lot of beautiful hotels in his time, but the Fairmont Jaipur was like a palace.

They entered through a massive archway with two towering wooden doors studded with rivets and strips of iron.

There was an ornate courtyard surrounded by high walls and lit by torches. As they pulled up to the main entrance, two men in crisp, blue-and-white uniforms with red turbans were playing enormous drums known as *nagada*.

Another, on a balcony high above the front doors, dropped rose petals to welcome the new guests.

A fourth staff member met the car when it came to a stop. His white uniform was accented with cream-colored cuffs, epaulets, and a sash. Atop his head was a brilliant orange turban, a piece of which had been allowed to hang behind him, almost to the ground. Unlike the two, who were clean-shaven, this man had the biggest mustache Harvath had ever seen.

Pressing his palms together, the staff member drew his hands to his chest, bowed ever so slightly, and wished them "Namaste," before opening Harvath's door.

He asked if he could provide assistance with any luggage. Vijay had checked in earlier and Harvath was fine wheeling his bag himself.

After he had retrieved it from the trunk, Vijay gave instructions to the valet in Hindi, and crossing the petal-covered threshold, the duo stepped inside.

Opulent didn't even begin to describe the interior. It was like stepping into a work of art. From the intricate frescoes and crystal chandeliers to the silver antiques and scalloped stone archways, every element of the design contributed to grandeur.

Vijay accompanied Harvath to the intricately carved front desk and waited for him while he checked in. Once he had his keycard, they agreed to meet in the lobby in twenty minutes.

Up in his room, Harvath unpacked and was about to text Nicholas a SITREP via the encrypted app they used, when he saw a message waiting from Lawlor.

"What happened?" Harvath asked when the man picked up.

"Nobody knows. It came on suddenly. Nicholas says he thought for a moment that he was having a stroke. But seeing the dogs impacted by it as well, he knew it was some sort of attack."

"Is he going to be okay?"

"They want to keep him at Walter Reed a little while longer for observation."

"Do they know what did this to him?"

"The symptoms track with Havana Syndrome."

Harvath was familiar with it. It was first reported by U.S. and Canadian embassy personnel back in 2016 in Havana, Cuba. Since then, it had happened in multiple other countries around the world, and the targets had broadened to include U.S. intelligence operatives, military members, and their families. "So, we're treating this as an attack, right?"

"One hundred percent," said Lawlor. "We just don't know how it was committed."

"Did you reach out to Bob McGee?"

McGee was the director of the Central Intelligence Agency and a close ally of the Carlton Group.

"I did. Immediately. They believe it's a directed-energy weapon of some sort."

"Who do they think is behind it?" Harvath asked.

"Even though they've been chasing this for the last six years, they still don't know. It could be the Russians. Maybe the Chinese. They're completely in the dark."

"Why Nicholas? Why target him?"

"Is that a serious question?" Lawlor replied. "That man has got an enemies list miles and miles long. The real question is who *doesn't* want harm to come to him?"

"But this has all the hallmarks of a state-sponsored attack."

"And Nicholas pissed off a lot of states, including China and Russia," said Lawlor. "Do I need to remind you that, in addition to the people he has pissed off, intelligence operatives have been targets in the past. Just because we're not the CIA doesn't make us any less likely for targeting."

It was a good point. If they could come after Nicholas, they could come after anyone at the Carlton Group, including family members. This caused him to ask, "What's Nina's status?"

"She was away visiting friends when it happened. She's back now."

Harvath had a rush of concern. Nina was a straight-up badass. She was quite fond of letting everyone know that she didn't scare easily and could more than take care of them both. "She's not staying at the house, is she?" he asked.

"No," Lawlor replied. "We've got her someplace safe. The dogs are with her, too. They've already been thoroughly checked over by their vet."

"And you've got a team on her?" Harvath clarified. "Just in case."

"Yes. On Nicholas, too."

That made Harvath feel a lot better. "What can I do?"

"Everybody's in excellent hands. Just focus on your assignment. That's the most important thing right now."

"You'll keep me updated?"

"I will," said Lawlor.

After giving Gary his SITREP, he took a quick shower and got dressed.

When he arrived back down in the lobby, Vijay was waiting for him. He was holding what looked like a bag from one of the hotel shops.

On closer inspection, Harvath realized it was from Cigar Diwan, the hotel's private cigar bar.

"For later," said Vijay, rolling up the bag and sliding it into one of the pockets of his safari jacket. "Ready to go?"

Harvath nodded and they walked outside to where the Jaguar had been parked. He was eager to get started. The sooner he picked up a trail, the sooner he'd be able to hunt down whoever had killed Ritter.

CHAPTER 23

As they drove out of the hotel's gigantic gate and headed toward Jaipur's Vaishali Nagar neighborhood, Vijay gave Harvath a rundown on everything he had been able to ascertain about Ritter's death so far.

"Mr. Ritter called downstairs at five twenty p.m. and asked the concierge to summon a taxi to take him to the Mahatma Gandhi Nagar Park. The taxi driver confirmed to police that he picked up an American matching Mr. Ritter's description from the hotel and drove him to the park. He dropped him off on the north side. They chatted about nothing in particular during their time together."

"Okay," replied Harvath, glancing back at the Fairmont and noting the position of its exterior security cameras. "What about the hotel's CCTV? Has anyone checked to see if he was being followed?"

"Jaipur is under the jurisdiction of the Rajasthan state police. Because of the nature of the crime and the citizenship of the victim, the case was immediately elevated to a District Special Team, known as a DST. The first thing they did after taking over the crime scene was to deploy investigators to the Fairmont to take statements, make copies of any and all video surveillance footage, and search Mr. Ritter's room. They found nothing suspicious. No one was following him that they could see."

"Maybe someone was out on the main road, beyond view of the security cameras."

Vijay nodded. "Which is precisely what they thought, so they began hunting down whatever imagery was available. They gathered footage from a series of private cameras as well as the city's traffic cams. From what they were able to stitch together, the taxi was not being followed."

"What about any cameras between the park where he was dropped off and the restaurant where he had dinner?"

"It's only about a kilometer and a half between the two, but Ritter took the long way. He either had a lot of time to kill, or he was trying to make sure he didn't have a tail."

"Did he?" Harvath asked.

"Based on the footage, no, he did not. There was no tail."

That left only three possibilities in Harvath's mind. The first was that someone who wanted to kill him had recognized him on the street. To his knowledge, Ritter didn't have any enemies to speak of. What's more, that would have been a hell of a coincidence—and coincidences were not something Harvath believed in.

The second possibility was that it actually was a robbery gone bad. But Harvath had too many doubts at this moment.

The third possibility was that the killer had known where Ritter was going to be. That idea was starting to gain traction in Harvath's mind. If it turned out to be true, it was going to create a lot of serious, and most definitely deadly, repercussions.

"Do you know with whom he was having dinner?" Harvath asked.

"Witnesses saw him eating with an Indian national, mid-forties, slim build, short hair, anywhere from five foot six to five foot ten, casually dressed. The restaurant didn't have CCTV and there are no exterior cameras nearby."

"How was the dinner paid for?"

"Cash."

"Of course. A credit card would have made it too easy."

Vijay nodded. "According to the file I was given at the embassy in Delhi, Mr. Ritter is an international business consultant?"

"That's correct."

"Hard to believe he came all this way just to see the sights and didn't try to get a little business done, isn't it?"

They were getting into dangerous territory. Harvath knew Ritter's real purpose in Jaipur, but he wasn't cleared to share it with Vijay.

"The State Department has already spoken with his office back in the U.S. They confirmed that this trip was a long-planned vacation and that he had no meetings set up. Sometimes it's just nice to get away from work."

"Fair enough," Vijay replied. "Maybe his dining companion was an old friend? Or an acquaintance who had said, 'If you're ever in Delhi, look me up.'"

"Could be. Or for all we know, it was a brand-new person he'd met after having arrived."

"Someone who may have lured him to the restaurant in order to kill him?"

Harvath knew who Ritter had eaten dinner with. He was an assistant to the foreign secretary in the Ministry of External Affairs—the agency responsible for India's foreign affairs. If, and it was a big *if*, he turned out to have been involved with Ritter's murder, he wasn't going to be hard to track down.

For the time being, Harvath wanted Vijay focused on the killer and steered him in that direction.

"All options are on the table, but I'd like to focus on the killer. When we find that person, we're going to get answers to a lot of questions."

"*When* we find that person," Vijay repeated. "There are one-point-four billion people in India. Over four-point-three million of them reside in Jaipur. I admire your confidence. I only wish I shared it. Very few murders like these ever get solved."

A critical skill for a spy was the ability to develop sources and build networks. It was something Harvath was exceedingly good at. What he had learned over the years was that it wasn't about gaining their trust—not at the beginning, but rather putting your trust in them.

"There's something you don't know about Eli Ritter," Harvath admitted. "Two things, actually."

As Vijay brought the Jaguar to a stop at a red light, he looked at his passenger. "Okay," he replied, cautiously. "I'm listening."

"He used to work for the State Department. Bureau of Economic and Business Affairs. His job was to level the playing field for American businesses overseas and to encourage foreign investment in the U.S. economy."

"Sounds like a cover position."

Harvath smiled. "You've been reading too many spy novels."

"What's the other thing I don't know about him?"

"He and I knew each other. We were friends."

The light turned green and it took a honk from another vehicle to shift Vijay's attention back to the road. As he accelerated he said, "First, I'm sorry for your loss."

"Thank you."

"Second, if there's anything else you want to tell me, now would be a good time. I can't help you, not really, if I don't have a full picture of what's going on."

Direct, smart, and to the point. The more time he spent with Vijay, the more he liked him. He took no enjoyment from keeping him in the dark. "You know what I know."

"Very well," said Vijay. "I understand. We'll leave it there for now. In the meantime, my job is to assist you, in any way I can, so what other questions do you have for me?"

"There was a witness to the shooting, correct?"

"Two, actually. A shopkeeper and his wife. I assume you would like to speak with them?"

"Yes," said Harvath. "I'd also like to see any forensic evidence, as well as Ritter's body. How soon can we do all of that?"

"We can visit the shopkeeper and his wife tonight. Accessing the morgue and the DST's evidence room would be easier during business hours, but I can make some calls if you want. Just understand that you'd be pulling people away from their Diwali celebrations. They'll be more cooperative in the morning."

"Then that part can wait. Let's retrace Ritter's steps, have dinner, and see the shopkeepers."

"Good plan," replied Vijay as he pulled up a route on his phone. "I've mapped out where all of the security cameras caught Ritter between the park and the restaurant. If at any point you want to stop and get out of the car, just let me know."

Harvath flashed him a thumbs-up and then reached behind the seat for the CD wallet.

Pulling out Average White Band's second album, *AWB,* he held it up so Vijay could see it. "Can I play this without us having another argument?"

The man smiled. "Sure. Go ahead."

Sliding it into the player, Harvath cued up the band's breakout hit, "Pick Up the Pieces."

As the saxophones began to play and Vijay sped up to pass the car in front of him, Harvath could have sworn he heard the man whisper under his breath, "Best R-and-B song *ever.*"

CHAPTER 24

Retracing Ritter's path from the park to the restaurant proved uneventful. A couple of times, Harvath had Vijay stop the car so he could check for extra cameras in certain spots that the DST might have missed, but they had been thorough and didn't seem to have missed any.

Arriving at the Tansukh, Vijay politely declined the table that was offered them and pointed out the one he wanted. It was in the back corner, near an exit, with a view of everything—the exact table Harvath would have picked. The waitress walked the men over, waited until they had sat down, and then handed them each a menu.

Harvath took one look and immediately set his on the table.

"Pictures too confusing?" Vijay joked. "Or is the English too complicated?"

"More like too overwhelming."

"Like I said, my job is to help out however I can. Do you want me to make some suggestions?"

"Please," said Harvath.

"Most important question—is there anything you won't eat?"

Back in Dushanbe, Leahy—who had been to India before—gave Harvath a rundown of things to avoid if he wanted to remain "operational."

"Nothing raw. No rice." Rice, Leahy had explained, was notoriously bad for cultivating bacteria. Uncooked fruits or vegetables, which might have been washed in tainted tap water, were also off-limits, as were ice cubes. Bottled water was the only way to hydrate.

"Got it," Vijay answered. "How are you with spicy foods?"

Harvath smiled. "I grew up less than twenty miles from the Mexican border. I can handle spicy food."

Vijay cocked a challenging eyebrow at him. "Are you sure?"

"Something tells me we're going to find out," said Harvath, cocking one right back.

When the waiter came over, Vijay ordered everything in Hindi. At the very end, he added, in English, "And a large portion of yogurt for my friend. Just in case."

The ex-cop was trying to mess with his head. Harvath simply smiled in return. Leahy had warned him that some Indian dishes were so far off the Scoville scale that they should come with a skull-and-crossbones warning. Should you suffer the misfortune of stumbling into one of those dishes, the best antidote was yogurt. Harvath didn't know what Vijay had planned, but it looked like they might be pushing the culinary envelope.

As a rule, Harvath didn't drink while he was working, but when Vijay asked if he'd like to have a beer with him, he had said yes. A bit of social lubricant could go a long way in cementing a relationship with a source.

"Do you like a good IPA?" the man had asked.

"An India Pale Ale?" Harvath responded. "Sure."

"Do you know where the name comes from?"

"To be honest, not really. I'm more of a lager guy."

"It comes from the Brits," he explained. "They used to have their beer shipped to India from England. That can be a pretty rough voyage, and in the beginning a lot of their beer spoiled. So brewers began experimenting. They made it more alcoholic and increased their use of hops. It resulted in a bitter but more aromatic beer that could safely make the journey. The British soldiers, in particular, loved it."

With Harvath's permission, Vijay ordered them each a popular, made-in-India IPA called White Rhino.

When the beers arrived, they said "Cheers," clinked bottles, and took a drink. Harvath, being a lager guy, was pleasantly surprised by the flavor.

It was smooth and not bitter at all. He said a small prayer and crossed his fingers that Vijay would perform as well on the food he had ordered.

The plates came out in waves. Laal Mass, a lamb dish in a tangy red chili sauce. Keema Baati, a deep-fried minced-meat pastry with fresh green chilies and green peas. Jaipuri Chicken, a chicken made with curry, cream, and lots of gravy.

They were all delicious. While the heat varied from dish to dish, there was nothing that Harvath couldn't handle. He was beginning to think he was going to make it through unscathed, when the waiter appeared with a fourth item.

It was a Bhut Jolokia chutney. When Harvath asked what he was supposed to eat it with and Vijay said, "Some people eat it all by itself, others put a spoonful of it on naan," he had a feeling this was the "surprise" dish— the one the yogurt had been brought out for.

"Aren't chutneys raw foods?"

"This one has been very specially prepared. Don't worry about it."

"Are you going to have any?"

"After you," Vijay replied.

That was all Harvath needed to hear. This was the *real* test. As spicy as everything else had been, he was now certain that this was the main event. Scooping some onto his plate with his spoon, he took a bite.

The first thing he noticed was the itching in his scalp. Then his nose began to run and his eyes water. It was at that moment that his entire mouth felt like someone had filled it with fire.

He tried to quench the burning with a long swig of beer, but it didn't even put a pinprick in the pain. Ignoring the laughter coming from Vijay, he helped himself to a massive portion of yogurt.

The only thing he had ever eaten that came close was a Red Savina habañero. This pepper blew that one away.

He washed down the yogurt with his bottled water and then grabbed Vijay's, opened it up, and drank that down, too.

"Do I need to call a doctor?" the man asked.

Harvath shook his head. "No, I'm fine," he said, his eyes still watering. "In fact, I think I'll try some more. This time on a piece of naan."

Vijay reached out his hand and stopped him. "I think it's better if you stop now. Trust me."

"If you insist."

"I very much insist."

The waiter brought over more bottled water and Harvath downed another one, along with some more yogurt. "What the hell does Bhut Jolokia mean?" he asked, finally beginning to recover.

"You have the same vegetable in America. It just goes by a different name. I believe you call it a ghost pepper."

"That was a ghost pepper? Are you serious?"

"I probably shouldn't have bought such expensive cigars for us," he said, laughing. "You're not going to be able to appreciate it now anyway."

"Oh, no," said Harvath. "I'm smoking that cigar, whether I can taste it or not. I hope you spent a fortune on it. You're also paying for this dinner. I don't care if you bill it to the embassy, take it out of your kids' college fund, or you need a loan from your mother-in-law. There's no way I'm going to finance my own torture."

Vijay laughed even harder.

CHAPTER 25

Once dessert had come—a dish similar to funnel cake called Imarti—and Harvath had asked for a bottle of water to go, Vijay pulled out his credit card and paid for the meal.

They stepped outside the restaurant and stood for a moment on the sidewalk, watching all of the Diwali revelers coming and going.

Everyone was smiling, dressed in their absolute best, and joyously making their way from one friend or relative's house to another. The intensity of the fireworks seemed to have been taken to another level in this part of town.

"You must wish you were back home," said Harvath, "celebrating with your family."

"It's one of our favorite festivals, so I do miss it a little bit, but I also quite enjoy my job. I don't know what I would do without it. Retirement from the Indian Police Service very quickly began to drive me crazy. I love my wife and I love my children, but not enough to be around them all the time."

Harvath smiled.

"How about you?" Vijay asked. "Are you married? Any children?"

It was complicated, but he tried anyway to explain. "I was married, briefly. But my wife died."

"How?"

"She was murdered."

"I'm sorry," Vijay replied. "Did they catch who did it?"

"*I* caught who did it," Harvath replied, as he looked across the road at nothing in particular. "All of them."

Somehow, Vijay wasn't surprised. There was more to the American than he was letting on. "I would ask what happened at trial," he stated, "but something tells me they never saw the inside of a courtroom, much less a police station."

Harvath didn't respond.

"Any kids?" the man asked.

"A beautiful little boy from my wife's previous marriage. He lives with his grandparents. I was able to spend some time with him over the summer. It was very nice."

"I think you'd make a good father," said Vijay.

Harvath looked at him. "Why do you say that?"

"Just a feeling," he responded. "How about now? Are you seeing anyone?"

"I'm engaged."

"That's wonderful. When's the wedding?"

"We haven't settled on an exact date," said Harvath. "Sometime between Christmas and New Year."

"You should do it here. In Jaipur. In fact, you should do it at our hotel. Were you aware that they will arrange for you to ride in on a beautifully painted elephant? Wouldn't that be incredible? I'm sure it would be a wedding that none of your guests would ever forget."

It sounded exotic and quite memorable, but there was no way Harvath and Sølvi were going to be able to fly all the way to India. They had their hands full simply coordinating friends and family in Norway and the United States. "Thank you for the suggestion, Vijay. I don't know if it will work with our schedule, but I'll definitely bring it up with my fiancée."

"Speaking of schedules," the man replied, "you should also talk to the wedding planner at the hotel. The sooner the better. Winter in Jaipur is very pleasant, and many ceremonies are scheduled during that time."

"I'll take it under advisement," said Harvath, who then changed the subject. "What about that cigar you promised?"

"Yes, yes," the man stated, removing the bag from his pocket and handing a Cohiba Robusto to Harvath. "Like I said, these were quite expensive. You don't have to smoke yours now."

"I feel like I do," Harvath replied with a grin.

Vijay shook his head, clipped the cap of his cigar, and then handed the cutter to Harvath.

After lighting his Cohiba, he gave Harvath a box of wooden matches so that he could do the same.

Harvath thanked him and the duo stood there for a moment, enjoying their Cubans, before Vijay spoke again. "Based on the DST's investigation, we know that Mr. Ritter purchased several of the same cigars at the hotel earlier in the day. Leaving the restaurant, alone—as far as anyone can tell—he lit one, turned to his left, and began walking."

The men headed in that direction as Vijay continued to narrate. "He made it two blocks before he was killed."

"Did Ritter or the killer get picked up on any security cameras?"

"Yes, they both did. Ritter is seen first. The killer doesn't show up until about a block down from here. But as you know, no one ever got a look at his face. He's wearing a helmet with a full visor. And the motorcycle he's operating was reported stolen a week ago."

"But it doesn't appear that he was waiting for Ritter outside the restaurant," Harvath stated.

"No, it doesn't appear so," Vijay replied. "Criminals, however, especially with street crime, work in teams all the time. They ID a potential victim and then one of them functions as a spotter, keeping an eye on their mark and relaying details via cell phone."

"Have there been a lot of armed robberies committed with a handgun in this area?"

"No. The most recent event involving firearms was a couple of months ago when two men held up the Central Bank of India—about ten minutes from here. In general, this is a relatively quiet district."

They continued walking, smoking their cigars, until they arrived at the spot where Eli Ritter was murdered.

Police tape still cordoned off the area, and a chalk outline of Ritter's body could be seen on the sidewalk, along with a large, discolored patch where his blood had seeped in and stained the concrete.

"I'll give you a minute," said Vijay, allowing Harvath to approach by himself in peace.

He had witnessed death in more forms than most people could imagine. Seeing a loved one, a friend, or a colleague killed was the worst. Not seeing it, but witnessing the scene shortly thereafter, was only slightly less disturbing.

Ritter was a very good man. He was also a very good American. Harvath could easily see himself in the same position—carrying out an important mission for your nation, only to have someone get the drop on you and take you out. As he liked to say, it was always better to be lucky than good. Because no matter how good you were, there was always someone better.

Parting the tape, Harvath stepped into the immediate crime scene area and looked around. He noted the position of where the body had fallen and then looked over his shoulder to hazard a guess as to where, specifically, the killer had been standing when he fired.

Even if Ritter had stumbled, he wouldn't have traveled far. That kind of shot, delivered right behind the ear and into the brain, would have been like pulling his fuses all at the same time.

According to the report, the police had retrieved a 9mm shell casing. While this kind of job could have been done with a .22, it was a much smaller round and took a lot of skill to pull off successfully. Whoever had done this was leaving nothing to chance.

He spent twenty minutes taking it all in, studying the scene from every possible angle. When he stepped out from behind the tape, Vijay was waiting for him.

"Thoughts?" the man asked as Harvath approached.

"My first thought is that I don't think it was a robbery."

"Why not?"

"Look at the foot traffic," said Harvath. "I'm assuming last night was as busy as it is right now."

Vijay nodded. "I would agree."

"Let's back up for a minute and say that this was a robbery. The whole purpose of using a gun is to intimidate the victim into compliance. If I'm the robber, I want you to know I have one, but I don't want anyone else to see it because I don't want them to call the police.

"If I'm approaching you from the front, I'm going to keep it under my shirt or jacket until the very last moment. Then I'm going to give you just enough of a look at it to let you know I'm in charge, I mean business, and you'd better stop right where you are.

"To the contrary, if I'm coming up on you from behind and you're walking, you can't see anything. I have to put my hand on your shoulder or grab your collar to get you to stop, while also letting you know I have a gun. If I put the gun to your head, everyone is going to see it. It's much better if I jam it into your lower back. That way, pretty much nobody is going to see it and my message is going to be delivered loud and clear.

"Nobody puts a gun behind someone's ear in order to rob them. Too much can go wrong. They can move their head. They can spin and attempt to take the weapon away. Witnesses can see it and scream. This wasn't a robbery. This was a hit job. A professional one. When a shooter places a gun behind someone's ear it's to kill them. Plain and simple."

Again, Vijay said, "I agree. Witnesses, however, saw the shooter remove personal items from the body."

Harvath had read the pertinent details in the file he'd been given. "His watch, wallet, and cash from his front trouser pocket, right?"

"And his sunglasses," Vijay added.

"But *not* his cell phone."

"Correct. Not his cell phone."

"Why not?" Harvath asked, testing him.

"Cell phones can be tracked."

"It takes two seconds to pop out a SIM card, which the killer could have done once he had safely made his getaway."

"Even without the SIM, they can still be tracked," said Vijay.

"Exactly," Harvath replied. "I know that and you know that, but does the average criminal?"

"Perhaps yes. Perhaps no. What's your point?"

"Ritter was carrying a high-end phone, which would have fetched more than a few rupees on the black market. The killer, however, was both smart enough and disciplined enough to leave it behind. That speaks to a high level of professionalism."

"As does taking the wallet, watch, cash—and even the sunglasses,"

Vijay stated, fully on board now. "Because it gives police a nice, tidy motive. Robbery."

Harvath nodded.

"Okay, so if the motive wasn't robbery, which I agree with you it looks
like it wasn't, then we're left with this being a murder."

"Correct."

"A murder over what? Why would someone want to kill Ritter?"

"Like I said, the killer is going to have a lot of our answers," replied Harvath. "But first, we have to catch him. Let's go speak to the shopkeeper."

CHAPTER 26

The shopkeeper hadn't noticed the shooter until he had raised his weapon and fired. Neither he nor his wife had any idea how long the helmeted figure had been there before pulling the trigger.

They both thought it was strange that on such a warm evening, the figure would be wearing a full helmet with a face shield—even stranger that the visor was tinted.

The method the assassin had used to disguise himself was of less interest to Harvath than the other details the couple had seen.

They spoke largely in Hindi with English words thrown in at random intervals, a common practice in India. Vijay, however, steered them toward speaking in all English so that he didn't have to keep stopping to translate. While their accents were a bit difficult to understand, Harvath quickly tuned his ear.

The husband said that the weapon used was a black pistol and that it absolutely had a silencer. His wife claimed that he watched too many movies and could not have been able to ascertain such a detail from where they were standing.

When they were both asked to indicate with their hands how long the weapon was, the results were inconclusive. There were lots of firecrackers going off at the time and had there been a gunshot, the husband was absolutely confident that he would have been able to distinguish it. Once more, the wife berated him for watching too many movies. Harvath actually felt sorry for the poor fellow. He also believed him.

There was no question that Ritter had been shot. The fact that neither the shopkeeper nor his wife had heard the telltale sound of gunfire while watching the killing take place bolstered the husband's assertion that a suppressor had been used.

They backed up the other witness accounts of the assassin removing items from Ritter's person. After which, they described seeing the figure hop on a motorcycle and speed off. Harvath gave them a few minutes to see if they could remember any other details that might be of help, no matter how small, but they were unable to offer any. He and Vijay then thanked the couple for their help and left the shop.

"I hate to say it," Vijay stated as they walked back toward the restaurant parking lot and his Jaguar, "but that interview went about as well as I thought it would. The DST are very thorough when they gather evidence and assemble witness statements. I'm sorry we weren't able to uncover more."

"Believe it or not," Harvath admitted, "sometimes it's helpful to look back under the stones people have already overturned. Things get missed— even by the best investigators. Happens all the time. Trust, but verify."

"So tomorrow, we'll examine Ritter's body. Do you have any expectations there? Anything specific you think they may have overlooked?"

"No. Not unless there's something weird."

"Such as?"

"Some kind of other trauma, beyond the gunshot wound. Something that doesn't belong there, like a puncture wound from a needle or unexplained bruising or lacerations."

"None of which you have reason to suspect, correct?" Vijay asked.

"I have zero expectations of any of that," Harvath replied. "Coroners, in my experience, are obsessively observant. Even the newest and most inexperienced. That field draws a special kind of person. They live for finding stuff that other people would miss. Especially exotic, out-of-the-ordinary things."

"And what about the DST evidence room? I've got to imagine there's even less to potentially find there. The bullet and the shell casing, according to what I've read, is all that they recovered that wasn't directly tied to Ritter."

"That and all the CCTV footage. But again, we won't know until we get there. I'm not holding out a lot of hope. So far, the DST appears to have been completely thorough and professional. Which is exactly what you want in a situation like this."

"Except, it's not moving us any closer to the killer," Vijay stated.

"We've ruled out robbery as the motive," said Harvath. "We know this was an assassination. No question. We know the hitter was a pro. Perhaps only a semipro, but a pro nonetheless, which means he was hired by someone. The trail right now may be tough to see, but it's there. Somewhere. We just need to find that one bent blade of grass, that one snapped twig, and we'll have a direction to pursue."

"I continue to admire your confidence. I still wish I shared it."

"A long time ago, I learned not to quit. No matter what. Sometimes confidence is all you have in these situations. But when you rule out losing, you quickly narrow your options to only one possible outcome—winning."

"You would have made a lousy cop," Vijay stated.

Harvath smiled. "Why's that?"

"You're too optimistic."

"We'll see. If you're right, I'll be out of your hair tomorrow and you'll be on your way home for Diwali."

"And if I'm wrong?"

Harvath's smile broadened. "Then things are about to get a lot more exciting."

CHAPTER 27

Working with Major Badal, Asha had quietly enlisted the help of the Coonoor police to identify the rooftop where the figure with the strange-looking weapon had been standing. Despite a thorough canvassing of the neighborhood, no one had seen anything. There was no CCTV footage, either.

It was a complete and utter dead end. Asha had then returned home.

After a fitful night's sleep, she had gotten out of bed early, worked out in her apartment, showered, dressed, and ate breakfast.

Heeding the warning Onkar Raj had given her, she once again tucked her Glock inside her waistband holster and headed to the "office."

She loved Delhi in the early morning—before the throngs of people began making their way to work, before the pollution from all of the cars, buses, and motorbikes could cloud the sky. It was fresh. Beautiful.

A rain had fallen overnight, slicking the streets and sidewalks like they were all part of a movie set. The lingering humidity amplified the fragrance of the flowers and the fruit trees along her route. Delhi, especially for those in tune with their senses, had so much to offer.

She moved deliberately, but with grace. More panther than automaton.

Her training, as all good training should be, had become second nature. She knew what to look for and how to look for it. The most dangerous threat wasn't the one you never saw, but rather the one you could see but failed to recognize. Because that threat came from a practiced, prepared enemy—one who had done their homework, had leveraged everything to their advantage, and had come to win.

That was why, when she saw the scene up ahead, her hand instantly moved to her weapon.

For anyone else, it would have appeared to be a terrible accident. A truck had struck a motorcycle, and the motorcyclist was badly injured. Except, it was all wrong.

Based on the direction of travel and the angle of impact, the motorcycle's handlebars, as well as its rear wheel, would have been pointed in a different direction. The truck's front bumper was damaged, but not where it should have been. There was also no motorcycle paint on the truck and no truck paint on the motorcycle.

In fact, the motorcycle, in her rapid processing of the scene, didn't seem to have any signs of damage whatsoever. It was as if someone had laid the bike down, and the driver next to it, just to make it look like an accident had taken place.

It was at that moment that she heard the sound—the hollow *thwump* of a Kevlar-encased beanbag round being fired from a twelve-gauge shotgun.

She had been so locked on the accident scene that she had failed to notice the figure behind the parked car across the street.

Whoever he was, he was a decent marksman. The riot-control round hit her dead center, in the middle of her chest, and knocked her over backward to the ground.

When she hit, she hit hard, cracking the back of her head against the pavement. She didn't see stars; she saw black. Practically pitch black.

But there was a little pinpoint of light and she clung to it, forcing her conscious mind, which was suddenly powering down, to pay attention to and follow it. And through absolute sheer force of will, she prevailed.

To anyone watching, it would have looked like the Terminator rebooting. Sure, she had gotten knocked on her ass, but shaking the cobwebs from her brain, she had gotten right back up.

Leaping onto her feet, Glock in hand, she began firing.

She started with beanbag. As he worked his way across the street, and before he could fire another round, she put two bullets into his chest and one into his forehead.

The sound of gunfire sent people scurrying, and Asha flipped her attention to the "accident" only a couple of car lengths ahead.

Not to her surprise, the heretofore injured motorcyclist was on his feet and moving in her direction. In his hand was a MAC-10 pistol. Next to him, with an Indian Army standard-issue CAR 816 "Sultan" battle rifle, was the driver of the truck. They both raised their weapons and began firing at the same time.

Asha took cover behind a parked car and crawled forward to maximize the protection of the vehicle's engine block. With a good mental picture of where her attackers were, she raised her arm over the hood of the car and began firing.

When her pistol ran out of ammo and she felt the slide lock back, she pulled her arm down.

In one fluid motion, she ejected the spent magazine, flicking it to the side, and slammed in a fresh one. She then released the slide lock, seating a new round in the chamber and rendering the weapon hot.

Though running Glock 17 mags in her Glock 19 meant they stuck out a bit beneath the weapon's grip, they allowed her to carry two additional rounds, which might end up being the difference between life and death. With her only spare mag the one now in her pistol, she had seventeen rounds with which to end this gunfight. Unsurprisingly, she suddenly wished she had brought a lot more.

But the idea of leaving her apartment with more than "one in the gun" and an additional magazine on her belt hadn't even occurred to her this morning.

Despite her outrage over the terrorist attacks in Mumbai, and how underprepared the first responders had been, she had stopped carrying multiple extra mags a while ago. She, like many others who had upped their game in the aftermath, had grown complacent. Dragging that extra weight around was a hassle. Ultimately, the Mumbai attacks had been an exception, a *horrific* exception, but not the rule.

Which begged a fair question—for how long should one be expected to leave their home every day, kitted out for war?

Of course, the answer was highly personal and depended upon what one could "reasonably" expect to encounter.

Never in a million years would she have expected something like this. Not here. Not so close to her apartment.

But right now, none of that mattered. This was an active-shooter scenario and *she* was the target. She needed to outthink these people and hurt them before they could hurt her.

Staying low, she tried to retreat, but the moment she did, her attackers began firing again, showering her with broken glass from the car she was hiding behind.

There was no way that they could have anticipated my move. They had to have seen me. But how?

She rapidly scanned her surroundings until she saw it—one of the side mirrors on the truck had been tilted in such a way that it allowed them to see her the moment she went to make her move.

Willing to expend one of her precious rounds, she took aim, pressed her trigger, and blew the mirror clean off.

But instead of moving the way she had originally intended, she reversed and pushed forward, taking the fight to them, rather than waiting for them to bring it to her.

A person standing near the door of a kitchen shop tried to peer out, and Asha waved for him to get back inside. The presence of civilians only made the situation more dangerous. She didn't want any civilians being harmed. Her remaining two attackers, however, were a different story.

Pressing forward, she continued to stay low and searched for any advantage she could find—a side-view mirror such as the bad guys had used, a reflective car windshield, a storefront window, anything. There was nothing.

Worse than nothing, the gunfire had been so loud that her ears were ringing. Someone could have come up right behind her and she wouldn't have heard them.

Pausing her advance, she stuck her gun under her left armpit and spun her head to look over her shoulder. *Fuck.*

Without even taking time to aim, she began firing.

The truck driver had come up from behind and was about to take her out. Instead, she stitched a racing stripe of 9mm rounds from his balls up to his bulbous, pockmarked nose, dropping him dead onto the pavement. That left only one more. *The motorcyclist.*

"Where the hell are you?" she whispered under her breath.

Then she saw something. A flash, in a puddle, just beyond the bumper of the car she was hiding behind.

Dropping to the pavement, she tilted her Glock to the side, aimed it underneath the vehicle, and held her breath.

For a moment, it felt like everything had stopped. There was no breeze, no traffic, no people, nothing. Until a boot came into view.

When the second appeared, she exhaled and pressed her trigger—shattering the motorcyclist's left ankle. She fired two more times, hitting him in the opposite ankle and shin.

Unable to bear any weight, the assailant fell over into the street. As he did, Asha continued to fire.

She shot him again and again. In the chest, the clavicle, the throat, and once through the side of his helmet.

Standing up, she crept out from behind the safety of the parked car and looked down on her attacker, lying in a pool of blood in the street. As she did, the man tried to raise his weapon and fire back.

Asha then shot him through his visor. Twice. They were the last two rounds in her Glock.

CHAPTER 28

"I have no idea who they were," Asha replied, shaken from the attack and feeling wiped out from the adrenaline dump. She handed her phone to Raj. "Maybe you can find something. I took pictures of the bodies."

She had snuck into the Blind Relief Association via the Delhi Golf Club, coming through the trees, making very sure she hadn't been followed.

Gupta handed her a bag of ice to apply to her chest, while Raj swiped through the photos.

"I don't recognize any of these men," he said. "But that doesn't mean somebody else won't. I'll get these uploaded and we'll see what we can find. In the meantime, the fact that they tried to subdue you first tells me that someone thinks you've got valuable information."

"Someone," Gupta added, "whom Asha wouldn't speak with unless she was forced to."

Raj nodded, still studying the photos.

"And the fact that they then tried to kill me?"

"They see you," said Raj, "and very likely us, along with what we're doing here, as a threat."

"You don't think this could be blowback from a past assignment?"

"No," said the man. "The timing would be too coincidental. And I don't believe in coincidences."

Ever the pragmatist, Gupta was already thinking ahead. "The first thing we need to do," he said, "is to scrub you from the scene. CCTV, shell casings, all of it. We also need to muddy up any witness accounts that might help identify Asha."

"But Delhi police must already be crawling all over the place," she stated.

"Don't worry about that," Raj instructed. "I'll make a couple of calls. In the meantime, we need to face the unfortunate reality that whatever we are up against, they have a much bigger reach than we had anticipated."

"Which means we need to be even more careful."

"Exactly. Unfortunately, any hopes I had of expanding our operational footprint, of bringing more people on board, are now dead and buried. This is going to have to be it," he said, pointing at them all. "The three of us."

"How?" Asha demanded. "This is a massive undertaking, not to mention that I was almost killed an hour ago."

"But you weren't killed," Gupta clarified. "You're very much still alive—a testament to your skill and training."

"My skill and training aside, we can't do this with just three people. It's impossible. We don't even completely know who and what we're up against."

"When a camel is at the foot of a mountain, only then judge its height."

"You're quoting Indian proverbs now? Seriously?"

"Trust me. Everything is going to be all right. We can do this and, Asha, we *must* do this."

It was the first time her boss had ever addressed her by her first name. It was jarring, but strangely reassuring at the same time.

"Okay," she replied. "How do we do it?"

"Let's start with the helicopter footage you brought back from Coonoor."

CHAPTER 29

Harvath had been glad to get back to the hotel last night. Vijay had been kind enough to offer to join him if he wanted a nightcap in the bar, but all he had really wanted to do was to get to sleep. He hadn't had a solid eight hours since before he'd gone into Kabul.

The next morning, he awoke refreshed, but not exactly one hundred percent. He was certain the discomfort he was feeling was thanks to last night's ghost pepper—on top of all the other spicy food.

After taking a nice, long hot shower, he shaved and ordered room service. Nothing too heavy—a stack of buttered toast and a pot of tea. Coffee was out of the question—even if it meant that less caffeine in his system was going to also make him less than fun to deal with all day.

When his breakfast arrived, he sat facing the room's arched windows and enjoyed the amazing views of the green Aravalli Hills, which stretched, uninterrupted, all the way to the horizon.

He had no idea if Sølvi had ever been to India, but he knew for certain that she would find this part of it incredibly beautiful and incredibly romantic.

Brushing his teeth with bottled water, he grabbed an additional bottle from the minibar and headed downstairs to meet Vijay.

The ex-cop was already sitting outside in his Jaguar, top down, with his sunglasses on.

"Good morning," he said as Harvath slid into the passenger seat, put his own sunglasses on, and leaned back. "How are you feeling? Any intestinal distress?"

Harvath could tell he was ribbing him. "Fuck you," he replied. "Drive."

Vijay, the flashy, larger-than-life ex-cop, roared with laughter and put his car into gear.

Driving out of the hotel's colossal gates, he pointed to the CD player. "I chose something special for you. Maybe it'll make you feel a bit better."

"What is it?" Harvath asked.

"You'll see. Go ahead, push PLAY."

Harvath did and heard the beginning strains of one of the best dance songs ever—the Gap Band's "You Dropped a Bomb on Me." As it played, he did feel a little better. He even smiled.

"Ah," said Vijay. "It's working its magic."

"The only thing that could spoil it," Harvath replied, uncapping his water and taking a sip, "is you mentioning the letters *R* or *B*."

The man smiled back. "We're going to have a good, productive day today. I'm not going to start it off with an argument."

Harvath was glad to hear that. "It sounds like someone found a little optimism under their pillow when they got back to their room last night."

"Actually, I got to thinking about what you said yesterday."

"Which part?"

"All of it. But especially the part about looking under stones that other people have already overturned."

Harvath looked at him, intrigued by the change in his mind-set. "Is there a particular stone or set of stones you've taken an interest in?"

"I'm not sure yet. Let's see what the morning brings."

• • •

Vijay didn't have to explain why it was better to visit the Jaipur city morgue first thing. It was an old building, with equally old air-conditioning. Thankfully, the temperature inside was still cool from overnight.

A medical examiner met them at the front desk and led them down a long hall to an autopsy room that smelled faintly of antiseptic. There, a body lay on a stainless-steel mortuary table.

The ME pulled back the sheet. Harvath stared at the face for a moment, trying to ignore where the top of the skull had been removed in order to withdraw the bullet from the man's brain, and then positively identified the corpse as Eli Ritter.

After pulling on a pair of latex gloves, Harvath examined the body. As he did, he asked the ME if she had found anything, beyond the gunshot wound, that was unusual.

"Other than the abrasions to the face, which are consistent with the victim having fallen forward after being shot, I didn't see anything," she said.

"Did you conduct a toxicology screen?"

"We did, but found nothing unusual. There was a trace amount of alcohol in his system, but that was it. It barely registered."

Harvath nodded and kept working his way along the body. He, however, didn't find anything out of the ordinary, either.

The ME gently lifted and tilted Ritter's head to the side so that Harvath could see where the round had entered. He studied the wound, but again, there was nothing to suggest anything was out of place.

Drawing Harvath's attention to the top of Ritter's skull, the ME described the path of the bullet, which parts of the brain it had passed through, and the location of where it was ultimately found and removed.

"His death would have been instant," she said, with an air of kind but professional detachment. "He wouldn't have felt any pain."

Harvath would make sure that information was transmitted to Ritter's family. There were very few things that loved ones could take solace in with such a violent death. The fact that he hadn't felt anything might relieve some of their grief. He nodded to Vijay that he was done.

The man approached the ME, thanked her, and they traded business cards. He told her that someone from the U.S. Embassy would be in touch to arrange repatriation of Mr. Ritter's body to the United States.

They didn't linger. There was no small talk to be made nor anything further they could learn from the ME. Harvath was glad to leave the building.

"I want to extend my condolences once more," said Vijay. "To know a friend has passed is one thing. To have to identify, much less examine, his remains is something quite different. I'm sorry."

Harvath held up his hand. "It's okay. Thank you. I'm good."

"If you want, there's a tea shop nearby. We can take a cup before we meet with the DST people. It's up to you. There's no rush."

"Let's keep moving. I want to dig into the rest of the evidence."

"Understood. Let's do it."

They walked back to Vijay's car and drove to the DST's office, but made the trip with the CD player off.

Harvath wasn't in the mood for music. In light of Ritter's service and his having made the ultimate sacrifice, it felt like some respectful silence was in order. Vijay, to his credit, could read the mood and remained quiet during the drive.

When they arrived at their destination, the ex-cop did all the talking, presenting his identification and asking Harvath for his diplomatic passport so he could demonstrate that they were who they said they were. Vijay had had a high-ranking friend in the Indian Police Service in Delhi call ahead so that there would be no runaround when they arrived.

They were shown to a small lab where an evidence tech was waiting, along with the few pieces of physical evidence they had gathered. Because chain of custody needed to be preserved, it was agreed to that Harvath wouldn't touch anything, but he could request that things be put under a magnifying camera, which would help him get a better view.

The first thing they examined was the round itself. It was a 9mm hollow point and had, as it was designed to do, "petaled," opening up like a flower as it passed through the skull and bored through Ritter's brain.

Next was the shell casing, which had been retrieved from the sidewalk, not far from Ritter's body. It showed signs of above-average "fouling," which was consistent with a round that had been fired from a suppressed weapon.

The suppressor succeeds in dampening the sound of the discharge by trapping the gases inside and forcing them back down into the breech of the weapon. Those gases are what cause the fouling or "dirtying up" of the shell casing.

In addition to the cigar he had been smoking, they had a bag with Ritter's password-protected phone, a few minor pieces of unhelpful pocket litter, matches, a cigar cutter, and his keycard from the Fairmont.

None of it was useful, and so Harvath thanked the DST personnel and asked if they could move on to the CCTV footage.

A conference room had been prepared for them. All the footage had been uploaded to a tablet in a series of folders. After explaining how to access the files and play them on the monitor in the corner of the room, Harvath and Vijay were left in private.

"Do you want one?" Vijay asked as he approached the room's coffee station and fixed himself a tea.

"I'm fine for right now," Harvath replied, holding up his half-empty water bottle. "Thank you."

The files on the tablet were organized chronologically. Opening the first one, he could see Ritter walking through the lobby of the hotel. The next one showed him exiting the main entrance and getting into the cab. Then the cab could be seen driving out the enormous gates, headed toward the main road.

After that, the footage was a hodgepodge of images captured by the cameras of homes and private businesses. Every once in a while, a feed from a city traffic camera popped up.

Ritter's journey played out just like Vijay had described. Harvath could not make out anyone who might have been following him.

He wondered if maybe someone had bumped Ritter at some point, sliding a tracking tag into his pocket or hiding one somewhere else on his person. But no sooner had the thought entered Harvath's mind than he discarded it. Ritter was highly skilled and very well trained. Not that it couldn't have happened, but the odds were so low that it wasn't worth too much thought. At least not right now.

He watched in jump cuts from different security cameras as Ritter wove his circuitous route from Mahatma Gandhi Nagar Park to the Tansukh restaurant. It was clear to Harvath that the man wasn't burning time, afraid to be early to his dinner appointment. He was running an SDR, making sure that he didn't have a tail.

The fact that Ritter went ahead with his meeting confirmed that he felt he didn't have anyone following him. What's more, his judgment was backed up by the CCTV footage.

Harvath then watched the footage gathered after Ritter's dinner and his exit from the restaurant. When he saw the motorcycle and the hel-meted assassin, he stopped and zoomed in.

He rolled the footage forward and back, looking for anything that might help them ID or track down the killer. After several minutes, Vijay stood up and headed for the door.

"Where are you going?" Harvath asked.

"I'm going to look under some other stones."

Harvath nodded and went back to poring over the video footage.

He slowed it down to frame-by-frame and then, once he had gone through all of it, went back to the very first file from the hotel and started all over again.

•   •   •

Forty-five minutes later, Vijay stepped back into the conference room.

"Time to go," he said.

Harvath pivoted in his chair and looked at him. "What's up?"

"I think I may have found something."

CHAPTER 30

As Vijay drove, he explained what they were getting into. "Sanganer is the most dangerous part of Jaipur."

"Because of the crime?" Harvath asked.

"And the cops," Vijay stated. "The police force in Sanganer is so corrupt that the powers-that-be have limited rotations to only three months, before officers are then rotated out."

"How the hell do you ever establish trust with the residents, much less solve any of the crimes in that area?"

"You don't. They have the worst case-closure rate in the entire state of Rajasthan. It's a hornet's nest of organized crime. The performance of the cops there is abominable. It's like there's something in the water turning them dirty."

"And why are we going to Sanganer?" asked Harvath.

"The motorcycle. The one the assassin was driving. It was reported stolen one week before Ritter's murder. It got me thinking."

"I'm listening."

"DST is looking for a killer. They're not going to put manpower on solving a stolen motorbike case. Like anywhere else in the world, stolen motorcycles are bought and sold every day in India. You know who else isn't going to pursue it?"

"The police in Sanganer."

"You are correct," said Vijay. "So, via the DST's computer system, I decided to do a little investigating on my own."

"And?"

"And you'll be shocked, I'm sure, to learn that Sanganer is a hotbed of vehicle theft, most notably motorcycles."

"You're right, I'm shocked," said Harvath. "*Shocked*."

"But it gets better. Because the Sanganer cops are so overwhelmed, most of their resources are tied up with high-profile crimes that garner news coverage and capture the public's attention. Murder, drugs, and sex trafficking being the most prevalent. You know what doesn't capture the public's attention?"

"Vehicle theft. And I'm going to guess, specifically motorcycles."

"Correct again," said Vijay. "So, knowing that neither DST nor the Sanganer cops were going to do it, I began running all of the reported motorbike thefts for the last year. It was like drinking from a fire hose, so I shrunk it down to the last six months and looked for patterns—what kind were stolen, where were they stolen from, were any of them ever recovered?

"I was trying to find a pattern—something that might tell us about the motorbike our killer was riding the night he assassinated Ritter. Then I found it."

Harvath's eyes widened. "What did you find?"

"There's a rather large extended family in Sanganer—the Kumars—who have been the victims of motorcycle theft at an unprecedented level. Looking at the data, one might almost conclude that the thieves are singling out the Kumars on purpose. Their motorcycles have been stolen at a rate almost three times higher than their neighbors'. But what's amazing is that the Kumars' bad luck appears to be contagious."

"What do you mean?" Harvath asked.

"They own a family business—a string of warehouses. The only residents of Sanganer who have experienced motorbike theft near the level of the Kumars are the people who *work* for the Kumars—their employees."

"So, it's a scam."

"It would appear that way," said Vijay. "Probably insurance fraud."

"As well as kickbacks from the sale of the stolen motorcycles."

"That, too."

"You've got a contact in Sanganer, right?" Harvath replied. "The one clean cop in the entire dirty force sort of thing."

"Unfortunately, in this instance, I have no contacts that can be of help."

Harvath shook his head. Police corruption really pissed him off. *"Corruptio optimi pessima,"* he said, citing a famous Latin phrase. "Corruption of the best is the worst of all."

"Agreed," responded Vijay. "We have a saying in India. Don't curse God for creating the tiger. Rather, be grateful that God didn't give it wings."

"I'm not sure I follow."

"While it's unfortunate that we can't seek any assistance from the police in Sanganer, there's an upside—neither can the people we're looking for."

"Which means we have a certain amount of latitude in how we approach things," said Harvath. "Correct?"

Vijay nodded. "Correct."

Harvath was continuing to like this guy.

They drove for a little while longer until they entered the roughest part of the Sanganer area. It was every bit as bad as Harvath expected it to be. An absolute slum. The flip side of the vibrant colors and exotic spices so often associated with India.

It was the side of the country that tore at people's hearts—filth, disease, crime, and absolutely grinding, abject poverty. They hadn't even set foot outside the car yet and Harvath was ready to leave.

"What's the plan?" he asked.

Vijay removed a printout from his breast pocket and handed it to him. "This is who we're looking for. His name is Pinaki Ali. He was the owner of the motorcycle used by Ritter's killer."

Harvath studied the driver's license photo and related information, then checked his watch. "Where do you expect we'll find him right now?"

"He's probably at work. The problem is, the Kumars have multiple warehouses and we don't know which one he's at. It would be better if we spoke with him outside his place of employment."

"So, the plan is to sit on his house? Wait for him to come home?"

"We're going to poke around a little bit," said Vijay. "See what we can learn in advance."

When they arrived at Pinaki Ali's building, Vijay didn't bother with a drive-by or a slow roll around the block. He pulled the Jaguar right up in front and parked.

"You want me to come in, or stay in the car?" asked Harvath.

The ex-cop looked at him. "Why would I want you to stay in the car?"

Harvath drew a pretend circle around his face with his index finger.

"Oh, no, my friend," Vijay replied. "I *want* them to see a white devil. This is serious business. I guarantee you that there hasn't been a white person in this part of town for years. Maybe even since the British pulled out. Your presence is going to send a big, shocking message. That's what I want."

"Well, you've got it."

"I also want some American currency. You have some on you, yes?"

Harvath pulled the wad of cash from his pocket. "How much do you need?"

"A one-hundred-dollar bill if you have one."

He peeled one off and handed it to him.

"Thank you," said Vijay, opening his door. "I left something for you under your seat. It's clean. Hopefully, you won't need it, but just in case you do."

Harvath reached around under the seat until his hand found the weapon.

"I assume they taught you how to shoot in the Navy?" the man asked.

"Most of the time we just worked on tying knots," Harvath replied with a smile. "But I managed to fire a gun once or twice."

Vijay smiled and got out of the car. "As long as you don't shoot me, we'll be fine."

Affixing the holster inside his waistband, Harvath stepped out of the car and joined him.

The ex-cop approached a couple of young kids kicking a weather-beaten, scuffed-up soccer ball outside the building. "No school today?" he asked.

"No, boss," one of them replied, lying.

"Nice car," said the other.

"It belongs to my friend," he said, pointing at Harvath. "He is a very important man. A *big* boss. He's also generous."

Vijay removed the hundred-dollar bill, showed it to the boys, and then tore it in half.

Handing half to the nearest boy, he said, "If you look out for the big boss's car, you get the other half when we come back."

Both boys stood up straighter and saluted. Vijay nodded for Harvath to follow him inside.

It was a rectangular, four-story building, covered in cracked, faded plaster, surrounding an interior courtyard.

Entering on the ground floor, Vijay scanned the mailboxes until he found Ali's.

"Which floor?" Harvath asked.

"Guess," the man replied.

"Top floor."

"Maybe you wouldn't make such a bad police officer after all."

Harvath smiled at him. "I don't think so. I'm not smart enough."

Vijay shook his head and moved toward the stairwell. Harvath watched as he paused, took a deep breath, and then began climbing. He was a retired cop with a cushy job at the U.S. Embassy, not some gym rat. They were in no hurry and Harvath didn't crowd him.

Electrical conduit, painted dark gray, ran exposed along the walls. Pungent cooking odors mixed with the scent of poorly functioning toilets. A cacophony of sound came from overly loud TVs and radios tuned to competing stations. Laundry hung to dry anyplace a line could be hung or a wire hanger placed.

At the fourth floor, as he had on each subsequent floor, Vijay paused to catch his breath. He looked at Harvath. "You're not a smoker, are you?"

"Nope."

"Me neither. Not anymore. If I were, we never would have made it up here so fast."

No matter what, the man maintained his cop sense of humor. Harvath appreciated that about him. Life really wasn't worth living if you couldn't laugh at and make fun of yourself.

"Have you had enough time to catch your breath?" Vijay asked once *he* had caught his.

"Sorry to slow you down," Harvath chuckled. "Thanks for indulging me."

"Let's just not make it a habit," the man responded. "Follow me. This way."

Harvath did as he was told.

All of the apartments' front doors and living room windows faced out onto a walkway with an iron railing that overlooked the courtyard below. No matter where you stood, you could see all of the other units.

Arriving at Pinaki Ali's apartment, Vijay removed the leather case containing whatever credentials it was that he carried, and delivered a solid, law enforcement pounding to the man's front door.

Moments later, a woman's voice said something from the other side in Hindi.

"Police," Vijay responded. "Open the door."

He stood directly in front of the door, apparently unafraid of being shot, with his credentials extended.

When the door opened, he made some pronouncement in Hindi, retracted his credentials, and then, nodding at Harvath, switched to English and added, "Special Agent JJ, USG Delhi."

An older woman stood inside the apartment, looking at both of them. For some reason, she didn't seem surprised to see them. Stepping aside, she opened the door wider and invited them in. Even from where they stood, the apartment smelled like burnt saffron.

"Don't say anything," Vijay directed Harvath. "I want to do all of the talking."

CHAPTER 31

"**M**rs. Ali?" Vijay asked, trying to reconcile the age of their suspect with the much older, graying woman with the deeply wrinkled face who stood before them.

"Yes, I am Mrs. Ali. I'm his mother," she responded, pulling her blue sari tighter around her. "What has he done now?"

"How do you know we are here about your son?"

The woman clucked and tilted her head from side to side. "Only a government employee would waste time with such stupid questions like this. I know my son. Why are you here?"

"We're here about his motorbike," said Vijay. "The one that was stolen."

"You mean *my* motorbike."

"Yours, ma'am?"

"Of course," she replied. "I paid for it. Doesn't that make it mine?"

"But it was registered to your son, Pinaki."

The woman waved her hand as if someone had expelled a cloud of cigarette smoke too near her. "Technicalities. My money. My motorbike. Why are you here? Have you recovered it?"

"No, ma'am, we—"

"Do you have an insurance payment for me?" she interrupted.

"No, ma'am."

"Then, Mr. Police Officer, why am I speaking with you? Hmmmm?"

She was a feisty one. Harvath tried to maintain a straight face.

"Ma'am, the motorbike was involved in a crime," Vijay stated.

The woman rolled her eyes at him. "A criminal steals a motorbike and goes on to commit more crimes. This is most unexpected news."

Vijay wasn't happy to have walked up four stories only to get danced around by the suspect's mother. "Where is your son at the moment, Mrs. Ali?" he asked.

"Wherever he is, I think we can agree that he probably isn't on a motorbike."

Trained to detect micro-expressions, Harvath saw the switch get flipped in Vijay before the ex-cop even spoke his next words. *Bad cop has arrived.*

"Two nights ago in Jaipur," said Vijay, his voice icy cold and firm, "an American citizen was murdered. The killer used *your* motorbike in the crime."

"*My* motorbike?" she stammered, realizing the severity of the situation. "All I did was give my son a small loan. He needed the motorbike for his work. It can't possibly be a crime for a mother to help her son, can it?"

"That is going to depend."

"Upon what?"

"Upon whether or not you answer my questions."

The woman smiled, revealing surprisingly more gold teeth than Harvath had previously noticed.

Vijay didn't smile back. "Your *son's* motorbike," he clarified, in hopes of securing her cooperation, "was used in the murder of an American citizen. We would like to ask your son some questions. Where might we find him right now?"

"He works for the Kumar family."

"I am aware," Vijay replied. "Where is he at this moment?"

"He moves around from warehouse to warehouse. It changes day by day."

"Are you dependent upon any medications, Mrs. Ali?" the ex-cop asked, changing the subject.

The question took the woman by surprise. "Medications? What do my medications have to do with—"

"You're refusing to answer me and are being purposefully evasive. Perhaps you'll be more forthright at police headquarters."

"*Police headquarters?*" she repeated. "Are you arresting me?"

"Only if you continue to resist."

"Me? Resist? Who's resisting?"

"Where are your medications?" Vijay asked, moving toward the bathroom. "Back here?" Looking at Harvath, he added, "She's obviously not going to cooperate. Go to the kitchen or the bedroom and find me a garbage bag or a pillowcase. Let's take any medication she has. I don't know how long they might want to hold her."

"I didn't do anything wrong," the woman protested.

"So then help us," Vijay replied. "Tell us where your son is."

"If I do, what will happen to him?"

"We just want to ask him some questions."

"Do you think he's the killer?"

It was a good question. Plenty of criminals, across time, had attempted to cover their tracks by reporting incriminating property missing.

"I can't know whether to rule him in or rule him out," said Vijay, "until I speak with him. But if you're asking me as a parent . . ."

"Yes," Mrs. Ali said, "I am asking you as a parent."

The ex-cop shook his head. "No, I don't think so."

The old woman's shoulders dropped, as if there was no longer a weight there she had to carry. "I think it would be better for everyone if he came to you."

"Excuse me?"

"It wouldn't be a good idea to go to his work. Not for you and definitely not for him."

Vijay looked at her warily. "What are you proposing?"

"A reason for him to leave and come home. A medical emergency."

• • •

Twenty-four minutes later, Pinaki Ali burst through the front door calling for his mother. He found her, not lying on her bed suffering from heart palpitations, but rather at the stove cooking.

"What are you doing?" he demanded. "You shouldn't be on your feet! I told you to call the doctor. To call an ambulance. You know how serious this can—"

Before he could finish his sentence, the old woman had turned from the stove, was yelling in Hindi, and beating him with a wooden spoon.

She might have succeeded in injuring the man had Vijay and Harvath not stepped into the room.

Vijay flashed his credentials, identified himself as being with the national police, and then put them away. He didn't bother introducing Harvath. Better to let the man wonder who the foreigner was.

"Just over a week ago, you reported a motorcycle stolen," said the ex-cop.

Pinaki looked at his mother and Vijay barked at him, "Don't look at her. Look at me. What happened to it?"

"I don't know," the man said.

He would have made the world's worst poker player. "He's lying," said Harvath.

"What happened to the motorbike," Vijay repeated.

"I told you, I don't know. It was stolen."

"Stolen from where?"

"Outside one of the warehouses at work."

Harvath nodded. While not much, that was at least true.

"Who stole it?" Vijay demanded.

"I have no idea. No idea," the man claimed. The micro-expressions were erupting off the man like a handful of corn kernels thrown into a pan of hot oil.

"Lie," said Harvath. "*Big* lie."

Pinaki had no idea what the hell was going on, but he knew whatever this was, it was no good. His eyes darted back and forth between the two men. Occasionally he glanced toward his mother, who only glared angrily back at him.

"Mr. Ali," said Vijay. "We know you're lying. However, I'm going to give you one last chance to do the right thing. So, I want you to listen very carefully to me. Your motorbike was used in the—"

"My *stolen* motorbike," the man interjected.

The ex-cop looked at Mrs. Ali, who drew her hand back and cracked her son in the mouth with the wooden spoon. "Don't talk," she admonished him. "Listen."

It was a pretty good whack. Vijay waited for the man to wipe the blood from the corner of his mouth before continuing. "Who stole your motorbike?"

"Who *specifically*? I am telling you the truth. I don't know."

The ex-cop had been at the game long enough not to need Harvath's feedback on that answer. "So, if not specifically, who in *general* do you believe stole your motorbike?"

Pinaki's pupils were dilated. His eyes darted from side to side. Harvath sensed the man was ready to bolt, and he moved slightly to his left to block the door in case he charged.

"I'm a dead man if I tell you," Pinaki said.

"You may very well be a dead man if you don't," Vijay replied, casting a subtle glance at Harvath.

"They will come after my mother."

"Depending on what you give us, we are more than capable of protecting you both. But this is up to you, Pinaki. You can do the right thing, or you can disappoint all of us, particularly your mother, and you can continue to be an asshole."

"It was the Kumars," the man said, needing no further time for reflection. "They told me where to park the motorbike and to leave the key in it. I don't know who took it. Once it was gone, I was told to go to the police and report it stolen."

"You never asked why you were being told to do this?" asked Vijay.

Pinaki Ali looked at the ex-cop like he was crazy. "Question them? Ask them to justify themselves to me? You obviously have no idea who the Kumars are or what they're capable of."

CHAPTER 32

Harvath didn't care who the Kumars were and neither did Vijay. They were a family of criminals and, judging by Pinaki Ali's fear, prone to violence. So was Harvath for that matter. And, Harvath suspected, so was Vijay.

The key to dealing with the Kumars was understanding what they feared and then to push on that, *hard*.

Like most gangs, it wasn't getting caught—it was getting cut out—losing territory, money, influence, or all three.

A conviction, even doing time in prison, was a stain on the conscience and standing only of *decent* members of society. Criminals wore those as badges of honor. If incarcerated, they used their time to develop deeper networks and further their criminal education by learning from other prisoners. It was like being sent to some kind of underworld graduate school.

The only thing people like the Kumars respected was force—sheer, brute force. And that was exactly what they were going to get. The only hiccup was what Harvath and Vijay should do with Pinaki.

Undoubtedly, his mother would have kept a closer eye on him than any parole officer. Had he attempted to leave the apartment, she probably would have beaten him with that wooden spoon until he couldn't move. He was a street rat, however, and when caged, rats could get creative. Ultimately, he could have snuck out a bathroom window or orchestrated some other type of diversion to sneak past Mrs. Ali. It wasn't worth the risk.

Downstairs, Vijay handed the two kids the other half of the hundred-dollar bill and told them to get lost.

Once they were gone, he opened the trunk of the Jaguar, pulled out a large, black duffle bag, and tossed it on the car's rear bench.

Then he looked at Pinaki, pointed at the trunk, and said, "Get in."

"In where?" the man replied. "In the dickie?"

"Of course, in the bloody dickie. You didn't think you were going to ride up front with us, did you?"

"But I'm claustrophobic."

"You're too dumb to even know how to spell *claustrophobic*," the ex-cop replied.

"No. Honestly, I am."

"He's lying," said Harvath. "Again."

"Please, sir. Just let me go and I won't say anything to the Kumars."

"I'm not letting you go and you're definitely *not* saying anything to the Kumars. Now stop wasting our time and get in."

Perhaps it was the looks on the men's faces, or the fact that Vijay's jacket was positioned such that his pistol was suddenly visible, but whatever the cause, Pinaki decided to cooperate and did as he had been instructed.

Once he was inside the trunk, the ex-cop had him roll onto his stomach and hog-tied him with flex-cuffs.

Leaning in, he gave the street rat a final reminder, that no matter what happened, he was not to utter a sound. He then slammed the lid and got into the car with Harvath. They had climbed the first rung of the ladder, but they still had their work cut out for them.

If what Pinaki had told them was true, however, he had provided some pretty good intelligence.

The patriarch of the family, Babul Kumar, was semiretired and more a figurehead than anything else. It was the eldest son, Rahul, who ran the day-to-day operations. He allegedly had a mind like an elephant—facts, figures, slights, grudges, and screwups . . . he never forgot anything. That was who they wanted to talk to.

On Thursday mornings, he could be found at the family's warehouse in the Malpura Gate neighborhood.

Because it was one of the buildings that didn't contain contraband or stolen property, it wasn't as heavily guarded as the others. Rahul normally traveled with a crew of three. One drove, one rode shotgun, and the other one sat in back with him.

All four of them, according to Pinaki, were dirty fighters and known for being particularly nasty. Harvath wouldn't have expected anything less.

He had asked Pinaki if he had any photos of Kumar on his phone. He did not. What Pinaki did provide, however, was an excellent description of the man—particularly his height. Kumar was so short, he was known as *Cheentee,* or "the ant," in Hindi.

Unlike at the building where the Alis lived, this time Vijay did conduct a drive-by. He was slow, without being too slow, and extremely thorough.

Once they had a good feel for everything, the ex-cop began to search for a place to park.

A little over a block down from their target was a row of derelict, abandoned buildings. Vijay pulled over and put the vehicle in park. Fifteen feet ahead of them was a perfectly shaded area.

"Really?" Harvath asked. It was hot and only getting hotter. "You're going to let poor Pinaki roast in the dickie? What would Mrs. Ali say?"

Reluctantly, Vijay put the Jaguar back in gear and rolled forward.

"You're a good man."

"No, I'm not," the ex-cop replied. "I just don't want to spend the rest of my life looking over my shoulder for that woman and her spoon."

Harvath grinned. "When I was growing up, the nuns all had wooden rulers and my mother had a wooden measuring stick."

"That's because the nuns were trained for close-quarters combat. Mothers need a tool that works on the broader battlefield—inside *and* outside. Especially if you try to run from her."

"I only made that mistake once," said Harvath.

Vijay smiled as he turned off the car's engine and stepped out. "I've found that if you make a big enough mistake, once should be more than enough."

Reaching behind his seat, he grabbed the duffle bag and carried it over to one of the doorways. Harvath exited the vehicle and joined him.

"Every cop I knew," Vijay continued, as he unzipped the bag, "always took a little something when they left the police service. Some people helped themselves to office supplies. Some took coffee and sweets from the canteen. I even heard of someone who lifted an expensive bottle of whiskey from a commander who thought no one knew about it."

"Why do I get the feeling," Harvath replied, "that I'm about to see what you took?"

"I don't like to use the word *took*."

"Huh," said Harvath, pretending to be confused. "Because that's what you just used to describe your colleagues."

"I prefer the term *liberated*."

"Huh," Harvath repeated. "*Liberated*. Like all you did was open the door and they walked out on their own."

"Exactly," said Vijay. "Allowing good equipment to languish in darkness is something no officer, neither active nor recently retired, should ever abide."

The man then stood back and revealed what was in his duffle.

Along with what looked like a couple of older, pump-action OFB shotguns, there were a pair of "liberated" raid vests emblazoned with the IPS logo, Indian Police Service armbands, more flex-cuffs, and cans of tear gas that looked like they originated from when Indira Gandhi was still prime minister.

Harvath accepted one of the vests and put it on. He adjusted it so that it rode high enough, allowing him to get to his pistol if need be. Next came an armband, followed by an examination of the shotgun he would be carrying.

Vijay had kept the twelve-gauge in excellent condition. It was clean and properly oiled. The ex-cop pulled out a box of shells and handed it to him.

"Are we expecting a firefight?" Harvath asked as he loaded the weapon.

"I always expect a firefight, especially with people like this."

Spoken like the true, experience-hardened, former law enforcement officer that he was.

Once they were all geared up and ready to go, Harvath tilted his head toward the rear of the Jaguar and said, "You know the minute he thinks we're gone, he's going to go to work on those restraints. I give him fifty-fifty odds if he's motivated enough. Then all he has to do is pop the trunk release and take off."

"Even if he can slip his restraints," Vijay replied, "the trunk release isn't going to help him, because I disabled it."

"Okay, how about punching out one of the taillights and sticking his arm out to get someone's attention?"

"Also not going to happen."

"Why not?"

"Let's just say he's not the first guest to have ridden back there. Everything has been reinforced. He's not kicking or punching his way out of there. And before you ask, there's plenty of ventilation. Even if he is claustrophobic and has a full-on panic attack, he'll have plenty of air. Any other questions?"

"Nope," said Harvath, shaking his head. "It looks like you have thought of everything."

"That's the problem with this kind of business," Vijay responded. "You can never think of everything. When that completely random or overlooked thing pops up, all you can control is how you react to it."

Harvath knew all too well what the man was talking about. *Murphy.* He prayed that they weren't about to meet him inside that warehouse.

CHAPTER 33

The men had agreed that walking straight up to the loading bay was a bad idea. Not only would they have been out in the open and exposed for too long, but there were also too many vehicles, as well as too many people who might pose a threat and need to be secured.

Their best plan of attack was to come in fast and as undetected as possible. Based on Pinaki's description of the layout, they decided to make entry via a metal side door fronting a smoking area.

The rust-covered door was allegedly propped open during business hours, allowing smokers to easily come and go. Even better, the area around it was overgrown and neglected, providing lots of cover. Trash and discarded items lay everywhere—including stacks of old pallets. It was a wonder that nothing had ever caught fire back there.

As they quietly made their approach, they were relieved to see that not only was the door indeed propped open, but also no one was outside smoking. So far, so good.

But just as they were about to go for the door, they heard voices approaching from inside and were forced to retreat behind a wall of pallets.

While they would never provide good cover, the pallets provided excellent concealment.

With Scot making sure no one snuck up on them from behind, Vijay watched and listened to the two smokers as they puffed and chatted in Hindi outside. When they returned to work, he gave Harvath an update.

"Apparently, their forklift is down. All hands are expected on the loading dock to help unload a truck that arrives in the next five minutes."

"Do you think that means Rahul?"

Vijay shook his head. "He's management. Not labor. I don't think he or his thugs do any honest work. My guess is we'll find them holed up in the air-conditioned office. That's the good news. The better news is that there should be fewer employees on this side of the warehouse to potentially see us and raise the alarm."

That was good news. Harvath only hoped that things would continue to break in their direction. Fast-moving, fluid situations had a way of going sideways quickly. And when they did, people got hurt. *Badly.*

He didn't want that to happen here, at least not to the wrong people. Kumar and his crew were one thing, but the hardworking warehouse employees only trying to support their families were another.

Looking at Vijay, he nodded. "Okay, let's do it."

It had been decided that the ex-cop would be on point. He spoke the languages and looked the part, two things Harvath most definitely couldn't lay claim to.

Readying his shotgun, he grabbed hold of the door handle. When Vijay gave him the signal, he opened the door and quietly followed the man inside.

The warehouse was hot, filthy, and smelled like animal dung. Masses of boxes sat stacked on rows and rows of what looked like pre–World War II shelving. To have called it "rickety" would have been a huge understatement. It was no wonder they left the side door propped open. One loud slam and the whole place would come crashing down.

They picked their way carefully across the back wall of the structure, avoiding the loading dock area and managing to stay out of sight. When they reached the office door, they took cover and paused.

Vijay indicated that upon entry they would divide the pie in half. He would hook left and Harvath would get any targets to the right. The rules of engagement had already been decided upon. Life was cheap in Jaipur and practically worthless in Sanganer. If anyone pulled out a gun, they were fair game. If someone pulled a knife—against two men with shotguns— they were either stupid or crazy, and as such were also fair game.

The hope, however, was that it wouldn't come to that. But with men like Kumar, and those he kept close, there was no predicting what might happen.

It wasn't getting any cooler in the warehouse and Harvath was itching to get going. He looked at Vijay, who in turn directed him to try the office door. It was unlocked.

The ex-cop counted down in a whisper from three. When he got to one, Harvath threw open the door open and they buttonhooked into the room.

Vijay yelled for everyone to get down on the floor.

Harvath saw one of the men nearest him reach into a drawer, presumably for a weapon, and he kicked it shut, shattering the man's wrist and hand.

Another one of Kumar's goons refused to heed Vijay's command, so Harvath gave him a little assistance by driving the butt of his shotgun into the man's stomach and then elbowing him in the base of his neck when he doubled over.

He then grabbed the guy with the broken hand by the collar, twisted him out of his chair, and took him down hard to the ground.

Looking across the room, he saw that Vijay had things well in hand. Both Kumar and his remaining bodyguard were on the ground and the ex-cop was patting them down for weapons.

Harvath did the same with his two. Then, pulling the office door shut, he locked it so that no one would stumble upon the meeting that was about to get under way.

Vijay found a roll of duct tape and tossed it to Harvath. As the ex-cop kept the four men covered, Harvath slung his weapon and went about taping wrists behind backs, followed by ankles.

The man with the broken hand made a lot of noise, forcing Harvath to place a piece of tape across his mouth before finishing the job. He decided, just in case, to gag the others as well. All of them, that was, except for Kumar. They had a lot of questions for him and it would be difficult, if not impossible, to understand him with a piece of duct tape across his mouth.

When he was done, he set up a chair in the center of the room, yanked Kumar up from the floor, and placed him in it.

"Someone is in big fucking trouble," the gangster stated. "*Big* fucking trouble."

Rahul Kumar couldn't have been any taller than five foot four, maybe five foot four and a half on a good day with thick socks.

The man wasn't filled with piss and vinegar; it was more like battery acid and snake venom. Flecks of spittle collected at the corners of his mouth as he raged. His eyes were wide with anger, showing their whites.

"I pay money, good fucking money, not to get raided," he continued. "Not to have some thulla I've never seen before burst into my business and hold me at gunpoint. And with a fucking Gora no less! What the hell is this? I don't even think you're cops."

"Clever, this one," said Vijay, explaining the slang to Harvath. "A *thulla* is a corrupt, incompetent cop. *Gora* means whitey, or simply a white person. So, he could have called you worse."

"I don't doubt it," replied Harvath.

"An American Gora?" the gangster exclaimed, reading Harvath's accent. "Who the fuck are you?"

"Let me put it this way," said Vijay, pointing at Harvath. "When this Gora shows up on your doorstep, it means that your day is going to get much, much worse."

Kumar looked at Harvath and then back at the ex-cop. "What is it you want? What are you doing here?"

"Part of me wants to rent you better bodyguards and sell you some cameras," Vijay responded, laying his shotgun on the desk. "It's unfathomable to me that your competitors haven't killed you yet and taken over your business. You don't know the first thing about security."

"Maybe I'll hire you," said Kumar. "Obviously paying off the local police isn't doing me much good."

"Sorry, Rahul. I don't work for men like you. You have no honor."

"Says the fake cop who, something tells me, isn't here on behalf of the IPS. Who are you working for then? The Gora?"

Vijay stepped forward and grabbed the gangster by the throat. "I'm not here to answer your questions. You're here to answer *mine*. Is that clear?"

"Teri-maa-ka-bhosda," Kumar responded.

The ex-cop cracked him with his opposite hand—the one with the signet ring, catching the thug just beneath his left eye. "You bring my mother into this once more," he warned, "and things are really going to get bad."

"Bhenchod!" the main exclaimed.

Vijay hit him again, harder. "The same thing goes for my sister."

Even from where he was standing, Harvath could see a nasty, blood-engorged welt swelling up on the man's face. One more blow and Vijay was going to open Kumar up like an Indian piñata.

"Now, if we're done talking about the women in my family," the ex-cop stated, "maybe we can get down to business."

Either because he had run out of insults or was wary of being struck again, Kumar remained silent.

"Good," said Vijay. "Business it is. To whom did you sell Pinaki Ali's motorbike?"

The gangster quickly looked away from him and then back. Not a good sign. He gave him another warning. "My friend, the Gora, is a human lie detector, but even I can see you're trying to come up with some sort of story to tell me. Take my advice—don't. If you lie, it'll get even worse than if you start insulting my wife or my daughters. Do you understand?"

Kumar nodded.

"After you 'stole' the motorbike, what happened to it?"

The gangster took a deep breath. "You don't want to know."

"Do I strike you as a man who doesn't want to know?" asked Vijay. "Because I'll gladly hit you again if it'll help clear things up."

There was nothing better than a smart-ass cop. As he had with Mrs. Ali, Harvath tried not to smile.

"Listen, Rahul," he continued. "You give us the information we want and we'll disappear. You'll never see us again. But if you don't give it to us, *you'll* disappear and no one will ever see *you* again. So, let's stop playing games. What's it going to be?"

Kumar was conflicted. "If I tell you what you want to know, I simply trade one set of problems for another. The person who arranged for that motorbike isn't going to cooperate with you. He's going to kill you. Then he's going to kill your Gora. And after that's done, he's going to come here and kill my entire family."

"Not if we kill him first," Harvath chimed in.

Vijay let go of the gangster's throat and stepped aside so Harvath could address him.

"Someone used that motorbike to kill a friend of mine. I'm going to settle the score."

Kumar shook his head. "Everyone who has gone after this person has failed. He has been shot, stabbed, poisoned, thrown from a building, and hit by a car—twice. It's said that he can't die."

"Believe me," Harvath stated, "if I decide he needs to die, he's *going* to die."

"And judging by the attempts on his life," Vijay interjected, "I'm guessing that you two know each other from the 'business' world."

Kumar nodded.

"And if he ended up disappearing, you might be able to profit from his absence?"

The gangster thought about it for a moment before warily responding. "We would be expanding into new territory, but nothing we couldn't handle."

"Is that a yes?"

"Yes."

"So here's how this plays out," said the ex-cop. "You're going to give us everything you have on this person and we'll take care of the rest. If you tip him off that we're coming, if you try to ingratiate yourself and cause him to be indebted to you, we will make sure you lose everything. And I mean *everything*—your business, your family, your life. *All* of it. Is that clear?"

Once again, Kumar nodded.

"Good," replied Vijay, picking up a pad of paper and a pencil from the closest desk. "Start talking."

• • •

Fifteen minutes later, they left the office and closed the door behind them. Upon it they taped a sign that Vijay had written: *Meeting in progress. Do not disturb. Do not knock.*

Back at the Jaguar, they re-stashed their gear in the duffle bag and checked on Pinaki. Even parked in the shade, it had gotten quite warm in the trunk. The man was soaked through with perspiration. Vijay cut off his restraints and helped him out.

"Is he dead?" the man asked.

"Who?" Harvath replied as he placed the duffle inside. "Your boss, Kumar?"

Pinaki nodded.

"A little worse for wear, but still alive."

"Does he know it was me? Does he know I told you where to find him?"

"He knows we were there about the motorbike," said Harvath.

"You mean he knows you were there about *my* motorbike."

"Technically," Vijay clarified, "it's your mother's motorbike. She paid for it."

"This is nothing to make fun of," the man protested. "You promised me that if I helped you, you would protect us."

Harvath looked at the ex-cop with a smile. "That is what you promised. You said that if—"

"I know what I said," Vijay replied, checking his watch. "Give me another hundred dollars."

Pulling the bills out of his pocket, Harvath peeled off another hundred and handed it to him. "I'm going to need a receipt for that. And from earlier."

Vijay ignored him and handed the money to Pinaki. "Go home. Pack a suitcase for yourself and one for your mother. Then I want you to take an autorickshaw to the Jaipur Junction railway station. Go inside, get something to eat. When you have eaten, use a different exit and walk to the Radisson hotel. Then take a taxi to the Fairmont hotel. There will be an envelope with a keycard and a room number waiting for you at the front desk. Go to the room and stay there until I contact you. Do not tell anyone where you are. Do you understand?"

"Yes," said Pinaki. "I understand."

"Good," said the ex-cop, as he closed the trunk. "Now hurry up. Get going."

As they watched the man jog off, Harvath asked, "How are you going to get them into the Fairmont? It's booked solid."

"They're taking your room and whoever it is that you're working for is going to pay for it. It's going to take me a day or two to figure out what to do with them. In the meantime, you and I are headed to Delhi."

"And what about the name Kumar gave us? It looked to me like you recognized it."

"I recognized it all right," said Vijay.

"So you know him?"

"Yeah, I know him," the man replied. "I'm the one who pushed him off the building."

CHAPTER 34

Basheer Durrani was odd by Pakistani standards. *Different*. Unlike many of his ISI counterparts, he had actually spent time outside of Pakistan. Lots of it.

The son of a Pakistani diplomat, a large portion of his formative years had seen his family moving from country to country, diplomatic outpost to diplomatic outpost.

Thanks to his father, he was a citizen of the world. Thanks to his mother, he was a citizen of Pakistan—a true and devoted son.

She kept him honest in his religious practices, devoted in his politics, and educated in his responsibilities to his homeland. No matter how far abroad they traveled, he always felt deeply connected to Pakistan.

His mother was exceedingly well-read, and she shared her love of reading with him. Her taste in literature, however, was considerably one-dimensional.

From leading theorists of violent jihad such as Sayyid Qutb, to political arsonists like Niccolò Machiavelli, she was, in the truest sense, an extremist. And if, as the saying goes, strong mothers raise strong sons, can it not be expected for extremist mothers to raise extremist sons?

She was a poised and polished diplomat's wife—stunningly capable for the daughter of a struggling textile merchant from Lahore. In her future husband she had seen a man of ambition, a man of potential.

It wasn't until after she had married him that she realized he had no aspirations beyond the diplomatic corps. Despite his immense potential, he had no desire to enter national politics. He was a bitter disappointment to her. It made her doubly determined that their son would not be.

While his mother had lit a passionate flame inside him for Islam and the maintenance of a true Islamic republic, he had also been taken by the martial arts, particularly the way of the samurai, via several years spent living in Japan.

There were plenty of embassies in Tokyo's Minato district, including Pakistan's. There were also a ton of corporate headquarters, such as Honda, Mitsubishi, Nikon, Sony, and Yokohama. Foreign company headquarters like Goldman Sachs and Apple were also there. Durrani hated it.

He hated it, not because his mother detested capitalism, but because all of the glass and steel obstructed the real Japan.

He had discovered *The Book of Five Rings,* by the Japanese swordsman Miyamoto Musashi, in the embassy library and had read it so many times within his first months there that he could recite it by heart. Written in 1645, that was Japan to him—pretty much anything up to the seventeenth century. After that, traditional Japan quickly began to recede.

The Book of Five Rings was Durrani's on-ramp, his gateway drug, not only into traditional Japanese culture but also its more esoteric martial arts.

Wandering far afield of the embassy, and utilizing his burgeoning knowledge of the language, he began navigating Tokyo's best dojos—often to be found in the city's roughest neighborhoods—and in those dojos he absorbed a wide array of art forms.

He studied Nami ryu, Kūdō, and Kyokushin. He mastered the skills that would make him a superb intelligence operative—humility, hard work, and a keen attention to movement and detail.

He learned to be patient. He learned to control his breathing, his emotions, and, most important—his thoughts. Because only by conquering himself could he hope to conquer his opponents. And he had plenty of them.

Within a year of haunting various dojos, he began to compete in matches. But not just any matches. He began to fight in nonsanctioned, underground competitions.

He was only a teenager and even in underground Tokyo, honor was still observed. He was only allowed to fight other teenagers. The bouts acted as a novelty before undercard matches in the lead-up to the night's main event. However, they were incredibly popular, with some teen fighters developing cultlike followings. Durrani wasn't one of them.

He lacked the showmanship, the personal magnetism necessary to attract a following. Even as a teen he was cold—disturbingly so.

His mother blamed it on having to uproot and move so often. His father disagreed. He believed that the boy might have antisocial personality issues. The embassy doctor helped them to find a psychiatrist. The doctor prescribed medication.

Durrani took the pills for a couple of months and studied their effects. He paid particular attention to which changes in his personality his parents were most pleased with. Then he stopped taking the pills. He had never liked how he had felt on them.

Instead, he worked at toggling the traits his parents liked, on and off, like a light switch.

He realized that he could convincingly project any quality or emotion that was called for—empathy, kindness, sorrow, warmth, friendship, even love. It didn't matter that he didn't feel any of it. All that mattered was that he could use these things to get what he wanted from other people. It was, in essence, his "superpower" and he maximized it to his advantage.

Durrani became so good at manipulating people that he didn't even need to think about it. It had become second nature to him.

He had all the makings of a perfect intelligence operative—remorseless, adaptable, and highly intelligent. And as was so often the case in the spy business, it took one to know one.

Shortly before his eighteenth birthday, Durrani was recruited by an ISI officer working out of Pakistan's embassy to the United States—his father's new posting.

The older man had struck up a friendship with Durrani over the Japanese game of strategy known as Go. Since leaving Tokyo, the teen had not had anyone to play with and the ISI officer had been a fan of the game for years.

He enjoyed being challenged by the teen and used the game to teach the young man about statecraft. Durrani was a quick study.

They stayed in touch while the young man attended university and upon graduation, the ISI officer made him an offer that was too good to turn down.

Durrani went through two years of intense, specialized military and intelligence training. He was then apprenticed under the older man, who taught him everything he knew.

The young man had dark hair, brown eyes, and an olive, rather than brown, complexion—provided he took care to stay out of the sun. His features allowed for him to pass as a member of any number of ethnic groups throughout South Asia, as well as in Europe, America, and the Middle East.

Eventually, Durrani had come to be based in India. His cover was working for an international aid organization based in New Delhi.

His work colleagues at the organization were a mix of Hindus and Muslims, so his faith, including his regular attendance of worship services at a local mosque, was not seen as unusual.

Via his credentials, he was able to move in and out of places like Kashmir, Bangladesh, Sri Lanka, Bhutan, and Nepal—not to mention all over India—with ease. He was an incredible asset to the ISI. But he also had a very disturbing shortcoming.

Technically, he had two. And clinically speaking, both were fixations.

The first, dacryphilia, was one of the most unusual sexual fixations known to mankind. It was a state of arousal brought about by the sight of tears or the sound of someone crying.

What made dacryphilia, also known as dacrylagnia, so unusual was that the scent of a woman's tears was known to lower testosterone and sexual desire in men.

This fetish was most often present in sadists who took pleasure in seeing others humiliated or in some sort of physical or emotional pain.

His other fixation was known as acrotomophilia—sexual interest in amputees. He found stumps incredibly erotic.

Put the two fetishes together—dacryphilia and acrotomophilia—and you had one very hard itch to "scratch." Crying, amputee sex workers didn't exactly grow on trees. Durrani, however, was resourceful. Better stated, he was well-connected. And in the world of rare and unusual sexual delights, the game was all about being as well-connected as possible.

As was the case with many spies, Durrani got some of his best information from others in the espionage game. That was how he had found a rather unique establishment in Bucharest called the "Terrace Club."

Because of the friendly relationship between their two countries, many Romanian officers cycled through Pakistan's School of Military Intelligence, outside Islamabad. That was where Durrani had met Alexandru Suliman. The two had established a nice friendship—or at least that was what Suliman had thought.

Wanting to further the relationship and see what intel he could pull from him, the ISI had sent Durrani to visit Suliman the following year. That was when his Romanian colleague had introduced him to the Terrace Club.

It was a veritable garden of mild to wild pleasures. Anything could be had at the Terrace, for the right price. And if they didn't have it, they would get it. The options were limited only by a customer's imagination, and his or her bank account.

The club was housed in a former palace built in French Neoclassic style by a family of famous Romanian bankers in the late nineteenth century. In addition to its walled grounds and broad granite terrace, it boasted forty bedrooms—perfect for a members-only sex club coupled with a particularly high-end bordello.

The price had been right as well. Because many places in Bucharest had been built on top of Roman ruins, some buildings ended up developing structural issues. The Terrace Club was one of them. Not only were many of the doorframes inside not right, but outside, the palace was quite visibly askew. Members liked to joke that the club tilted toward the wild side, which very much applied to Durrani.

As good as he was at controlling everything else, his sexual impulses, once indulged, began to take on a life of their own. They were an absolute addiction.

He didn't stumble into dacryphilia and acrotomophilia right away, but it didn't take him long to get there. Like any addict, each time he partook, he craved a bigger and more intense high.

His addiction both unnerved and excited him. In a world that appeared to him mostly in shades of gray, the Terrace Club provided amazingly bright and incredibly brilliant pops of color.

The only way he could fully "control" his addiction was to make a deal with himself. He would limit the indulgence of his predilections solely to his visits to Bucharest. At the club, and nowhere else, would he allow himself to be so disinhibited.

He started visiting multiple times a year. It required both lying and stealing. He found clever ways to extract money from the ISI for nonexistent operations, while simultaneously claiming to be anywhere but Bucharest when he was there.

It would have been difficult for most people to keep up the charade, but he was good at his job and that made him good at masking his addiction.

He knew, however, that at some point he was going to have to find the strength to give it up. A secret like this made him vulnerable. No matter how careful he might be, it was foolish to believe that it would never come to light.

Addictions, however, could be very persuasive. They had a way of clouding even the most intelligent and capable of minds.

He had talked himself into one more visit to Bucharest—one more time indulging his deepest, darkest desires at the Terrace Club. He would go after all this business with the Chinese was finished. That would be his reward. He would wrap up this operation and sneak off for a few days, with no one the wiser. Then he would return to Delhi and think about a change—some way that he could go cold turkey. In the meantime, he had work to do.

The next step in Beijing's plan was going to require precise execution. It was a spectacular attack. Perhaps even *too* spectacular.

He had tried to warn his superiors about all the danger it entailed, but they had simply waved him off. They not only loved to the idea of India suffering additional punishment, but he also suspected there was a large amount of Chinese money flowing into their bank accounts. The intelligence officers back in China weren't stupid. They knew exactly what they were doing. He had no choice but to follow his orders.

Nevertheless, he had a bad feeling about things. Something was off. It was more than just his discomfort with what Beijing expected to see done. He still hadn't heard anything on this morning's operation. No updates. Nothing.

That was a problem. And the one thing he didn't like were problems. Not when something this big was on the line.

Problems, he had learned, had a way of multiplying. No matter how small, once set loose into the world, they tended to grow. The only way to deal with them was to crush them—as soon as possible.

Looking at the time on his phone, he decided to give it five more minutes. If he hadn't heard anything from his contact by then, he was going to have to take matters into his own hands.

And if he had to take matters into his own hands, there was going to be hell to pay.

CHAPTER 35

N icholas hated safe houses. They were like sterile, corporate housing but with even less thought put into the comfort of the people staying there.

Nina was going to give birth soon. She needed to be at home, resting, in her own bed.

While he had no idea who had attacked him, he sure as hell wasn't going to let someone chase him out of his own house. No *fucking* way.

In his mind, however, the question wasn't *if* they were going to attack again but *when*? That was some of the worst pain he had ever felt. He had to think of Nina and the baby. Would she be able to withstand something like that?

Whoever was behind the attack had gotten his attention. *Most definitely*. But nothing had followed—no demand, no warning that if he didn't do what they wanted they'd hit him again, nothing. And that concerned him.

He was worried that they weren't done with him. That they would be back. When they did come back, he needed to be ready. But how?

Based on all the classified material he had been shown regarding Havana Syndrome, he had a loose idea of what he was up against. The key to foiling an attack was interrupting the flow of energy. In his estimation, there were only two surefire ways to do that.

The first, and worst idea, was to launch a drone of some sort equipped with a weapon of his own—a bomb capable of producing a significant enough electromagnetic pulse to knock out the attacker's weapon. In the process, however, it would likely fry all the electronics in his house, as well as those in all the houses in a three-mile radius. In addition to the damage, it would also create tons of legal problems. It was simply untenable. That left him with his second option.

The NSA had been experimenting with a new type of shielding for government satellites. Thus far, the results had been quite good against all forms of radiation. He asked Gary Lawlor to reach out to CIA director Bob McGee and for him to request as much of it as he could get his hands on.

When Nicholas returned from the hospital with his security detail, additional operatives from the Carlton Group were roaming the property. Sitting on the tailgate of a dirty, mud-spattered blue Ford Bronco was a man he recognized from the office.

His name was Wes Sutton. In his mid-fifties, he had been career Army before retiring and coming over to the Carlton Group. His expertise was in counterinsurgency. He had also been one hell of a sniper.

He was tall and thin with a full face of perpetual stubble. He had his credit card out and was entering information into his phone.

"Christmas shopping already?" Nicholas asked as he walked over to greet him.

Sutton looked up and smiled. "Renewing my subscription to The Blaze."

The man was an information junkie. He couldn't get enough. He claimed that his insatiable appetite for it was what had made him so good at his job.

Putting his phone and wallet away, he hopped off the back of the Bronco and shook hands with Nicholas. "If you've got a minute, there's something I'd like to show you."

"Did you find the spot?" the little man asked.

Sutton nodded. "I certainly did."

"Let me run inside real quick and then we'll go."

The man nodded and Nicholas headed inside. He wanted to check on Nina and grab the dogs.

Five minutes later, the garage door opened, and Nicholas pulled out in a black, off-road side-by-side vehicle. Like his van, it had been fully customized.

Argos sat in the passenger seat and Draco was in the second row. In the cargo area were a bunch of OD-green Storm Cases of various sizes.

Sutton offered to ride along in the side-by-side, but Nicholas said that he'd prefer the man drive his Bronco and that he would follow. He didn't plan on coming straight back. Once Sutton showed him what he wanted to see, he was going to be out there for a while.

The main reason Sutton had been sent out to the little man's estate was his human-tracking skills. He not only knew how a sniper thinks and acts, but he was also a distinguished graduate of the U.S. Army Combat Tracking School at Fort Huachuca in southeast Arizona, just fifteen miles from the Mexican border.

As the men drove, both dogs stuck their heads out the lowered windows and breathed in the fresh autumn air. Nicholas had been worried about them. But seeing them now, they appeared to be fine. The vet had provided some low-level pain pills and Nina—a vet tech by training—had been keeping an eye on them. So far, so good.

Though Nicholas had had a splitting headache and nausea, after a few hours in the hospital it had passed. It had felt like fighting off one of the worst hangovers of his life. IV fluids, anti-inflammatories, and pain medication had been a godsend, but he *never* wanted to experience that kind of pain again. He especially didn't want Nina or their baby to, either.

A few minutes later, when Sutton's Bronco came to a stop, Nicholas parked nearby and, along with the dogs, dismounted.

"So," Sutton began narrating as he walked and pointed things out, "there are a handful of things I was looking for. One, the shooter had to be able to see the target—aka you. He needed a line of sight to the house. Two, unless he time traveled, he would have arrived via some sort of vehicle, parked it, and hiked in. Based on the road system beyond your property, coupled with the view of the house, that made this area the most likely. So, this is where I started."

"And what did you find?" asked Nicholas as they trudged deeper into the trees.

Sutton led him to a specific spot, stopped, and pointed to the ground. "I found this."

Nicholas looked down, expecting to see something out of a movie that proved the attacker's presence—cigarette butts, a candy wrapper, a water bottle. There was no such evidence. It just looked like moss, grass, and fallen leaves. He couldn't see whatever it was that Sutton was trying to show him.

"Look at how this area is flatter," the man said, crouching down to point directly at what he wanted Nicholas to take notice of. "The grass here is bent and the twigs here and here are broken."

"I'm not doubting you," the little man replied. "But we've got more deer around here than we know what to do with."

"This wasn't deer," Sutton stated as he lay down in the same spot. "This was someone who had lain prone."

"Like a sniper."

The man nodded. "Like a sniper."

Nicholas turned and took in the view back to the house. This was as good a place as any, he supposed.

Sutton stood back up. "I also picked up his trail. I know where he entered your property and a couple of other hide sites he considered."

"Show me," said Nicholas. "All of it."

CHAPTER 36

I t took Sutton an additional twenty minutes to show him everything. After that, Nicholas thanked him and told him that he would be back up to the house in a little bit.

As the Bronco drove off, the little man began unpacking the Storm Cases from the cargo area of his side-by-side. It was hard, taxing work, but it needed to be done.

By the time he and the dogs returned to the house, a truck and a team from the NSA were waiting in the driveway. Putting his side-by-side away in the garage, he then showed the team inside, grabbed a Gatorade, and accompanied them upstairs.

The master bedroom not only had his-and-her bathrooms, but also gigantic his-and-her walk-in closets. In fact, the term *walk-in* was an understatement. You could have driven a truck through each of them.

Nicholas had used the majority of his closet to set up an at-home SCIF. Because of its steel paneling, it doubled as a safe room. He had decided that was where they would install the experimental shielding. If he could keep Nina largely confined to the bedroom, and something did happen, it would be a short hop to get into the SCIF.

The material the NSA provided looked like the Mylar blankets handed out to marathon runners and disaster victims, except that it was gold, rather than silver.

No matter how many questions he asked the team of geeks installing it, it was obvious that they had been instructed not to reveal anything about the makeup of the material.

They measured, noted, and photographed every square inch that was installed. At the end, many hours later, he was required to sign a ton of documents before they packed up their kits and left.

Once they were gone, Nina stepped into the closet and studied their handiwork.

"It looks like a bunch of crafters blew through here with a boxcar full of gold leaf and a couple dozen hair dryers," she said.

Nicholas chuckled. Next to her sky-high IQ and tough-as-nails attitude, he loved her sense of humor. "Baller that I am," he joked, "rose gold is much more my style, but if we need this and it works, color isn't going to matter."

"Good point," Nina replied. "Let's hope we don't need it."

"Speaking of needing things," said Nicholas, changing the subject, "what are you and the baby in the mood for tonight for dinner?"

"Will you make your special risotto for us?"

"With the poached egg?"

Nina nodded her beautiful head of jet-black hair and fluttered the lashes of her incredibly green eyes.

How could he say no? He was so deeply in love with her. Out of all the men in the world that she could have had, she had chosen him. He would have done anything for her. *Anything* at all.

Leaving her in the master, he headed downstairs, dogs in tow, to begin cooking dinner. Though he had offered to fix some food for the security detail protecting them, they had politely declined, sending one of their backup guys into town for takeout sushi.

Picking up his tablet, he returned to his playlist of favorite arias and pushed PLAY. As he gathered the spinach, leeks, fava beans, and chanterelle mushrooms that were the stars of his signature risotto, "Habanera," from Bizet's opera *Carmen,* began to play from the overhead speakers. It was one of the most beloved arias in the classical canon and one of his all-time favorites.

After getting the food going, he opened an exquisite white burgundy— a Domaine Leflaive Montrachet Grand Cru. He poured himself a glass and spent several moments breathing in the wine's aroma.

Then he took a taste. It was amazing. Buttery and complex. Worth every precious penny. Putting the glass down, he transitioned to preparing an accompaniment to the main course.

During her pregnancy, Nina's cravings for frozen French baguettes, which could be popped into the oven and served with slabs of salty, sunshine-yellow Irish butter, had gone through the roof.

Setting the oven to the right temperature, he pulled one from the freezer and set it on the counter.

The final notes of "Habanera" played and as they did, Nicholas had a pep in his step as he anticipated the next aria.

"Toreador Song," also from *Carmen,* was one of the most uplifting and energetic opera songs he had ever heard. No matter how good his mood, it could always be made better by this brilliant piece of music.

By the time the "Anvil Chorus" from Verdi's *Il Trovatore* came on, the risotto had been plated, poached eggs atop, and the bread had been pulled hot from the oven and wrapped in a linen towel.

As Nina was, rightly, abstaining from alcohol until after the baby was born, Nicholas downed the wine left in his glass, put the cork back in the bottle, and returned it to the fridge.

He took a moment and indulged in a deep breath. The kitchen smelled amazing. There was something about its design that seemed to concentrate all of the flavors of his cooking right over the island where he was working.

He loved this house. It really was the best home he had ever owned. And it was made that way because of Nina's presence. Everything would only get better once the baby arrived. Nicholas, truly, had never been happier.

Filling a pitcher with ice water, he placed everything on a room service–style cart, covered it with a crisp white tablecloth, and rolled it toward the elevator.

Knowing he would want an after-dinner drink and that Nina wouldn't begrudge him one, he paused at his liquor cabinet. In the mini fridge, he found exactly what he was looking for—a 1975 Chateau d'Yquem Sauternes.

Drinking the sweet French wine from Bordeaux was like consuming liquid gold, right down to the price tag. But, as far as Nicholas was concerned, price didn't matter. Life was too short to not drink fabulous wine.

He carefully uncorked the bottle and poured a dram of the beautiful nectar into a more than two-hundred-year-old Baccarat crystal glass recovered from a Russian shipwreck in the Black Sea and sold to him at auction.

It was all incredibly extravagant, but it was something that he felt he deserved. He owed this to himself. He had worked so hard, had come so far. If the parents who had abandoned him could only see him now— living in a castle, a beautiful pregnant wife upstairs, sipping wines worth thousands of dollars and drinking them from glasses that once belonged to royalty—wouldn't they be surprised? Shocked even. Though they had cast him out, their little boy had done well. In fact, he had done more than well. Despite everything being stacked against him, he had triumphed.

But that kind of recognition, that closure was never going to happen. His parents, he had discovered, were long since dead. He had no siblings, nor other living relatives. He was alone in the world, or at least he would have been had Nina not come along.

He tucked the bottle of Sauternes back into the fridge, set the glass on the cart, and signaled for the dogs to walk with him.

He entered the elevator, the doors closed, and the carriage was beginning to rise, when he felt the same, painful symptoms he had the night before. The damn weapon could penetrate the stone.

As his knees began to go weak, his dogs started howling. Upstairs, Nina had to have been feeling it as well.

He pulled out his phone and swiped to the app he had built, which was connected to the antipersonnel devices he had hidden throughout the woods. Placing his thumb atop the biometric scanner, he detonated everything.

The sound from the explosions reverberated across the estate. Tremors shook the elevator. Then it was quiet. Even the dogs had stopped howling.

His plan had worked. He had stopped the attack.

That was when he heard the most horrific sound in the world.

Nina was screaming.

CHAPTER 37

"G -Company," Raj said, projecting the arrest records and photos of the men Asha had killed that morning.

G-Company was the name that Indian media had given to the organized crime syndicate of mafia boss, drug kingpin, and wanted terrorist Zakir Rahman Gangji.

Gangji, the son of one of Delhi's most storied and honest police officers, had been on the wrong track since his early teens. His life in crime had begun in the late 1970s, when he had gone to work for a local smuggler.

The relationship had been profitable and amicable until years later, when, angry about police crackdowns, the smuggler had insulted Gangji's father.

Two days later, backed up by a crew of trusted confidants, Gangji and his men attacked the smuggler, along with his chief deputies, and beat them to death with soda bottles.

India had never seen such an attack. It catapulted Gangji to the head of the smuggler's organization and sent shock waves through the criminal underworld. The "Soda Pop War," as it would come to be called, made Gangji a celebrity in the gangster culture and the mere mention of his name inspired fear throughout India and beyond.

Soda bottles became G-Company's trademark and members wielded them with a viciousness that was unparalleled. Heads were bashed in, throats were cut, and faces were slashed. In some of the most extreme cases, Gangji had ordered bottles to be fully inserted into a victim's rectum and then shattered—causing a slow and agonizing death as they bled out.

Even those who made it to the hospital and survived lived in constant pain, as it was impossible for even the best of surgeons to locate and remove every shard of glass. "Cross G-Company, and you'll be shitting razor blades for the rest of your life," was a common warning among the criminal classes.

"Why would G-Company want anything to do with me?" Asha asked. "RAW would love to get its hands on Gangji for the Bombay bombings of the 1990s, but that was before my time. I've never worked a case that involves him."

Raj nodded. Gangji, a Muslim, had been behind a string of car bomb, scooter bomb, and suitcase bomb attacks in retaliation for a mosque having been illegally razed by Hindu nationalists. Over the course of two hours, twelve bombs had gone off.

Gangji had targeted the Bombay stock market, several banks, multiple hotels, the Air India building, and a passport office. Two grenade attacks also occurred.

In the end, 257 people lay dead and more than 1,400 were injured. While multiple G-Company members involved with the plot were either put to death or received sentences of life in prison, Gangji had never been apprehended.

He was said to have fled abroad. There were rumors that he was living in the Pakistani port of Karachi. Other intelligence pointed to Dubai. Still more reports suggested the Saudis had given him sanctuary.

The most persistent rumor was that Gangji hadn't left India at all. Instead, he had flown in one of the world's best plastic surgeons, who had totally transformed his appearance, right down to changing his fingerprints.

It was the stuff of Bollywood movies, of course, but for G-Company to continue to be a successful, feared organization, the threat of its founder hiding just around the next corner needed to live on.

"We believe," said Raj, indicating himself and Gupta, "that in addition to everything else Gangji's organization is into, they're upgrading their kidnapping and murder-for-hire operations."

"By going after a RAW agent?" she stated. "That's one hell of an up-grade. Technically, this means war. In any other situation, we'd bring the full power of the state down on G-Company and crush them for this."

"The key words being 'in any other situation.' Right now, that's not in the cards for us. We're off-book and we have to stay that way."

Asha didn't like it. What was the point of Raj being Raj if he couldn't swing the hammer when he needed to? Even covertly. "So we just let it go?"

"I'd hardly say it's been let go," Gupta interjected. "You killed all three of the men they sent. Consider it sending your dinner back to the kitchen. You'll get a chance to see the chef, just not yet."

"In the meantime," said Raj, "I want to discuss the likely actors who might have requested a capture-or-kill operation on you this morning."

Asha leaned back in her chair. "I'm all ears."

"The identity created for you to use down at Sulur Air Base was hastily prepared but should have passed scrutiny. Whatever happened, you caught someone's attention. Someone with serious resources. They were able to figure out not only who you are, but where you live. They were interested enough to try to take you alive to find out what you're up to or, failing that, to kill you on the spot to prevent you from getting any further.

"Our best guess at this point is that this is either elements within the Indian government who are against a defense alliance with the United States, or the Chinese themselves."

"Do you think it was elements within our government that took down the helicopter of the chief of defense?" she asked.

Raj shook his head. "I think it's more than likely, especially having reviewed the video you brought back to us last night, that it was the Chinese. We know they used some sort of directed-energy device in the Galwan Valley attack. We also have heard reports that they have been working on other sorts of similar weapons that do different things. One that scrambles aircraft electronics isn't out of the question."

"So if the Chinese knew when General Mehra was traveling and what his flight path was, that means they had to have had inside information; access to people on the ground, most likely at Sulur."

"Correct."

"This person or persons could have also leaked the information about the chief flight mechanic, Sergeant Siddiqui."

"To what end?" asked Gupta.

Asha looked at him. "We know from our own intelligence that China is threatened by India's growth. The better our nation is doing—whether it be economically or especially politically—the greater threat it is to Beijing. The Chinese want us to fail.

"The best way they believe to make that happen is to focus on fractures in our society and apply pressure. Religious tension is one of India's greatest vulnerabilities. An assault by one group against another can cause riots throughout the whole country. We're a tinderbox and the Chinese keep flicking lit matches at us.

"They're the largest creator and pusher of fake news in India. That's why, after Galwan, one of the first sanctions we imposed was to ban all Chinese apps from our cell phone market. It was a huge blow not only to their tech industry, but also to their propaganda efforts. With almost a billion smartphone users, India cannot afford Beijing gathering all that personal data, much less controlling our media narrative. That doesn't mean they aren't finding other means, which we know for a fact that they are, but it substantially weakened their efforts."

"I am prone to agree with you," said Raj. "The fact that the Chinese may have penetrated Sulur is a *major* problem. I am equally concerned, if not more so, over how quickly they were able to track you."

"So what's the plan?"

"Obviously, you can't return to your apartment, so you'll stay here."

Asha looked around at the makeshift operations center, with all of its mismatched furniture, lamps, and other odds and ends. "It's not the Oberoi, but I'll make it work."

"Good. Now, as far as a plan is concerned, if we can figure out who inside G-Company tasked the operation against you, we can start climbing that tree."

A smile began to spread across Asha's face.

"What is it?" Raj asked.

"I know exactly how we're going to get to him."

CHAPTER 38

While Asha didn't think G-Company would waste a lot of manpower on it, she did figure that they'd put some sort of a surveillance team on her apartment building in case she came back.

No true professional would return—not unless they were extremely prepared, which she was, thanks to Raj.

The hardest part was identifying the surveillance. How many were there, where were they, and how were they likely equipped?

A new tech start-up had been trying to get a meeting with Raj for ages. They were convinced that they could help RAW's Special Operations Division do better surveillance with fewer personnel and for less money than they were currently doing it. They had already gone through all the paperwork and had signed all the nondisclosure documents swearing them to secrecy. All they needed was to get in front of the man himself.

It wasn't that Raj didn't want to meet with them; initial reports from his surveillance specialists had been extremely positive, but with everything on his plate, he had been just too busy. Now he was willing to clear his schedule, and the tech people were willing to clear theirs.

He wanted proof of concept. They were ready to give it. The test would be to identify the full scope of surveillance taking place on Asha's apartment. Then everything would be up to her.

The tech people offered to pick up Raj and allow him to watch everything unfold in their mobile command center, but he opted for an encrypted feed that he could anonymously access from the basement of the Blind Relief Association.

Gupta wanted to be on-site to observe and to help out if needed, but didn't want anyone to know he was there. He chose a small tea shop down the street from Asha's and brought his briefcase with the latest novel from Saikat Majumdar. As long as he ordered something from time to time, they would let him sit there all day and read.

He had a perfect view of the front entrance of her building and, to the tech team's credit, he never saw any sign of them. *Zero*.

A surveillance op, as well as a countersurveillance op, was only as good as the people involved. You could have the best gadgets in the world, but if you didn't have experienced operatives behind them, at some point you were going to screw up and expose yourself.

By the time he got a text from Raj saying the tech company had wrapped up, he had already spotted two goons, who he assumed were part of G-Company. They were simply too low-rent and too out of their element to be anything else. Other than that, he hadn't noticed anyone else.

So one could imagine Gupta's surprise when the tech team identified seven people who were watching Asha's apartment.

"Seriously?" Gupta texted back to Raj. "Seven?"

It seemed like far too many. Three teams of two, plus a spotter in an upper apartment across the street. G-Company had to have known, like Asha, that she was a pro and that any pro who had been attacked so close to their home would not be back. They would go to ground. You wouldn't see them unless they wanted to be seen.

Why not simply leave a lookout and call for reinforcements, if and when she ever returned? He was worried. It felt like overkill.

But on the flip side, if they were subcontracting to Beijing, why wouldn't a criminal syndicate like G-Company inflate everything and try to get as much money out of the Chinese as possible?

That seemed like a perfectly rational explanation, but in situations like these, he always went with his gut. And his gut was telling him to be on guard.

Unlike with G-Company, manpower was where Raj's operation fell down. Keeping the circle tight was good for operational security, but not for carrying out any actual *operations*. Asha might have had exceptional talents, but one against seven was not a fight you wanted to have if you could avoid it.

She had been determined, however, and now that the surveillance report was in, the odds of success may have just tilted in her favor. It all came down to how she used the information.

The best course of action would have been to wait until night, when she could operate under the cover of darkness. But she didn't want to wait. She wanted to use the current intel and hit them now, ASAP. Gupta could only hope that she was making a sound tactical decision and not being motivated for revenge over what had happened earlier that morning.

• • •

Two blocks away, Asha had sat in the back of the tech company's mobile command center, appreciating its air-conditioning and watching all of the countersurveillance unfold.

The sophistication of the equipment was impressive. Miniature hive-to-target drones, acoustic and thermal sensors, X-ray cameras, refraction arrays, and passive particle beam units were only a part of what the team had brought with them and had put into the field.

The 360-degree picture of the battlespace they created was like something out of a science fiction movie. The heights of the buildings, the thickness of the walls, the layouts of the apartments inside, as well as the positions of all the people, right down to the cars on the street—it all came together in a fully explorable, precisely accurate, three-dimensional digital rendering.

"Let me see here and here," said Asha, pointing to two areas of the screen she was looking at.

One of the techs increased the magnification and zoomed in.

These people could literally see through walls. Now, thanks to them, so could she. Assessing all of the potential targets, she made her decision and contacted Raj.

She had a short but very particular list of gear she needed. "Give me an hour," the man had responded.

One hour later, on the dot, her phone rang. It was Raj. "Three cars behind you is a red, four-door Honda. Everything you asked for is in the trunk."

She thanked him and disconnected the call. As she did, one of the tech team showed her a small tablet. It was enclosed in a ruggedized polymer case by an American company called Juggernaut.

"This will allow you to continue monitoring everything. All I need to know is if you want it mounted to your forearm, or if you prefer flipping it down from your chest rig."

The primary weapon she had asked Raj for was an H&K MP5. Per her training, she would need to maintain two hands on the weapon at all times. Letting go with one hand, in order to roll her forearm over, as if she were checking a watch, was not tactically sound and was instantly out of the question.

"Flipped down from my chest rig," she replied.

The man set aside the straps he was holding and attached two mounts to the back of the Juggernaut case. "Just click these into your MOLLE webbing," he said, "and you'll be good to go."

Asha thanked him, exited the vehicle, and walked back to the red Honda. She recovered the fob from where it had been hidden and popped the trunk.

Everything was there. The Heckler & Koch MP5SD submachine gun with an integrated suppressor, an M68 Aimpoint red dot scope, a stack of thirty-round magazines, a plate carrier with one ceramic plate loaded in front, a two-shot Taser 7 CQ designed for close-quarter engagements, a fixed-blade knife, zip ties, a couple of distraction devices, just in case, and a handful of other odds and ends that might prove useful.

After putting on the plate carrier and attaching the tech team's tablet to the webbing on the magazine pouches, she distributed the rest of the gear across her body. Raj had also been kind enough to include a padded battle belt with Kydex holsters for her Glock and for the Taser. When she was done, she looked like she was ready to go to war.

Of course, she hoped that wasn't the case, but after this morning, she was leaving nothing to chance. Closing the trunk, she climbed into the driver's seat and activated the ignition. It was time to put her plan into action.

CHAPTER 39

If there was one thing Asha knew, it was her neighborhood. She knew it like the back of her hand because she had made it a point to.

Moving from Mumbai to New Delhi was a shock. She was used to a house always full of family and friends. And if she wasn't in her own, she was at any of dozens of homes around her Mumbai neighborhood that were buzzing with just as much life.

While RAW had discouraged having too many casual relationships, there was nothing casual that Asha felt about her neighbors in New Delhi. Family, even adopted family, was like oxygen to her. She was thoroughly Indian, and Indians thrived on social interaction.

She had created a whole new "family" and friend group in New Delhi, all within the neighborhood. She had been to their homes and apartments and they had been to hers. She had helped take care of children and pets, driven people to doctor's appointments and the airport, cooked for people when they were ill, and comforted people when they were sad or lonely. All of it she had done selflessly, and all of it had been returned to her in spades.

While she might have been tempted to say that she never imagined having to use one of these relationships, or knowledge of a friend's building, for her job, she would have been lying. One of the things they had been taught in training for RAW was that every person you interacted with and every piece of information you came across was valuable. If not today, then perhaps tomorrow, and you should treat all of it as if it were more precious than gold. Because at some point, it might just be.

That certainly applied to Asha's current situation. While she didn't know anyone in the building where the G-Company spotter had positioned himself, she knew several people next door. Best of all, the buildings had been constructed close enough together that you could jump from one rooftop to the other.

She found a spot near the front of the building and parked. At this time of day, almost everyone would be at work. That said, she needed to be careful. With the way she was kitted out, she ran the risk of creating a panic.

Placing her wireless earpiece in her left ear, she did a radio check. Raj heard her loud and clear. A moment later, Gupta, who had fished his earpiece out of his briefcase, confirmed that he had a clear signal as well. Everything was a go.

She had been to the building so many times that she knew the passcode by heart. Punching it into the keypad at the gate, she let herself in and headed for the nearest stairwell.

The roof was on the sixth story and she took the stairs as quickly as she could. During the whole way up, she didn't see another soul.

Hitting the door that led outside, she found it locked, but reaching above the frame—as she had done with her friends many times for drinks—she found the key and opened it.

Stepping outside, she paused, flipped down the tablet attached to the front of her rig, and gave Raj and Gupta a quick situation report. So far, everything was going according to plan.

She swiped through the various feeds and streams of data. Not much had changed since she had left the surveillance vehicle. The G-Company teams were still in the same places and, most important, the surveillance operative was still in the building next door. All Asha had to do was go get him.

Stowing the tablet back in place, she moved to the parapet and judged the distance. Then she backed up ten meters, took off running, and launched herself into the air.

The RAW operative landed on the other rooftop and rolled, taking particular care to protect the submachine gun and to make sure that she didn't damage any of her other equipment.

After a quick assessment, wherein she made sure that all of her gear was good and firmly secure, she headed for the service door that would lead into the building and downstairs.

When she got there and gave the handle a try, she found that it had been locked. She reached into a pouch attached to her belt and retrieved a set of lock-pick tools.

Expert lock picking had been drilled into her during her training. It was something that the more you did it, the better you got. Unfortunately, Asha hadn't done any in a while.

What's more, she had gotten spoiled by relying on a lock-pick gun for too many of her assignments. Raj hadn't been able to lay his hands on one in time, so he had substituted a standard set of picks instead. It took her a few moments longer than she would have preferred, but she eventually got the door opened and, readying her weapon, crept inside.

Flipping down the tablet, she checked to make sure all the G-Company thugs were still in place before continuing down the stairs. Once she saw that they were, she moved out.

The surveillance spotter was only one level down and still all alone. She moved quickly, but quietly—careful not to reveal her presence to anyone.

Hitting the landing, she scanned for any sign of life before hooking left and heading for the apartment. Anyone who was home was inside their unit, likely preparing more food in advance of another night of Diwali.

Coming up on the unit with the spotter, she slowed both her pace and her breathing. Once more, she checked the tablet. The lone figure was the only one inside.

How the man had gotten access to the unit was anyone's guess. Perhaps he had some sort of connection to the tenant. Perhaps the tenant was at work or out of town. There was also the distinct possibility that the tenant had been bribed or simply threatened to stay away until further notice.

None of that mattered to Asha. It wasn't any of her concern. All that mattered was getting into that unit and taking the man on the other side of its door alive.

Complicating matters was that this guy had six friends outside who would come running at the first sign of trouble. She had to be fast. She had to be efficient. Most of all, she had to be quiet. There was only one way she could think to do that.

Kicking the door in, or better yet, blowing it off its hinges, would have allowed her to be fast and efficient, but would have negated the "quiet" part of her plan. She was going to have to pick the lock.

She made her way to just outside the apartment door, stopped, and listened. Glancing down at the tablet, she could see exactly where the man inside was positioned—at a table of some sort near one of the windows, overlooking her building across the street.

Allowing her H&K to hang from the sling across her body, she pulled out her picks, crouched down in front of the lock, and got to work.

As she carefully inserted the thin pick, along with the tension wrench, she took great pains not to make any noise. She was concerned that even the slightest sound of metal scratching against metal would tip off the man inside.

So far, there had been no noise whatsoever. That made it quite unsettling when Raj said over the radio, "Freeze."

She did as he ordered, wondering what the hell was going on.

"Get out of there. Now."

Withdrawing her picks, she shoved them into a pocket, stood with her back against the wall, and readied her weapon as she whispered, "What's going on?"

"They're all converging on your location. They *know* you're there."

"How?" she wondered aloud, zooming out on the tablet, seeing exactly what Raj saw on his screen.

"There must be a camera somewhere in your vicinity. You need to get out of there. Do it now."

A camera? Damn it. She had purposefully kept her eyes open for cameras. But the technology had miniaturized them to such a degree that she could have missed one—or several. In fact, she could have been staring right into one as she worked on picking the lock and had not even known it. *Damn it,* she repeated to herself.

With the need to be quiet gone, and the element of surprise lost, all she had left was speed and efficiency.

"I'm going in," she radioed.

"Absolutely not. I'm telling you, for the last time, get the hell out of there. That's an order."

Technically, Raj was correct. It was an order. But it wasn't one with which she was going to comply. This was the only lead they had, and she would be damned if they were going to lose it.

Freeing up her left hand, she pulled a flashbang from her chest rig, removed the pin, and, stepping in front of the door, slammed it open and tossed the device inside.

When it detonated, she charged in behind it.

She swept her weapon from side to side, making sure—despite what the tech equipment had shown her—that there was no one else present.

The only person she saw was the man by the window. He was disoriented. Near his left foot was a pistol that he must have dropped. Asha wasted no time.

Letting her submachine gun swing on its sling, she transitioned to her Taser and fired, hitting the man with both barbed probes, dead center in his chest.

As he rode the lightning, his musculature seized up and he fell, groaning, to the ground.

She kicked his pistol across the floor, pulled out a pair of restraints, and zip-tied his hands behind his back before he could recover. Then she secured his ankles and, stripping away a lamp cord, bound all the restraints together so he couldn't move beyond rocking on his belly from side to side.

"They're coming up the stairs," said Raj, more concerned at this moment with her safety than the fact that she had disobeyed his order.

Asha looked at the tablet. "Confirmed. I see them." Four men were coming up the nearest stairwell, while two more were headed up the other at the far end of the corridor.

She scanned the apartment next door, which was empty. She also noticed something else—the units were mirrors of each other and shared the same Achilles' heel.

India in general, and New Delhi in specific, were plagued with substandard construction. Building inspectors were often bribed, or plans were submitted, only to be trimmed back and changed after occupancy permits were submitted. Apartments were frequently, and illegally, sliced in half, doubling a landlord's potential rental income.

When this happened, it was all about doing it on the cheap. There was no point in bricking over a narrow hallway when drywall could be used. And a narrow hallway, enclosed in drywall, made two halfway decent closets.

Grabbing a piece of decorative fabric draped over the couch, Asha gagged her prisoner and headed for the closet.

Once there, she didn't bother pulling the clothes out. Yanking out the rod, she let everything fall to the ground. Then, raising her H&K, she fired a barrage of suppressed rounds into the gypsum board.

She ejected her spent magazine, inserted a fresh one, and then, using the butt of her weapon, her booted foot, and her shoulder, punched her way through the drywall and into the closet of the apartment on the other side. Closing the door to the first closet, she quickly stepped into the adjacent apartment.

She had just officially recaptured the advantage.

What she'd do in the next ninety seconds would make all the difference.

CHAPTER 40

In the neighboring apartment, Asha had already cracked the front door. She had planned to ambush the four G-Company men as they ran past, maybe even get them killed in a crossfire if their colleagues in the other stairwell popped up and began shooting. Unfortunately, these guys weren't as dumb as she had hoped they would be. In fact, they were apparently quite disciplined.

The team of two at the far stairwell remained in place. Of the four men in the nearer stairwell, two came down the hall, while the other two hung back. This meant that if Asha stepped into the hall after they had passed, she would get shot in the back. That was a less-than-optimal outcome.

At this point, the only effective plan of attack she could see was to go back through the closet, reenter the spotter's apartment, and shoot the two men when they made their entry. They would, however, come in expecting an attack—especially when they saw their colleague gagged and trussed up on the living room floor.

There had to be another way, but not coming up with any, she hurried toward the closet and the hole leading through the wall back into the other apartment.

That was when Raj's voice came over her earpiece. "Help is on the way. North staircase."

Asha paused and looked at her tablet. Headed slowly up the stairs was a lone and somewhat larger figure than the others. "Is that who I think it is?" she asked.

"Yes, it's me," Gupta replied over his radio. "These fucking stairs are killing me, but I'm almost there. I can't see any of what you're seeing, so just tell me when, and I'll take out the two men at the top."

This was not at all how she had expected things to go down, but she appreciated the help and would take it however she could get it. Quickly she moved back to where she had been positioned at the front door of apartment number two.

Shifting her attention back to the tablet and the men coming down the hall, she gauged their timing and marked Gupta's location. "Are you in position?" she asked.

"Affirmative," he whispered.

"On my mark, then," she replied. "In five . . . four . . . three . . . two . . . one . . . *now*."

The north stairwell erupted in gunfire as Asha kicked open the door with her boot.

She caught both men, who were armed only with pistols, completely by surprise and couldn't have timed her attack any more perfectly. Just as they were beginning to spin to address the shooting behind them, she leaned out of the doorway and lit them up with her suppressed submachine gun, dropping them where they stood.

Before the men in the south stairwell could return fire, she had ducked back inside the apartment and had taken cover.

Bullets tore up the doorframe, but the shots were being fired one at a time; semiautomatic. Most likely, these guys were also using pistols.

Glancing at the tablet, she saw that Gupta had succeeded in ambushing the men at the top of the north stairs and had taken both of them out. That meant that this fight was now two versus two.

Her biggest question was what to do with Gupta. Have him hold and cover the north stairs, or have him drop down a floor, cross over to the south stairs, and attack those two shooters from below while she engaged them from where she was—essentially creating a pincer movement?

Unfortunately, she never got the chance to answer her own question. The two remaining shooters made up her mind for her.

Charging into the hallway, one fired toward Gupta's position in the opposite stairwell, while the other focused his fire on her door.

Asha risked breaking cover and ran for the closet and the opening to the other apartment. If these assholes were going to storm her position, the only thing they were going to get was practice.

As she ran, two rounds penetrated the door and slammed into her chest, hitting the ceramic plate. A couple of inches more to the side and they would have gone straight through her chest wall, puncturing her lung and maybe even piercing her heart—killing her on the spot.

The rounds were big and loud—.45 caliber, if she had to guess. It felt like being hit by a gorilla with a tire iron. The twin strikes had almost knocked the wind out of her. Nevertheless, her pace never slowed.

Charging through the closet and the hole in the drywall, she entered the spotter's apartment, weapon up, ready to engage. She paused only long enough to make sure the man on the floor was still tightly restrained and then headed for the door. The two shooters coming down the hallway were in for a surprise.

She told Gupta to stay where he was. He had already been more than helpful and she didn't want to put his life any further at risk.

Just as she had when leaving the spotter's apartment, she had closed the closet door of the second apartment on her way back. It wouldn't take them long to search the adjacent dwelling and find the hole, but she didn't need a lot of time.

Watching on her tablet, she waited until they entered the unit next door and then slipped into the hall and, avoiding the bodies, rapidly headed toward them.

She had one flashbang left. Letting her weapon hang, she retrieved the device from her chest rig and noticed the two holes where the bullets had penetrated the nylon plate carrier. One of them had nearly hit the flashbang.

Pulling the pin, she held the device in her left hand while securing the H&K in her right. Then, after ascertaining where the two shooters were via her tablet, she used the toe of her boot to nudge the door open and tossed the flashbang into the apartment.

It exploded with a loud bang and a blinding flash of light. As it did, she kicked the door the rest of the way open and rushed inside.

She double-tapped the man nearest to her and then swung her

weapon and double-tapped his accomplice. Both fell to the floor, dead, just as their comrades had out in the hall.

Asha kicked their guns away and then checked each man for a pulse, making sure that they were dead.

Though she had been able to avoid being seen by any of the building's residents, there was no way that the gunshots had gone unnoticed. The police were likely on their way and would be arriving at any moment.

She radioed Raj an update and told Gupta to get out of the building now, while he still could.

She had just one last thing to do—interrogate the spotter.

Transitioning back through the closet, she entered the other apartment and found the man right where she had left him. Rolling him onto his side, she unsheathed the knife attached to her chest rig and sliced the gag from around his mouth.

"I know you're G-Company," she stated. "I want the name of who sent you after me."

The man shot her an angry glare.

Asha didn't wait, she couldn't afford to. Taking the tip of her knife, she placed it against the man's groin and pushed. She heard the rip of the fabric and then the man's panicked cry of pain as the blade sliced through flesh.

"Aga Sayed!" he yelled. "It was Aga Sayed!"

CHAPTER 41

"Aga Sayed," Vijay explained as they drove from Jaipur to New Delhi, "is a vicious, lifelong criminal. He's into everything. And I mean *everything*. The worse something is, the more he's attracted to it. I'm not surprised that he's mixed up in all of this."

"So G-Company provided the assassin and the Kumars provided the motorbike," Harvath replied. "Who engaged G-Company to kill Ritter?"

"That's what we're going to find out," the ex-cop had replied. "But it isn't going to be easy. Not by a long shot. Sayed is one of G-Company's top people and extremely well insulated."

Changing the subject, Harvath asked, "How is it that you came to give him flying lessons?"

Vijay smiled. "Not my proudest moment. I was a young detective. Eager, filled with righteousness, and very quick—sometimes too quick—to anger.

"My partner and I were working a drugs case. A big one. We had an informant who was providing excellent information. He eventually wanted us to pull him in, to provide him protection. My partner, who was my senior, said no—not until the case was complete, we had dismantled the ring, and had made all of our arrests.

"The informant didn't like it, but he really didn't have any choice. He stayed in place and continued to provide us with intelligence. And then one day, he failed to make contact.

"That evening, we went to his house and found his body. He had been beaten to death. There was blood everywhere, but the blood wasn't all his. Some of it belonged to his family."

"Jesus," said Harvath. "They killed his family as well?"

The ex-cop shook his head. "Worse."

Harvath didn't want to imagine what could be worse, but knew Vijay was about to tell him and so he remained silent and waited for it.

"Aga Sayed had been sent to deal with our informant," the man said. "Not just to kill him, but to make him suffer. Before he died, our informant was forced to watch as his wife, then his mother, and finally his baby daughter were raped. Then, and only then, did Sayed's crew end his misery, along with his life."

"I would have thrown him off a rooftop, too," Harvath asserted.

"That's not the end of the story," Vijay continued. "It took us a week to track him down. We worked our way up through the sewers of New Delhi and the scum he associated himself with. No matter where we went or what we did, he was always two steps ahead of us. We were working around the clock, but couldn't catch a break. Then, we did.

"We found out that he was going to be at a gambling parlor to watch and bet on an important football match. That was where we decided we would confront him."

"*Confront* him?" Harvath repeated. "How about *arrest* him?"

"No one would agree to testify. Not members of his crew. Not even the informant's wife or his mother. Everyone was afraid of retribution. Without an eyewitness willing to go against him in court, we had nothing."

"So you decided to take care of things outside of court."

"We couldn't let the barbarity that he had committed go unanswered," Vijay replied. "Even if we lost our jobs, my partner and I were determined to make him pay."

Harvath understood the impulse. He had succumbed to it more than once himself. Good, capable men who did nothing in the face of evil were just as guilty of evil themselves.

"For the first time since we had begun our hunt," the ex-cop continued, "we were in the right place at the right time. We had him in our sights. But when we went to make our move, he bolted.

"It was monsoon season. The storm that night was horrible. You could barely see a foot in front of your face. My partner raced after Sayed and I took another route in hopes of cutting him off.

"When I got to where I thought he would be, the only thing I found was my partner, his chest and belly slashed wide open with a straight razor.

"I called for medical assistance, helped push his guts back inside his body, and tied my jacket around his midsection to act as a pressure bandage. I didn't want to leave him, but my partner was emphatic. Sayed needed to be stopped, once and for all. So, I resumed my chase.

"He had thought by forgoing the alleys and heading to the rooftops, that he could escape, but he was wrong. Like him, I had grown up in one of the city's rougher neighborhoods and long before I ever entertained the idea of becoming a police officer, I had run from countless cops and had used the rooftops to slip their grasp.

"He had a head start on me, but it didn't take long to catch up to him. Everything was soaked. Every surface was slippery and he was clumsy. Sayed had made just enough mistakes for me to reach out and grab him from behind."

"You put hands on some psycho with a straight razor?" asked Harvath. "From behind? My God, Vijay, if ever there was a reason to use your sidearm, that was it. Practically textbook."

"I know," the man admitted. "You're right. But I was young, dumb, and full of rage over not only what he had done to our informant and his family, but also what he had done to my partner. Putting a bullet in him would have solved one problem, but it would have created a mountain of others. Plus, it wouldn't have given me the satisfaction I needed."

Harvath appreciated that. "What happened?" he asked.

"He did just what you thought he did. He spun, I caught the glint of the razor—even in the storm—and he swung it at me. But I was expecting it."

"Meaning he *missed* you."

"Yes," said the ex-cop, "but not by much. He sliced through my coat, just below my left armpit. Almost got me."

"And you still didn't shoot him."

"No, I did not. But I did give him a little rooftop-to-rooftop counseling. I beat that piece of shit to within an inch of his life, tossed him to the next building, gave him a chance to catch his breath, and began the whole process all over again."

"When did he learn he couldn't fly?"

"On the last rooftop. I misjudged the distance. Didn't throw him hard enough. My bad."

Harvath chuckled. There really, and truly, was nothing like a smart-ass cop. "I'm guessing your partner wasn't afraid to testify against him."

"He was not. Aga Sayed countered by alleging police brutality and police misconduct. Unfortunately for him, there were no eyewitnesses to back up any of his claims, only the injuries he sustained while running from *this* detective.

"Sayed got lucky and pulled a judge who was soft on crime and hard on cops. His sentence was fifteen years. He served five."

"What about your partner?"

"That was it for him. His wife wanted him out. His kids wanted him out. And on a certain level, he wanted out, too. So he retired."

"What happened to you?"

Vijay smiled. "I got promoted."

Harvath shook his head and smiled. "Of course you did. Any other ending just wouldn't have suited that story."

"Don't the good guys always win?"

"Unfortunately," Harvath replied, "the only place that the good guys *always* win is in the movies."

"Well in this movie," the ex-cop exclaimed, pointing at the two of them, "there'd better be a happy ending. Because if there's one thing we demand in India, it's happy endings."

"And if there's one thing we demand in America, it's that justice be done before there can be any ending—happy or otherwise."

"Here's hoping both of our audiences get what they want," said Vijay, sticking out his fist.

Harvath gave it a bump and watched as up ahead of them the majestic city of New Delhi came into view.

CHAPTER 42

New Delhi was everything Harvath had expected it to be—congested, loud, frenetic, dirty, colorful, vibrant, energetic, and alive, overflowing with humanity. There were trees everywhere.

Scooters fought with autorickshaws, which fought with taxis, which fought with buses, which fought with trucks. It was a symphony of chaos. Everyone was in a hurry, jockeying for position, at least until the next red light, when drivers would lean out their windows and laugh and chat with each other.

Some of the things Harvath saw were on a whole other level of beauty—the colors of women's bright saris, the sidewalk carts exploding with fruits and vegetables, shrines and temples dripping with flowers.

Some of the things were heart-wrenching—the crushing poverty, the disease, the trash, and the filth.

Then there were the things he had never seen before—like traffic, on a major thoroughfare, patiently stopped, allowing a stray cow to cross unmolested. No one so much as honked. India was like no country he had ever visited.

Vijay explained that they were fortunate to have such a clean air day. When he had left New Delhi, he hadn't been able to drop the Jaguar's top until he was a half hour outside the city. The smog had been that bad. Harvath was receiving another grand introduction to one of India's most incredible cities.

The ex-cop had made and received multiple phone calls during their drive—all in rapid-fire Hindi, peppered with words in English. He was working his contacts, trying to get a lead on the whereabouts of Aga Sayed. So far, all of it had been a bust.

This was the part of any assignment that Harvath hated the most—when it began to stall.

While conducting surveillance or passing hours—sometimes even days—in a hide site was often mind-numbingly boring, having all of your leads dry up could turn out to be a death knell for an operation.

"If you were going to force his hand and flush him out into the open, how would you do that?" Harvath asked.

Vijay thought for a moment and responded, "I would take something that belonged to him. Something *very* important."

"Does he have a wife? Girlfriend? Kids?"

"These guys all have girlfriends. None of them rate very high on the importance scale. They're toys. Objects of pleasure."

"There's got to be something he cares about enough to risk everything for," said Harvath.

"I suppose if you interdicted a load of G-Company's drugs or stole a whole bunch of valuable contraband, he might expose himself. But more likely than not, he'd just send an army of thugs after you."

This was getting them nowhere. There had to be some way to get Aga Sayed to pop up. "If we can't take something from him, what can we bait him with? What would be too good for him, personally, to pass up?"

"That's entirely too easy," said Vijay. "We give him me."

"You?"

"Of course, *me*. I caught him. I got him sent to prison. And I did such damage when I threw him off that roof that he lives in a constant state of arthritic pain. Believe me, not a day goes by that he doesn't think of me; not a storm rolls in where he isn't cursing my name and wishing for my death."

"Unfortunately," Harvath replied, "that's a bridge too far. The United States isn't going to use you for bait. That goes above and beyond what you're being paid for."

"Then I quit."

"No you don't. You're one of the best FSN/Is I've ever worked with. The embassy is lucky to have you. They can't afford to lose you."

"When I drop you at your hotel, I'll write out my resignation by hand. You can decide what you want to do with it."

Harvath shook his head. "I already told you. It won't be accepted."

"That's the funny thing about resignations. If I resign, *I resign*. There really isn't anything you can do about it."

The man was right. However, Harvath didn't want to risk the ex-cop's life like this. There was no telling what Sayed would do if he could get Vijay in his sights. "We'll come up with another way to find him."

"Will we?" the man asked. "Maybe we can set up a sting like your NYPD does every several years. We can reach out to Sayed and tell him he has won season tickets to his favorite football or cricket team. Then, *if* he shows up in person to claim them, we can grab him."

Harvath smiled. "You know that was from an Al Pacino movie, right?"

"Does it have a happy ending?"

Harvath raised his right hand and tilted it from side to side as if to say, *sort of*.

"Is justice done in the end?" the ex-cop inquired.

"The good guy kills the bad guy by throwing him out of a window, so, yes, justice is done."

"Then it's settled."

Harvath looked at him. "What's *settled*?"

"We're going after Sayed. We're using me as bait. And this time, for justice to be done, I just need the right window, or a higher rooftop."

• • •

Vijay had called the embassy and had asked them to reserve Harvath a room at the Oberoi hotel, just adjacent to the New Delhi Golf Club.

Once the reservation was in place, Harvath texted Lawlor and asked him to keep paying for the Fairmont in Jaipur and to set up payment for the Oberoi as well. Lawlor confirmed the request and told Harvath to reach out to him as soon as he checked in.

"You won't get showered with rose petals," the ex-cop stated as they pulled up the broad drive in front, "but I think you'll find the service exceptional."

"Exceptional" turned out to be an understatement. The Oberoi was one of the most luxurious hotels Harvath had ever set foot inside. Between this and the Fairmont Jaipur, he was quickly becoming convinced that nobody did luxury like India.

Set on an extremely lush five acres of land, Harvath had been upgraded to a sleek, tastefully modern suite, with an incredible view over the golf course.

Setting his suitcase on the stand next to the closet, he called Lawlor via the encrypted app before he even began to unpack.

There was no friendly preamble; no chitchat. It was far too late at night in Northern Virginia. "What do you have for me?" the man asked when he answered the call.

Harvath gave him a brief but thorough SITREP, expanding on items only when asked for further clarification.

When everything related to his assignment in India had been addressed, Lawlor provided a SITREP of his own. "Nicholas was attacked again. Nina was with him when it happened."

"Are they okay? Is *she* okay? What about the baby?"

"When the ambulance got there, she was in labor and bleeding quite badly. She's in surgery now."

"Are she and the baby going to be okay?"

"The doctors aren't sure," said Lawlor. "Not yet."

"So they got hit at the safe house?"

"No. Nicholas had insisted they return home. He didn't want to be chased out of his own house. He wanted Nina to able to rest up for the delivery in their bed."

"He's prideful, that guy," said Harvath. "Nevertheless, he should have seen this coming."

Lawlor agreed. "He saw it coming all right. Sutton swept the woods and had pointed out where the attacker had set up shop the first time around. Nicholas then mined the entire area with antipersonnel devices. When the second attack happened, he detonated everything. He killed the attacker and triggered a new Northern Virginia record for simultaneous 911 calls."

"Is Nicholas okay? The dogs?"

"Everybody is fine, including his security detail. We're going to owe ATF a lot of favors for burying this, but if he hadn't done what he had, there's no telling how much worse it would have been this time around."

Harvath sat down on the edge of the bed. "What do you know about the attacker?"

"Chinese national. Twenty-four years old. Was on a student visa, studying applied physics at MIT. Had been absent from class the last couple of days."

"Anything else in his background?"

"You mean *her* background," Lawlor said, correcting him.

"The attacker was female?"

"Yep."

"Just like I—"

"Just like you projected," Lawlor said, finishing his sentence for him. "The Chinese are getting more desperate and their tactics reflect it. They're hoping that they can be more successful by utilizing female operatives."

"Didn't work this time, did it?"

"Judging by how much of her is scattered across Nicholas's property, no, it did not."

"Do we know anything about her background?" Harvath asked. "Was she working for Chinese military intelligence? State intelligence? Do we have anything at all on her?"

"She was unremarkable. Clean. No flags. She sailed right through the visa process."

Harvath shook his head. "One-point-four billion people. Welcome to the next fire hose we get to choke on. Beijing isn't going to send anything but *clean*, *unremarkable* operatives. They have an endless supply. We're fucked."

"Going forward, perhaps," Lawlor replied. "But right now, on this one, we lucked out."

"How so?" he asked, perking up.

"We got the weapon."

"You've got *the* weapon? The Havana Syndrome device?"

"Saint Nick's claymores really did a number on it," said Lawlor, "but yes, we've got it. DARPA is pulling it apart as we speak."

"And it's got MADE IN CHINA stamped all over it, right?" Harvath joked.

"It may be covered in blood *made in China*," Lawlor replied, "but our enemies are much smarter than that. I have no expectation that anything about that weapon is going to trace back to Beijing. Or Hong Kong. Or Shanghai. Or Huaibei. It's one of the first ghost guns of the twenty-first-century battlefield."

"So you got one gun. One operative. Well done," said Harvath. "But how do we know there aren't more? How do we know they aren't going to hit him again?"

"To be honest, we don't know."

"Exactly. Which is why I want you to bring me back."

"Now?" said Lawlor. "While you're in the middle of an op?"

"Send over Staelin and Haney. Send over Preisler. Jesus, send over Johnson. Even he couldn't fuck this up."

"Scot, I can't—"

"Gary, listen to me," Harvath interrupted. "I am the only family Nicholas has. He would drop everything to help me. Right now, I need to drop everything to help him."

"No."

"*No?*"

"Nicholas has Nina and they have each other, as well as the baby—who I have every expectation is going to be okay. Nick splattered that operative who was sent to attack him. News travels fast, but over long distances and in situations like this, it doesn't travel well. Beijing is going to have a hard time finding its footing and figuring out what exactly happened.

"There's going to be uncertainty up and down the ranks in China. We can use that to our advantage. The bottom line is that we're midstream and we are most definitely *not* changing horses. If you want to help Nicholas, complete your assignment and then return home. Is that clear?"

"Crystal," Harvath replied. "I just want one thing from you."

"What's that?"

"All of the stops get pulled out for Nicholas, Nina, and the baby. They get the best doctors, the best protection, all of it. Nothing is spared. No stone is left unturned. We do everything we can for them."

"Of course," Lawlor asserted. "Nicholas is one of us. We take care of our own."

"Good," said Harvath. "Thank you."

"And you? Can you remain focused on what you need to do?"

"Absolutely. But when everything is done, I want your promise that, even if it isn't connected to my assignment, I'll be allowed to go after whoever authorized targeting Nicholas and Nina."

There was a pause before Lawlor responded. "By all means," he said. "Something tells me that you won't have to work hard searching for a connection. It'll be there. The only question is, how much worse is every-thing going to get before we find it?"

CHAPTER 43

Colonel Yang Xin's stomach problems were growing worse by the hour. His American-based operative had missed her third communications window in a row. This was not a good sign. In fact, it was a very bad sign.

After her first attack on that little bastard, she had sent in an excellent situation report. She had given the Troll, as instructed, a full blast of the directed-energy weapon, completely debilitating him.

Then she had remained hidden in the woods at the edge of his property and had waited until the ambulance had taken him away, before departing herself.

Were there reasons she might not have reported in yet? Of course, but none of them were good. She could have been in an accident or detained by authorities, both of which might result in the discovery of her weapon.

Her number one priority, and it had been drilled into her, was *not* the targeting of the Troll and other Carlton Group members. It wasn't even staging a successful attack on Scot Harvath himself. It was to make sure that the weapon didn't fall into enemy hands. No matter what the cost, neither the Americans nor anyone else was to get anywhere near it.

Smuggling the weapon into the United States, piece by piece, had been a Herculean effort. There was only so much that could be done via diplomatic pouches.

Once all of the weapon's components were on American soil, it needed to be reassembled. That meant that one of the device's creators, someone from the Science and Technology Commission, had to be brought to the United States to oversee the process. This person had to be one hundred percent clean—not on the radar of any of America's agencies—and they had to have enough training in tradecraft so as not to arouse suspicion or fall under surveillance while inside the United States.

Then, finally, the weapon had to be tested.

While there were a plethora of test subjects clogging up Chinese prisons and concentration camps, America was different in that respect. Experiments needed to be carried out on subjects who couldn't, or wouldn't, report their symptoms.

Yang didn't want the American government to start seeing "Havana Syndrome," as they had dubbed it, on their shores, until he was ready to fully unleash it. And so they had focused the device on homeless persons, over a two-week period, up and down the eastern seaboard.

It had been an unqualified success. The Science and Technology Commission returned to China and Yang's Boston-based Yaomo operative began carefully targeting different U.S. government employees and officials. Panic instantly took hold and could be felt from the corridors of power in Washington all the way up to the United Nations in New York City. No one knew where or when the next attack was going to happen. Now neither did Yang.

If the woman failed to materialize for her fourth comms window, he was going to have to launch a salvage operation.

An operation of that nature, however, was one of the most dangerous he could authorize. You were putting another agent in harm's way and opening them up to a host of potentially disastrous outcomes.

Also, it wasn't just any agent who could be tasked with a salvage operation—especially one in which *both* men and matériel were at risk. It required an elite operator. Someone exceptionally skilled, with a single-minded determination to see the mission through to the end, no matter what came to pass and no matter what the personal risk. There was only one person Yang could think of who so perfectly fit the bill.

When the fourth window came and went without any communication, he walked over to his safe, opened it, and removed a file contained within a black envelope.

Setting it on his desk, he pulled out an old letter opener he hadn't touched in years. Once he cracked the thick, wax seal there would be no going back.

He stopped for a moment and ran his fingers over the crest and its raised lettering—*Joint Staff Department of the Central Military Commission Intelligence Bureau*.

Beneath it was a national security secrecy designation. The file bore one of the highest, most sensitive classifications in the People's Liberation Army. The contents of the folder were considered to be within the realm of state secrets that included China's space and nuclear weapons programs. Sliding the opener under the wax, he broke the seal.

Opening the envelope, he withdrew the file. The title page only held two, chilling words: *Codename—Carbon*.

Yang's stomach pain intensified. He felt like someone had just walked across his grave.

Nevertheless, he turned the page and began the activation process. He was about to open the gates of hell.

What would be talked about in the years to come was what the freshly unleashed demon had done in pursuit of its goal.

Yang, however, couldn't help but wonder how his role in helping the creature slip its bonds would be remembered.

His was but the turn of a key in a lock. However, as sure as the sun would rise, he would be responsible for every drop of blood that monster would spill. And the operative known as Carbon was the most bloodthirsty beast China had ever set loose on any of its enemies.

CHAPTER 44

NEW DELHI

Vijay had a plan in mind regarding Aga Sayed, but he needed to get a couple of things lined up. He also wanted to spend a few hours with his family. It was Diwali, after all.

He asked Harvath if he wanted to join them for dinner and experience a real Indian festival firsthand. Harvath thanked him, but said that after the ghost pepper incident, he probably wouldn't trust him ever again. Vijay had laughed and told him that if he changed his mind, he would still be welcome. Apparently, both his wife *and* his mother-in-law were excellent cooks.

As enticing as the offer was, Harvath relished the idea of a little downtime. Only two days ago, he had literally been hit by a truck—and he felt like it.

Calling down to the bell captain, he promised the man a seriously good tip if he would hit as many of the hotel's ice machines as possible and bring all the cubes up to his room. He wanted to take the world's coldest and longest ice bath.

As he awaited the bellman, he availed himself of the suite's minibar and poured himself a bourbon. Just a little something to take the edge off, numb the pain, and help him relax.

Once enough ice had been poured into the massive tub, he tipped the bellman, activated the do-not-disturb light on the door, and filled the vessel the rest of the way with water.

Sliding in was like taking the polar plunge. No matter how much time had passed since his SEAL training, he had never lost his deep and abiding hate for cold water.

With no access to pain pills, or a chiropractor to pop his myriad misplaced ribs and vertebrae back into place, this was the best medicine he had available.

Nursing his bourbon, he tried not to focus on the cold. The longer he stayed in the tub, the more restorative the torture would be.

He hadn't been this cold since the Russian helicopter he had been flying in had crashed into the ocean above the Arctic Circle. The only time he had been colder was when he had fallen through a frozen river in Russia and had begun hallucinating.

It was funny how, more than his SEAL training, the worst experiences he had had with cold had always involved Russia. That was a country that if he never saw it again, it would be too soon. He didn't have a problem with the Russian people. Their government, however, he despised with a passion.

The same went for China. Its people, by and large, were decent, honorable, hardworking. But the Chinese Communist Party was an absolutely horrific regime. They enslaved, slaughtered, and oppressed people on a scale that, much like Russia's atrocities, should have been a global embarrassment.

The fact that the United States remained so reliant on Chinese manufacturing was a black mark on its purported belief in individual liberty and human rights.

Harvath loved his country, deeply, but its relationship with China was a constant source of frustration and anger for him. And recent events involving Ritter, Nicholas, and Nina had done nothing but bolster his hatred of the CCP.

Taking a swig of bourbon, he tried to push the cold, as well as the godless Chinese communists, from his mind. It didn't work. The only thing that would keep him in the tub was being pissed-off, so he allowed his anger at both to flood through him.

Finally, when he couldn't stand it any longer, he got out and took a nice, long, hot shower.

Standing under the rain head, with jets shooting at him from the walls, he let the water pound him into a trancelike state.

He allowed his mind to let go of bad things. He thought of only good things. He thought of Sølvi in Oslo, their wedding, and of seeing her again soon.

He thought of Nicholas and Nina, and their baby, and hoped that all would be well.

And he thought of getting his hands on the person responsible for killing Eli Ritter and imagined what it would be like to watch him die.

While not on the same level of Nicholas's satisfaction in killing the person who had attacked him and his family in his home, he figured it would be in the ballpark. Harvath was nothing if not loyal. Plus, meting out vengeance was something of a specialty of his. No one wronged those he cared about without paying the full and maximum penalty.

Climbing out of the shower, he put on one of the Oberoi's famous bathrobes, shaved, and brewed an espresso.

The fact that he was shortly going to mix it up in the New Delhi underworld seemed almost surreal. From a cold, loud transport aircraft to two luxury hotels in a row, the espionage world was nothing if not inconsistent and totally unpredictable.

He set an alarm and closed his eyes, hoping to catch some sleep, but was only able to drift off for about twenty minutes before popping back up, wide awake.

His brain could be restless, uncooperative, when he was on assignment and trying to process lots of information. He would have liked to have caught a little bit more than twenty minutes, but he was glad to have had it. Twenty minutes was better than nothing.

Grabbing the menu, he called down to room service and ordered dinner. He didn't know when he was going to get a chance to eat again, and doing so now, at the hotel, meant he wouldn't risk getting sick later by ordering something from a street vendor on the fly.

The food came up on a linen-covered cart, with polished silverware and hand-cut crystal glasses. Everything he had ordered was there—multiple, high-protein appetizers and fully cooked vegetables. Per his request, there was no bread, or butter, in sight.

In addition to a carafe of coffee, there were two large bottles of water. Turning on satellite news to catch up on what was happening at home, he sat down and tucked into his meal.

Back in Washington, it was the typical bullshit. The two parties were unable to work together. Those representatives willing to reach across the aisle and attempt compromise were labeled by the fringes in their parties as sellouts and even "traitors."

Harvath hated the internet. He hated the political media complex even more. A bunch of loud-mouthed jackasses on the left and the right were getting rich by fomenting strife and convincing good Americans that their way of life was being destroyed by the other side.

The truth was that Americans had it better than any other people at any other time in history. The United States was at the peak of the mountain—lean too far left, too far right, forward or back, and we risked losing everything.

Instead of letting idiots on TV, radio, and the internet convince us that our good lives were terrible, we needed to be practicing gratitude. Only by recognizing how good we had it and being grateful for it would we ever hope to preserve it for the next generation. Frankly, there were days that the rampant stupidity in the United States made Harvath want to suck-start his Glock.

Lots of people were well-meaning, but they were lazy. They didn't exert the basic duties of good citizenship. They believed anything and everything that flashed across their phone or computer screen. They believed that if they were in a group, or a feed, of like-minded people, all the information being pushed at them was true. They didn't realize that the information spaces where you felt safest were where America's enemies loved to seed their propaganda and disinformation.

Harvath loved his fellow countrymen and women but loathed the ones who couldn't be bothered to fact-check what they were reading and hearing. Being a responsible steward of the American republic meant doing the hard work of being truthfully informed.

He was just finishing his meal when Vijay texted and told him he'd be downstairs to pick him up in a half hour.

CHAPTER 45

"That's your plan?" Harvath asked as he slid a Sly and the Family Stone CD into the Jaguar's player.

The evening air was heavy with humidity. Thunderstorms were in the forecast for later. Vijay had the top down and the AC cranked.

"I take it that you do not like it," the ex-cop replied as they pulled out of the hotel's driveway.

"It's not that I don't like it. It's that I hate it."

The man smiled. "It's not the quality of the trap that matters. It's the quality of the bait."

"Which is complete and total bullshit," said Harvath. "If we were dropping you into a snake pit, against just one snake, that'd be one thing. You'd at least be able to focus on the danger. But what you're asking for is to be dropped into a pit filled with God knows how many snakes. It's a horrible idea."

"I told you. Aga Sayed is well insulated. This is how we get to him. Now, ask me how my Diwali went."

"In all honesty, Vijay, I don't care how your Diwali went. I want to iron out this stupid plan of yours. Even if you were still an active cop, which you aren't, I wouldn't want to go into this with anything less than a whole police station full of officers backing us up."

"We're going to be fine," the man replied, tapping his steering wheel to the beat of the classic funk song "Thank You (Falettinme Be Mice Elf Agin)."

"You can say that a hundred more times, but it isn't going to make it any more true. This is a suicide operation. Your plan is to walk into a nightclub owned by Sayed, staffed by people on his payroll, and walk out—arms around each other—like a couple of newlyweds. You're nuts. It's never going to happen."

"To be clear," the ex-cop clarified, "I don't expect him to willingly walk out with me. That's why I have a gun."

"And if it doesn't work?"

"That's why you have a gun. The one I gave you."

"Is there a Hindi word for *lunatic*? For a person absolutely around-the-bend crazy?" Harvath asked. "Because if there is, I'm going to start using it. Maybe that'll get through to you."

He laughed. "*Chutiya* is the word that comes the closest."

"Laugh all you want, Chutiya. From the bouncers to any personal bodyguards, he could have ten or fifteen goons in there for us to contend with."

"Then you'll want the gift I have for you," the ex-cop said, pointing at the glove box.

Harvath opened it and pulled out the extra pistol magazine that had been placed inside. "That's it? One extra mag? And you waited until now to give it to me?"

"I didn't have it until now," the man replied. "I had to ask my mother-in-law for it. That's her gun you're carrying."

Harvath didn't believe him, not really, but there was a tiny part of him that did. The guy really was a *chutiya*. "Listen, Vijay, you need to think about what you're walking into. What's to stop them from taking you out back and putting a bullet in your head?"

"You," he replied. "And my mother-in-law's gun."

"I'm going to tell you right now, if that is what you're counting on, your movie is most definitely not going to have a happy ending."

"The minute anything goes wrong, all you need to do is to put two rounds into the ceiling and start a stampede. Everything else will take care of itself."

"Take care of itself, how?"

"Indians are conditioned to not only call the cops, but to also livestream everything via their phones. This place will be getting so much attention, Sayed wouldn't dare do anything stupid. Trust me."

It was a heavy gamble and Harvath didn't like it. If someone had thrown him off a roof, broken lots of his bones in the process, and then suddenly reappeared in his life, he'd kill the guy with a cocktail straw and worry about the fallout later. A stampede of customers waving smartphones in the air wouldn't make a damned bit of difference.

He didn't like their odds—he and Vijay against an untold army of gangsters. He wished there was some other way to do this, but try as he might, he hadn't been able to come up with a better plan. Nevertheless, this felt like a disaster waiting to happen.

As far as Harvath was concerned, his number one obligation was to get Vijay in and out alive. The man had been an absolute prince. It was obvious that he missed his old life as a detective and relished being back on the street cracking skulls, but at some point, enough could be too much. If anything happened to him, Harvath wouldn't be able to forgive himself.

"Despite my reservations, I'm going to go along with this, but only on one condition."

The ex-cop made a left turn, adjusted the volume, and replied, "Which is?"

"You make Sayed come to us—however you have to do it. You do not go anywhere with him or his people; not to his office, not down to the basement, none of that kind of thing. We do this out in the open."

"Agreed."

The man claimed to agree, but there was something about the way he said it that concerned Harvath. It sounded like he didn't really mean it.

If Vijay didn't mean it, they were about to saunter into a shit storm of epic proportions.

CHAPTER 46

Harvath hadn't thought it possible to hate Vijay's plan any more than he already did, but as soon as they got within spitting distance of Paharganj, that's exactly what happened.

Paharganj was the worst neighborhood in New Delhi. It made Jaipur's Sanganer look like Beverly Hills. When people talked about how terrible parts of India could be, this was the poster child for it. All of it.

Muggers, rapists, pickpockets, drug dealers, beggars . . . all slithering through a maze of dark alleyways and crumbling buildings. Harvath and Vijay were headed into a snake pit surrounded by an even bigger snake pit.

Known as New Delhi's "backpacker ghetto" because of its cheap hotels and even cheaper hostels, there was plenty of fresh, young tourist meat for local thugs to feed upon.

The main street was jam-packed with vehicles and the sidewalks were overflowing with humanity. Food vendors cooked over open fires. Stalls selling T-shirts and sandals sat cheek by jowl with travel agencies, which offered scooter and car rentals, as well as budget train and plane tickets.

Vijay found a place to park and pulled over.

After a quick chat with an incense vendor sitting in a plastic chair outside his shop, the ex-cop smiled at Harvath.

"Let me guess," Harvath replied. "Another hundred bucks?"

After paying off Vijay's new valet cum security guard, they pushed deeper into the neighborhood, where the congestion only became worse.

It would have been impossible to get the Jaguar through. He had been smart to leave it out on the main road.

In addition to the crush of people, honking motorbikes threaded their way through the crowds. Stray dogs, some terribly skinny and riddled with mange, roamed everywhere.

As a dog lover, Harvath hated to see it. According to Vijay there were upwards of four hundred thousand of them in New Delhi alone.

They passed a one-chair barbershop that was so narrow, if you stepped inside and held your arms out, you could span its width and touch both walls at the same time.

The barber was giving his customer a very unique, very kinetic head massage. At first, Harvath thought he was beating the customer. But as he watched the barber shuffle around the chair like a boxer and exhale large gusts of air, he realized something quite different was happening.

He looked at Vijay, who shrugged and said, "Many find it invigorating. Some barbers will even adjust your neck and spine for you. Do you want to try it?"

"Maybe later," Harvath lied. He had no desire to remain in Paharganj any longer than they had to.

The labyrinthine passageways grew slimmer the farther they went. So much wiring was strung from building to building that looking up in places it appeared as if you were walking under a thick, black net.

They passed a tiny bakery, a medical clinic, and countless other small shops selling everything from chips and sodas, to eggs, lightbulbs, and cleaning supplies. It was like an endless grimy bazaar.

Up ahead, Vijay spotted their destination and pointed it out to Harvath. The exterior of the Laid Back Lounge & Social Club looked every bit the dump that Harvath had expected it to be.

A third of the lights in its sign were either broken or burned out, half of the stained stoop in front was missing, and one of its two glass doors had a long crack that had been covered over with clear packing tape. The entire place just screamed "class."

Per the plan, Harvath had kept walking and had entered first, while Vijay had hung back. They didn't want anyone to know that they were working together.

The façade of the Laid Back barely hinted at how seedy things were inside. Harvath could feel the soles of his shoes sticking to the floor as he walked to the end of the bar and grabbed a stool.

He had passed a pair of bored, beefy bouncers on his way in. They were seated and both had been scrolling through their phones. They barely paid him any attention, which was fine by him. So far, the place was only a pit. No snakes. Yet.

Harvath had been fascinated to learn that only about a third of India's population drank on a regular basis. Those who abstained normally did so for religious or cultural reasons. Those who did drink, did so to get buzzed.

Spirits, especially whiskey, were the preferred libation, followed by beer. And if you were drinking beer to get buzzed, you wanted your beer to be strong. That was why "strong" beer, with an alcohol content ranging anywhere from five to eight percent, was the most popular.

Harvath looked at the list of bottled beers. There was one called Bad Monkey and another called Simba Strong. The fact that he was in some crime figure's bar, however, made the next beer on the list the one he had to try.

Godfather, like the two others, hovered right around eight percent. Harvath wasn't in the market to get buzzed; he just wanted to blend into the wallpaper, keep an eye on things, and not draw any attention. His plan was to take it slow.

When the barman brought it over, he politely declined a glass, paid the man with some of the rupees he had exchanged at the hotel, and told the man to keep the change.

Even in India, Thursday night was a popular night to party. The Laid Back had a good crowd, despite it not yet being even ten o'clock. It was a cross section of people.

Though largely Indian, the clientele also included a mix of young, Western backpacker types.

The beer wasn't expensive, but it wasn't exactly cheap, either. So, he figured there had to be another reason such a diverse crowd would be drawn to the Laid Back. It soon became obvious. The Laid Back was a bar that specialized in classic rock.

"La Grange" by ZZ Top had been playing when he had walked in and as it ended, the DJ began spinning "You Shook Me All Night Long" by AC/DC—much to the delight of a couple of female patrons who, well into their shots, simultaneously hit the stripper poles at the front of the dance floor.

If the presence of the poles themselves didn't indicate that this sort of dancing was encouraged, the fact that the DJ started a whole bunch of flashing red lights to encourage them should have.

By the time the ladies returned to their table for more shots, and "School's Out" by Alice Cooper started up, Harvath was pretty certain that he had the vibe of the place figured out. Definitely a rock bar.

He would've bet the next hundred bucks Vijay was sure to want from him for parking protection that the last song of the night, every night, was a raucous, standing-on-top-of-the-bar-and-tables sing-along to "American Pie" by Don McLean. It was just that kind of place.

If not for the provenance of its barbaric owner, it might have been the kind of place Harvath could grow to like. He enjoyed a seedy dive bar now and again. When he did, the more raucous, the better.

As if on cue, it was at that precise moment that Vijay stumbled into the Laid Back and began to give a performance worthy of an Oscar.

CHAPTER 47

Even from the other end of the bar, Harvath could smell the ex-cop before he had even seen him. He had no clue what sort of alcohol the man had briefly marinated in, but it was potent.

Taking a moment to steady himself, he then wobbled toward the bar, telling both the bouncers who tried to stop him to "Shut the fuck up" and "Go back to watching porn" on their phones.

He had everyone's attention at the front of the establishment. Plopping himself down on a stool, he pulled out his wallet and removed a two-hundred-rupee note.

As he slapped it onto the bar and demanded a Johnnie Walker Black on the rocks, his badge was clearly visible to the bartender as well as the bouncers, who decided to disengage and let the cop be.

"I'm sorry, sir," the barman informed him. "Johnnie Walker Black is a premium beverage. It is six hundred rupees."

Removing the rest of the cash from his wallet, Vijay ham-handedly placed it atop the bar and, with just the hint of slurred speech, replied, "Fine, then. Bring me two."

Scooping up the money, the bartender put it into the till and set to work making the drinks.

Harvath's gaze drifted from the ex-cop to the dance floor, paying about as much attention to the newly arrived drunk as he would in any other situation. It was important to know where the man was and if he was getting worse, but other than that, the best course of action was not to engage.

The barman arrived with the two drinks and placed them before his customer. Vijay made quick work of them.

After swirling the first one for a moment to release some of the water from the ice, he tossed it right back—one, fast, gluttonous gulp.

Wiping his mouth with the back of his hand, he reached for the second drink and knocked it over. That began what Harvath could only assume was a long string of curse words in Hindi.

The bartender told him that everything was okay and that he would make him another drink. Vijay nodded at the man and gestured to suggest that of course he would make him another drink. It was the only right thing to do.

If Harvath had been tending bar, he would have handed over the fresh drink, told him to enjoy it, and then told him to find someplace else to continue his evening. But Harvath wasn't the bartender and this wasn't your average watering hole.

This was, at best, a place where Aga Sayed laundered his ill-gotten gains and at worst, a location from which he ran many of his criminal endeavors. No one here would want any problems with the cops.

Before he had even finished his fresh, second drink, Vijay was setting his sights further upmarket. Eyeing the top shelf, he was surprised to see a bottle of Johnnie Walker Blue.

"Is that real Johnnie Blue?" he asked. "Or bullshit used to fleece your tourist customers?"

To his credit, the barman maintained his cool. Though he resented the accusation, he replied, "No, sir. It is most definitely legitimate Johnnie Walker Blue Label whiskey."

"Good," said Vijay, a little heavier on the slurred speech. "I'll have one of those next."

"Very good, sir. It is eighteen hundred rupees a glass. How would you like to pay?"

The ex-cop got his wallet back out, opened it, and feigned disbelief that there was no cash.

"Perhaps you have a credit card I could run?" the bartender offered.

Vijay threw his hand dismissively in the air. "I canceled them. Only cash. No paper trail for my wife's attorney to trace."

Patting himself down, he stopped at his breast pocket and removed a tattered business card.

Placing it atop the bar, he used two fingers and dramatically slid it toward the barman.

"What am I supposed to do with this?" the man asked, studying the Indian Police Service logo and Vijay's rank as an inspector general.

"I'd like to establish a house account."

"In other words," the barman replied, "you want us to let you drink on credit."

"Isn't that what a house account is?" Vijay said, a bit acerbically, but not enough to arouse suspicion and blow his cover.

"I'll have to talk to my manager."

The ex-cop nodded and drained his second drink. "You do that," he said, holding up his empty glass. "In the meantime, I want that Johnnie Blue. It would be a shame if your business got a reputation for being anti-police."

The threat was unmistakable. The bartender poured him a Johnnie Blue on the rocks and then waved the manager over.

They met at the other end of the bar, where Harvath was, and discussed the situation. Even though Harvath didn't speak a word of Hindi, he could sense the general gist of the conversation.

The barman then handed over Vijay's business card and the manager disappeared through a curtain of green, plastic jewels, presumably to head to the office and call someone higher up the food chain. Hopefully, that person was Aga Sayed.

While they waited for a response, Harvath was relieved to see Vijay barely sipping at his whiskey. He had no doubt the ex-cop had a pretty healthy tolerance for alcohol, but he was already two in. They both needed to keep their wits about them.

His Godfather beer all but gone, Harvath ordered a Bira 91, so named for India's telephone code, and even though it was a much lower alcohol content, reminded himself to go slow. Even with a couple of drinks, he could still handle things, but there was no use in taking on too much unnecessary risk.

He could only imagine what his after-action report might look like if things went south. We had a shit plan, with no backup and zero support, which we thought adding alcohol to would improve.

There was no way that was going to fly. Not anywhere. Harvath, though, got an internal chuckle out of it. A dark sense of humor, after all, was a sign of high intelligence and Harvath's was pretty dark.

When the DJ launched into "Sympathy for the Devil," one of his favorites, by the Rolling Stones, he had that feeling again that he'd had in Kabul, that somebody up above liked him and was smiling down. Then, Aga Sayed appeared.

Before pulling away from the hotel, Vijay had shown him the man's arrest photo, as well as the photos taken of him shortly before he was released from prison.

The five years inside hadn't been kind to him. They had really aged him, thinning his hair, carving deep grooves across his otherwise unremarkable face, and hollowing him out. Looking at him now, his time on the outside hadn't done much to restore his vigor.

He sported a potbelly that strained the buttons of his shirt. The belt beneath his gut was under such strain that it was rolling, trying to get away from his flab.

His records stated that he was forty-nine, almost ten years younger to the day than Vijay. But he looked ten years older. That's what the streets and prison were known to do to a person.

He wore lots and lots of gold. He even had a gold tooth. He made Vijay look like a piker by comparison.

The man moved slowly, deliberately. He was trying to put on the air of a badass, like a shark circling his prey, but Harvath knew what was going on. The barometric pressure was dropping outside. The man's body was killing him. And the person responsible for his pain was sitting behind a glass of Johnnie Walker Blue, right within his sights.

Harvath felt pretty certain that this scumbag Sayed had never seen *Casablanca,* but he couldn't help but wonder if a special form of one of its most famous lines wasn't tumbling through his mind: Of all the gin joints in all the towns in all the world, Vijay Chabra walks into mine.

Behind Sayed trailed a couple of knuckle-dragging gorillas. Much bigger than the dynamic duo at the door, they wore matching, poorly tailored suits. Pistols, in shoulder holsters, could be seen bulging beneath their coats. Harvath did the math.

The bartender was lippy but didn't strike him as a fighter. If he had to guess, the drink-slinger wouldn't have pissed on his boss if the man were on fire. He didn't get paid enough. The two bouncers, however, had no choice. They were paid enough and, more specifically, they were paid to get physical. They would do what they were told. That made the odds five to two.

What Harvath and Vijay continued to have in their favor was that no one knew they were partners. They also had Sayed out in the open. The next phase of the plan was where things were going to get complicated. Extremely complicated.

Harvath had to give Vijay credit. The ex-cop had not only dangled the most irresistible piece of bait ever; he had also picked the right pond in which to dip his pole.

But this was where the real work started. Harvath had agreed that if Vijay stumbled into the club, appeared to be hammered, and found a way to work his business card up the ranks, he might be able to smoke Sayed out.

It was what was supposed to happen next, however, that was going to be the hardest part. And it was where Harvath and Vijay had parted ways on the plan.

There was simply no way Aga Sayed was going to walk out of there with him. Even if the ex-cop put a gun to his head and tried to force him out, there was always a chance that the guy could do something nuts like tell his men to open fire and let the chips fall where they may. That was the bravado of the gangster, after all. It was the sine qua non of the underworld.

No, as far as Harvath was concerned, the only way to successfully navigate the situation was to split the proverbial baby.

Vijay had wanted to get the drop on Sayed, seize the upper hand, and force him out of the club. His backup plan, if things went sideways, was what he had instructed Harvath to do—start a panic. In a flash of inspiration, Harvath had decided to do both.

In his estimation, the greatest obstacle they faced was Sayed's bodyguards. The pair needed to be incapacitated quickly and to the degree that they couldn't interfere and give chase. It was going to call for some pretty dramatic action.

Speed, surprise, and overwhelming violence of action, however, were Harvath's specialties.

Unless the barman had a sawed-off shotgun hidden nearby, or the manager popped out of the office wielding a weapon, he figured his plan had a fifty-fifty chance of working.

Not the best odds, but handling these kinds of situations was also his specialty. As long as they could continue to keep Murphy at bay, they might just might pull this off.

No sooner had the thought popped into his mind than Aga Sayed did something that changed everything.

CHAPTER 48

"Thullas don't get to drink in my bar," Sayed spat, pointing his gun at the back of Vijay's head. "Not even former thullas."

The ex-cop turned around slowly on his stool until he was facing him. "Aga Sayed," he replied. "It has been a long time."

"Not long enough. Give me one reason I shouldn't shoot you right here."

"I'll give you about a hundred of them," Vijay replied, gesturing to all the customers who had their eyes glued on them. "That's a lot of people to bribe, intimidate, or murder."

"What do you want, Chabra? Why the fuck are you here?"

"I just came in for a drink."

"Bullshit," the gangster hissed, showing a flash of his gold tooth. "Once a thulla, always a thulla. What the fuck are you doing here?"

"We're expecting a storm tonight. I thought I would come by and check on you. How are your bones feeling? Probably not so good, eh?"

Enraged, Sayed charged at him, growling, "Mardachod." *Motherfucker.* He pressed the barrel of his pistol right against Vijay's forehead and continued ranting, "Phaad-doong-aa!" *I will fuck your ass.* "Do you hear me, mardachod?!"

From where Harvath was sitting, things couldn't have been going worse. Not only did Sayed have the upper hand, but Vijay was actively trying to piss him off. *What the hell is he thinking?*

Even if Harvath wanted to act, he couldn't, not with the gangster's gun at the ex-cop's head. This continued to be the worst plan ever.

"Rand ke jamai!" the man yelled. *Whore's son-in-law!*

Vijay had officially had enough. Snapping his left hand up toward his face, he pivoted his body, grabbed the gun by the barrel, and pushed it down and away.

At the same time, he let loose with his right hand and landed a solid uppercut right beneath Sayed's chin.

Then, as he put his right hand on the weapon, he did a quick flip of his wrists, joint-locked Sayed, and stripped the pistol from him.

"Nobody talks about my mother-in-law that way," he replied, backhanding the gangster with his signet ring.

It was one of the slickest takeaways Harvath had ever seen. The ex-cop most definitely still had it.

The moment Vijay pointed the pistol at the gangster, the bodyguards had theirs unholstered and were aiming at him. It was a Mexican standoff on the backstreets of New Delhi. It was also untenable.

Looking to intimidate Vijay into dropping his weapon, the two men moved in closer. Bad idea.

As soon as they passed him, it gave Harvath the opening he needed.

While he would have liked to have shot them both in the head, John Wick–style, if a single round went astray, it could have killed one of the innocent patrons. That brought up another problem.

There were already a bunch of phones out recording and, very likely, livestreaming the standoff.

In America, that would have meant police were inbound. In the Paharganj neighborhood of New Delhi? That was anyone's guess. Harvath was willing to bet that if the cops even came, it was going to take a while to get there.

That meant they had time. What they didn't have was invisibility. Vijay, the victim, had taken the gun off of an attacker. Clear as day on video. It was also clean—from both a legal and physical injury standpoint—minus the two raps to the face Sayed had received. Whatever Harvath did, he was going to have to be just as clean.

It was two against one. But even though the bodyguards were armed, he couldn't use his own gun, not now that everything was being filmed.

Vijay's plan was like a candy store that had been custom built for Murphy's law to step in. No matter how bad things got, this scenario kept finding ways to get worse. Harvath needed to put a stop to it. And that was exactly what he did.

Polishing off his Bira 91, he slid off his stool, eased from behind his spot at the end of the bar, and came up behind the nearest bodyguard.

Having gotten a little education from Vijay on the ride from Jaipur about G-Company's fondness for glass bottles, he thought it might be poetic to put one of their members on the receiving end of one.

To his credit, Vijay had not looked in Harvath's direction. Not even once. Undoubtedly, he was wondering when, or worse, *if* his American colleague was going to make his move. That question was answered with just as much speed as when the ex-cop had bitch-slapped Sayed and taken away his gun.

Harvath smashed his beer bottle against the bodyguard's right temple and drove his foot into the back of the man's right knee.

As the bodyguard began to fold, Harvath reached down and grabbed his right hand, which was holding his pistol, and spun the man toward his stunned partner.

When the partner raised his weapon and prepared to fire, Harvath used his own finger to help apply pressure to his guy's trigger.

Both guns went off at the same time. Each of the bodyguards were hit, center mass, dead center of their chests, right through their hearts. Ugly, bloody, and fatal.

No longer needing him as a shield, Harvath let his guy drop. The other bodyguard had already fallen to the ground. It was over. The stampede of panicked customers, however, had just started.

It had been bad enough to see men with guns pointed at each other. They had all been frozen in their place. The moment the shooting started, they ran for cover. And as soon as it stopped, they bolted for the exits.

It was absolute pandemonium. Though there was a ton of pushing and shoving as people tried to make it out the door, miraculously no one was trampled or seriously injured.

Vijay had Sayed up against the bar. He kept him covered while Harvath patted the gangster down for weapons and then secured his hands behind his back with a pair of flex cuffs.

They weren't in the clear, not yet, but they had definitely moved the ball down the field and were within striking distance of the end zone.

All that was left to do was to get Sayed out the back and to a nearby abandoned building that Vijay had identified. Once there, the fiend's interrogation could begin. The ex-cop had something very special and very painful planned for him.

They were halfway to the back door when Harvath, who was leading the way, heard a sound from behind them that stopped his heart cold.

A shotgun had been racked. Just as quickly, someone fired.

CHAPTER 49

"Come on, man," Trey Davis said as his colleague closed the door to Nicholas's garage. "You can't continue to keep those dogs in there."

In the aftermath of the attack last night, Nina had been airlifted to Walter Reed. Nicholas had accompanied her in the helicopter, along with part of their security contingent.

The pilot had said "no" to bringing Argos and Draco. There wasn't any room. The dogs had stayed behind with the remaining members of the protective detail.

Jack Hauptmann gave Davis a don't-fuck-with-me look and replied, "I brought their beds down from upstairs. They've got plenty of food and water. They've been out several times already. And that fancy garage is totally climate controlled. They're fine. Lots of people keep their dogs in the garage."

"Leave it to a Marine to be afraid of a couple of canines."

"A, I'm not afraid of anything. And B, have you seen the way those dogs sit and stare at you? Like they're just waiting for the right moment to attack."

Davis chuckled. "They're highly intelligent animals, prized for their speed, strength, and loyalty. That's why the Russian military and the East German Border Patrol loved using them."

"How do you know so much?"

Davis held up his phone. "Google, dumbass."

Hauptmann gave him the middle finger. "They creep me the fuck out, so they get to chill in the garage. There were plenty of days in the Corps when I would have killed for accommodations like that. Absolute luxury compared to some of the bivouacs I saw."

"Pussy," Davis replied, smiling.

"Let me ask you something. How do you know when your date with a PJ is halfway over?"

Interservice rivalries were par for the course, both when you were active duty, and even when you got out and were doing private contracting. Davis had been an Air Force PJ, short for Pararescue Jumper, famous for recovering and administering medical attention to personnel trapped behind enemy lines.

"I give up," he said, humoring him. "How do you know when the date is half over?"

"Because the PJ says, 'Enough about me. Want to hear about all the cool gear I carry?'"

Davis chuckled once more. "Do you know why everything in the Marine Corps has to be broken down into five-step plans? Because Marines only have five fingers on one hand."

"Only one of which really matters," Hauptmann responded, flipping him the bird again. Then, pulling out a cigar, he informed his colleague, "I'm going up to that nice rooftop deck and am going to have a smoke."

"Is that a Cuban?" the eagle-eyed former PJ asked.

"Yep."

"Where'd you lay your hands on one of those?"

"There's a humidor next to the bar."

Davis looked at him. "You stole it?"

"Relax," the man replied. "I'm a Marine, not a Green Beret. Nick knows I love cigars and he told me to take one as a thank-you for watching the dogs."

"Are you kidding me?"

"Nope. I'm as serious as a leaky septic tank."

"Nice," Davis stated. "What you are, however, is an asshole. Do you think he would have let you have one of his expensive cigars if he knew you were going to lock his dogs in the garage?"

"For crying out loud, Air Force. My God, you're sensitive. Try downloading a meditation app or something. I'll be back in fifteen."

Davis watched as his colleague left the kitchen, got into the elevator, and headed upstairs. He was tempted to let the dogs out, just to fuck with Hauptmann, but figured it wasn't fair to Argos and Draco.

They were probably stressed enough as it was with Nicholas gone. Not to mention the fact that they might still be experiencing aftereffects from not one, but two Havana Syndrome attacks.

Davis was a badass, but that didn't mean that he didn't love animals. He did and he felt for Nicholas's dogs. They were, first and foremost, employees—protection tools, but even cops and military members came to see their canine counterparts as family.

He knew that owners of these kinds of dogs were taught to launch them at bad guys and use the time and distance that was created as an opportunity to escape, but he couldn't imagine abandoning them in a fight, using them and their commitment to you, as cannon fodder. Nevertheless, that was what they were bred and trained to do.

Grabbing the tablet from the dock in the kitchen, Davis focused on getting back to work.

Nicholas had issued everyone temporary access to his home security system. He had perimeter cameras around the house, but had never thought to wire the woods until now.

He had reassured his detail agents that there weren't any unexploded antipersonnel devices anywhere that they might accidentally trip over. Those were all locked safely away. He was, after all, a responsible father-to-be and had baby-proofed the entire estate.

Tapping on the different camera feeds, Davis cycled through the various surveillance sight lines.

With each camera he selected, his anxiety began to build. When he got to the last one, he instinctively reached for his radio, but stopped himself and instead reached for his weapon.

Pulling his pistol from its holster, he moved away from the kitchen windows. Picking the radio back up, he hailed Hauptmann.

Expecting that someone who shouldn't be listening had a radio and *was* listening, he said the only word that summed up the situation and would warn him, *"Contact."*

CHAPTER 50

Upon being tasked, the first thing Carbon did was to anonymously scour the internet for any mention of the missing agent, the weapon, or the target of the attack.

Via a neighborhood Facebook page, he saw a discussion about a series of "explosions" in the vicinity of the property that he knew belonged to the little man called the "Troll."

Authorities had reassured residents, stating that improperly stored propane cannisters had been the source. They said they had spoken with the property owner, whose name and address were not given, and that no further action would be undertaken.

While the members of the Facebook group seemed to accept the explanation, Carbon didn't. A series of explosions? The night the agent went missing? In the same locus where she was to carry out her assignment? That was too many coincidences. Carbon knew better than to believe in coincidences.

Quietly, he reached out to his law enforcement contacts, but they had come up empty. No one knew anything. He decided to prepare his gear and visit the scene himself.

Driving to the property, he pulled off the road, parked his vehicle in a remote area, and then hiked in. As soon as he saw the damage, he knew what had happened.

Walking over to one of the shredded trees, he took out his knife and removed a piece of shrapnel.

A claymore mine contained seven hundred steel balls, one-eighth of an inch in diameter. It was effective out to one hundred meters and was like being shot with a sawed-off shotgun.

Judging by the destruction, multiple mines had been used. The agent never stood a chance.

Most probably, she had made the mistake of returning to the same position she had used for the first attack. Whether it was out of carelessness or necessity didn't matter. Someone had been ready for her and she had walked right into their trap.

There was blood, but no body. There was also no sign of the weapon. The powers-that-be in Beijing would be very upset.

They would want answers. More importantly, they would want proof that their agent was in fact dead. They would also, no matter what the cost, want him to recover the weapon.

Standing among the trees, mindful of tripwires or other sensors, he stared at the large, stone house. That's where he would get his answers. And the sooner he got answers, the sooner he would be able to complete his assignment.

He moved quietly through the woods, a predator, pausing now and again to identify a sound or to sniff the crisp autumn air. He was hunting.

All of his senses were keen and on alert. From off in the distance, he could smell the pungent odor of cigar smoke. Near the driveway, he heard two men speaking as they walked and made their rounds. They would be his first kills.

After a quick reconnaissance, he had identified two additional men. One was in the kitchen off the garage and the other, the source of the cigar smoke, was up on the roof. The man he had come looking for—the Troll—wasn't visible.

The killer carried a suppressed Ruger Mark IV pistol loaded with 42-grain, Gemtech subsonic ammunition. He had added wire-pulling gel to the baffles of the suppressor and was firing it "wet," dampening the sound to a point where it was barely audible.

The only drawback to the weapon was that for it to be truly lethal, he had to get in close. That meant exposing himself to the cameras. He chose the best spot available for an ambush.

Based on their bearing, the men were all private security. And even though he couldn't see their weapons, he had to assume that they were armed.

Those weapons, however, were under their jackets, not in their hands. His weapon was in his hand, and action beat reaction *every* time.

Adding to his advantage, he could choose when to strike. There were no rules governing the kind of work that he did. All that mattered was the outcome.

He secreted himself where they wouldn't see him until it was too late. Taking a deep breath, he steadied his heart rate and visualized what was about to happen. The man in the blue jacket would die first. Then, the man in the gray.

Like coworkers the world over, one was sharing the banalities of his life with the other. He had a son leaving for college.

As their shoes crunched along the gravel, the man talked about his child's exceptional College Board scores, his regret at not starting a financial plan earlier, and how he was going to need to take out a second mortgage to pay for everything.

By the time the pair drew even with him, he was ready to shoot himself in order to not have to listen to them anymore.

They were not worthy of respect in his mind. They were no longer human. They were pencil marks in a ledger; rungs on a ladder he was charged with climbing. Their deaths were a fait accompli.

Stepping out in front of them, he took a fraction of a second to savor the delicious look of shock on their faces.

As the man in the blue jacket started to charge, he shot him through his left eye. The bullet bore into his brain. The momentum he had started allowed him to take two additional steps before he collapsed to the ground, dead.

The man in the gray jacket had his hand on the butt of his pistol and was pulling it from its holster when the killer put a round into his forehead, just above the bridge of his nose. It was like throwing a circuit breaker. He dropped as rapidly as his colleague had.

He quickly pulled both men out of view of the cameras. Very seldom were residential security feeds being monitored in real time. Nevertheless, he didn't want to risk exposing his presence. He had at least two more targets, and hopefully a third, waiting for him inside. Taking a radio off one of the corpses, he listened for any communication that would suggest that he had been spotted.

At first everything was quiet. There was zero traffic. Then came one word that told him he no longer had the element of surprise.

"Contact."

CHAPTER 51

Using a Lishi tool to pick the lock, Carbon quietly opened one of the patio doors and slipped inside.

There was a flash of movement from the man in the kitchen. He had a pistol in his hand and was headed deeper into the house. The killer decided to follow.

Most probably, he was moving to link up with the other operative from the roof. Per Military Operations on Urban Terrain, or "MOUT" training, if the home had an elevator, the man coming down would not be using it—not in a tactical situation. It was a hard-and-fast rule.

In fact, in the early stages of Russia's invasion of Ukraine, the killer had been stunned to see CCTV footage of Russian paratroopers trapped in an elevator in the city of Kharkiv.

As soon as the doors had closed and the carriage had begun to rise, a clever group of Ukrainian soldiers had simply cut the power, imprisoning the Russians inside.

Then, after ordering the paratroopers to disarm—and verifying everything via the CCTV—the Ukrainians returned the elevator to the lobby, met the Russians with an overwhelming show of force, and took them all prisoner. It had been positively shocking to witness how flaccid and inept Russia's military actually was.

But right now, Carbon wasn't dealing with Russians, he was dealing with Americans. And, based on everything he knew about the Carlton Group, they only employed highly skilled, former Special Operations personnel.

He'd had the upper hand with the two men outside. They'd had no idea of the impending attack; no opportunity to prepare. The two men he was hunting now, however, were in fact prepared and likely *expecting* his attack.

There had been no sign, thus far, of the Troll. If he was inside the house, the men would be working to get him to a safe location within the structure and would be summoning backup.

If the little man wasn't in the home, it meant a different set of rules and an entirely different ball game.

The men wouldn't be sitting still, waiting for him to come to them. They would also be hunting.

And they had a distinct advantage. They knew the house inside and out. He was on their terrain.

As he crept cautiously forward, his pistol at the ready, he passed a well-appointed bar, its shelves stocked with expensive brandies and liquors.

Farther ahead, he saw a massive, ornately carved staircase, with an elevator rising out of its center, enclosed in wood paneling.

The elevator's door was closed but he could hear that it was moving. The only question was, was it going up, or was it coming down?

The killer didn't like it. It had to be a trap. Even if the Troll had trouble navigating stairs, his security detail would never let him use the elevator. They'd pick him up and carry him if they had to.

In a house this big and this expensive, there had to be a panic room. Considering the little man's inability to move quickly on such tiny legs, there was probably more than one.

If the killer had to guess, there'd be one adjacent to the Troll's bedroom, as well as his office or study. Maybe something off the kitchen or the dining room that could do double duty, such as a reinforced pantry. If the little man was in the house, one of those places is where the operatives would have rushed him.

What was the purpose of the elevator moving, then? A distraction? A means by which to hold the intruder's attention and buy themselves a little more time? Carbon soon had a partial answer.

The elevator wasn't on its way up. It was on its way down. Without knowing where the corresponding electrical panel was located, he couldn't do what the Ukrainians had done to the Russians and cut the power, potentially trapping any occupants inside.

But he was convinced that would also be a waste of time. Someone was trying to slow him down.

In fact, he wouldn't have been surprised if the elevator arrived, the door opened, and it was empty. Then, on closer inspection, he'd see that the trapdoor in the ceiling was unlatched and he'd waste further time investigating.

Or worse—and he wouldn't put it past Special Operations types—there'd be a claymore up there waiting to take his head off. He wasn't going to walk into that kind of a trap—or any other. He had a better idea.

Retracing his steps, he moved back toward the rear of the house. From his reconnaissance outside, he had seen a line of zigzagging windows. They resembled enlarged arrow slits and suggested an additional staircase leading to the upper floors.

In less than two minutes, he had found it. The circular stairs were cut from limestone, as were the walls. He took great pains not to make any noise that might radiate ahead of him and tip off his opponents to his approach.

At the second-floor landing he stepped into the hallway. Clearing rooms by one's self was an absolute worst-case scenario. No one in their right mind would do it solo if given the choice.

But Carbon hadn't been given a choice and there were many who believed he had never possessed a "right mind" to begin with.

Soundlessly, he advanced from room to room, looking for any sign of his quarry. There was none. Reentering the stairwell, he moved up to the next level.

The third story was the last full floor of the house. The only thing above it was the fourth-floor observation deck.

Carbon moved even slower now. Barely breathing. Not making any noise whatsoever. The men were close. Their scent was in the air. The lingering smell of cigar smoke, as if carried on someone's clothing, was unmistakable.

He made his way to the end of the hall. There, in front of him, was the arched stone entrance to the master bedroom. Its heavy, walnut door stood ajar. The killer paused.

Something felt off. It was too easy. The smell of cigar smoke. The open door. Even if there was a panic room within, why not close and lock the master entry? The door was almost three inches thick and, befitting a fortress, was replete with heavy iron hardware. He would have needed an axe and an afternoon to get through it. No, this wasn't right at all.

Now he was torn. Back up and wait them out? Or press on and potentially be drawn into a trap?

There was also the possibility that reinforcements were already inbound and they were trying to get him to spin his wheels until they arrived. But why leave the door open?

If the Troll was with them, their number one job was to protect him until the threat could be eliminated or he could be evacuated from the property and relocated someplace safe.

But, if he wasn't with them, why would these two guys be hiding? Why wouldn't they be bringing the fight to him? It didn't make any sense. He had his orders, which meant that there was only one thing he could do.

Carefully, he nudged the door open and did a quick peek inside. A jacket, much too large to belong to the Troll, had been tossed onto the bed. A stubbed out, partially smoked cigar balanced on the edge of the nightstand.

So, at least one of the men he was looking for had been in this room. The question was, was he still here? And where was the other one? He was going to have to commit to clearing the master to get his answer.

Making sure to avail himself of any cover and concealment, he pushed into the room, pistol up, ready for whatever might come. Nothing did. Something, however, did catch his eye.

Inside the Troll's enormous, walk-in closet, surrounded by infant-sized clothing, was what looked like a freestanding tornado shelter wrapped in some sort of gold metallic fabric.

It was rigged with an HVAC system and had massive amounts of cables and wires plugged into it. It was probably an SCIF of some sort, but not like any SCIF he had ever seen. Whether it was also functioning as a panic room at this moment was the biggest unknown. That, and whether hidden underneath the foil were any gunports from which he could be shot at.

Grabbing an edge of the foil with his free hand, he began tearing it away. He pulled the material off the front and then all the way down one side. There were no gunports that he could see.

He tried to open it, but it was locked. There was a keypad next to the door and he punched in a few random combinations, but nothing worked. Each attempt was greeted by a blinking red light and an error buzzer. He gave up.

The container appeared to be fabricated out of thick steel and probably offered a certain level of ballistic protection. He'd need a plasma cutter or, if it was thicker than two inches, an oxyacetylene torch to get in there. Despite everything else he had brought for this job, neither of those items had been on the list. He would literally have to "smoke" them out.

Taking a look again at the HVAC system, he realized that while the steel box might function as an impromptu panic room, that wasn't its primary goal. It was likely stuffed with computer equipment that needed to be kept cool. That was the container's Achilles' heel. If he could get a fire going in the system, the container would fill with smoke and they'd have no choice but to open the door.

He moved back into the bedroom proper, looking for anything that would be easy to burn and would create a lot of smoke.

That was when he heard a noise from the hallway.

It wasn't a groaning floorboard or a door creaking on its hinges. It was the telltale sound of battle rattle—one piece of tactical gear bumping up against another. And it had the effect of a starting gun being fired.

As Carbon dove for cover, the two men he had been hunting stepped into the doorway wearing chest rigs and carrying CZ Scorpion EVO 3 A1 submachine guns.

Somehow they had not only managed to evade him and sneak up on him from behind, but they had also completely upgraded their equipment. That was why the cigar smoker's jacket was on the bed. It was much easier to throw a chest rig on over a shirt. They probably had gear stored in the foil-wrapped SCIF.

The bullets from the Scorpions rained down like liquid fire and reverberated throughout the stone room like amplified thunder.

Everything was being torn up. Chips of stone, plaster, and splintered wood choked the air. Carbon was pinned down and had yet to return fire.

The two men took turns shooting, each covering the other while he reloaded. For the assassin, it was like being the target of some crazed helicopter gunship.

It was relentless. The intensity of the rounds coming at him was off the charts. These guys obviously had one very specific rule of engagement—no survivors. It explained the scale of devastation from the antipersonnel devices in the woods. In short, the Carlton Group didn't fuck around.

Neither did Carbon.

Transitioning his pistol to his left hand, he slid a fragmentation grenade from the equipment belt beneath his jacket, removed the pin, and prepared to hurl it toward his attackers, but he couldn't pull his arm all the way back. Something was wrong.

Looking down at his shoulder, he saw that it was drenched in blood. He had been shot.

He set his pistol in his lap, visualized the distance to the hallway, and, using his left hand, tossed the grenade through the oncoming fire.

It bounced against the doorframe, landed on the threshold, and before the two men could scramble to cover, detonated.

The hail of shrapnel had been close enough to do serious damage, but not close enough to kill them.

Carbon had used the explosion to scramble into the Troll's side of the his-and-her bathroom. He needed a towel, antiseptic, and medical supplies, but all of that would have to wait until he was sure he had neutralized the threat.

Passing through the other bathroom, he found a door that was open onto the hall. Both men were slumped against the wall, bleeding as bad as him. Their weapons lay nearby, but not in their hands.

Still deadly accurate, he stepped out of the bathroom with his pistol in his left hand.

"Who else is on the property?" he demanded. "Who's on their way?"

Davis looked at him and smiled, weakly. "Everyone is on their way. They're *all* coming."

"Where's the man they call the Troll?"

"Never met him."

Carbon kept his eyes locked with Davis, turned his pistol on Hauptmann, and shot him in the stomach.

The Marine roared in agony and struggled to get to his rifle. The assassin, his ears still ringing from the gunfight, kicked both weapons away and relieved the men of their sidearms.

"I'll ask you one last time," he said. "Where's the Troll? Tell me, or the next round goes through your colleague's skull."

Suddenly there was a voice from behind. Someone had climbed the stairs, but he hadn't heard them coming.

"I'm right here, motherfucker," Nicholas taunted.

The man spun, raising his weapon. Nicholas, however, was faster and shot him through his other shoulder, causing him to drop his gun. Davis kicked it away.

Then, signaling Argos and Draco, Nicholas gave them the command to attack.

CHAPTER 52

The driveway in front of Nicholas's home had become a sea of black Suburbans, red-and-white ambulances, and multicolored law enforcement vehicles.

Had Nicholas not returned home when he did, had he not ignored the orders of the two agents accompanying him to wait for backup, had he not released the dogs and charged upstairs, Davis and Hauptmann wouldn't have made it. They owed Nicholas their lives. And Nicholas knew they would have done the same for him. They were family.

The timing of his return had been fortuitous, to say the least. He had only come back to pick up some things for Nina and return to the hospital. It had been an incredibly difficult night.

Exposure to the Havana Syndrome device had sent Nina into painful, premature labor. She had screamed the entire flight and had almost given birth on the helicopter.

Nine minutes after arriving at Walter Reed, she delivered a baby girl. They had decided to name their daughter Caroline, after Nina's deceased sister, who had also been a dear friend to Nicholas.

But before either of the parents could hold their newborn baby, the infant was transferred to the neonatal intensive care unit with heart and breathing issues.

None of the doctors knew what was wrong with her, nor whether it would be permanent. Nina was the first pregnant woman to have ever been struck with Havana Syndrome. Both she and Nicholas were beside themselves.

In the chapel that had come with the house, he did something he had seldom ever done before: he got down on his knees and prayed.

He prayed for Nina, he prayed for their baby, and he prayed for the strength they would all need going forward.

Then, exiting the chapel, he set his mind on revenge. No matter who was behind these attacks, he vowed to make every last one of them pay.

CHAPTER 53

Upon hearing the rack of the slide, Harvath had turned around. He was just in time to see the manager of the Laid Back point his shotgun at Vijay.

But before Harvath could shoot him, someone else had put a round right through the man's head.

As the manager fell to the ground, Harvath saw a very good-looking woman holding a very serious, smoking Glock pistol.

"Sayed's my prisoner," she said, keeping both Harvath and Vijay within her sights.

"And who are you?" the ex-cop asked, tightening his grip on the gangster.

"None of your business."

"You want *our* prisoner. After we did the work of capturing him. I kind of think it is our business."

"I've got this, Vijay," Harvath stated, pointing his pistol at the woman. "Keep walking this way."

"I'm not going to say it again. Stop moving. I'm taking the prisoner," she ordered.

From the glass doors at the front of the club, blue police lights could suddenly be seen.

"Mr. Sayed must have good friends at the local police station to warrant such a quick response time," Vijay offered. "If we don't all go together, none of us is going to get out of here. And this asshole, whoever's prisoner he may be, is going to go free."

The woman thought about it for a moment. Then, lowering her weapon and pushing her way through to lead the way to the back door, she said, "Follow me. I have a vehicle a few blocks away."

"So do we," Harvath replied. "But that's not the plan. We're not doing that. Especially not now with the cops starting to pour in."

She looked at him. "What do you suggest, then?" she asked. "What's *your* plan?"

"Come," said Vijay as he nodded for Harvath to take the lead and keep going. "You'll see."

• • •

The abandoned building the ex-cop had selected was down a pitch-black alley less than two blocks away.

As expected, Sayed had been difficult to transport. At one point he had begun yelling and screaming for help. Vijay, however, had come prepared. Pulling a gag out of his pocket, he tied it around the man's face.

He warned him that if he strained against it or tried to cry out, razor blades, courtesy of his old partner whom Sayed had tried to gut, had been sewn into it and he was in for quite a surprise. Needless to say, the man didn't give them much additional trouble.

In the abandoned building, Vijay had pre-positioned a handful of supplies. As Harvath secured their prisoner to a chair, the ex-cop ignited a small camping burner and carefully placed a metal hubcap atop it.

The hubcap was filled with charcoal, which he ignited with a small kitchen torch. Once the coals were going, he dumped in the contents of a small plastic bag. There were nuts, bolts, nails, and what looked like roofing tacks, all of various sizes. Sayed, his eyes wide, was paying nervous attention to everything that was going on.

"Were you really a cop?" the woman asked as Vijay went about his work.

"For over three decades."

She pointed at Harvath. "What about him? Something tells me he doesn't work for the Indian Police Service."

The ex-cop smiled. She had spirit. He liked that. "No. He's with the U.S. government."

"And who gave the U.S. government the right to violate Indian sovereignty and deny rights to one of its citizens?"

"Oh, God," said Vijay. "You're a lawyer. This night just got a lot worse."

"I'm not a lawyer. Now answer my question."

Careful not to burn his hands, the ex-cop used a towel to lift the hubcap and shake the contents, making sure that everything was heating evenly, before placing it back on the burner. "Not until you tell us who you are."

"My name is Asha Patel," she responded, done playing games. "I work for RAW. Mr. Sayed is wanted for questioning regarding an attempted kidnap and murder plot."

"Of whom?"

She paused a moment too long, which caused Harvath to toss out an opinion. "He tried to have you captured, didn't he? I'll bet that was a mistake. How many of his guys did you take out?"

"Several," she stated. "What's your business with him?"

"He's wanted for questioning in the murder of an American citizen in Jaipur."

"So that's why the United States government is involved. Does my government know that you are over here investigating?"

"Yes," Harvath replied, cautious not to reveal too much. "And before we go any further, I want to—"

"What's your name?" she asked, taking out her phone and prepping a text to Raj.

"Joseph Sampson," he stated, providing the alias he was traveling under.

"Middle name?"

"John."

"But you can call him JJ," Vijay offered, winking.

Asha ignored him. "And the U.S. Embassy here in New Delhi will also vouch for you?"

Harvath nodded.

"Do you have a diplomatic passport?"

He removed it from his pocket and held it up.

"May I inspect it?"

"No," said Harvath. "Not until we get some proof as to *your* bona fides."

Asha looked up from her phone. "Fair enough. What would satisfy you?"

Harvath checked his watch. "Have someone at RAW contact the CIA station chief and confirm your identity for us."

"At this time of night?"

"If you are who you say you are and this is all legit, it shouldn't be a problem."

"Before I do," she declared, "what's the connection between you two? Why are you working with a retired IPS officer?"

"I work for the U.S. Embassy," the ex-cop interjected. "My name, in case you missed it in the bar, is—"

"Vijay Chabra," she replied.

The man smiled. She was good. "The station chief knows me. But feel free to have your people certify my identity as well."

"Give me a few minutes," said Asha as she stepped away to communicate with her boss.

"What do you think?" Harvath asked, once she was out of earshot.

"I think we may not have a lot of time with *our* prisoner. RAW isn't going to care about our investigation. They'll pull rank, a team will get sent in, and they'll help her take Sayed and move him someplace else."

Harvath wasn't so sure. "Why not do that from the beginning? If RAW, especially as an agency, is so interested in Sayed, why send her in alone?"

"Good point."

"I'm not exactly sure what's going on, but she's not being completely straight with us."

"Is this the human lie detector speaking?" Vijay asked.

"Just my gut."

"In my experience, you should always listen to your gut."

"Agreed," said Harvath. "And in case you're right, I think we should get started on Sayed."

The ex-cop shook the hubcap once more and checked the coals, which were starting to glow bright orange. Then, speaking loud enough for their prisoner to hear, he announced, "We're almost ready." Nodding toward the corner of the room, he asked Harvath for a favor. "There's a soda bottle over there. Would you be kind enough to fetch it for me? We're going to need it for what comes next."

CHAPTER 54

By the time Asha came back over and asked if she could have a moment with him in private, Harvath had already received a series of texts from Lawlor and had responded.

Checking out the coals in Vijay's hubcap, he stated, "Not hot enough yet. Keep working on those."

"If we get them too hot," the ex-cop replied with a smirk that Sayed couldn't see, "they'll melt the bottle."

"Then we'll just find another. There's plenty more."

Vijay nodded and gave the hubcap a few shakes with the towel as Harvath walked away to speak with Asha.

They stood near the entrance of the building, far enough away that Vijay and Sayed couldn't hear them speaking, and deep enough in the darkness that no one from the alleyway would notice them.

"I assume you've heard from your boss back in the United States?" she asked.

"I have," he replied. "And you, yours?"

Asha nodded. "So, may I call you Scot? Or do I have to call you JJ?"

Harvath smiled. "For right now, don't call me anything. It'll be easier."

Asha smiled back. "So, it sounds like we're in similar boats, with very little support, and pursuing a similar goal."

"With the stakes rising by the day. I'm sorry about the attempt on your life this morning. I didn't mean to make light of it."

"It's okay."

"I was also sorry to hear about the helicopter crash that killed your chief of Defense Staff. Do you have any more information on it?"

"We believe some sort of directed-energy weapon may have been involved," she replied. "The Chinese have begun fielding a couple of different kinds. We have a piece of video evidence, which we believe shows one in action in Coonoor."

"You should encourage your boss to share that video with my boss. We just recovered a directed-energy weapon that was being used against a colleague of mine back in the U.S. Our top scientists are currently all over it."

"I will encourage him to forward it. You know the Chinese also used some sort of energy weapon against Indian forces in the Himalayas a few months ago."

"I read the reports," said Harvath. "Some sort of microwave device. Heated up the water molecules under their skin, caused a lot of headaches, dizziness, and vomiting. Allowed the attacking Chinese soldiers to retreat."

Asha nodded. "I interviewed the Snow Warriors' commander. Gathering further intelligence about the event was part of my portfolio. His personal account is gut-wrenching. Both the telling of the attack and the aftermath. While I appreciate the political message it sends to China, I can't believe they've decided to winter in the Galwan Valley."

"It was the right decision. And I'm proud to admit that my organization had a little bit to do with it."

"*Your* organization?"

Harvath nodded. "The Snow Warriors are an amazing regiment. India is right to be very proud of them. But they lacked the infrastructure for a prolonged, high-altitude, overwinter deployment. We fixed that and sourced everything they needed—all premium, top-of-the-line gear. Insulated tents, camping stoves, snowshoes, subzero sleeping bags. We wanted your soldiers to have the absolute best."

"There was a lot of speculation in the ranks as to where it came from," she replied. "No labels. No made in 'X' country."

"We employed a team, around the clock, for two weeks that removed all the tags and erased any signs of origin. While we hate Beijing as much as you do, Washington wanted this to be off the radar."

"Like the negotiations over an Asian version of NATO."

Suddenly she was striking right at the heart of why they were both standing in this abandoned building, ready to let Vijay do whatever he was about to do to Sayed.

Harvath nodded. "Yes."

"And why shouldn't America and India formalize an alliance?" she asked. "The threats to democracy are only growing. From Pakistan's relationship with China and Iran, to what the Russians have done to Ukraine. We can't pretend that strong coalitions don't serve as the ultimate bulwark and aren't absolutely necessary."

He really liked the way she saw the situation. "Agreed. India is a natural partner for the United States. As our ambassador to the United Nations has said, you're a nuclear power with over one million troops, a growing navy, a top-tier space program, and a proven history of economic and military cooperation with the United States. Together, with Japan and Australia, we wouldn't just maintain our global strength, but expand it."

"It also makes a lot of sense on our end," Asha replied. "The Chinese Communist Party has been providing far too much support to our number one enemy, Pakistan. Through the China-Pakistan Economic Corridor, Beijing has not only shored up Pakistan's faltering electrical grid, but has provided medical supplies, and helped ease Pakistan's growing national debt. At this point, there isn't anything China could ask that Pakistan wouldn't do."

"And," said Harvath, "there's all the ways we can assist each other in the cyber realm. We got hit by a crippling Russian attack on one of our major pipelines recently and the Chinese hit you with an electrical grid attack that cut off power for twenty million residents in Mumbai. It just makes sense for the world's oldest and largest democracies to be aligned."

Asha now nodded. "I agree. And, more importantly, my boss agrees and wants us to work together."

"Good. That means that everything comes down to what we learn from Aga Sayed."

"I'm with you."

"Are you?" Harvath asked. "Because I agree with Vijay. A couple of minutes ago, you were sounding a lot like a lawyer. When we go back in there, it's not going to be anyplace a lawyer wants to be. I'm just going to warn you."

"A couple of minutes ago, I didn't know what I do now. In India, knowledge is a virtue. As a wise person once said, we cannot control the direction of the wind, but we can always control how we trim our own sails."

"So you're going to be able to handle what is going to go down in there?"

"Meaning can I stomach it?" she asked.

Harvath nodded.

"I don't know. Maybe we should go back and ask the manager of the Laid Back. How about you? Are you going to be okay with it?"

He nodded again.

"Just ask Sayed's bodyguards," Asha replied. "Right?"

Harvath smiled. "You'll be fine. Let's go."

CHAPTER 55

O ut of a canvas bag, Vijay produced a pair of long metal tongs—the kind you might see in a foundry or a glassworks. It didn't take much time to understand why the tongs were present.

One by one, he picked up each of the red-hot pieces of metal from the pile of glowing coals in the hubcap and examined them. As he did, Aga Sayed continued to watch.

Harvath walked over to him and loosened the gag. There were cuts at the corners of his mouth and along the sides of his face. The ex-cop hadn't been lying. He really had sewn razor blades into the gag. Harvath was impressed.

"Okay, Sayed," he said. "Collectively, we built a pile of dead bodies getting to you. If you think that somehow you're leaving this place without telling us what we want to know, you are sorely mistaken. So, question number one: Who killed Eli Ritter in Jaipur?"

Sayed looked up at him and replied, "I don't know."

"Not a good answer. Who killed Ritter?"

"Fuck you. That's who."

Harvath nodded to Vijay that it was time to begin.

The ex-cop used the tongs to retrieve a blistering-hot bolt from the coals, walked over, and paused as he decided where he was going to brand the son of a bitch who had gutted his partner.

"This is just the start, Sayed," said Harvath. "You know why he asked me to get the soda bottle, right?"

"Fuck you," the man spat, looking to his left, trying to anticipate what Vijay was going to do.

"Don't look at him," Harvath admonished. "Look at me. I'm the one you need to talk to. I'm the one you need to convince you're telling the truth."

"Fuck you," the gangster repeated.

Harvath looked at Vijay. "I love when they do that. It's so brave. So macho. And," he said, grabbing Sayed's jaw with his hand, "so fucking pointless because they have absolutely no power. Do you understand that, Aga? You have zero power here. No one is coming to save you. I decide what happens to you. I decide how much pain you experience. I decide whether you live or whether you die. So, last chance. Who killed Ritter?"

"Fuck you. Fuck him. And fuck her," Sayed said, singling out each of them.

"Okay," Harvath replied. "Just remember, you asked for this."

Stepping back, he nodded once again to Vijay and watched as the ex-cop moved in and pressed the red-hot bolt against the monster's left nipple.

The man screamed like a stuck pig.

Actually, he screamed worse than a stuck pig. It was some of the worst wailing Harvath had ever heard.

He let the man wallow in his pain for a few more moments and then leaned in and asked, "When you had your men rape the wife, mother, and baby daughter of Vijay's informant, do you think they cried louder or softer than you?"

Sayed didn't reply. He sat there, strapped to the chair, hyperventilating, while tears streamed down his face. The bolt had burned right through his shirt and had seared his sensitive flesh like a branding iron.

"That piece of pain," said Harvath, "was just the beginning. We needed to make sure that everything was hot enough. And judging by the results, it's looking pretty good.

"Now, because I'm not a monster like you, I'm going to give you a choice. We brought a small amount of burn cream with us. You can use it over the next half hour of things we're going to do, or you can save it for the grand finale.

"And by grand finale, I mean when we put the remaining pieces of hot metal into the bottle and shove it up your ass. That's the G-Company signature, right? The people who survive it are said to shit razor blades for the rest of their life, right?

"Do you offer them any lube? I'm guessing you don't. I probably shouldn't, either. It's really best if you get a true taste of your own medicine. Vijay, however, wanted as much hot, sharp steel as we could get in you as possible. He didn't think it was right that you only thought of him when a storm was coming. He wanted you to think of him all the time.

"But if you ask me, I think he's overthinking it. There's no way you're going to survive. And best part of all, when the tabloids find you here, with your pants around your ankles—and they will find you first, because we're going to call them—no one is ever going to look for us. We're going to get off scot-free, because everyone—even the cops and the people in your own organization—are going to believe that you deserved it and that it was carried out by some rival organization that no one will bother wasting the time to investigate.

"So, you need to understand that you don't have a single card left to play. If you don't cooperate with me, you're going to experience pain the likes of which you have never imagined before tonight. I am going to make you pay for every sin you have ever committed. And at the very moment you think you can't take any more, not a single, additional ounce of pain, I'm going to see to it that you do. Are we clear?"

Harvath waited for the gangster to respond and when he didn't, he said to Vijay, "Okay, time for round two."

This time he selected a metal nut from the coals. "Ear canal or nasal passage?" he asked.

Harvath looked at Sayed to see if he had a preference. Once again, the man didn't respond.

"If you shove that in his nostril," said Harvath, "he'll only be able to snort cocaine on one side. By the same token, if you stick that far enough in his ear, he'll probably go deaf and not be able to hear anyone who sneaks up on that side. If it were me, I wouldn't want to lose my hearing. So, definitely shove that thing as far as you can into his ear. You pick which one."

Sayed had absolutely no reason to doubt that the ex-cop was going to do it. He was already in more fucking pain than he had ever been since that asshole had tossed him off the building. He couldn't go on. He needed to make it stop. These people were completely psychotic.

"Stop," he pleaded.

"Sorry, Aga," Harvath replied. "It's kind of like a children's party. Once you remove a treat from the bowl, it can't be put back. You're going to have to take your medicine. Maybe next time I ask you who killed Eli Ritter, you'll be a little more polite and a hell of a lot more forthcoming."

"I don't know who killed him," the man insisted.

"And herein lies our problem," said Harvath. "You want me to do something for you, but you're absolutely unwilling to do anything for me. You're not really a good negotiator, are you?"

Sayed became even more insistent. "I cannot tell you his name because all I did was make arrangements for him."

"What kind of arrangements?"

"If I tell you, will you let me go?"

Turning back to Vijay, Harvath instructed, "Pick whatever ear you want and let's get this over with."

"The gun!" Sayed yelled as the ex-cop closed in on him with the tongs and the flaming-hot piece of metal. "The gun, and the silencer, and the hotel room, and the motorcycle. All of it."

Harvath signaled for Vijay to wait. "And who asked you to make these arrangements?"

"He is a very bad man."

"People who arrange murders usually are," Harvath replied. "For your sake, I hope you've got a name to give me."

"I do," said Sayed. "I do. Just don't let him put that in my ear."

"There's nothing I can do if you don't come out with it. Hurry up."

"All I know is that he's originally from Pakistan and he goes by the name Malek Hamid."

Harvath doubted that was everything Aga Sayed knew. But he wasn't worried. Vijay had brought lots of additional surprises and they had all night to get to the bottom of things.

CHAPTER 56

"Malek Hamid is one of multiple aliases he uses," said Lawlor. "His real name is Basheer Durrani. He's a deep-cover operative working for the Pakistani ISI."

Harvath had been feeding information from Sayed's interrogation back to his boss in Northern Virginia.

When Lawlor gave him the update, his first question was, "How'd we get our hands on that intel?"

"*You* actually secured it."

"Me?" replied Harvath. "When?"

"When you helped get Topaz and his family out of Afghanistan. He had uploaded a trove of encrypted data to the cloud. Once they landed in D.C. and were handed their American passports, he gave us all of the passwords.

"While Pakistan might have been one of the first nations to recognize and formally establish diplomatic ties with China, Beijing has been trying to wrap Afghanistan in its tentacles.

"China signed a thirty-year copper mining agreement for the Mes Aynak deposit outside Kabul—the second largest in the world—and is spending fifty million dollars to help set up a Taliban-controlled TV and radio network, and is dangling the construction of a nationwide railroad network as part of bringing Afghanistan into the Belt and Road Initiative."

"For which," Harvath said, "Beijing will not only have the government in Kabul by the throat, but I imagine the CCP will demand a lot of dirty work in exchange."

"Correct," Lawlor replied. "They want the Taliban to agree to help crush an al Qaeda–affiliated group of Uyghur fighters formerly known as the East Turkestan Islamic Movement and now called the Turkestan Islamic Party, or TIP. Pakistan has already agreed and is actively helping China in this regard. The TIP has cells in multiple countries. It has been agitating for independence of a large portion of Xinjiang, which shares a border with a handful of nations including Afghanistan, Pakistan, Russia, and India."

"So it's kind of a reverse extortion racket. Afghanistan gets money and infrastructure and in return China gets its Muslim terrorism issue cleaned up."

"More or less," said Lawlor. "But there's also the U.S. Defense Department study that projects Afghanistan is sitting on deposits of various minerals including copper, rare earths, and lithium valued at over one trillion dollars. So, the sooner China can get its hooks into Afghanistan, the better."

"With all of the blood and treasure we spent over there, the United States should own a permanent piece of any money that comes out of that ground."

"I know a lot of people who would agree with you. But you and I know that's not how we roll. We went with the objective of denying terrorists a sanctuary, got caught up in nation building, and then pulled out. It was never about plundering another nation's resources."

Harvath understood the argument. The same could be said for Iraq. He had lost a lot of good friends in both countries and couldn't help but view both wars through that lens.

Be that as it may, he—like them—was a soldier. He would do what he was ordered to do. Right now, he had a mission to accomplish.

"Did Topaz have any other information on Durrani?" he asked.

"The dossier he uploaded was thin, but we've got a photo, as well as the NGO in New Delhi he allegedly has been working for as a cover."

"Send it to me."

"I will. There's also something else that may be of interest."

"What's that?" Harvath asked.

"A Romanian intelligence officer named Alexandru Suliman. He met

Durrani while studying at Pakistan's School of Military Intelligence and introduced him to a pretty wild brothel and swinger's club in Bucharest called the Terrace Club. At some point, the two drifted apart. Suliman thought Durrani's predilections were grotesque and quite cruel. It offended his sense of honor.

"He also didn't like that Durrani kept making visits to Bucharest, claiming to the ISI that he was coming to groom Suliman as a double agent against Romanian intelligence. So, he decided to screw him.

"Suliman tried to sell a blackmail packet to Afghan intelligence. When they passed, rumor has it that he sold it to the Chinese. It's all in the file."

"Good copy," said Harvath. "I'll read everything and get back to you."

Disconnecting the call, he approached Asha.

"Is everything okay?" she asked.

"We may have a lead."

"Leads are good. What is it?"

"We've been able to get our hands on a dossier that belongs to the man Sayed referred to as Malek Hamid."

"That's fantastic," said Asha. "Who is he?"

"A deep-cover operative for the ISI, based here in New Delhi," he replied, watching as her face flushed with anger.

"So, it was the *fucking* ISI who tried to have me killed?"

"The Chinese were probably involved as well. Listen, I need a favor."

"I'll trade you for the dossier," she offered. "My boss is going to want to see everything you've got on this guy. So will I."

"I think that can be arranged," Harvath responded. "But first things first. I don't think Sayed has much more to offer either of us. That doesn't mean Vijay can't squeeze some more out of him that might help the IPS regarding various criminal activities. But the bottom line is that we can't cut him loose, not right away. If we do, he's going to find a way to warn our ISI operative. We also can't keep him here. We need someplace else."

"What did you have in mind?"

"To be honest," said Harvath, "I don't really care. A broom closet would work, provided it was secure and nobody knew where we were holding him. Do you have any suggestions?"

Asha smiled. "Actually, I have the perfect location."

CHAPTER 57

Harvath had to give Onkar Raj major credit. Hiding a black operation beneath a school for the blind was beyond brilliant.

And what was ironic was that Harvath was staying at the hotel right next door, and he'd had no idea any of it was there.

By moving Sayed out of the abandoned building in Paharganj and stashing him at the Blind Relief Association, they not only improved their security posture, but were able to establish shifts where someone would always be watching him. Harvath had laughed out loud when Gupta offered up an actual broom closet to keep him in.

Gentleman that he was, and knowing that it might still be dangerous for her to return to her apartment, he offered Asha private use of his hotel suite in case she wanted some downtime and a chance to clean up. She thanked him but said that before she did anything, she wanted to see the dossier on the ISI operative they were after.

Lawlor had signed off on sharing the dossier, provided that Harvath didn't reveal how the United States had come into possession of it.

In exchange, Raj had provided a copy of the video footage believed to show the downing of General Mehra's helicopter over Coonoor.

Once Harvath transmitted the footage to Lawlor so that he could forward it on to the CIA and DARPA, he sat down with the group and watched as Raj projected the contents of the dossier onto a screen at the front of the eclectically furnished war room.

Ever the thorough spymaster, Raj combed through every piece of information and examined each in meticulous detail, starting with reports of the boy traveling with his family from diplomatic outpost to diplomatic outpost, all the way to the most current information the Afghans had assembled on him.

When he had gone through it once, Gupta asked him to start over from the beginning, but to go slower this time.

Harvath could feel his stomach grumbling. Dinner had been hours ago. He had seen all he needed to see. What he needed now was a bite before bed and maybe a drink before turning in.

He asked Asha if she wanted to avail herself of his shower while he got something to eat down in the hotel bar. He was still being a gentleman, but he also wanted to do a little old-fashioned tradecraft—build rapport, learn more about her organization, and tease out further information on where India stood on the proposed military alliance. Asha agreed . . . to using his shower.

Saying good night to Raj, Gupta, and Vijay, they exited the Blind Relief Association from the rear and walked through the woods over to the Oberoi.

The doorman smiled warmly as they walked up and welcomed them back to the hotel.

"He thinks we're together," she said with a smirk as they entered the lobby.

"Why does he think that?"

Asha smiled at him. "He's Indian. I'm Indian. And you're a white guy. They look at you different in a situation like that."

"A," Harvath clarified, "we could be work colleagues, which technically we kind of are. And B, I find 'white guy' highly inappropriate."

Concerned that she may have offended him, she stopped walking. Turning to him, she apologized. "I didn't mean to insult you. I'm very sorry."

"Thank you," Harvath replied, trying but failing to keep the grin off his face. "I prefer you use the proper term when speaking about me."

She didn't know where this was going, but being possessed of a pretty good sense of humor herself, she was willing to play along. "And exactly what would that term be?"

"I'm offended to even be asked. But if you must, the appropriate term is *Gora*."

Asha burst out laughing. "Vijay taught you that, didn't he?"

"Not really. He served more as my translator on it."

Her eyes widened. "Someone called you Gora? To your face?"

"Yep. It really hurt my feelings."

"I doubt that," she said, smiling. "Is this person still breathing? That's not a very nice thing to say."

"Don't worry, I've been called much worse."

"Have you? Like what?"

He thought for a moment. "Smart-ass. Pretty boy. Gym junkie. People can be incredibly cruel."

"How terrible for you."

He sighed and shook his head. Then, removing a keycard, his room number written on its paper sleeve, he handed it to her. Pointing toward the lobby bar he said, "I'll be in there, burying my pain and insecurity with food. Take all the time you need."

Asha accepted the card and replied, "Thank you. Promise me you won't do anything rash while I'm gone?"

"I'll try."

He was only human, and he was a guy, so he watched her as she walked away. She was a beautiful woman.

She was also highly intuitive because she glanced over her shoulder and caught him.

If it bothered her, she didn't show it. In fact, he could have sworn he saw her smile. He would need to be careful. He didn't want to send the wrong message. He was more than happy with Sølvi and the wonderfully crazy relationship they had together.

Sitting down in the bar, he was handed a cocktail menu, as well as an extensive food menu from the adjacent restaurant.

As a Southern California native, he was immediately drawn to the sushi, but he remembered Leahy's warning of not eating anything raw and staying as far away as possible from rice.

Instead, he opted for another Southern California favorite—Mexican. He was always hungry after an op, and a blackened chicken quesadilla sounded perfect, even if he did have to err on the side of caution and pass on the guacamole and pico de gallo. Better safe than sorry.

While he waited for his meal, he asked for a Woodford Reserve, neat, with a bottle of water on the side.

Sitting back in his chair, surveying all the glamorous patrons, he could see why it had been dubbed the drawing room of the crème de la crème of Delhi society and luxury international travelers.

The waitress brought his beverages and a place setting. Once everything was set up, she departed and he added a splash of water to his bourbon.

There were a million questions banging around in his brain and, for the moment, he was content to let them keep banging. Sometimes his best breakthroughs came when he wasn't even trying. It was also healthy to put work to bed for a little bit.

He sipped at his bourbon and enjoyed the people-watching until his quesadilla arrived and he dug in. It was delicious—even without the guac and pico de gallo.

He was on his last bite when Asha materialized, fresh from her shower.

"Thank you," she said, putting his keycard on the table and sliding it over to him.

"You're welcome," he replied, tucking it into his pocket. "Hungry?"

"No, thank you. But I could go for a drink."

Harvath gestured the waitress over. Asha placed her order—an espresso martini—and he asked for another bourbon.

Once the waitress had left, he said. "I have to ask. How'd you end up in Paharganj tonight?"

"RAW has an informant in G-Company. He told us where to find Sayed. What about you?"

"We got lucky."

"Well, you know what they say, better to be lucky than good."

Harvath did know. That was one of his favorite expressions. "There wasn't a Plan B, so all's well that ends well. Speaking of which, any thoughts on what to do with Sayed, long term?"

"Obviously," she replied, "nothing you extracted from him tonight would be admissible in court. And my presence, though I'd never admit

I was there, makes it problematic to get him prosecuted for coming after me—not once, but twice today."

"So, he'll walk."

"No. We'll use him to track down and take out G-Company's founder, Zakir Rahman Gangji. Then we'll finger him for it and watch the organization implode as all the senior leadership go to war with each other."

"Sounds like fun."

"Just another day in the office," she said with a smile as the waitress brought their drinks over and set them on the table.

Once she had walked away, Harvath continued. "Who do you think put you on Durrani's radar? How many people even knew you went down to Coonoor to investigate the crash?"

"Only Raj and Gupta. I used an alias while I was there."

"A clean alias?"

"Brand-new," she replied.

"How solid was its backstop?"

"I was posing as a senior investigator with the Defense Security Corps. The helicopter had just gone down. Raj had to work fast to build my cover. I don't think my file was super thick."

"Was there a service photo in there?"

"Probably."

"If I were suspicious of you, that's where I would have started. It doesn't take a lot of computing power to set a facial recognition program loose to search for a match. And, if you do have elements within your government sympathetic to the Chinese, it's conceivable that they could access any of India's databases."

Asha didn't like it, but she knew he was right. "Here's to tomorrow being a better day," she stated, raising her glass.

"Come on," said Harvath, as he raised his glass. "I came all the way to India. I want to learn the most common drinking toast."

"Cheers," she said, clinking his glass.

"Seriously? *Cheers?*"

"Yep. That's it."

They each took a sip of their drink and before he could ask her another question, Asha steered the topic away from work. "Married?"

"Excuse me?"

"Are you married? I don't see a ring. Or are you one of those wheels-up, rings-off kind of guys?"

"Definitely not one of those guys," he replied. "I'm engaged."

"Second time around?"

Harvath didn't respond.

Asha was excellent at reading people. "I'm sorry," she said, instantly pivoting off what was obviously a painful subject for him. "Tell me about your fiancée. Tall? Short? Blond? Brunette?"

"Tall and blond."

"*So* American."

"She's actually Norwegian."

"Where'd you meet her?" Asha teased. "On the ski slopes?"

"Through work."

"Is she an intelligence officer as well?"

He nodded and took another drink. Asha was good. He couldn't tell if she was playing him, so he tightened up his game a bit.

"Okay," she conceded, no work talk. "Do you two have a song?"

"What do you mean, *do we have a song*?"

"Aren't you a romantic. Yes, a *song*. You're engaged to be married to this woman. You have to have a favorite song together. It's a law."

"It's not a law," he said with a laugh.

"It's Asha's law. Now, what's the song?"

"There's a lot of songs we both like."

"Pick. One. Something significant. Something special for both of you. Take your time. I'll wait," she stated, enjoying another sip of her martini.

Harvath thought for a moment and then replied. " 'Into the Mystic' by Van Morrison."

"Why?"

"Why not?"

Asha rolled her eyes at him. "What's significant about it?"

"That's what was playing the first time we ever danced. We were in a little dive bar in Oslo."

"Did you ask her or did she ask you?"

"She asked me," Harvath admitted. "I'm not much of a dancer."

"Why am I not shocked? But you did get up and dance because she means that much to you."

He nodded.

"Maybe you are a romantic after all."

"What about you?" he asked, changing the subject. "Married?"

"Nope. And before you ask, not engaged and no boyfriend—much to my parents' displeasure. Marriage and family are a really big deal in India. Too big, if you ask me."

"So why not? I can't imagine you have any trouble finding dates."

She held her glass up, signaling the waitress that she was ready for a refill, and said, "Dates are precisely the problem. My calendar is full. I'm too busy."

"So you are married," he said. "To the job."

"Did my mother send you? You can be honest. I won't tell anybody."

Harvath smiled. "She did not. But I think she would want me to tell you that the days are long and the years are short."

"Meaning?"

"Meaning, when your head is down, when you're consumed with the work, you don't notice the passage of time. When you finally do pick up your head and look around, you're stunned by how much has passed. If you wait too long, you're doubly stunned by how little you have left. Life is short. Don't waste it."

"Good advice—even if my mother didn't send you."

Harvath smiled again. "I've got a couple of years on you and—"

"A *couple of years*?" she teased.

He absorbed the jab with good humor and continued: "You may have Asha's law, but I've got Harvath's three rules for happiness. Something to do. Someone to love. And something to look forward to. Ours is a rough business. It'll take everything from you. But only if you let it. My advice—don't let it."

"Do you always wax this philosophical with women you've just met?"

"Only the ones who point Glocks at me and try to steal my prisoners," he said as he smiled once more and took another sip of his bourbon.

The waitress returned, set down Asha's drink, and asked if Harvath wanted another. He politely declined and asked for the bill. If he didn't apply the brakes now, they'd be down here all night.

"So, tomorrow," he said. "What's the plan?"

"We know what Durrani looks like and we know the organization he is using for his cover. We'll set up surveillance first thing in the morning, before people start showing up for work."

"*We?*" Harvath asked. "Just the two of us?"

Asha nodded. Then with a smile she added, "I have some surveillance tech that I think you're really going to like."

CHAPTER 58

For a fraction of a second, Harvath had thought about offering to share the suite with Asha, with him taking the couch in the living room. But then he realized what a kind but stupid idea that was.

It wasn't that he didn't trust himself; it was that any appearance of impropriety was unprofessional.

Asha was incredibly attractive and no one would believe that they had shared a hotel room overnight and nothing had happened.

Sølvi would believe him, but why would he ever want to put her in the position of wondering? Even the smallest of doubts had a habit of growing and festering over time. He chalked his undelivered offer up to the bourbon talking and welded shut his mental suggestion box.

He did, however, offer to walk her back to the Blind Relief Association. She thanked him for the drinks, politely passed on the escort back, and told him that she'd be in the lobby at six a.m. The plan was to grab a quick breakfast and then head out to the target.

Upstairs in his room, as the storm that had been forecasted blew in, he transmitted a SITREP to Lawlor. Once it had been received, he asked for an update on Nicholas, Nina, and the baby.

Lawlor didn't bother texting a response. It was too much to put into writing. What's more, Harvath needed to hear every detail and be able to ask as many questions as he wanted. He suggested they do a call.

Harvath agreed and as the rain lashed his windows and lightning lit up the New Delhi sky, the pair spoke for more than an hour.

He didn't know how to react. He was angered by the attack, outraged at the injuries and loss of life. He was also incredibly proud of how Davis and Hauptmann had comported themselves, not to mention Nicholas. Had he arrived a few minutes earlier or a few minutes later, things could have turned out much worse. It was the epitome of right place, right time.

The fact that the baby had not yet improved also troubled him. After all that Nicholas had been through in his life, he deserved a happily ever after. Harvath could only hope that the next update would bring better news.

Getting into bed, he was so wiped out that he was asleep almost the moment his head hit the pillow. Had he not set the alarm on his phone, he would have slept right through meeting Asha in the lobby.

After a shower and a shave, he was downstairs waiting for her. She strode into the hotel promptly at six a.m.

"How'd you sleep?" she asked.

"Actually, I—"

"I was joking," she said, interrupting him. "I slept on an army cot with a wool blanket that had to have been from World War One. You slept on a mattress that easily cost over thirty thousand rupees and sheets with a thread count so high, it gives me a nosebleed just thinking about it."

Harvath smiled. "Breakfast?"

"Coffee first," she replied, leading the way toward the restaurant. "Then breakfast."

The hostess offered them a beautiful table with a gorgeous view near one of the windows, but Harvath and Asha simultaneously pointed to a booth in the corner, close to the entrance of the kitchen, and asked for it. They were both cut from the same cloth. Though she thought it an unusual request, the hostess smiled and obliged.

"Any updates from overnight?" he asked as they waited for their waiter to bring them coffee.

Asha removed a folder from her backpack and handed it to him. "A list of everyone who works at the Universal Relief Initiative with Durrani."

"Photos and bios as well," said Harvath. "Nice job."

"Open-source intel for the most part. NGOs put a lot of information about their people on their websites. It helps them tell their story and raise money."

"Or, in Durrani's case, it can also help backstop a cover."

"Agreed."

"What are these?" Harvath asked, holding up two profiles that had extra pages attached.

"We ran all of the employees, looking for anything unusual that we might be able to leverage."

"And?"

"The first one you have there is Jaya Devi. She is the organization's director of finance. While there haven't been any allegations of impropriety with regard to the Universal Relief Initiative's books, her home is in foreclosure and she is behind on her car payments."

"Interesting," said Harvath, studying the grandmotherly-looking woman. "What about the second?

"The second is Amit Paswan. He's from a small village in West Bengal. He was studying chemistry at the Indian Institute of Engineering, Science, and Technology in Kolkata when his twin sister was brutally attacked by a group of men who sexually assaulted and murdered her. The trial was a shambles. All five of the men went free. Over the next eighteen months, all of them wound up dead."

"Did this Amit Paswan kill them?" he asked, staring at the photo of a geeky, bespectacled man in his thirties.

"He was investigated, but always had an alibi from someone at school. He was never charged."

"So, then why'd you include this information on him?" asked Harvath.

"Because unlike the investigators in West Bengal, I kept digging. Each of his alibis came from someone who had been the victim of sexual assault or had an immediate family member who was."

"Jesus."

"He also never finished his degree. After the last man accused of murdering his sister was killed, he dropped out of school. He only had one term remaining. He never went to work in the field of chemistry. All of his employment has been in service organizations; NGOs and the like."

"Because he's doing penance," said Harvath. "That's the person we want."

"We also have this," said Asha, removing another folder and handing it to him.

Harvath opened it. There were high-tech schematics and 3-D renderings of the Universal Relief Initiative's offices as well as other buildings and businesses up and down the street.

"Impressive," he remarked. "You, Raj, and Gupta do good work."

"We had a little help with the surveillance. There's a very unique company that has been trying to get Raj's attention. They put this together overnight."

"They did a hell of a job. What's this here?" he asked, pointing to a spot across the street from the NGO that had been highlighted.

"That's where you and I are headed right after breakfast," she replied. "That's going to be our surveillance post."

CHAPTER 59

The surveillance post was an "intimate apparel" shop on the second floor, across the street from the NGO. It was closed while its owner was away visiting family for Diwali. Gupta had been able to quietly arrange for them to use it.

"This doesn't make you feel uncomfortable, does it?" he asked as they brought their gear in and set it down.

"No," Asha replied, exaggeratedly stroking a piece of risqué lingerie. "Why should it? Does it make *you* feel uncomfortable?"

"I've got about a half-dozen terrific comebacks about me doing some of my best work in the presence of ladies' lingerie," he said. "None of which I'm going to use right now."

Asha laughed. "You kind of just did."

Harvath stifled a grin and walked over to the window. "This is the part of the job they never dare mention during recruitment."

"The long hours of boredom punctuated by random, brief moments of excitement?"

"Precisely."

"What kind of fool would sign up for that?" she joked. "There's a reason the intelligence agencies so love the James Bond movies."

"The ultimate government program: six decades of somebody else doing their work for them."

They both laughed and began unpacking everything. As Asha set up a tiny wireless camera at the window, Harvath powered up the tablet they would be using to monitor the NGO. Things had come a long way from trying to stay hidden behind venetian blinds while peering through a huge pair of binoculars.

On the table in front of them they laid out all of the pictures of the Universal Relief Initiative's employees. There were only two, however, whom they were interested in seeing.

Target number one was Basheer Durrani himself. Harvath had already begun running scenarios in his head about how they could apprehend him if he showed up.

Their consolation prize was Amit Paswan. They both felt certain that they could convince him to assist in their cause if need be.

Regardless of which target presented himself, Harvath was determined to spin them into gold and drag his mission across the finish line. He was ready for it to be over, to get out of India, and to return home.

"Contact," said Asha, recognizing a face down on the street and expanding their image on the tablet.

"Who do we have?" asked Harvath.

She looked at the faces on the pieces of paper on the table and then tapped the corresponding one. "Katrina Kapoor."

Harvath took out a pen, leaned over, and marked the time of arrival on her profile.

They went back and forth like this eight more times, logging in employees, before Amit Paswan showed up.

Harvath marked down the time of arrival on his profile sheet.

"Now what?" Asha asked.

"We wait and see if Durrani shows up?"

"And if he doesn't?"

"We do what any good intelligence operative would do. We improvise."

"In other words, we hope to be lucky rather than good."

Harvath smiled. "Like James Bond, I plan on being both."

"Now *I'm* the one who's uncomfortable."

• • •

After another hour, Harvath was giving up hope of seeing Durrani. Perhaps the man was on sick leave, or had taken some vacation time in order to carry out his assignment. Whatever the reason, Harvath didn't think he was going to show up.

"I'm going to the café down the street for coffee," he told Asha. "Do you want one?"

"Yes, please. Black."

"Like your ops," Harvath replied.

She rolled her eyes. "If you're waiting for me to make a bad coffee pun in response, you're going to be standing there all day."

He smiled. "Call me if anything starts percolating."

Asha pointed at the door. "Get out of here before I pull my Glock on you again."

With a laugh, Harvath headed downstairs and over to the café. He was reading the menu, written on a large chalkboard behind the counter, when his phone rang. It was Asha.

"What's up?" he asked, activating the call.

"Amit just left the building," she replied.

"Which direction is he headed?"

"Toward you."

"Okay," Harvath replied, turning around and looking out the window, trying to catch sight of the man. "How far away is he?"

"About twenty meters."

"May I help you, sir?" the barista asked, interrupting.

"Yes," he replied, turning back to the counter. "Two coffees. To go. Both black, please."

"I think he may be headed to the café," Asha said on the phone. "What do you want me to do?"

"Nothing. I've got this. Just keep your eyes peeled for Durrani."

"Will do," she responded. "By the way, he's almost at the door. Good luck."

Harvath disconnected the call and returned his phone to his pocket. When he heard Amit Paswan enter, he didn't turn around. Instead, he stood facing the counter, waiting for his coffees.

Once they were ready, he paid and left a small tip, thanking the staff.

On his way out, he walked right past Amit, then stopped and backed up. They locked eyes.

"Universal Relief Initiative, right?" Harvath asked.

Amit nodded, trying to place the stranger's face. "Yes. Do we know each other?"

With two coffees, Harvath wasn't able to shake hands, but he offered the man an elbow in greeting. "Joe Sampson. CARE International."

While his name was a lie, the organization was legit. Harvath knew the director and had conducted an operation on their behalf.

"To be honest, I don't remember us meeting, but I've never been good with faces to begin with. Amit Paswan," the man said, returning the elbow bump.

"Kashmir. Bangladesh. Afghanistan. Who knows, right?"

"Are you meeting someone?" Amit asked, looking at the two coffees.

"Actually, I was taking these back to my room. I'm staying nearby. I have a report I'm supposed to write and my brain doesn't really kick in until the second cup. I figured this was more efficient than just coming back in twenty minutes to buy another. How about you? Do you have time to sit and chat?"

Amit looked at his watch. "I've got a few minutes. Let me place my order."

"Terrific," said Harvath. "I'll grab us a table."

Sitting down in the corner, away from the rest of the customers, he shot Asha a quick text, letting her know what he was up to.

The table was a two-top. In a move that was uncharacteristic for him, Harvath sat with his back to the café and left Amit the chair with its back to the wall. A few moments later, the man appeared with his cappuccino and sat down.

"What brings you to New Delhi?" he asked.

"You're never going to believe this," said Harvath. "In fact, I don't even believe this. I'm here hunting a killer."

For a moment, the man appeared at a loss for words. Finally, he found a few. "As in a pathogen like cholera or Ebola?"

"Nope. I'm looking for a human killer."

The color drained from his face. "This meeting isn't an accident, is it?"

"Actually, it is. I was across the street watching as you arrived at work this morning. I'm technically on break right now. I had no idea we'd end up in the same café. This does, however, make my job much easier."

"I'm not comfortable with this conversation," said Amit, trying to stand.

Harvath shoved the table into him, pinning him against the wall. "I'm not here to talk about your sister. And if I were, I'd tell you that I think you did the right thing."

"I don't know what you're talking about."

"Cut the crap, Amit. All of your alibis were from people who were not only sympathetic to your situation, but who took vicarious satisfaction in you avenging your sister. But like I said, that's not why I'm here."

He relaxed his posture and Harvath eased the table back enough for him to sit down.

"Then why are you here? Why are you bothering me?"

"I think you may have information that might be valuable to me."

"About a killer?"

Harvath nodded.

"You don't work for CARE International, do you?"

"No, I do not."

"How would I know anything about a killer?"

"You work with him."

The shock on Amit's face was instant. "At URI?" he asked, using the NGO's acronym.

Once again, Harvath nodded.

"That's impossible."

"Is it really?" he asked, raising an eyebrow.

Amit caught the not-so-subtle meaning of his remark and rephrased his question: "What specific information is it that you want?"

Sliding his phone from his pocket, Harvath pulled up Durrani's photo and showed it to him. "I want to know everything you know about this man."

"You want to know about Wasim? Wasim Younis? He's the killer you're looking for?"

"First of all, yes. And secondly, his name isn't Wasim, it's Basheer Durrani. He's a Pakistani intelligence agent and he is very dangerous."

"But he's a good man," Amit protested. "I have been in the field with him. We've been on countless relief missions together. He really cares about people."

"It might have appeared that way," said Harvath. "But that's part of his job—making people believe what he wants them to believe. URI is nothing more than a means to an end for him, a cover organization that allows him to avoid suspicion as he moves through various countries doing the ISI's bidding."

"And why do you care? You're American. It might make sense if I was speaking to someone from one of the Indian intelligence services about this."

"Mr. Durrani is responsible for the death of an old friend of mine. An American."

"So this is about revenge?" asked Amit.

"If it were, would that be a difficult concept for you to grasp, Mr. Paswan?"

While unnecessary, Harvath had hit him right between the eyes with that one. The look on the man's face told him everything he needed to know about how the rest of their conversation was going to unfold.

"If I help you, what happens to me? Who else knows what you know?"

Harvath was honest with him. "Only one other person. But it's someone I trust. And you can, too. If you cooperate, and if it leads us to Durrani, we'll bury everything back where we found it. You've led a good life, Amit. You have a chance to do the right thing. I wouldn't be here if we didn't have absolute confidence that your Wasim Younis is who we say he is."

"But you could be wrong. He could look like the guy you're searching for. Their names could have been mixed up in some database somewhere, right? I mean, that's a possibility. Isn't it?"

"Amit, look at me," said Harvath, his tone icy. "I don't get sent halfway around the world on *maybes* or *possibilities*. My people don't traffic in mistaken identities. Your colleague Wasim is the person I'm looking for. He is a killer."

CHAPTER 60

G upta had warned against moving too quickly. He wanted to work with police, establish a cordon, and send in a crack team from Special Group, RAW's special forces unit. Raj had sided with Asha and Harvath.

There simply wasn't enough time to wait. They knew where Durrani was at this very moment. A chance like this might not come again. They would be foolish not to jump on it.

Durrani was in the volatile, Muslim-majority area of Delhi's North East district known as Jafrabad—recently ground zero for a massive, six-day riot where fifty-three people had been killed, including a policeman and an intelligence officer. Gupta wasn't wrong to have wanted to proceed with caution.

The whole district was a tinderbox waiting to go up in flames at even the mere mention of the word *spark*. One wrong move and they could send the city into chaos.

Harvath wasn't surprised that Jafrabad was where Durrani had set himself up. The best place to hide a needle was in a haystack full of them.

What did surprise Harvath, however, was that a man like Durrani had allowed himself a piece of discernable routine. In tradecraft, it was considered something to avoid at all costs.

Of course, plenty of spies broke that rule, for various reasons, such as picking up or dropping off kids at school, taking night classes at a university to get closer to a target, or hitting the gym at the same time as a potential asset in order to develop rapport.

But Durrani wasn't breaking the rule for family—he didn't have one—nor did he appear to be doing it in service of his mission. It was an ideological position he had taken.

During the riot, two-thirds of the people killed had been Muslims. They were shot, stabbed, slashed, beaten, and set on fire. Sure, he could easily hide among them, in their neighborhood, but he wanted to do more than that. He had wanted to help them learn how to defend themselves.

According to Amit, Durrani taught a Friday morning martial arts class at a dojo in Jafrabad. The Universal Relief Initiative encouraged a flex schedule, so management had no trouble with employees moving their hours around as long as they put in their forty a week and didn't miss key meetings.

A question that had always plagued Amit was, if he had been there—could he have successfully protected his sister? He wore that insecurity like a badge of shame.

On a mission trip, in the wake of a typhoon striking Myanmar, he and Durrani had shared a room together. They had discussed their interests and hobbies.

Amit had talked about his love of science, Durrani his love of martial arts. One thing led to another and an invitation was extended to the Friday class. Amit accepted and ended up training with Durrani for several months, before switching to a different dojo, closer to his apartment.

Now the only time he interacted with the man was through work. That injected a potential problem into Harvath's plan.

They needed Amit to identify the dojo, which meant he was going to have to come along. But if Durrani spotted him in a car with two other people, he was absolutely going to run.

In fact, Harvath was pretty sure that just seeing Asha would be enough to make him rabbit. There was no question in his mind that the ISI operative had assembled a dossier before hiring Sayed to go after her. Durrani knew what she looked like. Hers wasn't a face that a man easily forgot.

That brought Harvath to his own face. A Gora in Jafrabad was going to stick out worse than a sore thumb.

In short, none of them could afford to be seen by Durrani. This whole thing would be like eating an elephant—an expression, Harvath realized, that probably wasn't too terribly popular in India. Nevertheless, they were going to have to tackle this job one bite at a time.

The first bite involved convincing Amit to come along. He had strongly resisted, but when Harvath, who could be quite persuasive, made it clear that this wasn't an either/or situation, the man gave in. He also agreed to turn over his cell phone. Until they were done with him, Harvath was not going to trust him or turn his back on him. Not for a second.

Asha pulled the car Raj had arranged for them around and they exited the café. Amit sat in front. Harvath sat in back, where he could keep an eye on everything.

Morning traffic in Delhi sucked. It made Los Angeles look like nothing but free-flowing carpool lanes.

To her credit, Asha maneuvered through it quite well. When she was able to open it up, she opened it up. When she could "safely" blow a light without causing an accident or drawing any immediate police attention, she did so.

Whoever owned the car was going to receive more than a few redlight tickets in their mailbox, but that would be Raj's problem to solve.

As they entered Jafrabad, Harvath had hoped sitting in the backseat would provide him with a little lower profile. He still got lots of stares and what he and his teammates used to refer to as the "stink eye." It was obvious he was not welcome in this part of town.

They threaded the vehicle through the squalid, pothole-punctured streets.

"That's his mosque," Amit said as they passed a rather weather-beaten structure. "His class is timed so that the students can be done before the midmorning prayer service."

"Dhuhr," said Harvath, using the correct name for the prayer. Pulling out his phone, he did a quick internet search for prayer times in New Delhi. "We've got twenty minutes."

"Does he walk to mosque with his students?" Asha asked.

"No. He normally gets cleaned up, prays on his own inside the dojo, and then heads to the office."

Asha met Harvath's eyes in the rearview mirror. "So, we take him inside?"

"Or we could wait until he leaves and hit him with the car."

She looked around. "While there's a certain beauty to the simplicity of that plan, we don't have enough real estate. Too many cars and other obstacles. It'd be a one-in-a-million shot. And that's me being generous with the odds. I say we take him inside."

"It's his turf. He knows it. We don't."

"Amit knows it," she replied.

"Good point," said Harvath, reaching his hand over the seat and placing it heavily on the man's shoulder. "If it were you, how would you do it?"

CHAPTER 61

"We should have sent him right up to the front door and had him knock," said Asha as they crept up on the dojo.

"And if it were you inside, instead of Durrani?" he asked. "How would you react?"

"I'd have my weapon out, a few millimeters from the door so it could cycle, and I'd begin shooting the moment I saw anybody else but Amit."

"Which is why we're not using Amit and he's facedown, zip-tied, in the trunk. Speaking of which, why didn't you tell me you had a whole other bag of tricks in there?"

"Raj is our quartermaster. When we went up to the lingerie store, I handed you all the cases that were coded for surveillance. I knew you had a weapon and I had a weapon. That was all that mattered. The bonus bag was just Raj being Raj. He's famous for saying, 'Whatever you do, don't *underdo* it.' It's a joke, but there's some practical wisdom to it."

"Vijay had a duffle like yours. It was filled with a bunch of stuff that magically 'walked' out of IPS the same day he did. I'm beginning to think that Indians are obsessed with only three things—marriage, music, and mass quantities of tactical gear."

"Are you absolutely sure my mother didn't send you?"

Harvath shot her a quick grin. "Something tells me your mom and Vijay's mother-in-law would probably get along well."

Asha smiled back, but it disappeared the moment she made ready to reach for the front door. The time for jokes was over. It was now time to get to work.

Harvath had been in his share of dojos. From how Amit described the layout, it was pretty standard—which, in this case, was a tactical nightmare.

The front door opened onto one big room where everything happened. In the back were a men's locker room and a women's locker room, both with toilets and showers.

There was no rear exit, because there was no true urban planning in this part of Delhi. Houses and buildings were built right up against and on top of each other. While there was an occasional gangway, there were no organized alleys providing access for garages and trash pickups as there were in the United States.

This was a slapdash, unregulated district, erected with little to no oversight or forethought. A testament to well-organized urban planning it was not. That was good and bad for Harvath.

It was good, in that by their controlling the front door, Durrani had no means of escape. It was bad, however, in that to go in and take him, they had to move through open space with no cover and no concealment.

The ISI operative would ostensibly have every advantage—save for one. Surprise.

Harvath would have killed for submachine guns, rather than pistols, but you went to war with the gear you had, not the gear you wish you had.

While he would have also killed to have had a few flashbangs, Raj had seen fit to at least provide them with two smoke grenades—both green, for some unfathomable reason. Among multiple other pieces of kit, Harvath had one smoke grenade on his vest and Asha had the other on hers.

That was the extent of their distraction devices. Two green smoke grenades. The only other thing that they might have going for them, and Harvath prayed that they did, was that the water in the dojo shower was exceptionally warm and that Durrani would take his time enjoying it.

He had, without question, done hundreds more hostile entries than Asha ever had, or would. That made him the most experienced operator on scene and she had agreed to defer to him. She wasn't stupid. She didn't want to run in and get shot in the face.

Harvath was of two minds. If they were lucky enough to enter when Durrani was in the shower, he might not have any clue that they had slipped inside.

If, however, Durrani somehow did know that they had made entry, they could be walking into a trap. So, Harvath decided to split the baby.

If Durrani was in the shower, he'd never notice the smoke from the grenades. If he wasn't, Harvath and Asha would be damn glad to have the concealment. Smoke might not stop bullets, but it made their targets a lot harder to hit.

Harvath signaled for Asha to hand him her grenade. Once she had, he nodded for her to go ahead and hit the door.

Pulling the pins from both her smoke grenade and his, he watched as she counted down from three and then quietly pulled the door open.

As she pushed her pistol into the space to cover him and counter any threats, he tossed both active smoke grenades into the dojo, making sure they landed soundlessly, on different corners of the mat.

Watching the grenades was like watching a couple of smokestacks at a steel mill. The volume of smoke they produced and the rapidity at which they produced it was astounding.

With his pistol up and at the ready, he pushed into the dojo and motioned for Asha to follow.

As degenerate as Durrani was, they didn't expect to find him showering in the women's locker room, and so they pressed on toward the back, left-hand corner of the building, where Amit had told them they would find the men's area.

The thick green smoke was filling the space. It was dense and extremely heavy. Disorienting even.

Harvath looked back to make sure Asha was still on his six, but he couldn't see her. That's when he heard the first shots ring out. They had come from the direction of the men's locker room. Durrani knew they were there.

Backtracking to where he hoped he would find Asha, Harvath fired repeatedly in the ISI operative's direction. He was supposed to take Durrani alive, but at this moment Harvath had crossed into don't-give-a-fuck territory.

Despite the heavy smoke, he found Asha. She had been hit. The bullet had struck her in her right thigh.

"You okay?" Harvath asked.

"I'll be fine," she snapped. Though she was bleeding, it didn't appear the round had hit an artery. "I can't find my damn gun in all this smoke."

Harvath turned, felt the toe of his boot bump something, and bent down to retrieve Asha's pistol. Handing it to her, he quickly helped her up and said, "We end it right now. Can you move?"

She put some weight on her leg and nodded.

"Good," he stated. "On my mark."

Harvath counted backward from three and the pair charged, shredding the locker room area with rounds from their pistols.

But no sooner had they started than they were met with an even deadlier response. Durrani had picked up a machine gun and was firing from the shower area into the dojo.

As the bullets popped and whizzed around them, Harvath tackled Asha and took her to the floor.

In so doing, he saved her life as a bullet that was headed for her brain instead only creased her scalp.

Even so, as head wounds often bled the worst, the blood poured profusely into her eyes, making it hard for her to see.

Using a damp, matted clump of her own hair to wipe the blood away, she reloaded and begin firing again. But she only served to act as a beacon for the machinegun fire, which pounded her again and again and again in the chest, like a psychotic John Henry, hell-bent on knocking every molecule of oxygen from her body.

Asha fell back again to the floor, guppy-breathing like a terminally ill or end-of-life senior citizen, about to cross over. Harvath fired the last two rounds of his one and only spare magazine.

The green smoke was beginning to dissipate.

Out of ammunition, Harvath could see through the haze as Durrani stepped out from the shower area holding an AK-47.

Harvath looked at Asha, hoping to pick up her gun and finish the ISI operative off, but the slide of her Glock was locked back, out of ammo. There was no way he could reload her weapon fast enough.

Pulling the Taser off her vest, he aimed at Durrani's feet and fired.

The probes landed in the puddle of water he was standing in and lit him up like a Christmas tree.

Goon that he was, he stood there growling, foaming at the mouth, and shaking, but refused to face-plant like a properly felled redwood.

Harvath pressed the trigger and hit him with another burst of electricity, encouraging him to ride the lightning once more.

As he seized up again, Harvath moved forward.

When he was right in front of Durrani, Harvath engaged him again. This time with the Taser's second shot. The barbed probes tore right through Durrani's shirt and embedded themselves in the flesh of his chest.

This time he was powerless to fight the baseball bat to his neurological fuse box. He fell face-first and broke his nose when he hit the floor.

Normally Harvath would have been looking for toilet paper or tampons to shove up his captive's nostrils to stop the bleeding, but right now he didn't care. Raj could deal with the stains in the trunk.

After placing Durrani in flex cuffs, he checked on Asha. Her wound was worse than she had let on. She wasn't exsanguinating, but she needed medical attention.

Removing the tourniquet from his vest, he applied it to her thigh and marked the time. Every minute would count.

CHAPTER 62

"Let me explain how this is going to work," said Raj as he sat down on the edge of the metal table to which Basheer Durrani had been handcuffed and chained. "There are a series of rhetorical doors available to you. I will explain what is behind each one and then you will need to choose. Keep in mind that choosing not to act, to simply sit and remain silent, will be interpreted as an action. There is a door for that as well."

Harvath sat in a comfortable chair, a cup of coffee in his hand, on the other side of the one-way glass. Gupta sat next to him, taking notes on a blue pad of paper, puffing away on his pipe.

Raj had allowed Harvath to witness the interrogation, with the caveat that if things drifted too far into matters of state security, he might be asked to leave the room for a bit. Harvath had agreed to the terms.

It was fascinating to watch Raj work. For a man known for being tough and abrupt, those were not the traits he was exhibiting now. He came off more like a math tutor moving a reluctant yet capable student through the concept of linear equations. These were not insoluble problems he was presenting. The student had the pertinent data needed to come to the correct conclusions. It was all about having the will to do so.

That was Raj's job—to help Durrani find his will and get him to make the right choice. If Durrani didn't make the right choice, things were going to get ugly for him very quickly.

"Just so you understand," Raj continued. "The downing of that helicopter was an act of war, by Pakistan, on India. It was completely unprovoked. I say that because I want you to know what the stakes are here. We are talking about our two nations going to war. *Again.* And believe me, if India chooses to do so, we are going to strike with such force that Pakistan will be reeling for years to come."

Removing a handkerchief, the director of RAW's Special Operations Division cleaned his glasses, completely comfortable with the silence in the room.

Then, placing them back upon his face, he said to Durrani, "Now, let's talk about those doors I mentioned. Choose the right one, cooperate fully, and you can walk away a free man."

• • •

The interrogation went on for hours. At one point Gupta leaned over and showed Harvath a text from Asha. No bone or arterial damage. She had been stitched up, bandaged up, and discharged.

Harvath was relieved to hear that. It had been a hell of a shuffle getting Amit out of the trunk, getting Durrani into it, and placing Asha on the backseat for the scramble to the nearest trauma hospital.

Once they had arrived, all he could do was drop her at the ER and wave a group of nurses over to assist.

After telling them how long the tourniquet had been on, he had leapt back into the car and driven off. Asha had insisted. She knew the importance of getting Durrani back to Raj and Gupta. And she had been right.

Putting Amit behind the wheel, they had driven straight to the Blind Relief Association. The men were outside waiting for them.

Harvath handed Amit back his phone and thanked him. Gupta then pulled the NGO worker aside, gave him money for a taxi, and delivered a very stern warning about national security and what would befall the man if he ever mentioned, to anyone, what had taken place.

With that loose end sufficiently tied off, Raj popped the trunk and took a picture of Durrani as Harvath double-checked the ISI operative's restraints.

With Gupta then driving, they headed for the high-security detention and debriefing facility manned by the personnel of Special Group.

While Durrani was transferred to an interrogation room, Raj arranged for a team to retrieve all the surveillance gear from the lingerie shop. He then asked Harvath to take a walk with him as he smoked a cigarette.

"You saved Asha's life," Raj said. "Thank you."

"She would have done the same for me. I don't doubt it."

"You also saw the mission through. Thank you for bringing us Durrani. What can we do for you?"

Harvath knew exactly what he could do for him. "I want to know who killed Eli Ritter and I want to know who has been pulling Durrani's strings. Either you get him to talk or I will. I'm not leaving without that information."

Raj looked around at the high, concrete walls, the razor wire, and all of the black-clad men toting machine guns. He smiled. "I think that's the least we can do for you. Anything else?"

"Not at the moment, but I'd like to reserve the right to make one additional request sometime in the near future. Let's see how everything pans out."

Raj had nodded and they shook hands. He then laid out the ground rules for allowing Harvath to sit in on the interrogation and, as soon as they had each gotten coffee, Durrani's questioning began.

Once he had made his choice and had agreed to cooperate, the details he revealed were mind-blowing. He knew the Indians had him against the wall. If he didn't play ball, he'd spend the rest of his life in a deep, dark hole. Making a deal was the only way to go.

The extent of the network he had built throughout India was beyond impressive. He was one of the best recruiters Harvath had ever seen.

When Durrani identified the man hired to kill Eli Ritter, Harvath turned to Gupta and said, "I want everything you have on him. Including an address."

Gupta pulled out his phone and sent a text. Twenty minutes later, there was a knock on the door of the observation room. There was a brief conversation and then the man closed the door and handed Harvath a file.

As Harvath read through the file, Gupta received another text. Flipping to a clean sheet of paper on his pad, he wrote something down, tore off the page, and handed it to the American seated next to him.

Harvath looked at the note, folded it, and put it in his pocket. He then settled back and watched the rest of the interrogation.

One of the most stunning things Durrani revealed was that the person who had brought down the helicopter carrying the Indian chief of Defense Staff was the same person who had been responsible for accompanying Asha during her investigation at Sulur Air Base—someone named Lance Naik Kamal Khan.

Khan had been suspicious of Asha from the jump. She wasn't like any investigator he had ever met. The stunt she had pulled in relation to helping the Siddiquis was outrageous.

When he couldn't find enough about her in the DSC database, he had suggested to Durrani that he use his contacts inside the Indian government to figure out who she was and what she was up to. That search had led to hiring Sayed and his men to go after her. The Kamal Khan story, however, didn't end there.

The Chinese had sent over a specialist to teach Khan how to use their secret directed-energy weapon. He was smart and had proven an adept student.

In two days' time, Khan was set to bring down another aircraft. This one was much bigger and even more dramatic.

With national elections looming, India's biggest politicians had been crisscrossing the country. There had been a pause for Diwali, but campaigns were about to ramp back up.

When they did, the party of India's hottest political star was expected to launch into overdrive. Rishi Puri was rich, handsome, and referred to in the media as the future of Indian democracy. They called him the "Rising Tiger" of Indian politics. He intended to smash corruption, shake everything up, and lead India to prominence. He also was a fan of India deepening its military ties with the United States, Japan, and Australia.

In other words, the idea of an Asian version of NATO could not have hoped to have had a more sympathetic Indian prime minister than Rishi Puri. For that, Beijing wanted him out of the picture, permanently.

Durrani went on to explain that Khan had already traveled to Delhi, had the Chinese weapon with him, and was staying in a safe house that Durrani had arranged for him.

Durrani was willing to give him up, not only in a bid to secure his own freedom, but because he was angry with him.

Hoping to spark religious violence, it was Khan who had leaked the chief flight mechanic's personal information and had incited the mob to attack the Siddiquis in their home.

Even though Raj couldn't see Gupta through the one-way glass, he had stared right at him and Gupta had received the message. Picking up his phone, he summoned the Special Group's commander. They were about to launch an incredibly important mission and needed to begin preparations immediately.

Harvath hung around and listened as Raj kept trying to get Durrani to provide the name and related information about his Chinese contact. No matter how many ways he asked the question, no matter how many angles of attack he employed, Durrani wouldn't give it up. It was his ace in the hole. Until he was confident that the terms of his deal with the Indians would be honored, he wasn't giving that information up.

As he sat in the observation room, Harvath traded a few texts back and forth with Vijay and even had a nice exchange with Asha. She had thanked him for getting her to the hospital and even had the nerve to joke about how tightly he had affixed the tourniquet. "Like all Americans," she typed, "you overdo things."

He had responded right back. "I learned from the best. Like Raj always says, whatever you do, don't underdo it."

That had prompted a string of laughing emojis and a few more pleasantries.

As Raj continued the interrogation, he moved Durrani into the realm of current Indian politicians and civil servants who may or may not be serving the interests of Beijing.

The moment that line of questioning began, Gupta pulled the pipe from his mouth, turned to Harvath, and said, "I think we should call it a day. Can I arrange a ride for you back to your hotel?"

Two Special Group soldiers drove Harvath back to the Oberoi in one of their brand-new, blacked-out Bharat Forge/Paramount Group armored vehicles.

The looks on the doormen's faces when he climbed out told Harvath that not a lot of guests had been dropped off in such a dramatic fashion.

When he got up to his room, he texted with Vijay. It was the last night of Diwali and he had accepted an invitation to celebrate with the ex-cop and his family.

They set a time to meet and Harvath asked if the man could fulfill a small request for him.

Vijay agreed and ninety minutes later pulled up under the hotel's portico, where Harvath was waiting.

It was a gorgeous evening. The storms from the night before had moved through, bringing cooler, dryer air. The sky was clear and beginning to fill with fireworks. Vijay had the top down. "Boogie Nights" by Heatwave was playing.

As Harvath slid into the passenger seat, the ex-cop handed him a small gift. "Happy Diwali."

"Thank you," Harvath replied, handing him the piece of paper Gupta had given him. "Here's where we need to make a quick stop."

Vijay memorized the address and handed it back. "It'll take us about twenty minutes to get there."

"Perfect," said Harvath.

As the ex-cop eased the Jaguar away from the Oberoi, Harvath pulled out the empty magazines for the pistol and began reloading them with the box of rounds Vijay had given him as a gift.

They didn't talk much on the drive. They enjoyed the music while Harvath took in the sights and sounds of Delhi.

Because Diwali was such a family-oriented celebration, he had been concerned that the man he was going to pay a visit to would either not be home, or would be home but surrounded by family. Gupta had assured him that it wouldn't be a problem.

The man was a contract killer without close, personal relationships or affiliations of any kind.

When they pulled over near the entrance to his building, Vijay turned up the Jaguar's stereo. "I'll just be here, listening to music. See you in what? Ten minutes?"

Harvath got out of the car. "If I'm not back in five, I'm not coming back."

Closing the door behind him, he walked up the street to the apartment complex and stepped inside. At the mailboxes, he searched for the man's name and unit number, cross-referencing it against the information Gupta had given him. It was a match.

Climbing the stairs, he slid one of the fresh magazines into his pistol and racked the slide, making the weapon hot.

Everything about the building's construction was cheap and bottom of the barrel. That was a good sign.

Reaching the killer's floor he walked down the hall, stopping to touch a couple of other apartments' front doors.

They were crappy, thin, and flimsy. Unless the killer had gone to the trouble and expense to reinforce his, it would be exactly the same.

Arriving at the man's door, Harvath was pleased to see lights on inside and to hear what sounded like a television.

He positioned himself where he could see the peephole and knocked. When a shadow appeared on the other side and stepped forward to peer through the hole, Harvath kicked the door in.

The door slammed right into the man's face and sent him tumbling backward. Harvath stepped into the apartment and, before the man could raise the weapon in his hand, shot him twice in the chest and twice in the head.

When Eli Ritter's killer fell to the ground, Harvath shot him again, just to make sure he was dead, and then left the building.

"All good?" Vijay asked as Harvath got back into the Jaguar.

"All good," he replied. Holding the gun out, he offered it to Vijay. "Please tell your mother-in-law that I appreciated the loan."

The ex-cop put the car in drive and pulled away from the curb. "You can tell her yourself when we get to my house."

• • •

Vijay's home was alive with family, music, cooking, and laughter. There were so many people there, Harvath couldn't keep track of them all. A couple of them, however, stood out.

His wife was a lovely, demure woman, a bit on the quiet side. She obviously loved Vijay and he loved her right back. She welcomed Harvath and was extremely gracious, attempting to explain all the traditions as brightly garbed relatives and joyful chaos swirled around them.

When an older woman walked into the kitchen to check on the food, Mrs. Chabra excused herself and went to see if anyone needed a refill on drinks.

"I'd like you to meet my mother-in-law," Vijay said proudly.

"This is the man from the office?" the older woman asked, approaching Harvath and taking his face in her hands. "I don't know what you have been doing, but keep it up. I haven't seen him this happy in years."

Harvath accepted a hug and then, making sure no one else was watching, removed the pistol, dropped the mag, and locked the slide back, catching the round that had been in the chamber. He handed the weapon to her. "I understand this is yours."

The woman accepted it and raised it to her nose. "This has been fired recently. You couldn't have been bothered to clean it?"

Vijay humorously scolded her for being rude to their guest. She smiled, pocketed the magazines, and took the pistol back to her bedroom to lock it away. Harvath accepted a cold beer from his friend.

"I found Pinaki Ali's mother a job here in Delhi," he said.

"That's great," Harvath replied. "Where?"

"At the embassy, on the kitchen team, provided she can pass the background check."

"What about Pinaki?"

"He's been harder to find employment for. Very few companies will hire somebody with a record like his. That being said, I think I have a lead on a sanitation job. We'll see what happens."

"You're a good man, Vijay."

The ex-cop smiled and pointed to one of the many dishes on the kitchen table. "You should try that. You'll like it."

Harvath paused. "Hold on. Are there any ghost peppers in it?"

Vijay laughed and shook his head. "It's called Onion Bhaji. Spicy, but not too bad. And it's deep fried, so I know it's on your list of approved foods."

He picked one up and gave it a try. It was delicious. Spicy, but not too spicy. He was reaching for a second when he saw a familiar face enter the kitchen on crutches.

"Look who's here," said Vijay as he walked over and gave Asha a hug. "I'm so glad you accepted our invitation."

"It was very kind of you," she replied as Harvath walked over and gave her a hug as well.

"How are you feeling?" he asked. He could see the bandage on her head and assumed that beneath her sari her right thigh was pretty well wrapped.

"Exhausted."

Vijay pulled out one of the kitchen chairs and motioned for her to sit. "What can I get you to drink?"

"Can you make a martini?"

"I have an excellent martini maker," the man said. "I'll be right back."

As the ex-cop walked off, Harvath asked, "Who pulled guard duty for Sayed tonight?"

"They transferred him to the Special Group facility," she said. "Neither Raj nor Gupta wanted to spend the last night of Diwali keeping an eye on him and I obviously couldn't do it. They're going to decide what to do with him on Monday."

"Have they briefed you on anything coming out of Durrani's interrogation?"

She nodded. "I couldn't believe it when I heard about Kamal Khan. That floored me."

"You never know in this business."

"So true," she replied. "Special Group is hitting the safe house he's in tonight. They're going to attempt to capture him and the directed-energy weapon."

"Hopefully," said Harvath, "they'll be successful."

"I hope so, too."

There was a pause in the conversation, before Asha added, "I also want to thank you for putting the tourniquet on and getting me to the hospital."

"Don't mention it. I'm sorry you had to be the bullet sponge."

Asha smiled. "I think that guy has an issue with strong, confident women," she joked.

Harvath laughed. "I agree. So, what about you?" he asked, changing the subject. "What's next?"

"Besides some serious desk duty? Let's see," she responded, ticking the items off one at a time on her fingers. "Right off the bat, there's a high-jump competition tomorrow and then I have the New Delhi Marathon on Sunday."

Harvath laughed again. "Good. Something to do and something to look forward to."

"All I need now is that third thing."

No sooner had the words left her mouth than Vijay reentered the kitchen with one of his most handsome sons in tow. "Okay," he stated, "who's looking for a martini that will absolutely change their life?"

CHAPTER 63

On a gravel road outside of Bucharest, the headlights from three SUVs sliced through the darkness. A cold front was coming.

When the icy winds met the warm Dâmbovița River, curtains of swirling, spectral fog would be born. Colonel Yang Xin wanted to be back on his plane and wheels up before that happened. He did not want to get grounded at the airport—especially not when transporting such sensitive cargo.

He couldn't believe what a colossal mess everything had become. Operations sometimes went sideways, but this one had gone sideways, backed up and run over itself, and then had gone sideways all over again.

Not only had Carbon completely fallen off the grid, but so had Durrani. No one had heard from him—not even his superiors at the ISI back in Islamabad.

Then, finally, word came. It wasn't good. Indian intelligence, specifically those bastards at RAW, were onto Kamal Khan. Durrani claimed to have no idea who had tipped them or what Khan may have done to draw their attention. He'd had to choose between saving Khan or saving the weapon. He had chosen to save the weapon. For that Yang was grateful. But his gratitude was short-lived and, he soon learned, misplaced.

Concerned that Khan would eventually break and tell the Indian authorities everything, Durrani had fled.

He couldn't go back to Pakistan. India was going to demand his head on a platter. To avoid war, the Pakistanis would either hand him over or kill him themselves.

Durrani alleged to have headed to Bucharest because of his contacts within Romanian intelligence. Yang knew better. He had chosen it because of his obscene, inhuman sexual proclivities.

The ISI operative had decided that he was going into early retirement and he made it crystal clear that he expected Beijing to fund it. He would ransom their own directed-energy weapon back to them.

The payment he demanded was exorbitant. The window to close the transaction far too short. And the terms were near to unacceptable. He had twisted Yang's arm up and behind his back so far that you could hear the cartilage popping and the sinew tearing as he wrenched it from its proverbial socket.

But it was nothing compared to what Beijing would do to him if he lost the weapon. Durrani had been quite forthright about his willingness to sell it to the highest bidder, which likely meant the Americans. In short, Yang had been given no choice. Assembling a team, he had sprung into action. And now here he was.

Using elements from the Chinese Embassy in Bucharest, he'd had the location for the meeting placed under surveillance. Nothing unusual had been observed.

Riding next to him in his SUV was the scientist who had assembled the weapon and had taught Khan how to use it. Yang wasn't about to hand over any money without a one hundred percent positive confirmation that they were getting the actual weapon back and not some facsimile thereof.

If it were up to him, Yang would have much preferred to double-cross Durrani and have a member of his security detail put a bullet in him.

The Pakistani, however, had anticipated this possibility and had gone into lengthy detail about the information he had buttoned down. Like a suicide bomber, should he be captured or killed, his thumb would come off the button and there'd be an explosion of blackmail material laying out everything he had been doing for the Chinese.

Yang's only way out of this was to verify the weapon, hand over the money, and get the hell out of Romania before any new misfortune popped up and tried to fuck him over.

Pulling onto the farm property, they rolled past the house, as instructed, and toward the barn. Seeing their approach, Durrani opened the large barn doors.

The convoy came to a halt and Yang's security detail debussed first. After patting the Pakistani down for weapons, they conducted a sweep of the perimeter.

Once they were satisfied that everything was safe, they allowed Yang and the scientist to exit their vehicle.

Inside the barn, atop a wooden table, were two hard-sided cases. Durrani walked over to them, opened their lids, and then stood to the side.

No one spoke. There was nothing to be said. This was a business transaction. The sooner it was over, the better—for everyone involved.

When his examination was complete, the scientist nodded to Yang. The weapon was legitimate.

The Chinese intelligence officer then signaled to his men, who removed a large aluminum suitcase from the back of the nearest SUV and wheeled it over to Durrani.

Laying it on its side, he opened the lid and removed random stacks of banded currency, fanning the bills to make sure that Yang hadn't ripped him off.

Satisfied, he closed the case, stood it upright, and wheeled it through the barn. He opened the opposite set of doors, revealing a parked car.

Popping the trunk, he put the suitcase inside, closed the lid, and got behind the wheel. Not once did he look back.

Starting the engine, he put the vehicle in gear and drove off. He had what he had come for. If he never saw Colonel Yang Xin again, it would be too soon.

Yang felt very much the same way. He gave orders to his men and a small wave of relief washed over him as they closed the two cases, lifted them off the table, and carried them toward the SUVs.

He had done it. He had gotten this weapon back. The knot in his horribly pained stomach loosened ever so slightly. He still didn't know what he was going to do about the one in the United States, but he had the whole plane ride back to Beijing to think about it.

Unbeknownst to him, he wasn't going to make that flight, or any other, ever again.

As long, wispy tendrils of fog began to roll across the farm, a team of heavily armed men stepped silently from their hiding places.

A woman's voice issued a one-word command via the earpieces connected to their radios. "*Execute.*"

Before Yang or any of his men could react, they were cut down in a hailstorm of suppressed rounds.

After all of the Chinese nationals were confirmed dead, Asha and her team of Special Group commandos disappeared back into the darkness.

CHAPTER 64

Harvath hadn't intended to let the woman suffer one second longer than necessary. She had already suffered enough. It would all be over soon.

Her name was Olena. She was a Ukrainian refugee. The fact that she had made it out in her condition was a miracle.

What the Russians had done to her was horrific. What she was now being subjected to, just to survive, was abominable.

Harvath had scaled the wall and dropped into the garden. Via one of the French doors at the end of the terrace, he entered the building.

According to his intel, the room he was looking for was on the third floor. He spun the suppressor onto the barrel of his pistol as he climbed the service stairs.

He had no intention of drawing this out. There wouldn't be any long soliloquies. He was here to do a job. Once it was done, he'd be gone.

Stepping onto the third floor, he crept silently down the hall until he found the room he was looking for. He listened, but couldn't hear any sound from the other side. Gently, he tried the handle. It was locked.

He removed the key he had been given and slipped it into the lock, which, along with the door hinges, had been recently oiled.

The key turned soundlessly; the lever and the dead bolt moved softly into place. When he felt the lock release, he applied pressure to his trigger and pushed the door open.

The room was empty. Or to be more precise, *almost* empty. Olena's prosthetic limbs sat on the bed. An aluminum suitcase sat behind a dressing screen near a rust-stained sink.

Where is this motherfucker? he thought to himself. Then he heard muffled voices coming from somewhere toward the other end of the hall. A woman was sobbing. A man was berating her. *Gotcha.*

He moved quietly down the hall and stopped when he arrived at the palace's grand staircase.

Durrani was humiliating Olena, making her painfully climb the stairs with her stumps.

She had once worked in a flower shop in Mariupol, a job she had loved, creating arrangements that brightened people's lives and brought joy to the world.

But now this was what she had been reduced to. This is what she had to do to survive. The tears were streaming down her face.

Taking aim, Harvath said, "Pssst."

When Durrani looked up, Harvath shot him in the dick.

As the man began to cry out, he then shot him in the head, killing him. He watched as his lifeless body crumpled onto the landing and his blood began to stain the purple runner.

Olena was in shock.

Securing his pistol, he walked down the stairs to where she was. Her eyes were wide with fear and she was trembling.

"It's okay," he said, bending down to pick her up. "Everything is going to be okay. Put your arms around my neck."

He didn't know if she spoke English, but she understood enough to do as he had asked.

He carried her back to the bedroom, placed her on the bed next to her prosthetic legs, and told her to put them on. Again, she did as he asked.

Removing the aluminum suitcase from behind the screen, he set it on the bed next to her, opened it, and showed her what was inside. He removed several stacks of bills and slid them into a small backpack he had brought along.

"This is yours now," he told her, pointing at the rest of it. "I'm going to help you downstairs, you're going to take this money, and you're going to disappear. Okay?"

The tears had returned to Olena's face, but they were no longer tears of pain and anguish. "Thank you," she cried. "Thank you."

She threw her arms around him and hugged him. Harvath allowed it for a moment, before saying, "We have to go. Are you ready?"

Olena nodded and Harvath helped her down the service stairs, while he carried the suitcase. A car was waiting for them around the corner.

After helping her get into the backseat, he put the suitcase in the trunk and then tapped the roof, letting the driver know he was good to go.

He stood there, watching her watch him through the rear window as the car vanished in the ever-thickening fog. She mouthed the words "Thank you" again and again as she disappeared.

Shouldering the backpack, he disappeared into the fog as well.

A few blocks from the Terrace Club was a pub called Terminus.

It had the oddest mix of customers he had ever seen. From organized crime figures to intelligence operatives, there was something about this dimly lit bar with its snug leather booths that appealed to people who plied their trades in secret.

At one of the coveted back booths, Harvath found his companions.

"Mission accomplished?" Asha asked as he sat down.

"Mission accomplished," Harvath replied.

"Did he try to cite our deal as a reason for you not to do it?"

"It wouldn't have made a difference. Your deal was your deal. I didn't have any such arrangement with him. I was never going to let that guy go on breathing."

"Understandable," the RAW operative responded. "Did he say anything at all?"

Harvath shook his head and waved a waitress over. "I never gave him a chance. How about you? How'd your op go?"

"Mission accomplished," she replied.

Harvath smiled. Scanning the bottles behind the bar, he selected the best bourbon they had and then, pointing at Alexandru Suliman, said, "And make sure he gets the bill."

The waitress nodded and walked away to place the order. Once she was gone, Harvath unzipped the backpack and placed it between himself and the Romanian intelligence officer. Inside was the pistol, extra magazines, and suppressor the man had provided as well as the multiple stacks of cash taken from Durrani's suitcase. "For the madam, the people who own the farm, plus whoever you use to scrub the scenes and any local law enforcement issues."

Suliman nodded, zipped the pack up, and put it on the floor between his boots. "The hope at my agency is that America and India will become even closer partners with Romania, particularly in terms of intelligence sharing."

Harvath was all about deeper partnerships. Romania was a fellow NATO member and had proven invaluable during the war next door in Ukraine. He only wanted to see that relationship strengthened.

He hoped the same for India. An Asian version of NATO was a fantastic idea on so many levels. One of their first steps forward was going to be a technology swap. DARPA would be sharing everything it knew about the Havana Syndrome device and India's Defense Research and Development Organization, known as DRDO, would be doing the same with what it learned from the directed-energy weapon Asha would be transporting back to New Delhi.

After a nice back-and-forth with Suliman, Harvath looked at Asha. "So, Vijay's son Akshay, there've been how many dates so far?"

"We've been out twice. Coffee and a lunch. I don't know that I'd call either of those a 'date.' "

"You just don't want to call them dates," Harvath replied with a smile.

"What about you?" she asked, changing the subject as the waitress set down his drink.

"I just found out that I'm going to be a godfather."

Nicholas and Nina's baby had fully recovered and they were planning a christening in the chapel of their home. They had asked Scot and Sølvi to both be godparents and were hoping the ceremony could happen when Sølvi came to the States for the wedding, sometime between Christmas and New Year's.

"Congratulations," said Asha, raising her glass.

Suliman and Harvath raised theirs.

"To having something to do," she continued, "someone to love, and something to look forward to."

The trio clinked glasses and Harvath smiled. He did have something to do. He also had someone incredible to love. And there was so much coming up for him to look forward to.

He couldn't wait to get home and hold his goddaughter and he couldn't wait to be back together again with Sølvi.

He was blessed, beyond measure. And he was going to take time to enjoy it.

ACKNOWLEDGMENTS

I have long been fascinated with India, especially the geopolitics of the region, which is why I chose it for the setting of *Rising Tiger*. I think we are going to be hearing a lot more about it in the years to come.

Each year, my goal is to bring you a better book than I did the year before. I not only want you to enjoy an exciting read, but also to close the novel a bit wiser about what's happening around the world.

My thrillers would not be possible without you, my fantastic **readers**. Thank you for all of your phenomenal reviews, the incredible word of mouth, and all of the great interactions on social media.

To all of the fabulous **booksellers** around the world who help place my novels into the hands of eager readers, thank you. I wouldn't be able to reach all of those lovely people without you.

In my two decades in this business, I have been blessed to have developed some amazing friendships. The following brilliant people were indispensable in the writing of this book.

Ambassador **Robert C. O'Brien**, former Special Envoy for Hostage Affairs and former U.S. National Security Advisor, has been a dear friend for many years and has helped with many of my thrillers. He freely shared his knowledge of India and its strategic importance throughout the writing process. I am much in his debt. Thank you, Robert.

Another dear friend, **Chad Norberg**, U.S. State Department, provided some terrific insight from his time stationed at the United States embassy in New Delhi. On-the-ground color details really help bring a novel, especially one set in such an exotic location, to life. Thank you, Chad.

Author, Diplomatic Security Service Agent (ret.), and good pal **Fred**

Burton was incredibly helpful on multiple fronts over this past year. His nonfiction novel, *Ghost*, about his time in DSS, is one of the most gripping books I have ever read, and I highly recommend it. Thank you, Fred, for all of your help.

Sean Fontaine and I have been friends since we were little kids. Not only has he risen to the call every time his country has asked him to step forward, he has also picked up the phone every time I have called. He has always been willing to answer my questions and offer amazingly helpful suggestions. Thank you, Sean.

U.S. Navy SEAL (ret.) **Pete Scobell** has had an astounding career. He seems busier now out of the SEAL Teams than when he was in. Nevertheless, Pete is a terrific friend and always makes time to help me out on the books. His assistance continues to be invaluable. Thank you, Pete.

My good friend **Sidney Blair**, Senior United States Federal Air Marshal (ret.), United States Marshal Service (ret.), and United States Secret Service (ret.) has assisted on many of my books and was there again for me on this one. He always has great advice and terrific tactical suggestions. Thank you, Sidney.

Steve Tuttle is another great longtime friend who has helped me tremendously over the years. He's one of the founding members of Taser International and Axon Enterprise. I think the TASER is an amazing tool, and I love coming up with outside-the-box ways for Harvath to use it. Whenever I do, I always run the scenario by Steve to make sure I'm on point. He always has great feedback for me. Thanks, Steve.

You never appreciate a good laugh or someone checking in to see how you're doing more than when you're in the thick of writing a challenging book. In addition to Pete and Sidney above, I want to thank **Marcus** and **Morgan Luttrell**, U.S. Navy SEALs (ret.), **Paul Craig**, U.S. Navy EOD (ret.), and **Dan Moran**, USMC (ret.) for their consistent good humor (even if 95 percent of the jokes are at my expense). Thanks, guys.

In Chapter 54, as Harvath and Asha discuss the importance of a strong military alliance between the United States and India, Harvath makes note of remarks by a United States ambassador to the United Nations. These remarks come from real-life former ambassador **Nikki Haley** and Congressman **Mike Waltz** in a ForeignPolicy.com OpEd titled "It's Time to Formalize an Alliance with India," which I highly recommend.

Simon & Schuster's outstanding **Jon Karp** has delivered another incredible year for S&S, as well as for all the authors fortunate enough to be under his stewardship. Jon, I continue to be grateful for everything you do for me day in, day out. Thank you.

One of the reasons I am able to raise the bar year after year is because of my phenomenal editor and publisher, **Emily Bestler**. Her encouragement to keep pushing, and to keep delving into new and uncharted terrain, supercharges my creativity. This year, we celebrated the twentieth anniversary of my first thriller, *The Lions of Lucerne*. Emily, thank you. You are the absolute best. There is nobody else I would rather be working with. Here's to the next twenty years!

The extraordinary **Lara Jones** is a consummate professional. It is an absolute pleasure to work with her and the rest of the awesome **Emily Bestler Books team**. Without them, you would not be holding this book in your hands. The tally of what they do every day is incredible. Thank you.

My astonishing Atria publisher, **Libby McGuire**, and associate publisher **Dana Trocker** keep pushing the envelope in new and totally creative ways. I am very thankful for all that you both have done and continue to do for me. Thank you, and I look forward to seeing you soon.

David Brown is, hands down, the absolute best publicist on the planet. He is tireless when it comes to promoting his authors and never rests on his laurels (or the author's). He approaches each new book with boundless enthusiasm and energy. He's a fantastic person to work with, and I am proud to call him my friend. Thank you, David.

I am now officially two years behind in bourbon drinking with another good friend at S&S, the spectacular **Gary Urda**. Gary and I go back so many years together, and one of my greatest joys has always been visiting New York and getting together with Gary for drinks. It's not only a nice way to catch up and renew our friendship but also to say thank you for all that Gary and his awe-inspiring team do for me throughout the year. Fingers crossed that we'll see each other soon. Thank you, Gary!

Jen Long and her crew at **Pocket Books** continue to be absolutely sublime. As the marketplace continues to change, Jen and her team are always ten steps ahead. You all are amazing. Thank you for everything.

One of the hardest working people I have the pleasure of knowing is the miraculous **Al Madocs**. He and the rest of the **Atria/Emily Bestler Books production department** are willing to do whatever it takes to get it right and get it done. Any errors in this novel are mine and mine alone, but I guarantee you that there are a lot fewer of them because of Al and his team. Thank you, all.

In addition to all of my S&S family members listed above, there are a host of other wonderful people who kill it on my behalf on a daily basis whom I miss seeing in person. I want to thank the following people, many of whom I have known, loved, and deeply appreciated for years. This includes **Suzanne Donahue**, **Karlyn Hixon**, **Alaina Mauro**, **Liz Perl**, **Janice Fryer**, **John Hardy**, **Paula Amendolara**, **Colin Shields**, **Gregory Hruska**, and **Stuart Smith**. Thank you.

I also wish to thank the formidable **Atria/Emily Bestler Books** and **Pocket Books sales teams**. You all are out there crushing it every single day! I am incredibly grateful for you and for all of your hard work. Thank you.

This year, I had the pleasure of working on the *Rising Tiger* jacket from square one with the amazingly talented **Jimmy Iacobelli** of the **Atria/Emily Bestler Books and Pocket Books art departments**. I wanted us to incorporate a set of gorgeous brass doors from the City Palace of Jaipur, and Jimmy made it happen, all while delivering an energetic, eye-catching, super-cool look. Thank you, Jimmy!

If you enjoy audiobooks, as I do, there's simply no one better at producing them than the superb team at the **Simon & Schuster audio division**. My thanks go out to all of them, especially rock stars **Chris Lynch**, **Tom Spain**, **Sarah Lieberman**, **Desiree Vecchio**, and my longtime narrator and friend, **Armand Schultz**. Thank you.

Copyediting is tough work, but my splendid copy editor, **Tom Pitoniak**, did a terrific job. Thank you for helping to take the book to the next level.

It has been a hell of a year, and I am blessed to have had my magnificent agent and devoted friend, **Heide Lange** of **Sanford J. Green-**

burger Associates, by my side every step of the way. We have so many things to be thankful for this year, Heide, and when I count my blessings, you are right there at the top of the list. Thank you for everything, large and small, that you have done for me. I value you more than you will ever know.

And I cannot mention Heide without mentioning her splendid assistants, **Iwalani Kim** and **Madeline Wallace**, the outstanding **Charles Loffredo**, and the rest of the astonishing SJGA team. You all are key players in every phase of my novels, and I cannot thank you enough.

I want to give a very special heartfelt thank-you to the incredibly exceptional **Yvonne Ralsky**. As Executive Vice President, Yvonne is integral to everything that happens at Thor Entertainment Group. This year, we have seen not only big leaps on the publishing side of our business but also in Hollywood. That is thanks, in no small part, to you, Yvonne. In addition to your talent and professionalism, I also deeply value our friendship. Thank you for each and every thing. Here's to another incredible year!

This last year has brought both heartache and joy. One of my greatest joys is that my friendship with my marvelous entertainment attorney, **Scott Schwimer**, has only grown stronger. That, and the fact that he kicked absolutely incredible ass over the last twelve months in Hollywood! We have some amazing announcements coming up—so stay tuned. Scottie, I love you more than I will ever be able to say. Thank you for an outstanding year and all the goodness we have coming down the pike. You're the best!

And while we're on the subject of "the best," I want to thank my awesome **family**. Writing a novel involves having to spend a lot of time locked away in my office. They are so supportive and selflessly seek out new and caring ways to make my life easier. I love being an author, but I love it even more because I have their backing. Thank you for all that you did so that this novel could happen. Now it's time to celebrate!